Lewis and Clark
Murder on the Natchez Trace

Booklocker.com, Inc.
2010

Lewis and Clark
Murder on the Natchez Trace

Thomas Berry

Dedication

This book is dedicated to my wife, Colleen, and my
children, Brendan, Colin, Nolan, Kathryn, & Patrick,
for their support and encouragement.

I would like to send a heartfelt thanks to:

Colleen, Kevin, and many others who contributed their time
and efforts in polishing my manuscript.

Angela, my editor, for her constant guidance and patience.

Todd, who created the cover art, for his creativity and
technical expertise.

My wonderful family, far and near, for helping me reach for
the stars!

PROLOGUE

March 15, 1803
Paris, France

"**D**amn the English!" shouted Napoleon, his fist pounding the large map table in his inner office.

The room was expansive and lavishly decorated, the only room in the building permitted such luxury. Two ornately carved chairs sat opposite a large, heavy table over which the diminutive leader stood. His own chair was large and soft; its velvet exterior colored a deep burgundy which almost matched the red in the man's flushed cheeks. Heavy draperies covered the large picture windows behind him, letting in only a stream of the light outside.

The French leader looked up at his second-in-command, General Jacques Chartes, an expression of anger and frustration clearly etched on his face. Chartes, a tall, balding man bordering on six foot, felt the mood in the room grow a little colder as he stood there before his leader and friend. Deciding it was better to show his subservience at the moment, he took a seat in the chair behind him.

"The treaty with Britain will hold for the moment," Chartes offered carefully.

"But they ignored the substance of the Amiens treaty and encourage protests against the republic across Europe!" Napoleon shouted once more. "And they'll take any excuse to continue the fighting!"

Napoleon Bonaparte, First Consul of the French republic, kept his momentum going. Chartes knew him to be demonstrative and ambitious, fighting at Napoleon's side for most of last few years. While the French

1

leader's temper was fierce and legendary, he had done great things for France and Chartes had prided himself with knowing how to deal with the ebbs and flows of his personality. Others who had crossed Napoleon often found themselves on the cutting edge of the infamous guillotine. Chartes had no wish to join them.

Napoleon had led his country to new heights, with largely successful campaigns on several important fronts in Russia, Egypt, and Germany. But Chartes knew it was their island neighbors to the north that taxed his commander more than any other.

"The British Navy will start with blockades on our main ports, if that happens," Chartes said matter-of-factly. They had had similar discussions like this before, and both understood well the ways of their English counterparts.

The shorter, sandy haired man stood at a window high in his castle tower, overlooking the republic over which he ruled. "We need more money for such a fight – the republic is nearly bankrupt." The verbal acknowledgement of his dire financial situation was a clear sign that he was worried. If there was to be further war with England, who would pay for the Armageddon?

"We could sell the land in North America." Chartes volunteered. "Since we can't use it to supply the sugar cane plantations on the island of Santa Domingo, it's really of no use to us now."

Napoleon turned towards him, almost violent in his actions, his left hand raised in anger, forcing a surprised Chartes to recoil impulsively. It was not wise to anger such a man as Napoleon – even his second-in-command was not immune to his wrath, a fact Chartes acknowledged reluctantly.

But his superior surprised him yet again. Napoleon, his hand raised towards his friend, was about to make a sharp retort then stopped himself. His eyes, full of wild desperation and anger just a few seconds ago, visibly and slowly returned to normal. His face took on a calmer demeanor and Chartes thought the storm had past. The French leader was quiet for a moment, clearly thinking it out in his head.

Chartes seized the moment. "The attack to reacquire Santa Domingo failed miserably. Between the yellow fever and the defenses that L'Ouventure put up, we couldn't get it back."

"I had been hoping to use the Louisiana Territory we acquired from Spain to supply those lucrative sugar crops, but now..." Napoleon's words trailed off.

"We can sell the land and get solvent again! Use the money to fight the British!" Chartes countered, his confidence growing by the minute. If

Napoleon could listen to reason, perhaps there was a chance to make this work.

"But what about the Americans?" Napoleon questioned. "Would they want the land?"

"Of course, sir. They have been in dispute with Spain for years over the rights to the Mississippi River and the city of New Orleans. If they get the land around that, they will be able to control their own commercial trading."

Napoleon looked at his friend, his face decisive and firm. A good omen, Chartes thought to himself. "Get our foreign ministers to open negotiations with the American ambassador, Robert Livingston. Ask him how much they would be willing to pay for a little bit of land."

The small man spread his hands over the map table. It was covered with heavy parchments adorned with ornately painted drawings of territories both claimed and unconquered. Napoleon fumbled with the documents until he found the object of his search. He pulled it out and placed it on top.

A map depicting the territory of North America lay before him. The Americans owned the eastern third. Colonies won with French help, he reminded himself. The great territory to the west had been won by Napoleon himself from Spain.

Now he would sell it to the Americans, an incredible purchase if they could afford it. Doubling their current landholdings in a single transaction. President Thomas Jefferson would undoubtedly want it – it might even be the single largest victory in his government's history. His ambassador, Livingston, was in Paris and would relay his offer to the American president.

Chartes bowed his head and trudged through the heavy oak doors, closing them behind him.

Napoleon Bonaparte turned and stood at the windows, determined to prepare for the changes in store for all of them.

Chapter 1

"I hope the accommodations will be sufficient, Mr. Lewis." The woman smiled coyly as the tall man looked around the sparse room. She absently brushed a long strand of dirty brown hair back behind her right ear and ran a slender hair over her cotton dress.

"Yes, they will do quite nicely, thank you Priscella. I'll only be here for a day or so. I'm waiting for a few people who should be joining up with me shortly. I hope to get some hunting in tomorrow morning, and then I'll be on my way."

"I'll prepare supper in an hour or so, Mr. Lewis. My husband should be back from Memphis tomorrow morning and you can settle up with him then. Feel free to make yourself at home." Her eyes twinkled as she turned and walked away slowly. Lewis couldn't help but admire how beautiful the woman looked, her brown hair falling loosely over her shoulders, while her simple blue dress showed off her slim waist and ample bosom to an appreciative audience.

He smiled as he closed the door, alone to his thoughts. Meriwether Lewis looked around the small room. The dirt floor was dry at least, despite the recent rain. A small wooden frame bed was pressed against the far left wall, next to a stout looking stump that served as both chair and desk. There was a medium sized open window along the back wall overlooking the woods thirty feet away. He placed his case containing his traveling clothes on the stump and a smaller case that held his papers next to it. His rifle, a state-of-the-art air

5

gun he had purchased at Harper's Ferry before the expedition, stood in the corner by the back, near his belongings.

He sat down on the bed which squeaked noisily in protest. He was tired, so tired. He closed his eyes and rubbed the bridge of his nose. He hoped James would get here soon – the Indian agent had with him an herbal potion that often alleviated Lewis' headaches. But those damn horses had gotten away last night during the storm and the pair of Chicksaw Indians they had hired as guides seemed more clueless in the wild than most of the city bureaucrats in Washington. Staying behind to help find the strays, James had encouraged Lewis to continue on ahead to Grinder's Stand. At the time, he didn't argue the point, but now…*perhaps I was too hasty in leaving them…*

Captain James Neely was an Indian agent who worked for the government, and had been assigned to the governor for the past few years. Lewis had left it up to him to contract guides for this dangerous stretch of Indian trail known as the Natchez Trace – he was a capable man and Lewis trusted his judgment. But events over the past several days had gave him considerable alarm over his personal safety, as well as that of the men who rode with him – enough to voice his fears to Neely.

James had been very calming and level-headed – assuring Lewis that the stress of the government inquiry was playing tricks with his mind. He accepted it at the time…but now the fears were beginning to return and they wouldn't go away. He got up, and paced the floor, wringing his hands together over and over. His stomach felt like a knife was being twisted inside him, a constant reminder of the stresses of his office. *Where did I go wrong? How had it come to this?*

He dreaded what the next week will bring. A formal inquiry by the Treasury department. Being deposed and interrogated to what end he could not fathom. The headache beneath his left eye was becoming worse and it would not go away.

Maybe a good hunt was what the doctor requires. Despite having traveled the past week through the densely wooded Trace with nary a civilized person in sight, he still longed for the great outdoors over the confines of his St. Louis governor's mansion. He felt more comfortable in the elements than in the big city and he enjoyed getting out as often as he could. Away from the bureaucracy of Washington and the politics that its minders enjoyed so much. They can have it!

Lewis rose from his bed and opened the door. It was almost dinnertime and Priscella said she would have a decent meal on the table shortly. He was the only guest at the small country inn at the moment and he was thankful for the isolation. He wasn't sure if he could stand making polite small talk with a large group of people in his present state.

The sun was hanging low on the horizon, fighting with the darkness in a losing battle for domination. Soon the night would overtake them and he would rest again, battling the demons that plagued him in his dreams. His future, once so promising and open, now lay in disarray, his career coming to a halt faster than he had ever considered possible.

He walked slowly to the white clapboard building next door which was identical to his own. The paint was peeling badly and many of the wooden boards were stained with mildew and water damage. Priscella Grinder was standing outside, a water bucket in her right hand. She was looking off towards the rear of the property, her attention focused on something in the distant.

"Mrs. Grinder," Meriwether said amicably.

Startled, his hostess turned towards her guest, dropping the bucket and spilling a small amount on water on the packed earth. Her worn coat was open; her thin cotton dress barely able to conceal the gentle curves of her figure. He smiled awkwardly, and apologized for scaring her.

"What can I do you for, Mr. Lewis?" she said, picking up the bucket once more.

"I'd like to do some hunting in the morning, but I'm fresh out of ammunition and powder. Can I buy some from you?"

"Oh, certainly, certainly. I can sell you a day's worth for a nickel, if that's ok."

"That will be fine. It's worth the price, I guess, if I can get out and do something productive. Can you recommend a decent spot for finding elk or deer? Even a rabbit will do nicely."

"Sure, come on inside and I'll get you squared away, honey." Her gaze drifted back towards the rear of the property one last time before ushering her guest into her own building.

An hour later, having eaten a light dinner of tomato and carrot stew which Priscella had prepared, and obtaining his ammunition, Lewis was in a better mood. He wasn't entirely comfortable around his flirtatious hostess without her husband present – he wondered on more than one occasion how it would look to someone coming upon them, and would be grateful to be on his way tomorrow when James and the servants arrived. Such social situations vexed him to no end – he enjoyed the peacefulness of the outdoors over complicated dramas any day. Even his headache seemed to have vanished now that he had eaten and relaxed somewhat.

The daylight had finally succumbed to darkness, and the moon was reigning its fullness over the earth. The white buildings of the little inn stood in sharp contrast to the thick woods that surrounded it. The activity of the nocturnal animals were in full swing now, as owls hooted in throaty calls, crickets chirped in a high pitched mating dance, while small animals scurried unseen in the tall grass and bushes all around him.

If I close my eyes, I can picture myself back there. Lewis imagined the woods of years ago, thousands of miles away from here. The rivers that coursed their way through the heartlands of this great country, emptying their waters into parts unknown. Great mountains of frozen rock rising higher into the air than any white man had ever seen on the North American continent. Feeling the salty air of an ocean unseen by any American, whose horizon extended far off into the great reaches of Asia and beyond.

He pictured familiar faces in the line of men as they walked on foot and horseback, riding in canoes and large pirogues – men whose fate lay in his hands. Men whom he had come to trust and admire. It was a time that occurred only a few years before and sometimes, like today, the memories came back crisp and clear, as if he had left these men only yesterday.

He opened his eyes, suddenly alert. He had heard a noise that seemed out of place, even predatory. He looked around but saw nothing – the moon did not penetrate the darkness of the woods. Trees, tall and thick, covered the ground in an impenetrable blackness.

Meriwether Lewis heard a snapping again, this time to his right towards the rear of the cabins. A wolf? A bear? Or perhaps it was James returning with the horses.

"James?" There was no answer. It was most probably an animal of some sort.

He decided it would be prudent to retire for the night, not wanting to be caught outside if the nocturnal animal wanted a part of his hide. Bears were always hungry it seems as settlers moved in, disrupting their habitats, scaring away their food sources. Men diverted rivers and spoiled ponds, causing the animals to seek their basic necessities elsewhere. Even if it leads them into human territory.

He opened the door to his small building and entered, closing and locking the door behind him. There was no light anymore, save for a scant sliver of moonlight coming from the rear window. He was glad the window had no glass in it – not like the stuffy houses he was used to in the city. He liked to feel the cool breeze on his face, and the smells of nature surrounding him. It made it easier to go to sleep. He removed his coat and shoes, and lay down on the bed, using only a thin blanket to cover his tall, wiry frame. The bed was small and the straw mattress thin, forcing him to curl his legs slightly to stay comfortable. Within ten minutes, his tense muscles had begun to relax and he drifted off to a fitful sleep.

When he awoke, the dawn was just beginning to shine its light into the room. What time was it? 7? 7:30? He was always an early riser and was surprised he had slept as long as he had. He remembered the dreams from the night before – and sighed deeply. The details were fading fast, but he noticed he was sweaty and his heart was beating rapidly. He was hoping the briskness of the fresh air and the different scenery would help him sleep better, but some events in his life have shown him that they will not go away so easily. He forced himself to calm down, then after a minute stood up and stepped towards the bag on the stump. He put on a fresh shirt and ran his hand through his short brown hair.

He walked over towards the wall and gripped the barrel of his rifle, cold steel against his flesh, checking that it was loaded with the bullets he purchased last night from his host. It would be effective for what he asked from it today. The specially made air gun was the same one he had brought with him on the expedition several years ago and he smiled as he was reminded of how impressed the natives would be when they saw this remarkable repeating wonder. He was proud of the air rifle and brought it with him on such outings where he might want to hunt…or protect himself from nature's hunters.

Meriwether Lewis saw movement from the woods in back of his cabin and walked slowly over to the window, peering out into the darkness of the thick trees. Was the animal from last night still out there? During the last moments of his life, he thought about how much he loved the woods, how much he longed to give up his career in St. Louis to be a part of it again, how much he wanted to be free…

Chapter 2

The glint of the sharp metal tip reflected in the sunlight. The Blackfoot warrior took the arrow shaft from his leather case and silently notched it into the bowstring. His bare chest was lean and well muscled, his hair dark as the night and falling halfway down his back. Leather pants protected his legs, and comfortable shoes made from soft buffalo skin kept his footfalls quiet. His only decoration on this outing was some black paint which he had carefully adorned his forehead and cheekbones. He focused on the spot where he was told his quarry would come into view and waited with practiced patience.

Running River looked up at the sky, judging the time from the last reported sighting and configuring his own internal clock. He was right on schedule. Overlooking the water below, he knelt on a small bluff, prepared to unleash a clean shot. He permitted himself a slight smile. This was going to be fun.

The canoe was silent as the two men made their way down the small creek. Their wooden paddles made a slight swirling dip in the water, perfectly in sync with each other. The weather was warm for this time of year and the animals were starting to come out of their winter habitats.

John Colter and John Potts, both recently released from the tour of duty with the Lewis and Clark expedition a few years earlier, examined their beaver traps they had left beside the stream earlier in the week. Beaver hides were their stock and trade now. A fur pelt could be sold for a good deal depending on the size of the animal and the condition it was in. Adequate care was important and Colter was one of the best traders in the business.

"Did you hear something?" Potts asked quietly. "Sounds like buffalo." Scattered trees stood like sentries on each side of the creek but the majority of the land was dry and arid. Cactus plants dotted the landscape and the sun beat down hot upon the two men. The creek stretched about 20 feet on each side towards a small muddy shoreline, but its depth was deceptively deep. The direction of the current ahead turned almost seventy degrees, its headway blocked by low level hills.

Colter had indeed noticed the change in noise, but to him it wasn't the sound of heavy buffalo. This was more muted, more like... "I think it's Indians, John. Perhaps we should go back." Reflexively he reached down for his rifle he carried alongside him in the bottom of the canoe.

But Potts pressed on. "Nah, I'm sure it's buffalo. We've hunted enough of them to know. Besides we'll be done with these traps in a few hours. Don't want to turn back..."

As their canoe rounded the next bend, Potts stopped talking and simply stared at the scene before him. On either side of the small creek were more than six hundred Indians and more arriving fast. Potts, who was in the front of the canoe, looked back with an anxious expression at his friend. Colter's face was impassive, but his eyes betrayed his fear.

The Blackfoot Indians, one of the most aggressive and hostile tribes in the western plains, looked ready to pounce. The warriors were armed with spears and arrows, and as Colter looked around him, he saw a few Blackfoot warriors on elevated terrain, their arrows notched and ready. This was clearly setup up as an ambush – not just an innocent encounter along the waterway. There would be no easy escape. Colter understood these warriors, probably more than most white men who lived in the western plains. Violence was not the way out of this one – but perhaps they could negotiate.

The Indians gestured for them to bring the canoe alongside, and the two men felt helpless to do anything else. Running or fighting their way out was suicide. But as Potts, who was in the bow of the boat, hit the shore first, one of the Indians grabbed his rifle.

Colter was a foot behind him and something about the Indian's demeanor triggered an alarm in his head. Instinctively he jumped out of the canoe and grabbed the rifle from the startled native. This was one of the only weapons they had and their only bargaining chip. The way the Indians were set up told him they had one thing on their agenda and it wasn't to let these two white men escape alive. He handed the rifle back to Potts and reached for his own in the canoe. Potts, his fear quite evident on his wiry frame, quickly pointed it in sweeping semi-circle at the Indians, hoping to scare them off.

Suddenly Potts let out a cry and tried in vain to push off again in the canoe. He knew what happened to captives of the Blackfoot and didn't want to be remanded to that terrible fate. But as he started down, several pairs of hands grabbed the canoe and he turned around quickly to face them. He made a fateful decision and, cocking the rifle, pointed it at the nearest Indian and fired into the man's chest.

Running River watched the events with interest from his perch on the hill to the right of the canoes. His instructions were clear – don't shoot unless fired upon. Take them alive. He really didn't think these white men would be foolish enough to make a stand. But his trigger reflexes took over the millisecond Potts fired his weapon. His fingers let the sharp, gleaming arrow fly and he hit his target dead center of the chest. Other warriors did the same, raining the air with arrows until the body of the unfortunate man tumbled over into the water, blood already spreading out in a circle around him.

He looked quickly at the other man, now held tight by Nesting Eagle and Patient Thunder. The white man's frightened eyes were growing wider by the second. Good. He must be taught a lesson, and Running River vowed to make it a good one. He silently stood and jogged down to the river to meet the newcomer.

Colter tried to wrestle away from the Indians but it was useless. Why didn't they just kill him and get it over with, he thought. He knew why. These types of warriors were very territorial and wanted to make sure white men learned to stay off their lands. And his idea of pain tolerance was going to take on a whole new level. At least Potts was able to take the easy way out, he thought grimly.

The Indians were talking amongst themselves but Colter didn't quite understand them. He had lived among different tribes from time to time, and shared the land with them, but he didn't understand the words of the Blackfoot. But the gestures they made towards him were unmistakable. He tried to look around for any sign of a leader. Maybe he could be reasoned with. It was his only hope.

Soon some warriors moved aside and a middle aged chief, his war bonnet reaching halfway down his back, full of eloquent feathers and beads, came up to him. He didn't speak but made a gesture the rest understood immediately. Colter was moved towards the nearest large tree and tied there, his hands secured around both sides for good measure. Then one of the larger

Indians stepped forward, brandishing a sharp knife. Colter looked him in the eyes – if he was going to meet death, better to see it clearly, he thought.

Running River held the knife in front of the man, his dark black eyes burning like coals in the deepest embers of the war fire. He was slightly amazed that this white man had the audacity to look at him, his conqueror, in the eyes. No matter, he would make him suffer.

But first, the prisoner had to be humbled. Chief Tukamansha made his instructions clear. Running River took the knife and twirled it between his fingers, grinning at the man like an evil demon. Then he took the man's white cotton shirt and, using the knife, cut it away with two quick strokes. Then he did the same with the man's pants until the prisoner was naked. The Indians laughed at the sight and took the discarded clothes, waving them around, whopping and hollering.

Still, Colter's gaze did not waver. Humiliation was just the start, he knew. Would they use him for target practice? He had seen bodies of men killed in such a way. Perhaps they would put him to the rack, and burn him slowly? Burning was a horrible way to go.

After what seemed like an eternity, the warriors again parted to allow the chief access to the prisoner. Colter shifted his eyes from Running River to the new leader who spoke some words to the warriors. Running River took his knife and came around to the back of the tree. Without a word, Colter felt the bonds holding his wrists slacken and he quickly untied himself.

Several Indians grabbed him by the arms and together they followed the chief out into the field beside the river. The hundreds of warriors watched in silence. As he walked past, Colter noticed something different about the Indians, their demeanor slightly more excited – more agitated - than before, but he didn't know if it was significant or not.

After about a hundred yards or so, the small group stopped. Colter shook off the hands that held him and, after a sharp word from the chief, his guards did not restrain him further.

"Walk with me," said the Chief, his first English words he had spoken since the ambush. Colter, a little shaken, stepped forward and started walking into the meadow, the chief beside him. The guards remained where they were.

"What is going on?" asked Colter, trying to remain calm. "You know English, I can see that. Tell me what is happening." He was stark naked and felt more than a little vulnerable. Standing just over six foot in height, Colter was a solid fixture of sinew and muscle. His wavy brown hair fell to his shoulders and his beard of four days lay like a thin carpet on his angular face.

The aged Blackfoot leader stopped walking and turned towards his captive. "You run fast?" he asked in halting English.

Run fast? Colter thought. What kind of game is this? Desperate to bide some time, he decided to lie. "No, I don't run fast. Bad leg," he replied.

"End come quickly," the chief stated. From under his cloak, he produced a wooden stick. Striking the prisoner on his bare rump, he calmly announced. "Run!"

Colter looked behind him and saw, with a sickening feeling of dread, over six hundred warriors armed solely with spears, give a horrible yell and start chasing after him. The whooping and hollering was so loud, he covered his ears and turned away.

Without another word Colter, barefoot and naked, ran for his life.

Chapter 3

He headed straight across the prairie, knowing the Jefferson River, roughly six miles away, provided his only chance. He had lied to the chief about his running. Among the trappers and hunters of his generation, he was one of the fastest. If he had known the truth, the chief might have second-guessed his choice of sport but, after all, there was really no hope of escape, was there?

The arid land of the prairie was littered with cactus needles and briar patches and his bare feet were bleeding badly after only a mile, but Colter never gave himself the luxury of stopping. The yells and screams of the approaching warriors spurred him to run faster and harder still.

By the fourth mile no one had yet to catch him and he still had another two miles until he reached the river. Once there, he would just have to improvise, but it was his only hope. He dared one backwards glance at this point and saw to his amazement that most of the warriors were about half a mile back, but still running hard. Only one warrior was close to him and he realized with sudden clarity that he would not reach the safety of the river in time. The warrior had his sharp spear held high, but was keeping quiet and soft-footed as he made his approach. Colter decided to grit it out and ran even harder.

Running River was almost there. He knew where the white man was headed and was determined to get to him before he reached it. The rest of his tribesmen would be here soon, but this kill was all his. He smiled at the thought of the man lying helpless on the ground, his spear sticking out of him like a pig on a spit.

By the fifth mile, Colter was exhausted and his body was bleeding and thoroughly worn out. The Indian was almost on him, perhaps thirty yards away, and he had to do something. Suddenly he felt blood explode from his nose and saw red patches appear on his sweaty chest and seep into his mouth. He had run so hard, he realized he must a blown a blood vessel. *This is it. I'm done.* Colter stopped suddenly and turned around, his arms outstretched, ready to end this here and now.

Running River held his spear high – he was only twenty feet away from his quarry – his prey as they liked to call the captured men forced to play this killing game – and he felt the bloodlust rise up in his head. It was the ultimate pleasure for him – the feeling of a trapped animal who must submit to his own death and beg for mercy. To which none would be given. It was true, this one was especially troublesome and he was forced to run harder today than he had in a long time. The sun would be setting soon, probably within two hours, so it was best to get it over with and return to the village by dusk.

Without warning, he was brought up short. The prey – this white man who had put up a valiant run over the prairie – had stopped and turned to face him, now no more than five feet away. His long spear, which was an effective weapon for mid-range shoots, would be useless here. He tried to throw it down and grab his knife tied on his waist, but in his haste, his feet tripped on the long shaft and he fell head over heels at the foot of his enemy.

Colter, in the span of seconds, saw the Indian approach, the warrior's eyes wide with disbelief as he tumbled forward. The hunted man, seeing salvation where there was none before, grabbed the spear lying on the ground and without a second's thought or hesitation, drove it straight down into the chest of the warrior. The Indian grabbed the shaft with both hands but the spear had gone straight through him, pinning him to the hard earth beneath. Colter bent forward, laying his weight on the spear, exhausted. The eyes of the brave warrior looked up sightless, his face a mask of confusion and incredulity.

But the whooping of the Indians still coming up across the plains brought Colter back to full reality. They had seen from a distance the killing of their tribesman, and would surely be out for blood in the worst way. Already some spears were flying towards him and he turned and ran hard and fast, trying to cover the last mile to the river.

The last mile was probably the longest of John's life. Six hundred warriors who wanted nothing more than to kill him over and over, hang his bloody scalp on their war belt, and dance on his grave, chased him the final distance at a dead run. As he approached the river, the trees began to get more abundant and thicker, undoubtedly benefiting from a good source of water.

As he approached the river, he noticed right away a small island where driftwood had piled up as it came down river. Without missing a step and using the trees for cover, Colter plunged into the river, the cold water stiffening his muscles and gripping his chest like a vice. He came up amidst the driftwood floating in the river and tried to remain as quiet as possible. He remained in the water, keeping his head between two large logs hidden from view. Just as he came up for air again, the warriors reached the river.

They scanned both sides of the river, with some running north and others running south along the banks. Many of the Indians wore black paint on their face or chest in similar fashion to Running River, with leather pants, shirts, and shoes. They had lost their quarry, at least for the moment, but with such overwhelming numbers they had plenty of opportunity to reacquire him. Many Indians waded out into the cold water to search the driftwood.

Others reached the island, which was covered with bushes and smaller trees, searching in vain for the white man. The white man who had killed Running River, one of the bravest and proudest warriors in the tribe. Who wanted to tell Chief Tukamansha that his own son was dead and six hundred of the tribesmen had failed to find the single naked white man who did it?

Colter moved around silently, as he felt the Indians searching the driftwood, sometimes going underwater for very long breathes as he tried desperately to remain hidden. The night was fast approaching now, and he knew eventually the Indians would have to give up. Would they find him? How long could he stay hidden? Wild, horrible yells were heard from all over the river and its banks as angry warriors realized the white man might have slipped out of their grasp! If they only knew how close he really was, Colter thought with a slight smile. But his smile stopped cold when he realized what they would do to him once they found him. They would never allow him a second chance.

As time wore on, the yells from the warriors became louder and more feverish as the frustrated Indians realized they could not keep up the search in the dark. Colter couldn't see them from where he was hidden but he kept his ears open for the next several hours until he made sure the Indians had finally left.

Four hours after darkness fell, the half moon was at its highest point in the sky, illuminating a small part of the river bank. Colter decided it was time to take a look and, seeing no one, he swam to the river's edge on the far side and dragged his body onto the muddy shore.

He had calculated in his mind where the nearest safe haven would be, and decided on Fort Manuel, roughly 300 miles distant. Leaving the Blackfoot warriors behind, Colter spent the next seven days and nights walking along the Jefferson, until he finally came upon the trading post, half-starved, naked, sun burnt, and utterly exhausted. But alive. Yes, Colter thought, as he reached the gates of the post. "I am alive."

Chapter 4

The bow of the large wooden ship sliced through the water like a hot knife through butter, sending large waves in both directions as it pushed relentlessly towards its destination. The salty air hung over the deck and filled the lungs of the crew, reminding them of what it means to be alive. The sails were unfurled and the wind was providing good headway toward the distant horizon, the dark red hue of sunset giving way to a black night full of stars. But the men on deck hardly noticed the time, so intent were they on their tasks at hand.

The deck was an orderly chaos, thought Lt. John Ordway, as he stood near the front cannons under his command. It was cool up here and he wore his wool blue jacket, to keep out the biting sea air. A man tall in stature and fair complexion, Ordway was a product of New England and loved the mountains and lush greens of the countryside. Men moved high up above on the three large masts, tending to the rigging and sails, while others below them kept the six forward cannons and sixteen mid and aft cannons in top shape and ready for battle.

The men walking past carried a nervous but excited air about them – for many, Ordway knew this was going to be their first real battle. He took another look forward and saw their quarry was closer than before. *We're gaining on them.*

Just then a whistle pierced the clear air, and Ordway snapped to attention. The captain had arrived on deck.

A tall, lean man approaching fifty, Captain Isaac Hull strode briskly up the stairwell and onto the deck. Without having to say a word his presence commanded respect and authority, and officers quickly leapt to attention. He walked toward the stern of the great warship and stood by the helm, a large wooden steering wheel, now tended to by a uniformed officer as was custom during times of battle. The appearance of the captain told the others the time for action was drawing near.

The thirty or so officers, Ordway included, gathered in four lines in front of their captain awaiting further instructions. Captain Hull looked them over and then, speaking loudly, explained the situation.

"We have identified the vessel we are pursuing as the British warship, the H.M.S. Guerriere, who we know has preyed on our ships out of Boston and Charleston for the past few months. Our orders are to engage and capture her. She is a ship not to be taken lightly – but one from which we will not run."

Hull looked out at the evening sky. It was close to 1700 hours and night would not be far behind – only one or two hours of daylight remained. If we didn't catch her by then, he realized, the Guerriere might very well slip away. The ship appeared below the horizon, its full sails carrying her crew and ship away from the Americans. Hull made a decision and turned back towards his men.

"Night approaches and we cannot afford to let the Guerriere escape. We must close and engage her within the hour. All hands, prepare for battle! Lt. Rosenburg," he said, turning his attention to a young, thin officer in the front row, his closely cropped hair hidden beneath his smart white cap.

"I want you to steer us a course alongside the Brits' starboard side, where we will open up with our gunners. They will try to maneuver away from us, but you must keep us close. It's the only way to slow them down."

"Ordway," he said, looking out among his officers, until he found the tall, blond man in the second row. "Make sure our forward guns on our port side are ready to fire, with enough ammo to last us a good long time. Relay the command to the gun deck below, all port side guns ready to open fire at my command. Let no one forget the name, U.S.S. Constitution!"

Ordway, while being a new lieutenant himself, was no stranger to battle situations, and was confident in his ability to lead the gunners under his command. He walked with the air of a man who has stared death in the face and was not afraid of it. Well educated, and raised in New Hampshire, he was the consummate naval officer, a position that served him well. But his experience came from another frontier, one that he longed to return to, and it existed far away from the frigid waters of the Atlantic.

"Gunners, front and center!" Ordway yelled as he approached the bow, the focal point of his own command. Six large bow chasers surrounded the forward spar mast, 198 feet tall, and second longest on the ship. These impressive cannons were often the first stage of an attack upon a ship, charged with shooting away the masts and sails of the enemy. They were the only cannons on the whole ship that could be rolled on wheels and be maneuvered into other open gun ports in the stern if necessary. They were essential in the upcoming attack. *Could his men handle the stress of battle?* For most of them, it would be their first time fighting a more-experienced and disciplined British frigate. There was only one way to find out, he mused.

"Gentlemen," he said loud enough to be heard by his crew of twelve. "We will engage the enemy within the hour. Ensure all guns are cleaned and ready, and be prepared to fire the port chasers at my command. I will ensure we have enough gunpowder and magazine cartridges for all the cannons. Blanco! Waldrop! You will accompany me." The lieutenant left his crew and he walked to the nearest stairwell, followed close behind by the two crewmen. Dressed in a more casual light blue uniform, the crew was grateful for the warmth the interior of the ship afforded.

As the three men descended to the gun deck below, he looked out over the sea of men and machinery. For as many cannons as was visible topside, the gun deck had many more. Thirty-two carronade cannons, each capable of firing round shots of thirty-two pounds each, crowded this deck, their short snouts protruding through small hatches in the wooden hull. Besides each cannon lay a pyramid of cannon balls and barrels of gunpowder.

Young men, affectionately known as powder monkeys, continually re-supplied the crew from the magazine hold far below decks. It was here that Ordway was headed. He gazed down the stairwell and continued his descent.

"Ordway!" a voice called out as he passed the next deck. He looked up and saw the young surgeon, a man by the name of Vogel, come up to him in a hurry.

"What's the matter, doc?" Ordway asked cautiously. He didn't have time for interruptions – not now at least.

"Just wanted to ask you if you've gotten any word about the battle? Are we expecting many casualties?" he asked. As the primary doctor onboard, he wanted to make sure he was prepared for the worst.

"Well, I'm hopeful we can do this without too much bloodshed. You can never tell. We might even loose them in the blackness and miss the fight all together. But I wouldn't count on it," Ordway said stoically.

It was darker down here, with only artificial light to see by. The sickbay was in the bow of the deck, with the crew hammocks located behind them in the mid section. Ordway's own quarters, along with the other officers, lay in the stern, the most senior holding up in separate rooms. Of course the captain's room was the largest but Ordway had never been invited in there, so he had only heard about it through the grapevine. Under normal conditions, there would be several men asleep at this time, who would work the night shift topside when the rest of the crew was sleeping. But the battle brought everyone on active duty and the deck was pretty deserted right now. Ordway wondered how many of those men might not come back here tonight. Would he?

"Well, I need to get to the magazine room," Ordway said suddenly. Time was growing short. "I'll be seeing you." Then he realized what he had said and added hurriedly "But not professionally, I hope!"

He descended once more through the hatch, the laughter from the good doctor following him from above. At this last floor, the light was so poor he could barely see anything. He felt along the deck heading towards the back, Blanco and Waldrop following close behind. He avoided coming down here as much as he could – he felt more claustrophobic when he couldn't see around him. Sweat broke out on his forehead and he wiped it away hurriedly. As he reached the back, he felt himself get shaky and he tried to calm down. It was not something he wanted his men to notice.

Suddenly there was movement behind him, and someone ran by, scaring him. Damn powder monkeys! They had a job to do, and they had to do it quickly, but did they have to scare him so much? *It's only because you're nervous down here, John. I'm being irrational – I know that. Just get to the business at hand and get out of here.*

The magazine room was actually accessed by a hole in the floor – a hatchway for those small enough to make it through. Fortunately, Ordway had no need or desire to squeeze into the small compartment himself. Instead he called out, "Franklin! It's Ordway from topside!"

A head suddenly poked out through the hatch. "Oh, John! Didn't see you!"

"Of course not, you oaf!" Ordway replied back sarcastically. "If you ever get better lighting down here…"

"We've been over that, Johnny boy. You know we have to keep the magazine powder safe and dry...and spark-free!" Franklin laughed. "You want more lighting – we'll light up the night-sky for miles around, if you bring a lantern down here!"

"Well, the capt'n is demanding my crew be fully stocked – and we're looking to engage within the hour. I've brought two men here to carry more gunpowder back with us."

"The boys will bring up extra munitions for you," Franklin said. "I'll pass up a barrel and your guys can take it with you." His head disappeared once again.

"Much obliged," Ordway said quietly to himself. He looked around, sweat pouring off his forehead now. *I hate coming down here! Why did I do this?! You know why, John. You have a duty! Now fulfill your duty!*

Quickly he backed up, muttered something to Waldrop as he went by, and almost ran back towards the bow...and the stairwell that would bring him out of this hellhole. A few minutes later, he was breathing in great, deep gasps of air, just below the topside stairwell. It was much better lit but the men couldn't see him. He couldn't risk that. He was an officer after all. He straightened his shirt, and wiped his brow one more time. Then he climbed the last remaining stairs and walked calmly and quietly up on deck.

It was here, out in the open air, where he found himself most effective, more at home. It was here, among the gunners topside that he was at his best. And once more, he vowed never to go to the bottom deck again.

The Guerriere was closer now, probably no more than 100 yards away, and off to port. They were trying to maneuver away, but Captain Hull was keeping contact with them as close as possible. Within another twenty minutes, the first shots might be fired. He found himself actually anxious for the battle ahead. *Don't try and compensate for your behavior below. Just do your job effectively and don't push it.*

Chapter 5

Ordway looked at his men with pride. They were a good group and he had trained them well. They reminded him of his last command, a group of adventure-lovers who needed some discipline in their lives. The fact that both of his commands had taken boys and turned them into mature, hard-working men was a testament to his own leadership abilities. *You did a good job with them, John. Now it's time to see what they can do.*

Seventy-five feet. Fifty feet. He looked behind him at his captain, waiting for the signal to fire. But Captain Hull stood his ground. Night was almost upon them and they had to be dead on, or risk losing them altogether.

When the distance closed to twenty-five feet, Hull gave a curt nod. His second-in-command called out loudly, "Port chasers! Fire one!"

Ordway gave the signal to the three gunners on the port side. Their cannon balls were already loaded and the powder was packed. All that was left was to light the powder on the firing hole and hope for the best. A thin line of gunpowder was laid out in a groove on top of the cannon before finally entering a small hole on top that lead to the explosive charge inside. As the spark from the first cannon reached its mark, a decisive and loud crack could be heard, and the cannon recoiled sharply in response. The second and third cannons fired in quick succession.

Cannon shot from the Guerriere followed and although one landed on deck, perhaps twenty feet from Ordway's position, there were no injuries. Ordway could see the mizenmast in the stern of the enemy ship and realized it was listing to starboard. It looked like it had taken at least one hit and that would seriously slow them down even further. He smiled to himself.

The two ships came alongside each other in a matter of minutes, each vessel exchanging cannon fire from very short range. The impact velocity from these heavy cannons was great, and although he could see considerable damage to the British frigate, there was hardly any on his own. Two cannon balls had reached the top deck of the Constitution, and three men had been injured. But the masts were still intact, and that meant power.

After the first pass, the American ship took the lead and did an about face, coming head to head with the Brits, ready for a second pass. The Guerriere was injured, Ordway knew, but this would only make them more desperate to turn the tide against the Americans. Grimly, he ordered his men to reload, and to concentrate the firepower on his starboard cannons. Their goal would be to come at them again, keeping their barrage on the damaged starboard side of the British frigate. With luck, they would be able to take out another mast or, perhaps, deliver the enemy a fatal blow.

Ordway looked out at the horizon. The setting sun was almost gone – there was perhaps only twenty minutes of remaining light, and it was waning at best. This last pass had to work!

As the Americans edged closer to the slower Brits, the enemy tried to maneuver away from them, making a slow turn towards port. For a few minutes, their damaged starboard side would be exposed and Ordway realized they had to make their charge now while the opportunity presented itself.

"Capt'n!" he cried. "They're turning to port! Now's the time to fire!" He realized the gunners were not finished prepping their cannons and he raced over to assist. Lifting one of the heavy iron balls, he dropped it into the open end of the cannon, and then watched as the gunner's mate took a long pole and packed gunpowder in afterwards. The second gunner's mate poured more powder in the grooved fuse line on top of the cannon.

"Keep it short, Waldrop! We don't want a long delay."

Then Ordway heard the order given from the second-in-command – the order to fire. The lieutenant repeated the order to his starboard gun crew and watched them light the fuse. First one cannon roared, followed by the second. The third however remained silent and Ordway looked down at the cannon, quickly searching for the cause. "It's the fuse line – it's clogged! Clear it out and relight now!" he bellowed.

The gunner did as he was commanded and this time they were both rewarded with a clear crack of the mighty weapon discharging its deadly volley. Ordway looked at the enemy ship and wondered if they had been too late.

Captain Hull took binoculars from one of his officers, and surveyed the damage. Ordway could tell, just by casual observation, that the mizenmast was now shot away completely, and the main and foremasts were also listing and damaged. Without their masts, the British ship would be without power or maneuverability and they would be in dire straits.

"Come along for one more pass, helmsman." Hull ordered, "But stay out of range of their guns." He ordered Ordway's gunners to reload and fire once more, to send a message to his British counterpart just who was in command.

"Sir, did you see that exchange?" Waldrop said to Ordway, as he set the gunpowder charge after the cannon ball. "I saw several shots just... bounce off our sides! We hardly got damaged at all!"

"Our sides are as wooden as theirs, Waldrop. The only metal we have is a few lines of copper sheathing below the water line. It did seem as though they bounced off, though. Must be from your thick iron heads!" Ordway joked.

"Give a huzzah for Ol' Ironsides!" Blanco called out, a cry that was repeated by many others that night. A new name was born.

Just then a remarkable sight occurred. First the main mast of the helpless Guerriere listed more to port and then split with an audible crack, followed by a few seconds later by the foremast. The lines of rigging and the weight of the sails must have contributed greatly to their ultimate demise, but Ordway knew his crew had played a hand in this incredible victory.

Within half an hour, a boat had been lowered alongside the Constitution, with an officer and a few crew members onboard. They rowed the short distance to the Guerriere which now lay in darkness and adrift, as helpless as a newborn baby in a rough sea. Ordway knew many a cannon shot had found its mark and pierced her side. It was very likely she would be gone by morning, sitting at the bottom of the Atlantic.

A short time later, the small boat returned, this time carrying with it a special visitor. The American officer, Lieutenant Reed, approached Captain Hull, his British visitor walking briskly behind him. Ordway came over to witness the exchange, one he will never forget.

"Captain Hull, I introduce Captain James Richard Dacres," he said with ceremony.

The British captain, appearing stoic in defeat, stepped forward, presenting his sword out as a gift. "As commander of the Britannic Majesty's Frigate, the Guerriere, I surrender my vessel to the United States frigate Constitution."

A cheer erupted from all around him, as Ordway felt happier than he had been in a while. A great victory for him, and for the United States. Old Ironsides – a good name!

Chapter 6

October 5, 1813
Chatham, Ontario

The man stood tall on the hill overlooking the grassy prairie below him. His shoulder-length red hair flowed out from beneath a coonskin cap and his weathered face squinted in the mid-morning sun. His dark brown leather jacket and pants blended in perfectly with the natural forest setting behind him, where his six-foot three-inch frame seemed more in keeping with the behemoths growing nearby.

He turned and called out quietly to the men assembled around him, some still in the tree line. "See those tracks in the grass, boys? They came through here, probably only a few hours ahead of us. We'll see if we can catch up with them. Let's go."

"Sir?"

Sergeant William Bratton turned around, his look quizzical.

"Yes, Frank?"

"Is it true we're...we're goin' after...Tecumseh?"

Bratton smiled. These green boys from Kentucky had not seen much action as of yet, but they sure heard the rumors about the feared Indian chief. They had heard the stories of the great Tecumseh leading the Tribe of Five Nations against the white man. Heard stories that would make your blood crawl. Heard tales of torture and painful death...but Bratton knew not to believe everything you hear.

"Yes, it's true that Tecumseh has aligned himself with the British general Henry Proctor. Harrison's men are chasing both armies at the moment. However, our mission right now is a little different."

He waited until the twenty men were fully assembled and giving him their undivided attention. He wanted to say this only once. The tall green grass and surrounding old forest gave off the smell of sweet honeysuckle and pine needles. Bratton breathed in the enticing aroma deeply.

"You have been hand selected for this mission by Isaac Shelby himself, the very governor of the great state of Kentucky. He picked you for your tracking abilities as well as your stealth and marksmanship. We've been on the move since this morning, as you know, tracking down supply wagons for the Brits." He looked at Frank, and then said in a voice an octave lower than normal, "We have word that Tecumseh's men are guarding the shipment."

"But..." Frank started to say, and then quickly stopped short when Bratton held up his hand for silence.

"We are members of United States army under the command of General William Henry Harrison, and we live to serve our country," said Bratton sternly. "Neither Indians not Brits will detour us from accomplishing our mission. Is that clear, soldier?"

Frank looked up and saluted smartly. He was learning fast, Bratton smiled to himself. He gave instructions to the men to track the wagons but warned them to be wary of traps set by the crafty Indians. He had seen enough damage done to a human body to last him a lifetime.

When most men were out of earshot, he strode up alongside Frank and put his arm around his shoulders. "Son, listen to me. I promised your father I would look after you, and I will. You have my word on that. You can't believe all the stories you hear – they were probably started by the Indians themselves just to frighten guys like you."

"I...I'm not frightened, sir..." stammered the boy.

"How old are you now, son? Fifteen, am I right?"

"Yes...yes, sir. Fifteen last month." Frank tried to brave a smile but it didn't stay long on his face.

"Wow. When I was fifteen, I was tracking rabbits in the forest and shooting squirrels with slingshots, not chasing Indians and redcoats. It's alright to be afraid. You just need to know how to use it – turn your fear into a defense - a heightened sixth sense, if you will. Don't let it eat you up inside. Use it – don't let it use you."

"Sir, you sound like my pa." the boy replied with a laugh. "He was always saying stuff like that."

"Yeah, I guess that's what pa's do. Well now I'm your pa. At least out here." The tall man stopped and gripped the boy on the shoulders, looking him square in the eye. "And don't you forget it, Frank. I have your back..."

28

"And I have yours. Sir!" the boy said grinning. His short blond hair and youthful face was tucked underneath a homemade hat from the skin of an animal known to none but himself. Possible beaver, Bratton reckoned. Or maybe raccoon. He'd have to ask him about it another time.

As the team spread out through the tall grass, they came to another crest of a hill. They slowed down, and stayed quiet, careful not to allow themselves to be spotted by prying eyes.

What they saw gave Bratton a start. Four wagons were moving across the valley, covered by two lines of Indians on both sides, perhaps ten in all. Fortunately for him, the wagon train seemed to be focusing on putting as much distance between them and their pursuers as possible, and not being too careful about the trail they left behind.

"I've got an idea," Bratton said excitedly, and his men gathered around him, eager to see what the red-headed outdoorsman would come up with. He quickly laid out what he had in mind and then looked at Frank when he was finished. The boy swallowed hard, then gave a nod. He was in.

Half of Bratton's forces, with Frank in the lead, scrambled into the tree line to the right, intending to make their way the short distance into the next clearing where the valley curved around, and the wagons would be coming upon them. The remaining men kept pace with the receding caravan from behind, making the two sided pincers complete.

When the wagons rounded the bend ahead, Bratton waited calmly, hoping, expecting Frank and his men to do their part as he had instructed. He only had to wait about twenty minutes until the wagons had reached the target zone and then he heard the first rifle shots and the initial yells from the Brits.

"Wait," he said, holding up his hand. "They have no idea how many men we have in front, and they will be expecting far greater numbers than we really have. When they double back our way, we'll lay into them. Just await my signal."

True to his word, the Brits started their turn and headed back up the valley, trying to coax every bit of speed from their tired horses. The Indians had been contracted to stay with the supply wagons, and so, after firing back a few volleys of their own, made their own retreat.

Upon reaching the curve in the valley once again, the wagons came under the deluge of firepower from the second half of the Americans and, finding themselves pinned down, hunkered under or around the four wagons as best they could. The Indians, for their part, realized they had run out of options and took off into the woods, leaving the Brits to their fate.

Bratton smiled as his plans came to fruition just as he had planned. With an incredibly small force, he had stopped and captured the British supply wagons, a great victory for him and his men. But before he could claim his prize, he had to force their surrender. *Don't count all the eggs in the basket, quite yet.*

He called for a cease-fire and the silence that followed was almost as loud as the barrage they had initiated. He wanted the Brits to sweat a bit, to see they had no other choice. The last thing he wanted to do was show his cards at this point. *How are you at poker, Sarge?*

"Attention!" he called out as loud as he could. "You are surrounded by the armed forces of General William Harrison. You are ordered to throw down your weapons and surrender immediately. Failure to do so will be suicide. You have..." he looked at a man next to him who held up five fingers. He shrugged, and continued "five minutes to comply."

"Why five minutes?" Bratton asked his friend, a fellow Kentuckian by the name of Bradley Barker.

"My kid turns five today," he smiled. "It won't last that long anyhow."

True to his word, the Brits were quick to come out of hiding, their spirit gone and their guns piled in a heap on the ground. Bratton and several men came out to collect them, making sure they had their backs covered at all times. The Indians could be lurking just in the tree line waiting for them. But he didn't think their allegiance with the Brits would stretch that far. No, most likely they were halfway to Tecumseh by now, wherever he was.

Bratton came upon the hapless lot of about fifteen prisoners, who sat in a circle, surrounded by a few guards he had posted. He was looking for their leader and found him easily enough, dressed in a wool overcoat with brass buttons. His regimental cap and uniform gave away his rank of Major. The American addressed his counterpart with a salute.

"Major?" Bratton said. "I thought we might have a word."

The British officer gave him the once over, and clearly did not like what he saw. "And who might you be? A fur trapper?" He laughed at his joke but it quickly died in his throat as a fist shot out from this leather-clad American and struck him square in the face. He went down hard holding his nose, as it started to bleed profusely. The prisoner looked completely befuddled, his eyes staring in disbelief at Bratton.

But the major wasn't done. He suddenly smiled through red-stained teeth. "Just you wait..." he sneered. "Just you wait till your band of upstarts reach McGregor's Creek – then you'll get what's coming to you."

The American sergeant looked at him hard, and suddenly realized what he needed to do. Leaving the prisoners to their fate, he pointed to Frank and Barker, and together they set off at a run.

Chapter 7

They entered the forest and kept up the pace, not bothering to slow down – time was running out. Bratton knew that the rest of Shelby's forces were planning to cross a portion of mighty Thames River at a bridge that spanned McGregor's Creek. But if the Brits or Indians had already planned for that, the Americans could be running right into a trap. *I have to warn them – it could be the difference of life and death!*

Within twenty minutes of this blistering pace, he started to encounter small pockets of Americans as they neared their destination. With the American forces standing at over three thousand men, with another thousand cavalry troops, finding a place to cross the river was of utmost importance. What could the Indians do? Bratton knew Tecumseh has only about five hundred warriors with him and Proctor had no more than a thousand British forces, so they were outnumbered by the Americans almost three to one. What better way of leveling the playing field than to not let them on at all?

How would they do that? *Destroy the bridge!* That had to be it! The Indians would be looking to destroy the bridge!

He ran on, until at last he reached the water's edge, just ahead of the most of the American forces. A sudden dread filled him. Just as he feared… the wooden bridge that would have carried them across the fifty foot span of water was now lying in rubble in the water below. He could see movement in the tree line on the opposite shore and realized it was a trap.

The first rifle shot struck a tree near him and he quickly dove for cover. He called out to any who would listen, "It's a trap! Go back!" but most of the men were still arriving and didn't know what was going on. Frank and Barker stayed with him, and he finally settled down.

"Okay, the bridge is down. I can't stop the men from coming…and besides there is no alternative route anyway. Somehow we have to overcome the Indians and get across this creek. And we need to do it now. Any suggestions?"

"Well, sir, if we put up a two sided front and start picking off the Indians from here, they might retreat. The key is to stay hidden ourselves," Barker replied.

Frank snapped his fingers. "And then we can put together a makeshift bridge – maybe get some logs and…hey, with all these men, it should come together in no time!"

Bratton smiled. "Alright, let's see if we can coax these redmen out from their cover." He called out hasty instructions to those around him, and the word was quickly passed on. With the Indians massed together on the far side just inside the tree line, Bratton sent one group of fifty men up north and another smaller group of twenty men south. Then, as one unit, they opened up on both sides on the Indian's hiding places, forcing them deeper into the woods.

At the same time, more men felled trees, both large and small, and lashed them into a workable bridge that was long enough to span the water.

A few brave souls even decided to wade through to the other side of the creek further downstream and came up on the far side, shooting at anything that moved in the forest. Within an hour, they had seen the back of the last Indian as he retreated with his comrades and a cheer went up on the American side. The bridge was quickly laid down and the long procession started to cross.

"Sir, how close are we to…you know?" Frank asked carefully as they walked together an hour after the crossing. A long line of men followed them and stretched into the distance ahead. Three thousand men, Bratton marveled. *I hope to see the same sight tomorrow.*

"Well, I'm not rightly sure, but it all depends on how eager they are to fight us. They keep up the pace and we follow, but sooner or later – hopefully sooner - they will turn and fight. When we captured their supply wagons - that had to inflict some damage to them. There was food there to last a long time – without it, they'll be down to half-rations by now. They might have to turn and take a stand soon."

"If you were Proctor, where would you do it?" Barker asked, as he walked behind his friend.

"I don't think it's a matter of where…but when." The veteran soldier replied. "He needs to do it soon, or he'll find himself without an army."

By nightfall, word from the scouts ahead indicated the British and the remaining Indian forces were settling in and preparing for a morning fight. The Americans made camp for the night, setting up temporary tent villages along the damp foothills of the Thames. The air was chilly and sleep was hard to come by. The tension in the air was heavy and thick with anticipation, as each man began to wonder – would they make it back alive? Would they survive yet another day? Bratton thought the British must be thinking the same thing, and he was suddenly glad he was on this side of the line.

Chapter 8

There was a meeting scheduled for 2100 hours and Bratton reported to the large tent with two minutes to spare. It was good size – enough to fit thirty men standing comfortably. And it was overflowing tonight. He entered quietly, looking around at the assembled officers. While some heads turned his way, most averted their gaze. While he was technically a sergeant, he did not exactly look or dress the part, and, for some, that was enough to distrust him. *Let them think what they want. I'm not strictly regulation but I've got more experience in the woods than all of these desk pushers put together.*

"Attention!" a voice bellowed out. Immediately officers in the tent stood up straight, as the striking figure of General William Henry Harrison strode into the room. He was dressed smartly, with a crisp, clean uniform and polished black leather boots – a sharp contrast with many of the men in the room, who had spent the greater part of the last month walking in the rain and mud up through Canada chasing Proctor and Tecumseh at the general's discretion.

"At ease," Harrison said. He walked towards a table and chair made available to him, but did not sit. Instead he leaned on the table with his fists and looked out among the assembled group.

"Tomorrow. We attack tomorrow at dawn," he stated as if to answer the question on everyone's mind. Men turned to look at each other, but no one interrupted their commander.

"The scouts have determined the location of the enemy and where they stand." A large map of the area lay on the table and he pointed out the spots that indicated where the enemy soldiers were situated. "The Brits have aligned themselves about two clicks north of the Thames, where the valley narrows slightly. Tecumseh, we are told, has positioned his army to the left next to the river, in the swamps while the Brits have guns on the high ground above on the right. They are ill equipped and running on half rations. But they are desperate and might put up a fight."

A young man wearing captains bars spoke up. "General, how will we be positioned for the attack?"

"We will be set up to charge on two flanks. Colonel Richard Johnson will lead his team of twenty cavalry volunteers against Tecumseh followed by the 500 man infantry. I stress that these men are volunteers because they will be taking the brunt of the initial Indian attack." He turned towards a man sitting near him, and nodded in his direction. "Colonel Johnson, the floor is yours."

Johnson, a middle aged man with a streak of gray in his brown hair, bowed slightly at his superior and approached the table. Bratton knew of his reputation, and that of his military family. In fact, he was not the only Johnson represented here tonight.

"Thank you, general. As you know, it's our duty to engage the Indians and show Tecumseh and his warriors a thing or two about American military. In my advance squad, which I will lead personally, each horse will have two riders, and each man will be equipped for both horseback and hand-to-hand combat with a rifle, a hatchet, and a knife. With luck on our side, we will draw the Indians away from the forest and into the open where our infantry can engage them more easily."

Heads nodded in appreciation from many assembled members, as Johnson continued. "While we charge Tecumseh, I have ordered my brother, James, to lead the cavalry against the British forces on the right. We have gotten word that the British 41st battalion are setup in the forest on the right, and I know the best way to deal with them is to lead our own Kentucky backriders against them. No one rides the woods better than the boys from Kentucky!"

Bratton smiled at this comment, for although he was not part of the cavalry, he appreciated the nod toward his fellow statesmen. *And given half a chance, I'd beat most of them myself.*

"We all know what happened when our army was wiped out by the British and Indian forces at the Raisin River in Michigan last January. We must let that be our rallying cry! We must use that as our personal motivation when all else is gone! I urge you all tonight, tomorrow, and forever, to remember the River Raisin! Do not let it happen again!"

36

A great cheer went up in the tent that night, and word was spread through the American forces that a victory tomorrow would avenge the death of so many lost to us in battle. *Remember the Raisin!*

By early morning, the American forces were up and moving again, with Bratton and his men marching with the first line of Kentucky cavalry under direction of Captain James Johnson. Young though he was, he came from a well-respected line of military officers, and he was well liked. And he was smart too, a trait not every officer shared.

The men in blue assembled in small groups just below the rise in the hill that would lead them on a direct charge against the waiting redcoats and their long cannons. Although the British soldiers were undoubtedly tired, hungry, and disheartened, their cannons remained as deadly and violent as ever.

Bratton waited with the rest of his men, including Frank and Bradley. Each man was formally outfitted with a rifle, but the Kentucky men never went anywhere without their own knife or axe, a habit picked up by necessity of outdoor living. Suddenly a bugle sounded in the distance and stopped, only to repeat a moment later. The charge was on!

Bratton shouted to his men and, as one, they ran over the hill and down the other side. The Kentucky cavalry were riding very hard in front, determined to get behind the enemy lines as quickly as possible and neutralize the dreaded guns. To this end, they proved very effective.

By the time Bratton could pick out and engage the first British soldier, the guns had gone silent and the redcoats were in a state of disarray. His spirits picked up a bit as he saw the British line scatter and fall back, once, twice, and then suddenly there was no where to go. Within ten minutes, the British had surrendered. Bratton looked around and could identify no causalities on the American side. A few bodies of redcoats lay on the ground but their numbers were no more than a handful. Bratton shifted his attention to the other side of the valley floor now, where the Americans had engaged the more determined forces of the Indian Shawnee chief Tecumseh.

"Men!" Bratton shouted suddenly. "Follow me! The rest of you, join us!" And without looking back, he ran as hard as could towards the swampland where a more bloody campaign was being carried out nearby.

While still a good hundred yards away from the nearest Indian, Bratton could tell the fight wasn't going well, and he saw several bodies lying on the ground, almost half of which were wearing the blue coats of the Americans. Shouts rose up, both in anger and in fright, as the Indians, outnumbered and outgunned, put up a determined fight alongside their famous leader Tecumseh. The man who orchestrated the union of five separate Indian nations into a single fighting unit, who trusted his friendship with the British in the hopes of driving out the encroaching white Americans, this man fighting by their side, on this day, at this hour... This was the man that both sides respected. This was the man who drove them on, and engaged their will to fight.

This last bastion of Indian strength was in the thick of it, directing his warriors onward, his long black hair draped down his back, his clothing decorated with the symbols of the Shawnee – a wooden necklace, cords of beads and feathers. His bare chest and head was adorned with war paint, both black and red, and his body was in constant motion. Bratton could see the other warriors were inspired by him and took direction from him – a trait which made him particularly dangerous to the white men he faced. He was more than one man – he was their rock.

There were only two men still on horseback now, the other riders having fallen or jumped off their wounded steeds. Bratton saw the cavalry commander, Col. Richard Johnson, was still astride his white stallion, despite bleeding from several different places. He stayed in the foray with his sword raised, sometimes sending it crashing down on the heads of the Indians around him.

Now everyone was fighting hand-to-hand with the redmen and Bratton joined in the fray, his rifle finding its mark, once, then twice. Suddenly there was a great shout that rose above the rest, and all at once every head turned towards the sound, as men on both sides stopped their attack. A circle of men slowly backed away from a figure on the ground, and suddenly someone shouted "Tecumseh...is dead!"

Bratton could not see the body clearly but he noted that it seemed to unnerve the rest of the Indians, many of whom broke off the attack and headed into the forest trees. As more and more retreated, they gave off a shout that seemed both anguished and chilling – the passing of their leader marked the end of their campaign here – and perhaps the end of their way of life as they knew it.

Many soldiers chased the Indians into the forest but Bratton stayed behind, and indicated to the men in his command to do the same. The fighting was over – a wise man knew when to put away the sword. Only a fool rushes headlong into danger unnecessarily.

There were hundreds of men milling about, some caring for their wounded compatriots, and others covering up the dead. The ground was soft and muddy, a perfect place for the Indians to have set up their attack, Bratton realized. Horses would get stuck and their riders would find themselves surrounded and defenseless. He took off his hat and said a small prayer for those brave men who would not make it home tomorrow.

Tecumseh was dead, and the British had surrendered. The great American victory was sweet for a day. Tomorrow would bring another battle, another chance to give one's life in this blasted war. But today, they would celebrate. The bloodshed was over. Sgt. William Bratton replaced his hat and walked off across the valley floor.

Chapter 9

"**D**ouble-time, soldier! Pick up the pace!" a gruff voice bellowed, close to his ear. Charles "Chip" Parker, a young lad who celebrated his sixteenth birthday last week, and hoped to celebrate his seventeenth someday, ran faster.

"That's it, people! Keep up! Don't let me catch you slacking off!" the voice continued unabated. "Only ten more miles to go!"

"Permission to speak! Sir!" called out a strong voice that came toward the front of the long line of men in blue.

"What is it, *private*?" the voice asked, the last word dripping with sarcasm.

"When did you get to be such an ass?"

At the sound of that startling retort, several heads turned suddenly to see the reaction from the man giving orders.

Sergeant Patrick Gass, jogging along beside his men, surprised them. He stopped in his tracks and stood there, then gave into a hearty laugh that rooted him to the spot.

Stocky and well muscled, the 43 year old staff sergeant suddenly bolted into a dead run, passing the man who dared to utter such a remark to his superior and slowed down to a jog beside him.

"I think you need a refresher course in basic training, Gavigan." Gass said. "Now you just take that attitude of yours and stow it away real quiet like. No need rustling up my feathers now, ya hear?"

"Loud and clear, sir!" Gavigan replied in earnest. Then he turned and smiled at his commanding officer. "But you're still an ass."

The two men laughed together and Gass replied, "I know, but you wouldn't have it any other way."

"No, sir!" Gavigan said. Tall and lean, this string-bean of a man hailing from Tennessee, often enjoyed needling Gass whenever he could. But he understood where, and, more precisely, with whom, to draw the line.

As part of the two thousand-strong American brigade under Major-General Jacob Brown, Gass lead his company of forty-four men south along the Niagara River in Southern Canada. Having stayed part of the summer months up north outside the British Fort George in the small town of Queenston, they had faced daily harassment from both Indians and British forces.

Unable to attack the fort due to limited reinforcements, the Americans held their position for a time, but then Brown received word that their supply lines were being intercepted. Deep in hostile territory, Brown had ordered them back to the relative safety of the Chippewa River and from there, towards the city of Burlington to the west.

Still several miles from the Chippewa, the men were taking their state of affairs gamely. Tired from the strain of the last few months, Gass' men were looking forward to relaxing a bit in more friendly territory. And the good sergeant was determined to keep their heads high.

"What I wouldn't give for a little steak…" said one voice quietly nearby.

Another chimed in, the eagerness evident in his voice. "Forget the food, I'd like some little…"

"We'll all be home soon enough," Gass said amicably. Their company passed others in front and was the first to reach the destination for the night, a flat field under a starry sky, only 100 yards from the Chippewa River. The Chippewa extended 75 yards across to the other side but it was not the intentions of the Americans to cross the span. Tomorrow they would head west along its banks and make their way to Burlington, a town that marked their return to American soil.

As the hot July afternoon drew on, more and more men arrived to the site, and within the hour, Gass saw the flags of General Brown and his contingent of officers appear. But the officers tagging along with the general were talking in earnest to each other and Brown himself did not retire to his tent as was his custom after a long march. Scouts were continuing to arrive, looking more worried than Gass would have expected. After all, they were leaving the British behind. Weren't they?

Gass decided to find out what was going on but before he could get close to the general, he was accosted by another officer, a lieutenant whose name Gass did not remember.

"Did you hear?" the man said worriedly. "The Brits are coming down after us! Word has it than Lt. General Tucker had a brigade of men coming down the east bank! Brown might have us go back towards Fort George again!"

Back where they came from? Gass had known leaders to pull such stunts but he had hoped to put this Niagara campaign behind him tomorrow. Maybe it's just a rumor. *The boys are anxious to get home and I don't blame them.* In a matter of hours, though, the rumor was confirmed.

"But Sarge!" one young man said after hearing the news of their impending northward return march.

"Can't help it, Roberts." Gass explained. "Brown wants to keep them off our backs by making a march back north against the fort. They can't cross the Niagara yet so they'll have to pull back to protect the fort. We'll get back here eventually."

"We don't need 'em hounding us all the way home, either," Gavigan chimed in. "I like Brown's thinking. Show a little aggression, and maybe they'll back down."

"Maybe," replied Gass. "Maybe."

The next morning, the sergeant woke up before sunrise, feeling the dew on the tent. It covered everything it touched like a cold blanket; the rays of the sun were still an hour off.

He roused his men, as was his custom, and then sat back to watch the sunrise. He loved the outdoors, and he felt more comfortable in the back woods than in a big house. *This is God's playground after all.*

Over the course of the next few hours, the camp slowly awoke and started making preparations for their campaign back up north towards Fort George. General Brown had received word last week that the fort was to change leadership sometime soon, with British Lieutenant Governor Gordon Drummond personally coming to take charge. It was unclear when he would arrive or how he would take to his new command, but Gass would not put it past Brown to try and shake up the new commander if he could.

By mid-afternoon, a column of men in blue uniforms were seen snaking a course back up the path they had just traversed the previous day. Walking in small groups, the two thousand strong army tried to stick to the dirt road paralleling the Niagara River. For the past half hour, the river and the road weaved through a small forest and the men followed it dutifully. It was one of many they had traveled the last few days.

Gass led his company near the front of the parade, just behind the 25th infantry from Connecticut, led by his friend Daniel Ketchum, a rare breed of a man who ruled with unbridled discipline and passion. The 25th infantry, under his command, had been transformed into an elite, special-forces squad, one of the first of its kind in the American army.

As the men continued to march northward, the sergeant began to hear the roaring coming from the river to his right. The dampness in the air gave him an unmistakable sign of the turmoil occurring just behind the trees. *The great waterfall of the Niagara.* They were probably only a few hundred yards away at this point and Gass didn't want to get any closer than this. One wrong move too close to the edge...and you would plummet over a sheer drop that granted certain death, albeit a quick one. No, it was best to let nature alone when death can come from so many other ways.

Despite the summer heat, Gass did not permit himself or his men the luxury of a respite – the English were near, most likely just across the river themselves. He wondered, not for the first time that morning, how long they'd be forced to march northward before turning back. The strategy of the march was not so much to make an actual attack on the fort – but to put the suggestion in the minds of their counterparts and force them to make a defensive move. Another two days, most likely, just until...

The roar of the cannon fire could be suddenly heard above the quiet rush of the river, off to their left – and broke the silence of the men who were nearby. The sheer number of large trees all around them prevented the Americans from seeing where the cannon fire had started, but as more Americans came up from behind him on the narrow road, Gass felt a dreadful sense of entrapment. *Can't go forward, can't go back, and chaos all around us. Just great.*

But Gass quickly rallied, and gathering his men around him, directed them towards the tree line off the side of the road on the left, away from the river. They didn't want to expose themselves to the enemy but he needed to see what they were up against. After ten minutes of walking painstakingly slow among the tree line, the sergeant put up his hand, a silent signal for his men to halt. The cannon fire had continued every few minutes and now all the men could hear the cries and screams of the Americans caught under its deadly bombardment.

Gass looked out and saw a large clearing ahead, with a series of small hills looming in the distance. Figures dressed in red were standing on the top and no less than three cannons could be seen pointed down towards them. Smoke from the cannons had not dissipated in the heat of the day and it made visibility difficult. The open fields stretched for perhaps 200 yards before beginning its gentle slope up the hills.

Across the fields between the two forces of men stood wooden picket fences and tall waist-high grasses, good for cover, but not for much else. The tree line skirted around the hills on both sides, giving the Americans some cover if they stayed there. But out in the open, they were sitting ducks. He saw dozens of bodies already in the field, cut down in their tracks. His own anger began to rise, and he forced himself to calm down.

Where are we, anyhow? He wondered. Then he recognized the area from the topography maps he had examined on the way down. *This must the hilltop road called Lundy's Lane.* He remembered there being an old cemetery on top of the hill with what looked like a good vantage point over the valley. He remembered passing the house of the elderly Mrs. Wilson a half hour before, as she sat on her front porch silently watching the procession. She had allowed some of the men a drink from her well on their march south yesterday and, judging from her posture this morning, was none too keen on seeing them again so soon.

Grimly, he realized the British must have marched a group down *both* sides of the river and setup an ambush along the ridge. Did the Wilson lady know about this and remained silent? He hoped she had not known – he didn't want to end this day, or his life, being deceived by an elderly civilian. Not when he could have done something about it. *Forget her. Get on with it, Patrick!*

He saw members of Ketchum's company, the elite squadron of the 25th infantry, alongside Brigadier General Winfield Scott on horseback, and decided it was time to strategize. Their own forces were building up in the forest and he knew Scott would be looking for advice and a plan of action.

Over the next ten minutes, Gass set about convincing the old commander of his plan, and how it was looking to be a quick and dirty affair. Gass could tell, just by how the general's green eyes grew a little bigger and how he stood straighter in the saddle, that he was accepting the idea from the upstart Irish sergeant.

"I've had captains who I don't think could come up with something half that brazen, Sergeant, but I'll let you do it. Combine your men with Ketchum and have a go."

Gass kept his enthusiasm to himself, for there was a very good chance his idea would not pan out. But it was their best shot.

"Come with me, boys!" he cried out, and Ketchum's company of thirty-one men followed along with his forty-four, giving him a small but strong punch to deliver.

Chapter 10

It was time-consuming work, as they picked their way through the tree line skirting the open fields. Gass could see columns of men running out into the open, trying to climb the fence, dodge the bullets and avoid the cannon fire. Few succeeded in getting very far and those who did, were quickly dispatched at close range by the watching redcoats. Many of their bayonets were already stained with blood.

Within twenty minutes, he and his men were in position, as yet undetected by the enemy. Their current position put them on the side of the British, just down the hill from their guns which were pointing away from them. Gass gave silent instructions to each man and, when he was ready, brought his arm down in a gesture of action. At this point, stealth was the key, the element of surprise the only way to climb the hill before being cut down themselves.

The smoke that covered the valley helped the Americans to hide until it was almost too late for the British to react. Their quick and silent attack was devastating, as each American found a target and delivered their own brand of justice. Many of the guns were captured and the British, fearing a larger number of forces, started retreating off the hills towards the north.

There were a few British officers on horseback and it was evident that they were taken completely off guard by the assault. A few started circling around their own men, urging them to regroup and defend, some of whom complied.

One of the officers was only about twenty feet away from him, his torso hit several times with musket shot and bleeding considerably. Gass signaled to three of Ketchum's men to go after him. An officer such as this one, who was pretty decorated from the medals that adorned his uniform, would raise a good ransom. Provided he lived through the ensuing battle.

Such captures and post-battle payments for their release were common practice among both sides, and Gass saw an opportunity he didn't want to see get away. No one would pay much for a foot soldier, but an officer, maybe a lieutenant or a captain? There was something to be said for that. Despite their disadvantage on the ground, it didn't take the Special Forces trio long to dismount the officer from his steed and truss him up like a Thanksgiving turkey.

The three men carried their prize back into the tree line, a gift to General Scott. Gass remained on the hill, hoping the British would forget the battle and keep going north. But within ten minutes, he realized this would not be over that quickly.

A rallying cry was heard from the north end of the hill and several of Gass' men tried vainly to move the enemy cannons before they were overrun by the returning British. They disabled one by breaking its wheel but they were forced to leave the others behind. What was left of Ketchum's company and Gass' men, made a quick exit back to the tree line just as redcoats began swarming the hill again. Their retreat was successful and they were not followed. But the guns that had briefly been theirs were once again back in enemy hands. Gass felt badly about the outcome, but he hoped some good could still come out of it.

Once in the tree line, he was able to survey the field below. He had momentarily forgotten the men trying to cross the open field and was surprised and heartened by the sight before him. Hundreds of men had now managed to cross the wooden fence, and were either now climbing or starting to climb the hill now retaken by the British. At this range and this angle, those mighty long range British cannons would be almost useless. In fact, he could already see the redcoats moving away from them and starting to engage the Americans in hand-to-hand combat among the tombstones of the hilltop cemetery.

After another fifteen minutes of a careful descent back through the tree line, Gass and his men quickly made their way to the new command center. General Scott paced up and down between two trees and he smiled when he saw who had just arrived. They took the prisoner inside and set about addressing his wounds.

Ten minutes went by as Gass waited for instructions from his commander. He was itching to get into the action and protect the men.

"Sergeant!" Scott said loud enough to be heard from at least several yards in any direction. Gass came over and saluted smartly.

"Sir!" he said, while his men stood at attention behind him. Suddenly, Captain Daniel Ketchum, his friend and leader of the elite 25th, came out of the nearby tent, a broad grin spread across his face.

"Tell them what they've won, captain," the general said smugly.

"I guess won isn't the right word here. Perhaps captured would be more to the point." Ketchum said. He slapped his hand smartly across the broad back of the Irishman. "You hit the mother load, my friend! You just captured your very own British General! He's been shot several times, and in a bad way, but none of the wounds seem life-threatening. At least not now."

"A general?" Gass exclaimed, not quite believing it himself.

"Yes, sir. Major-General Phineas Riall, who is in charge of this sortie on Lundy's Lane here. A prize catch, indeed." Ketchum said with pride.

"Good work, sergeant. And you as well, captain," Scott said, nodding his head in their direction. "Now that you've stopped the guns, it's up to us to take that hill. Round up your men and let's have at 'em!"

He didn't want to be the one to tell the general the British cannons were technically not eliminated and still remained in enemy hands, but if they managed to take the hill for good, it would be the same thing. The British advantage over their position would be gone. He turned towards his own men, forty-two still standing. Private Jeff Grossman has been injured and he had sent him back towards the rear of the American column. And Private Jackson... well, what was there to say? He had given his life in defense of his country.

"Men, the momentum is ours now, and let's take this hill and drive them all the way back to England!" Gass said with gusto.

The men took up the rallying cry and together they sprinted across the valley floor, using the paths through the tall grass that previous columns of men had stomped down before them. When they reached the wooden picket fence, they tore down what remained and kept going. They had the advantage of knowing that there would be a minimum of shooting aimed at them for now. The big guns were silent, the small musket flashes ahead being the only indication of where the soldiers were. Smoke and fog had enveloped the valley and the hill by now, and as darkness fell, it became almost impossible to identify friend from foe.

Gass halted his men just before the cemetery hill. Individual fights were taking place around them, but he wanted them focused on the task at hand. Be careful who you trade shots with, he instructed them. Be sure it's one of the

British, they of the bright red coats. If in doubt, call out your own identification first, and hopefully they'll do the same. The English are honorable...at least most of them. But if in serious doubt or if you feel in danger, shoot first and we'll sort it out later.

"Now go!" he said, and turned on his heels and ran up the mountain into the face of the enemy. The further he rose into the hills, the same ones he had been at just an hour earlier, the thicker the smoke became. He coughed and put a scarf around his mouth and nose in order to breathe better. He saw just in front of him a looming figure and he raised his pistol to ward off the attack!

Then a shot rang out and he heard a cry from behind him. Gass whirled around and saw a British soldier kneeling in pain, clutching his chest, blood beginning to seep through his fingers. The sergeant dove to one side behind an ancient tombstone and the shooter ran on as if Gass had never been there. He realized just then how close he had come to killing one of his own in self-defense, and how close he had almost come to being killed himself. *Gotta watch out, Patrick!*

He tried to block out the cries of pain as the wounded fell around him, as metal shots tore away both stone monuments and people's lives. The battle seemed to go on forever, darkness surrounding them, with no light at all save for those instruments that delivered the deathly firepower. Men rushing around through the haze, not knowing who they were up against, or even if they would live to see the morning's first light. He had been in many conflicts during his career, but he was not afraid to admit that, on this night, surrounded by hundreds of men, he never felt more alone.

At close to midnight, near as he could tell, Gass heard a bugle sound to his left, and he got up slowly from where he had fallen. The man who lay under him did not rise, and the sergeant could tell that he never would again. A knife stuck in the dead man's chest and Gass pulled it out slowly, taking the time to close the man's staring eyes. He knew the sound of the bugle meant retreat, and he had had enough of the fighting to last a lifetime. Without looking around him, he headed back quickly towards the sound. His body ached in more places than he cared for, and he wanted to get as far away from this place of despair as fast as possible.

Hours later, the light of morning dawn had brought the grim realities of the previous night into a clearer focus. As the Americans headed south once more, their numbers had been almost cut in half. General Scott himself had been wounded badly when he had come upon the hill fighting alongside his men, and had been rushed away ahead of the retreating column. Gass was covered in cuts and bruises but would certainly live to tell the story – of one of the deadliest fighting in the campaign that year. Of his men, only thirty of the forty-two remained alive and walking. Four were wounded but could manage on their own. In all, a grim and deadly reminder of the tragedies of this war.

Chapter 11

August 20, 1814
St. Louis, Missouri

The letter was old, penned eight years, five months four days ago to be precise. The holder of the letter was careful with it, gingerly refolding it and pressing it back between the pages of the journal from where he had been keeping it all this time. He closed his eyes as the memories of the past continued to wash over him, threatening to drown him with their own intensity and excitement. He welcomed them for, in truth, they were all he had left of his friend, Meriwether.

A hollow rapping jolted him from his momentary reflection and his bright blue eyes flew open, then darted away quickly from the sunlight that cascaded through the glass picture window. Those eyes sparkled in their brilliance and he smiled as the memories slowly retreated from his consciousness. The man rose from the couch, all six foot two inches of him, solidly built, and dressed to the nines. He gathered himself mentally then spoke in a soft voice that almost seemed out of place for the man.

"Let them in, York."

The two heavyset white doors leading into his office opened as one, and a large black man, dressed in a fine looking suit and tie, announced the visitors. "Mr. Clark, may I present Mr. Colter, Mr. Ordway, Mr. Bratton, and Mr. Gass." His mouth moved into a half smile. "I'm sure you have much to talk about." He shut the doors behind him, leaving his master alone with the newcomers.

"Come in, gentlemen!" William Clark said with genuine affection. He held out his arms wide and the four men, with hats in their hands, quickly came over and shook hands with him. Smiles and heartfelt greetings took up the next few minutes.

"Well, well, tell me what you've been up to lately." Clark said as he took his place behind his solid oak desk. It was large and uncluttered, the way he liked everything in his life. Wide open, no limits. He indicated that the four men should take seats opposite him.

"Well, governor," Ordway said, looking around at all the assembled men as he spoke, "as you probably know, I accepted an offer to go sailing around New England with some of the newer ships the union has put out. Caught some big fish too."

"Did ya' save any for the rest of us?" Colter asked deadpan.

"I know you didn't drain the ocean 'cause I found plenty of the English variety up north myself," chimed in Gass.

"What about you, William?" Clark asked.

"Well, sir, I don't think I've done as much fishing as these here gentlemen," Bratton said slowly, drawing on each word. "But I've managed to keep busy with the natives."

"Didn't you do some fighting with Boone a year or so back, John?" Clark asked the trapper.

"Yes sir, I had a farm in New Haven, Missouri, when the war started, and signed up rightly. My new wife Sallie, didn't particularly care much for the idea – said I already done my service. But I saw it different. Nathan Boone was my commandin' officer. His father is a big senator now, but used to be quite the frontiersman, I hear. Daniel, his name was. Maybe you heard of 'em."

Clark nodded in understanding. Truth be told, he knew exactly what each of them had been doing for the past several years. For he would be derelict in his duties to go forward with the information he had, without knowing their backgrounds thoroughly.

"Well," he said, sitting back in his chair, as he surveyed the four men sitting before him. "I guess you all want to know why I've asked you here today." He got up slowly and walked around the table toward them.

"Well, I 'spect you didn't call us out of bed to talk about fishin'" Colter said dryly.

"You are correct, my friend." Clark said softly, almost to himself. Gass looked at Bratton sitting next to him, a slightly worried look in his eye.

"I have brought you here on behalf of Meriwether Lewis."

"Mr. Lewis?" Ordway asked, puzzled. "I heard he died a few years back."

"Yeah," Colter interjected, "some paper I read said he bought it on the Natchez Trace, down in Tennessee. Maybe '08 or '09".

"It was 1809. October 11 to be exact," Clark said.

The four men looked at him, expectantly. Rising to his full height, he straightened his starched shirt and looked at them, each one in turn. "Meriwether was my friend for many years. He was your leader on one of the greatest journeys ever taken by modern man. An expedition that will define a new nation. He was a great man."

"Here, here!" Ordway said loudly.

"Mr. Lewis held my post, as governor of the Louisiana Territory, back in '08-'09. Of course now, they call it the Missouri Territory. Same place, new name. Politicians," he said dismissively. "What can you do?"

He paused here, thinking of the time when he first heard the news himself. "Mr. Lewis was traveling along the Natchez with a small party, on his way to the capital, when he stopped at a local inn. The Grinder's Stand. It was here that he met his... untimely fate. Marshals were called in when his traveling companion, Captain Neely, reported his death, and they found him at the inn. I was notified by Captain Neelly on the 13th by courier."

"What did they say killed him?" Colter asked.

Clark looked down for a moment, as he thought of the best way to phrase it. "He was shot, and the rifle was found nearby, so they thought it might be suicide. The door was locked from the inside. The owners of the inn, a married couple who lived in an adjacent building, said they heard nothing out of the ordinary. At the time, the authorities did little else. They sat on it for a while, had a preliminary inquiry, interviewed some witnesses and took statements, and they eventually closed the file on the case. Officially, the cause of death was gunshot, but no one was ever held responsible. He was buried on a bluff near Grinder's Stand where he died."

The men were silent for a moment, deep in thought about the revelations surrounding the death of their friend and former commander.

"I was devastated, when I heard, of course." Clark continued. "I came down to see for myself but the marshals didn't want me involved. He was my friend, but I felt...powerless to do anything. Nothing would bring him back. A few years passed, and I was given this post last year, July in fact, 1813. I felt honored to take his old position, and oversee the same lands he once held dear. As did we all."

"I think a part of us never left, sir." Bratton said softly. "I think we're all, in some way, a testament to that." He gestured his arms wide to include everyone around them. "We've traveled far and wide since those days, yet we've found our way back."

"Speak for yourself. Some of us were summoned back against our will," Colter replied.

Ordway gave him a sour look. "Look, John, you may not like it, but would it pain you to show a little respect?"

"Respect? I'll show you some respect!" Colter said explosively. Then he took a moment to calm himself. "I've got nothing 'gainst you, Mr. Clark," he said in a quieter tone, "but I get rankled by authority figures when they interfere with my livelihood, so to speak. I had to cut my tradin' season short to make this little excursion down here, and probably lost a good month of pelts."

"And you are the only one who ever sacrifices?" Ordway said reproachfully. "How about the rest of us? I know Patrick was up in the north country just last month, fighting for his country. I don't see any stars and stripes on your sleeve."

"Gentlemen, let's not get into it," Clark said. "You sound like you did the first time you two met. Do you remember that? I had to lock you in the stockade, Mr. Colter, for insubordination. And, you, sergeant," he said, nodding towards Ordway, "had a lot to learn about leading men. Let's hope you both learned something since then, or there will be no point in going further with my plans today. Maybe ever."

"Plans, sir?" Bratton asked. "What plans do you have for us?"

"Well," the governor began, then stopped suddenly to cough discretely to one side. "Pardon me. I think that, despite the warm weather, I have a bit of the bug. That's what I get for landing a desk job."

Colter looked like he was going to make a remark at this, but stopped himself. Ordway noticed, and permitted himself a slight smile.

"In my new position as governor, I have made friends with some members of Congress and others in certain high places over the last year. I took it upon myself to re-examine some evidence regarding the circumstances of his death. What I have found recently has given me more determination than ever before to uncover the truth. I owe it to him. As do you all. And it is to you that I am turning. For it is you, who have walked with me during an extraordinary journey and charted the vast reaches of this great country, that I alone can turn to. I entrusted my life to you years ago and you to me. I am commissioning you to discover the truth surrounding the death of our friend, your commander, Meriwether Lewis."

The four men didn't speak for a while, trying to assimilate what he had just asked of them. Finally Patrick Gass spoke up.

"Sir, what makes you think we can do what the marshals couldn't? We don't have the authority to get most of the stuff we'd be lookin' for."

Clark stood up smartly and held up his right hand. He asked the four men to do likewise. "I, William Clark, governor of the Missouri Territory, hereby deputize you all, Patrick Gass, William Bratton, John Colter, and John Ordway, to serve as my consul and with my authority, investigate all manners pertinent to the death of Mr. Meriwether Lewis, passed away October 11th, in the year of our lord, 1809." He lowered his hand and then said. "I have document papers all ready in order which you will get to keep, granting full authority in all manners of the investigation. Up to the highest reaches of government. All I need is your agreement. Do I have it?"

"When do we start, sir?" Gass asked with a smile.

Clark smiled and looked at the four men assembled in front of him. *That excursion of ours bridged more than oceans, chartered more than forests and rivers. It forged a link between men so strong that death itself could not break them.*

Chapter 12

"Thank you, gentlemen," he said. "There is much to discuss. Much to relate to you concerning the new evidence I have uncovered. Why don't we retire to my dining room where we can sort it out over a good meal? It might be the last decent meal you'll get in a while."

Clark walked to the wooden doors from which they had come, opened them, and ushered his guests into the hallway. He turned left, guiding them past several closed doors, their footsteps echoing softly on the hard wooden floors. They emerged onto the patio terrace, where a table had been setup for them. York stood off to one side, awaiting their arrival. Once they were seated, he slowly wheeled out a cart, from which emanated a fragrant and delicious aroma.

While the men dined on roasted pheasant, potatoes, and sweet corn, the governor laid out the facts as he had them. The four men listened to him carefully, only occasionally interrupting with a pertinent question.

"After Captain Neelly's summons, an army team arrived from Fort Pickering near Memphis to Grinder's Stand to investigate on his death. They did a cursory examination on the body, before burying him nearby. The army reported in official records he had shot himself with his rifle in the head, at point blank range. Somehow he misjudged the angle and managed to give himself only a grazing wound, not life-threatening. Then he took the same rifle and shot himself again in the chest, just below the sternum. They said the death was officially a suicide."

Clark stabbed at a piece of lamb and put it to his mouth, savoring the juicy meat. He chewed it slowly, not looking at the others for a short time, leaving his guests to wonder if that was all he had to say on the matter. But they knew him too well.

"So, what gives…sir?" Colter asked after a time. He had eaten his fill and was waiting for the story to pick up speed.

"Patience, my good fellow," Clark replied. "All in good time." He put down his fork and wiped his mouth carefully with a cloth napkin before replacing it on his lap. He continued his narrative as suddenly as he had stopped it. "It appeared to all that suicide was the official cause of death. I, for one - and I know his family felt the same – knew Meriwether wasn't one prone to such actions, despite the host of personal and professional issues he was dealing with at the time. So, on a recent visit to our new capital this year, I took the liberty of talking with one of the officers who took part in that visit, and was listed in the official inquiry. A major by the name of Higgins. He just reiterated what the report said, which did me no good. I was leaving his office, when another man pulled me aside, and said he worked for Higgins and wanted to share with me what he knew. I had to pay him for his time, of course, but it was money well spent."

"What did he say?" asked Ordway. "Was his account different from the official version?"

Clark smiled. "Indeed. He said after the initial investigation, Higgins confided in him that Lewis' head wound was not so grazing after all. The bullet was lodged in his brain, never exiting the body. A man suffering from such a wound could hardly turn around and shoot himself again in the chest, I dare say. Neither wound showed concentrated powder burns, indicating some distance between himself and the shooter. Hardly suicide, under those circumstances."

"Why would they alter the official finding?" Colter asked.

"A very good question, one that you will be entrusted to find out."

"Not bloody likely he would be able to suffer such a head wound as you spoke of, and then reload and fire this rifle a second time." Gass said.

"Not unless he had help," growled Colter.

"Did I mention the diaries?" Clark asked suddenly, once several of his guests pushed back their plates, their appetites thoroughly satisfied. The four gentlemen looked at each other, and Gass shook his head slowly.

"No, not recalling ya did," the Irishman said evenly. "I know he wrote diaries during the expedition. I even published my own memoirs a few years ago – named the expedition the "Corps of Discovery", I did. That was back in '07'. Sold for a dollar each outta Pittsburg."

"Well, Meriwether was, as you know, constantly taking notes on everything – and everyone - he could find," Clark replied. "And once the expedition was complete, he was under pressure to publish his finding."

"Who was pressuring him?" Bratton asked.

"Well, from what I'm told, President Jefferson was keen on getting his hands on the material," Clark said. "After all, it was he who authorized the expedition to start with. I am sure he wanted to see what came of it."

"But how does that affect the circumstances of his death?" Ordway asked.

"Because, my dear fellow – the diaries are missing." Clark responded. The room grew quiet as the four newcomers absorbed that shocking detail. It was Gass who spoke up first.

"They've been missing since…his death?"

"Officially, yes," Clark said. "The officers who first found him reported that only his small satchel of clothes was in his room. No papers of any kind… which strikes me as highly suspect since he was going to Washington to meet with the treasury secretary. It is my belief that they were taken by whoever committed the crime. But, alas, don't allow me to cloud your impartial judgment. I want you to conduct your own investigation. Find out what happened. Was he murdered? If so, by whom and why? Perhaps his missing diaries and papers have nothing to do with it. But it might be a clue – a clue worth checking into."

Governor William Clark slowly rose to his full height and the others followed suit. "And with that, gentlemen, I wish you Godspeed – and good hunting."

Chapter 13

September 6, 1814
South of Nashville, Tennessee

The four horses walked two by two, their riders quiet and reflective in the late afternoon haze. It had taken two weeks to cover the 200 mile journey to Nashville and a journey of three more days with borrowed mounts, for the newly deputized investigators of Governor Clark to ride seventy miles into these dense woods. The narrow dirt path through the forest was barely ten feet wide. The temperature had peaked at 101 degrees by noon and still showed no signs of letting up. The humidity was worse, bringing swarms of mosquitoes which were having a field day with one rider, sweat trickling down his back like its own version of the Missouri River.

Colter took off his hat and wiped his forehead with his already soiled shirt. "So, this is the Natchez Trace. Man, I've been all over this country and I ain't never been so miserable as I am today."

Gass just chuckled. "Yeah, I believe that one. Fat off of the good governor's finest dinner, sleeping under the stars each night, and enjoying the wonderful company of yours truly – I can see why you're so ornery."

"These freaking bugs are as big as the pimple's on your mama's rump, Ordway," Colter continued unabated.

"Don't go dishin' my mamma, you maggot," the sergeant replied sternly. "You definitely don't want to go there."

"Gentlemen, if you please." Bratton said, holding up his hand for quiet. "If I'm not mistaken, we are near the Grinder's Stand." He urged his horse forward into a slow trot, as they rounded a bend in the trail. The dirt path of the Natchez, no more than four feet wide now as they made the turn, cut through the thick woods like a runaway jigsaw. Branches on both sides threatened to reach across and completely block the path if they didn't move fast enough. It was a dangerous road for travelers who were frequently besieged by thieves and Indians lurking around in the shadows of the tall poplars and maple trees. It was best they stick together.

After they rounded the bend, the tree line widened considerably, and a small, but unmistakable pair of low-lying buildings came into view. The first building was only about thirty feet away, the second one about ten feet beyond that. The area of cleared land was no more than a third of an acre across, and the forest floor showed evidence of continued attempts to retake the clearing. The buildings were painted white with a single door on each, and the windows in front had small glass panes. More common in the city... but not usually found in the sticks. No one seemed to be outside.

"Wonder if anyone still lives here?" Bratton asked as the four men rode into the small clearing. There was no sign anywhere announcing the inn but it was clear they had found the right place. "Let's look around quietly..."

"Hallo! Anyone home?" Colter cried out suddenly. Bratton shot him a dirty look but the man simply grinned back at him, reminding everyone of a boy who refused to grow up.

"Well, so much for surprise," Ordway muttered as a man came out of the nearest building, casually holding a hammer at his side. He was a man who has seen better days, as his weathered face, slightly stooped appearance, and scraggly beard attested to. But his clothes were somewhat clean so perhaps he had someone to help him around here. There was supposed to be a wife around - at least there was four years ago.

"Greetings, sir." Bratton said earnestly, dismounting his horse. He approached the innkeeper, shaking hands with a strong grip. It was evident the older man was unaccustomed to such formalities, as he backed away slightly as the tall red-headed giant came closer, his own hand being swallowed by this newcomers large fist. But his smile was genuine.

"Well, well," he said after a time. "What brings you gentlemen to these parts? Far cry from Nashville for a pint of ale."

"Are you Mr. Grinder? Robert Grinder?" Ordway asked, still on his mount. To someone on the ground he looked formidable and dangerous; a combination he hoped would secure him some authority.

But the man didn't acknowledge the name right away. "Who's askin'?" he replied evenly.

Bratton, standing next to the innkeeper, opened his waistcoat and removed an official looking document. He presented it to the man, saying "We represent Governor Clark from the Missouri Territories. My name is Bratton. William Bratton. My associates and I are here to ask Mr. Grinder some questions. Now you wouldn't be he, would you? Because if you are not, we'll be more than happy to turn this establishment upside down to find him." He put on his best smile for the man.

After looking at them in turn for a moment, he sighed noticeably. "That will not be necessary. I am Robert Grinder. I own this little inn and you are more than welcome to stay for the day, if you wish."

"Is there a Mrs. Grinder? I believe Priscella was her name?" Gass asked.

It was clear Grinder would much rather keep her out of the situation but these men knew a little more than he thought. He finally nodded, "Yes, I got a wife. She's out back cooking up some supper. Roasted rabbit. Well, half a rabbit actually. There's just the two of us. Would you like to join us, gentlemen?" At that moment, a striking woman appeared from between the two buildings, her small frame adorned in a worn but clean, white, cotton dress and her long auburn hair was pulled back into a ponytail.

"Gentlemen, allow me to introduce to you my wife, Priscella." At the sight of the woman, the remaining three newcomers dismounted and made their introductions to the couple, shaking hands all around. Colter's demeanor was the most changed of all of them, a fact quite a few of his compatriots noticed.

He smiled for the first time in hours, and even went so far as to take off his hat when he introduced himself.

"Pleasure to meet you, kind sir," she said.

"The pleasure is ours, ma'am."

Gass gave him a curt look and then explained their intentions to the couple. "We're here to investigate the death of a colleague of ours, Meriwether Lewis, who passed away on these very grounds, October 11, 1809. Perhaps you remember him?"

Robert Grinder was a careful man but even so, he could not stop the look of fear from showing in his eyes, even if it was a brief second. Gass was looking for it, and smiled in satisfaction. The man said, trying to remain casual, "Oh yes, I remember. I wasn't here when it happened but my wife rented him a room for the night. Gave him supper, then he retired to bed. I came home the day after, and all hell had already broken out. Hard to forget when the cavalry rides into town, threatening you."

This time it was Gass who showed surprise. "Threatening you? By what grounds do they have to lay presumption on you?"

Robert was about to speak but his wife beat him to it. "When they seen him lying there, they started saying I did it. Can you believe that? Well, I gave them a piece of my mind, I did, and set them straight. Told 'em it was all very simple. Poor man checked in one night, and the next morning he was dead. Shot 'imself. Heard tell later on, he had some personal problems or somethin'."

"Hm, that's interesting. From the reports, it says you provided him the gunpowder and bullets. Does that ring a bell?" Bratton asked.

Priscella looked at Robert, who just nodded. "Well, of course," she explained, "when he asked me for some ammunition for hunting, I sold him what he needed. It was just for hunting he says, so I figured, what the harm? How was I to know he was planning to off himself?"

Robert looked at Priscella and shook his head side to side. "Poor man. When they left we thought that was the end of it. Four years go by and you show up today. You can see why we're a bit surprised."

"Gentlemen, if you excuse me, I have to finish the supper. Perhaps you will care to join us? We don't have much but you are welcome to it," Priscella said.

"Thanks, ma'am, we'd be much obliged," Colter replied, with a slight bow as Priscella retreated back around the corner of the house and disappeared from view.

"Mr. Grinder, perhaps you can begin by showing us exactly where you found Mr. Lewis?" Gass said.

"Of course, of course. Well, my wife and I live here," he said, nodding in the direction of the first cabin. "And we rent out rooms to guests in this adjacent building. As you can see, they're pretty close."

He walked over to the second building, covered in peeling white paint that hadn't seen a new coat in probably twenty years. It was unlocked and he entered, pausing outside to let them in. Colter stepped in first, followed by Gass. Ordway paused before the door and let the innkeeper go in ahead of him.

"As you can see, it's not very spacious but it suits a man for a night's sleep," he said amicably.

The men said nothing for a few moments, as they surveyed the room. A medium size wrought iron bed was in the middle of the room with its large headboard pushed against the back wall. The floor was covered with wooden planking, not altogether common in these parts whose poor inhabitants often sleep on dirt floors with straw mats. On the far left wall a fine, four-foot dresser stood, and on the right wall, a wooden desk and chair.

"If I didn't know better, I'd say I was in New York," replied Gass, who couldn't wholly hide the surprise in his voice.

"Well... my wife ran into some inheritance a few years back and we fixed up the place some," Grinder replied.

Ordway looked at Gass, who simply smiled and nodded to no one in particular. "Ah, inheritance. I understand. We'd all love to fall into a little more money now and then," he said. "But I'm curious, Robert. You have fixed up the place so nice and fancy on the inside, yet you don't seem to have touched the outside paint in years. Why keep all this finery someplace people can't see it?"

"Unless you don't want people to know you have it." Colter said, speaking up for the first time. "I'd say someone paid you off after the incident with Mr. Lewis and you wanted to keep it hidden."

"Why...," Grinder sputtered, "that's not true! It's the injuns! If they knew what we had here, they'd be in to take it all! We had to downplay things a bit, at least on the outside."

"Indians? Where are their settlements?" Colter asked warily. "What tribes live nearby?"

"Well...I'd rather not go into that right now. It has nothing to do with anything," the innkeeper said, backing off from the trio of men. He looked around, and suddenly his eyes grew wider. Someone was missing.

The door suddenly burst open and Priscella was roughly thrust into the room. Bratton filled the doorway, his long red hair spilling down around his shoulders and his soft hat sat lazily on his head.

"Excuse me!" Robert Grinder growled at him, but his voice registered more fear than bravado. "What is the meaning of manhandling my wife like that?"

The giant kept quiet for a moment and then said softly "I found her out back, but it wasn't a rabbit that she was tending to. It was a Cherokee. She told him something and he ran off into the woods. I don't think he saw me, and I couldn't tell what she said. But I know it musta been a warning of some kind. 'Bout us."

Chapter 14

The giant of a man looked at her, and bowed his head. "Sorry for the rough treatment, but I don't take kindly to people who see fit to betray me."

"I wasn't warning anyone, you lout!" she replied in anger. "Sometimes we get Indians from nearby tribes that come and go. Some stay for food or ale, and we even trade with a few. But I would never betray anyone, let alone to one of them!"

"Then perhaps you can tell us what you were doing?" Gass pressed.

"Well, it's…it's all very simple really," she said, her cheeks flustering a bit. "One Indian who comes by occasionally saw the horses out front and naturally was curious who the strangers were. Times being what they are, who can blame him? So he came to me and I told him you were officers from Nashville just asking some questions about something from long ago. Nothing to get all excited over."

Ordway looked at the large man in the doorway and could tell he was fuming. Perhaps her story didn't quite jive with his version, but for now, he was keeping quiet about it. Giving her one more stern glare, Bratton turned around and stormed off.

Grinder was upset but he wasn't turning tail either. Keep him talking. "Well now, it seems everything has been cleared up," Gass said evenly. "Let's continue, shall we?"

"So if this furniture is fairly new, how was it setup when Mr. Lewis was here? And where did you find him exactly?" Ordway asked.

Grinder looked around the room for a moment before speaking. "Well, we had a smaller bed over there," he said pointing to the far left wall. "The floor was dirt – didn't have the money to cover it, you see. No dresser or nothin'."

"And the body? Where was it?" Ordway asked again.

"Well, as I recall, it was lying on the floor there, face up." Grinder said. "The rifle lay beside him, yes it was. The marshals who came still hadn't moved the body before I arrived that day. I could tell he had shot himself in the head and then the chest. I found him there, looking at the ceiling."

"Hm, shot himself in the head." Colter said. "Must have been a lot of blood on the ground. I can see why you'd want to cover the floor afterwards."

"Yes, lots of blood. 'Course I wanted to clean it up." Priscella said with conviction.

"And the chest wound would have been pretty bad as well, pooling blood around the body like that." Gass said.

"Yeah, that was bad too. What a mess."

"And you were the first to find him, Mrs. Grinder? What time was that about?"

"Well, as I had told the marshals who came that day, I was asleep in my bed, and I heard the first gunshot early in the morning. Then I heard him cry out for water and help, but I was afraid, you understand, don't you? I stayed where I was… until I heard another gunshot a little while later."

"What did you do, then, Mrs. Grinder?" Ordway asked.

"Well, Mr. Lewis had two servants who arrived late and I put them up in a barn we have off in the back. They were carrying some trunks of his and didn't get here till after dark. I ran and summoned them and together we looked in on Mr. Lewis. The door was locked so we went around to the back window and saw him lying there. It was a dreadful sight!"

"When did Captain Neelly arrive?" Colter asked. "I heard it was he who reported Mr. Lewis death to the authorities and summoned them here."

"Well, he arrived about an hour after sunup, and I immediately brought him to the body. I had one of the servants – I forget his name – crawl in through the open window and open the door. I wanted to make sure he was dead, you know."

"I took the time to read up on the initial investigation that occurred shortly after his death, Mrs. Grinder." Gass said evenly. "After they took statements from everyone, they discussed their findings back in Washington and filed their reports. While they officially ruled it a suicide, they did allude to…other possibilities."

"Other…? Just what are you referring to, Mr. Gass?" Robert Grinder interjected.

Gass whirled on the man, who took a step back in surprise. "You claim you arrived back here the next day…when the marshals were already here in fact. That had to have been close to evening on the 11th of October by then, is that correct?"

"Well, yeah, I suppose so…"

"How did you feel about Mr. Lewis staying the night alone with only your pretty wife here for company? Sometimes men get lonely…have urges…"

"Why, you swine! Don't say another word about my wife!"

"Let me paint anther scenario, for you. You arrived home early that morning, and catch your wife off guard. Perhaps she was in the middle of a tryst with Mr. Lewis; perhaps it was an idea that was only in your own twisted head. But you were jealous! You were angry that another man might look at your wife in such an intimate way! You took your own rifle and killed Mr. Lewis yourself! Shot him in the chest and then in the head for good measure!"

Robert Grinder's face was red with twisted fury. "That's a lie! I never seen the man before I got back! He was already dead, I tell ya!"

"Or was it a simple robbery? But this time the perpetrators weren't in the woods at all, but here standing before Mr. Lewis all this time!" Ordway chimed in. "You must have seen a money bag, a watch that looked expensive enough to pawn for a few dollars. You kill him and make it look like he was done in by his own hand!"

"You got it all wrong, I'm tellin' ya!" Priscella cried out. "It wasn't Robert or me, I swear!"

"Perhaps it was Captain Neelly, or one of Mr. Lewis servants? Or perhaps the two Chicksaw they had hired as Indian guides? The list of suspects is growing by leaps and bounds."

"It was suicide, I tell ya. You'll just have to take our word for it. It was a long time ago – nothing left to investigate…Marshal Gass." Robert said, trying to keep himself under control.

Patrick smiled. "Oh, but you are wrong… Mr. Grinder. We have new evidence now – we know his head wound was not the graze that you made it out to be. It was a full impact shot, leaving out the possibility of a second strike to his chest. It had to be delivered from a third party – someone with a motive and an opportunity – and you had both!"

"I don't know why they did it!" Robert said angrily. "But it wasn't us! We were just told to keep quiet about it…we got a few bucks to keep our mouths shut. That's all we know, really!"

"You fool! Don't tell them anything! They'll kill us!" Priscella wailed, and suddenly it was too much for her, and she burst into tears.

"We won't harm you, ma'am." Colter said, coming over, as she collapsed on the bed.

"Not you! Them!" she pointed outside, her arm wavering as if caught in a maelstrom. "The Cherokee! They…" but then she buried her head in her hands and refused to say more.

Gass looked over at Ordway who kept his eye out the back window. Without turning away, he replied, "There are two of them out there. They've been hanging around since we got here, just out of sight among the trees."

"So it was the Cherokee who put the hit on Mr. Lewis?" Gass said to Robert. "But why?"

The innkeeper looked at the ground, trying not to notice his wife crying on the bed next to him. "Don't know why they did what they did, but they told Priscella to stay out of it and not tell anyone. I showed up later that day, as I told ya. The marshals were already here, asking questions. But they were gone in under a day, and told us to keep our mouths closed. Say to go along with the official inquiry findings that it was a suicide. Then a few weeks later – we get this telegram from Nashville saying our ship has come in. We're rich! But we're not stupid. Some bad stuff went down that night and…well, we've kept our mouths quiet. Until you showed up today."

"Under the circumstances, I don't think arresting you would serve the public any good. If you are truthful in what you say, and I think now you finally are, then the perpetrators are someone from the Cherokee camp. Perhaps we should pay them a visit."

"I have one last question," Ordway said, still looking outside. "When Mr. Lewis was staying here, did he have any papers or books with him? Money of any kind? Or when the army came, did they find anything like that?"

Priscella Grinder sat on the edge of the bed, wiping away her tears with the sleeve of her white dress. She looked as if this thought had never occurred to her before. "You know, no one ever asked about his effects before now. Not about papers and such. But I do believe he did have something like a small case of some kind when he arrived. And I never did see it again. I know the Cherokee did not take it – they were never in the room. Actually they fired from outside that window there," she said, pointed out towards the back. "The door was closed and locked from the inside until I had one of his servants crawl in through there and open it up. When the soldiers left, it was cleaned out."

Gass looked at his friends. "Well, now we're getting somewhere."

Ten Years Earlier

The Lewis and Clark Expedition

Chapter 15

August 16, 1804
Near present-day Sioux City, Iowa

The soft morning light peered lazily from between two trees and the forest floor glittered from the starry dewdrops that clung to each blade of grass. The doe stood twelve hands high, not quite fully grown but it would gain another foot or so before winter. Bending down, it pulled at a large leaf that stubbornly refused to break away from the small bush that held it firm.

Suddenly a snapping branch caused the majestic animal alarm; its ears twitched, and its head rose in response, straining to catch the sound again. Its mind screamed 'run' but instinct told it to wait, and get its bearings. It paused for several moments, trying to ascertain where the sound came from. When the sound did not recur again, it looked around one final time, then bounded back the way it had come.

"Darn it, Charlie!" said Nathaniel. "I almost had him in my sights! Now we'll never get another one for hours!"

"Sorry, cous'," the younger man said. "I just stepped on a branch – lost my balance, I guess. I'm sure it won't happen again – honest!"

"Sergeant, report," came the authoritative voice of Captain Clark, walking up behind them. Nathaniel looked at his commander and saw the half dozen men trailing behind him, rifles slung over their shoulders. The last two men, brothers Joseph and Reubin Field, led two pack horses with them. But they won't be carrying any food back to camp this morning. Nathaniel sighed.

"Captain, we had a deer in our sights, but she got spooked and ran off. We'll keep on her trail. I'm sure we'll catch her later on. Sir," he said, standing at attention. His posture was ramrod straight and his demeanor showed proper respect. Clark liked that in his officers. Sergeant Nathaniel Pryor was one of his best men, and why he wanted him leading today's hunt.

"It was my fault, sir," Charlie spoke up. Nathaniel's cousin, Sergeant Charles Floyd, was the second of Clark's three officers, and although he didn't have the experience of his older cousin, he was well-liked by everyone on the expedition. He was also an avid outdoorsman and hunter, and if anyone could bring success to a hunt, he could think of few others.

"What happened?" Clark asked.

"I got a little dizzy for a moment…lost my balance and stepped on a branch. Feel terrible about it," Charlie said, his voice trailing off dishearteningly.

Clark frowned. He didn't care about the deer right now – there would be others, certainly. What he didn't want was one of his men getting ill. Deep in the wilderness was the last place on earth a sick man should be. "Sergeant Floyd, please go see the doc. Have him check you out."

"I'll be alright…" he started to say, but one look from his commander changed his mind quickly. "Ok, I'll see what he can recommend." He saluted smartly and walked off.

"What do you advise, Sergeant?" Clark asked, turning his attention back to Pryor. "Shall we keep going? Do you have an idea of what we'll find if we keep heading north?"

The sergeant was thoughtful for a moment and then nodded his head. "I think we should keep going. I can track that deer and maybe she'll lead us to a bigger prize." He smiled at the thought. "Maybe even bring back a grizzly."

"Don't go thinking over your head now, Sergeant," Clark scoffed good-naturedly. "Just stick with deer and we'll eat well tonight."

"Then we'll have to make sure to cover up Bratton's red hair or the giant will give us all away!"

The party continued in a northerly direction, with Pryor leading the way. His cousin hung back to talk with Private Patrick Gass, the expedition's carpenter who also doubled as country doctor when the need arose. Gass had the tools required for both trades, and was sometimes called upon for minor medical issues. Major ones would be left to the hands of the Almighty, and so far there had been none of those. But the expedition was just beginning. To Clark, the future looked like a great big…dark void.

What will they find? What will happen to these forty-eight men whose lives he held in his hand? Questions…or fears perhaps…often filled Clark's mind as his other senses were busy tracking their elusive prey.

The horses were passed off to two young privates, George Shannon and George Drouillard, who led the pack animals deeper into the undergrowth. Bratton, his home-made musket slung across his back, walked several paces in front of them. An hour passed, then two, and the trail became harder to follow. The brush thinned out until the party came into a large field. The grass was tall here and small bushes dotted the landscape, but their attention was quickly drawn towards the horizon. Pryor, who was scouting ahead about twenty yards, held up his hand once, stopping the procession in their tracks.

After a minute or two, he walked back and approached Clark. He spoke softly. "There are about two dozen buffalo about a thousand yards ahead. We're downwind of them and they don't see us so we have the element of surprise – for now."

Clark smiled and nodded his understanding. Perhaps there might be some meat after all. The journey ahead was long, and they needed to get their supplies in order, as soon as they could.

The captain gathered the hunting party around him and explained his plan. Two teams were formed. One, led by Pryor, would include Privates George Shannon, William Bratton, and Joseph and Reubin Field. They would head east of their location and try to flank their large prey.

The other team consisted of Private George Drouillard, Patrick Gass, Clark, and his personal slave, York. Drouillard and Shannon tied their horses to a nearby tree, and hurried back. Floyd was instructed to stay behind and lay low. He was getting weaker the farther they went and, for now, his current state of health would only be a hindrance if he participated.

As Pryor and his men headed out, keeping down in the tall grass, Clark settled back in the tree line and waited. He glanced at Drouillard, then at Gass. Both men were intelligent and capable, and he trusted them. What he was about to do might be frowned upon back in civilization, but here in the wilderness, he alone was in command.

He unslung his own rifle and held it out to York. The black man looked surprised for a moment, and then slowly grinned as he gripped it by the fine wooden stock. He nodded towards his master. He would not let him down.

"Sir...?" asked Drouillard hesitantly. "Isn't that against regulations to arm a... a slave? Sir?"

"Private, I trust my man, York, here more than most people on this expedition," came the terse reply. "Out here, I am in command, and I make the decisions. York will do as he is told and do it better than most. He has my complete trust. Is that understood?"

"Yes, sir," the private responded.

"And one more thing, young man. If you ever question another one of my decisions again, I'll have you disciplined for insubordination. Is that clear?"

Drouillard stood up straighter and spoke softly but with no hesitation. "Sir! Yes, sir!"

Clark turned his attention back to the matter at hand. He could see Pryor's group begin to complete their circle around the herd. In a little while, he would initiate his own move. Would it work? The captain closed his eyes and said a quick prayer. A prayer for a successful hunting day. A prayer for a fruitful expedition during the coming months. Most importantly, a prayer that they would all come back alive and well.

The commander and those waiting with him watched as Pryor's group made their way around the herd up ahead, taking the time to step quietly and carefully – like the deer, there would be no second chances once the prey was on the run. After about twenty minutes, the men were in place and Clark nodded to his own team. Together they rose and crept forward slowly.

When they were within two hundred feet of the large beasts, Clark held up his hand and then gave the signal. All at once his men charged forward, hollering and whooping it up. The buffalo, the tallest standing at least twenty hands at the shoulder, looked up, startled at the sudden intrusion. They made a quick turn away from Clark and his men, looking for a hasty retreat – and ran straight into Pryor's company.

Several shots rang out over the tall grass and the agitated animals could be heard bleating and snorting loudly, as they changed direction at the last second heading to the west, away from both parties. Clark saw one animal, a medium size one that stood almost to his own height, falter in step, then stagger to the ground as the rest ran past. It was Joe Field, one of his privates, who ran up and finished it off.

"Great work, gentlemen!" Clark said as the men gathered together. "Mr. Field, congratulations on earning the expeditions first buffalo kill! Why don't you start off dressing the beast? You deserve the honor."

Chapter 16

Field beamed, and he eagerly set to work on skinning the buffalo. They would preserve the hide and use it later for leather work. Bratton and Joe's brother, Reubin, then teamed up to slice off the meat for transport back to their camp. Pryor called to Shannon to bring the horses up for loading. As the young man ran off, the sergeant turned to his captain, a smile on his face.

"Well, it wasn't deer, but bison have more meat on 'em anyway. We'll be okay for a good while, as long as we have days like this," Pryor observed.

He looked over at the three men working on the carcass. The process would take a while but they'd still be home before night fell. He smelled the air and took in a deep breath. He loved the outdoors and the adrenalin rush of the hunt. He looked over towards the woods, his eyes following the young lad, and realized with a start that something was wrong. Shannon was coming back... empty handed.

"Captain...," Pryor said quietly, as Clark looked up at him. He followed his gaze and frowned, his face growing more concerned with each step Shannon took. Where were the horses?

"Private, report. Where are the horses?" Pryor asked, his voice carrying more irritation than he wanted to show.

The boy looked down and kept shaking his head. "I...I don't know, rightly sir." He suddenly looked up at his sergeant, almost imploring him to believe his story. "They were tied up when we went after them buffalo – me and George did it – but...they're gone! Must' a gotten spooked and run off!"

"Drouillard!" Clark shouted, standing next to Pryor. The private ran over, his face a question mark.

"What's going on, Capt'n?" he asked.

"Private Shannon says the horses have run off. Now you two tied them in the woods. You better find them, understand?"

"Run off?" Drouillard repeated, incredulously. He looked at Shannon who continued to look down at his feet. "Well, we'll find 'em sir, don't you worry. We'll round 'em up, we will. Let's get going, George," and the two privates walked away hurriedly.

Clark sighed heavily. The day was going so well too.

As the hours passed with no word from the pair, Pryor became more irritated with the situation. It didn't help matters that his cousin's symptoms were getting worse as the day went on, and although he tried not to show it, he knew Clark was worried too. By early evening light rain began to fall, and he knew they needed to make a decision.

"The men are done with the dressing, captain," he said as he stood next to his commanding officer. "But with the horses gone, I think is best to carry what we can ourselves and try and make it back to camp. Shannon and Drouillard are probably heading back now with the horses."

"How's Charlie?" Clark asked quietly. He stood looking out across the wide expanse of the west, deep in thought. But his mind was always on the matters at hand.

"Well, Private Gass originally thought it was just nothing, maybe lack of sleep or something. But Charlie's been having more pains in his stomach, although he'd never admit it to you. He's not one to put on a show, though, so you're not going to get much out of him. But it's become harder for him to walk without stopping for a rest." He paused as he considered his next statement. "I think we need to get him back to camp. At least he'd have a shelter and food."

Clark nodded. "It's a shame we don't have the horses though – even with ten of us, we'll bound to leave a good deal behind." He gave the word and Pryor had them divide the meat between the men into their knapsacks. He and Gass stayed close to Charlie as they made their way back into the deep woods.

Several hours dragged on and the men, to their credit, never complained about the extra load nor the wet conditions. They were all in this adventure together and had suffered far worse on their own back home. But as they approached their encampment, and could hear the roar of the mighty Missouri River in front of them, they picked up their pace. The rain clouds had disappeared and the moonlight shown through. The trees and grass were filled with crickets playing their high-strung melodies and the air permeated with the smell of recent rain.

"Welcome home!" a voice called out, just as the first man walked into the clearing. Three large canoes were pulled up on shore, with a large covering stretched between the first two. These vessels, what the natives called pirogues, were each equipped with a sail and benches and measured roughly 40 feet in length and nine feet across. Meant to travel the big rivers, they were capable of transporting nine tons of cargo and many men. This was their home – for now – until they were ready to continue their expedition further along the river. No white man knew what lay beyond its shores. But it was their assigned duty to find out.

Clark looked around as he came into the clearing. He saw men come up to greet the hunting party, and help them with their loads. Two men approached Charlie, and Gass directed them to place him under the temporary shelter of the pirogues. But Clark did not see what he'd hoped he would. He spotted a sergeant who had stayed behind and beckoned him over.

"Sergeant Ordway, have Privates Shannon and Drouillard returned yet? They were out looking for two horses that had run off and I was hoping they had made it back before us."

"Sorry, sir, they haven't returned. You and your group are the first to come back to camp. I'm also sorry to see Charlie in such a state. But we'll pray that he recovers fast."

"Thanks, Sergeant," Clark replied. He looked over beyond the last pirogue and spotted a figure squatting besides a small leafy bush, not far from the waters edge. He walked towards him, a smile spreading across his face for the first time in hours. As he approached, a large, dark brown, Newfoundland dog came over to greet him, wagging his tale in excitement. Clark bent down to scratch him behind the ears, saying "Hi, Seaman, were you good for your master while I was gone?"

"Meriwether! What are you up to?" the captain said loudly, announcing his arrival. The man kneeling in front of him remained silent for a few moments, recording his last notes in a small black covered journal. Finally he shut it, and stood up, turning around to look at Clark. Seaman ran over to Lewis but before he reached him, the dog jerked his head suddenly, and the animal took off into the underbrush.

Lewis watched him go with an amused expression. "I was recording the foliage of the region, in particular this small and peculiar bush, whose equivalent I have not seen in the east." The man had short hair the color of burnt umber, and his face was angular with a long nose. His slender frame stood almost to Clark's height, falling perhaps two inches shorter.

"You never cease to amaze me – you find the greatest pleasure in the most minute details," he said with a chuckle. "How goes the preparations for the journey?"

"The men have collected and re-supplied the essentials, which are stored on the boats. The sail on boat two has been mended and everyone is anxious to get started. Can I assume your hunt was successful?"

Clark hesitated. Do I tell him the good news first or the bad news? He settled for a compromise. "Well, we did get bison meat but two horses wandered off and we couldn't bring it all back. I left Shannon and Drouillard to fetch the beasts. They should return soon, I would hope."

Lewis frowned. "That is a shame. But we'll store what you did bring and wait for their return in the morning. We'll open the barrels of salt and pack the pieces carefully. They should last us a while."

By morning, the pair had still not arrived but Clark remained stoic. They would be fine, he reminded himself, and would be along shortly. He was certain they rested for the night and would be on the move again by now. Shannon was young but Drouillard would provide direction and reason.

"Capt'n, may I have a word with you?"

Clark turned and looked into the weathered face of his carpenter and part time doctor Patrick Gass. A natural with his hands, the small, powerfully built man could create buildings or boats, and anything in between. He had an eye for the mechanical and could draw plans as well as implement them, a gift that was of the rarest commodity in the western frontier. He also was great with the men, able to easily interact with both officers and enlisted alike. At the beginning of the expedition, it was Clark himself who offered him the extra duty of doctorin' for a slightly higher wage.

"Sir, Charlie isn't doing so well," he said. "I can sew up a wound or set a broken leg...but his problem is inside him, and I can't fix that with what I have. It's his gut – maybe bad spirits or his insides are all twisted up, but...it's getting worse, not better."

Clark looked towards the canopied boats where the young sergeant lay and tried not to think about losing him. He had seen many a man die from sickness or wounds while on the battlefront, but this was different. Charlie Floyd was an experienced hunter and outdoorsman, and one of only three sergeants he had under his command. His importance to the expedition was not to be slighted, and he did not know how his cousin, Nathaniel would take the news. It could derail everything...if he allowed it. *Have to keep things moving forward.*

"Has Nathaniel been told yet?" he asked suddenly.

"No, sir, he doesn't know quite how bad off he is…yet. But he will eventually. Do you want me to tell him?"

"I'll do it. It might do Charlie some good to walk around some – we don't want to have his insides any more twisted up."

The challenges of command, he thought dryly and he went off to find Nathaniel.

By evening the two privates had still not shown up, and Clark was thinking of sending more people after them. Charlie continued his downward spiral and could barely sit up now, let along stand. Nathaniel and Gass remained at his side throughout, and to his credit, young Charlie bore up well.

"He must be in constant pain, but he is trying his best not to show it," Nathaniel said to the commander when Clark asked for an update. "He's one tough young man."

Clark nodded in agreement. All these men were brave, or they wouldn't be here. He had handpicked them and they were the best in their fields. But now that the expedition was approved and ready to go, they had complications. The waiting is the hardest part. Waiting for his sergeant to improve… or not. Waiting for his men to return… or not. He spent his days worrying about his men, and the logistics of transporting forty-eight men and hundreds of pounds of equipment up thousands of miles of unknown territory over the course of many months. *It would drive a normal man mad, I tell ya.*

"Captain, someone's comin'!"

Clark turned around, as did all who were within earshot. Forty five pairs of eyes looked towards the bushes that slowly parted. The evening twilight did nothing to reveal the figure that emerged. Only when he spoke, did the company realize who had returned.

"Captain?" he said carefully. "I'm back."

Chapter 17

Several men descended on the newcomer, patting him on the back triumphantly, and shaking his hand vigorously. Clark remained where he was. Lewis, who was in the shelter with Charlie, came out and stood by his friend.

The large group slowly gave the man room and he quietly made his way over to stand in front of his commanding officers.

"Welcome back, Private," Clark said to George Drouillard.

"Is...is he back yet?"

"Who, Shannon?" Lewis said. "No, he's not. He was supposed to be with you. What happened?"

"Ah, for the love of...," Drouillard said angrily to himself, then stopped as he realized the company he was with. He paused, making a conscious effort to remain calm. But his eyes beheld his misery. "I told him to stick with me, but...we had been following them tracks for hours it seemed, and then we came to a fork, where it divides, you know?"

"Go on. Where is Shannon?" Clark said evenly. He was relieved that Drouillard returned but even more worried now about the fate of young Shannon, alone in a dense woods hundreds of miles from any civilization.

"Well, he wanted to head down the south trail towards the river, and I wanted to head west. The tracks were very slight at that point so it was really anyone's guess. He said he just wanted to check if the trail picked up farther down and that he would be back soon. I know I shoulda gone with him, capt'n, but I never thought..." He paused again then said the words no one wanted to hear. "He never came back."

"Didn't you go after him?" Lewis asked, allowing just a trace of irritation in his voice.

"Yes, sir! I called down to him after a while, and then I went off looking for him. But the night overtook me and I remained where I was 'cause it was almost impossible to see and I wasn't getting no response from him. In the morning, there was still no sign of him, and I thought…maybe…he had made his way back here."

"Well, that's just great! Fine job, George!" came the sarcastic retort from a man nearby. "We've barely gotten started, and you can't keep tabs on one kid!"

"Knock it off, Colter," Sergeant Ordway said sternly. "Or I'll send you after him myself."

"That's not a bad idea." Lewis said. "Maybe not Private Colter, but the Field brothers may be up for it."

So it was quickly arranged. The next morning, Joe and Reubin Field set out in search of the missing lad, and Clark returned his attention to his most pressing problem.

"Has Charlie regained consciousness yet?" he asked the man's physician, after they cleaned up from their brief morning meal. The sun had not yet risen to its full height but the captain already could tell it would be a hot one. Gass shook his head.

"His fever is quite high now, and he's pale and sweaty. York has been up with him all night. Charlie's showing little to no response to me, and I…" he paused, looking as lonely and out of sorts as Clark had ever seen him. "There's nothing more I can do for him. I'm sorry, Will. I'm really sorry."

The captain struggled to remain calm, but his will was being tasked to the breaking point. "I know. You're doing all you can. How…how much time?"

It was the big question no one wanted to ask, and Gass has hoped to avoid it altogether. But it sat there like an elephant in their mist and there was no way around it. "Could be soon. Tonight, tomorrow. At the latest probably." He sighed heavily. "Not long."

But the next morning, as Clark went to check on his patient, Charlie Floyd was sitting up, trying to keep down some biscuits that Gass had given him. When he saw the young man, the captain was nothing less than shocked.

"Charlie, how are you feeling?" Clark asked earnestly, as he knelt beside him. "I was told you were on your deathbed." He looked up at Gass who simply shrugged his shoulders in bewilderment.

"Well I thought so too, Capt'n, and I'm still a little sore in my stomach, but I feel a whole lot better this morning," Floyd responded. "And I'm hungry cause I ain't had nothing to eat in I don't know how long! York fixed me up some soup to put in me, and some cornbread. Not bad if you haven't eaten in a while!"

Clark spent the afternoon getting ready to move out in the next day or two. He still wanted to get more meat- what they carried back from the buffalo hunt wouldn't last forever – but he was leery about risking any more men, after what happened with George Shannon. But he finally relented and assigned half a dozen men to start another hunt in the morning.

The group waited throughout the day, as Lewis used the time to examine and record more of the surrounding trees and animals they found. By the evening meal, the Field brothers made their return.

Clark was the first one to meet them. "Did you find him?" he asked directly.

"Well, we traveled along the path that George indicated and walked several miles," Reubin said. "We did see tracks made in soft clay made by a man… presumably Shannon…as well as tracks made by a horse. But they were several days old. Eventually the tracks petered out in the underbrush and the path got rockier making it impossible to keep on his trail. The forest around those parts got pretty thick and we called out many times…but we didn't get no answer."

"Capt'n, if he's out there, I don't think he's going to make it back," his brother continued. "He's traveling away from us and from all indications, he's become impossible to find."

Clark began to pace, his anger and frustration quickly mounting. With Charlie Floyd's improvement, it would have been a coup de grace to get Shannon back, but that didn't seem to be developing the way he had hoped. *Control what you can and keep moving forward. Good advice.* He sighed deeply to regain his composure. Then he faced his men once again, his expression one of determination.

"Thank you, gentlemen," he said. "It's frustrating to lose someone who, given adequate hindsight, I could have saved. Horses are not worth a man's life, no matter the circumstances. Let's pray for his return, but for now, let's focus on our preparations."

As the men quietly dispersed, Gass approached him and took him aside gently. The sun was not yet set and Clark could see the dwindling sunlight cast an eerie shadow over the doctor's features.

"Charlie's developed a fever again."

Clark felt as though he'd been sucker punched. "What…? He seemed better this morning. How…?"

"I've seen it only once before, back in Kentucky." Gass said. "Man has stomach pains, gets fever, but then he improves…for a short time. Then the fever reappears and…he was dead within a fortnight."

"But what was the cause…with that man?" Clark asked, trying to get his mind around this new development.

"Well the doctor said it was bilious colic, a sickness in his intestines, where food passes through. There was nothing he could do, and probably not much we can do either."

Clark felt numb all over. With Charlie's improvement, he had started to look positively at their situation again, but now things were unraveling once again and he felt powerless to stop it. He closed his eyes and prayed. Hard. A calm slowly descended over him and he opened his eyes again. He breathed deeply then went in search of Lewis.

The hunting party was rewarded for their efforts that evening with a young stag, only four antlers, but its meat would be stored and used for many meals during the journey. After dinner Drouillard and another private named George Gibson broke out their fiddles and gave everyone an hour of enjoyable diversion with many tunes and songs, including Clark's favorites "The Bold Soldier" and "Greensleeves".

Clark awoke the next morning with a start. The sun was shining overhead and he could tell from the noise outside his tent that most of the men were already having breakfast. He put his head down again on the pillow, trying to gather his thoughts. The merriment of the previous night began to dissipate as he pondered on the weightier issues before him.

Meriwether was the first to corner him when he emerged from his tent. "Good morning, William," he said amicably. "There is news about young Charlie," and before Clark could get any more out of him, Lewis was already walking off towards the shelter of the boats.

Clark followed, hope rising with each step. Maybe it wasn't the colic as Gass had said; maybe he'll wake up this morning as good as before. Maybe…

But as he arrived at the boats, the mood was anything but jovial and he saw Nathaniel, Charlie's cousin, sitting next to the boy holding his hand, talking to him softly. He turned to the doctor. "Well, Patrick, how's his condition?"

Gass took a breath, and then let it out slowly. "Charlie Floyd just died," he said quietly.

Chapter 18

William Clark closed his eyes and bowed his head in resignation. He knew it was coming – had known since yesterday – but hearing the actual words brought a tightening in his chest and a weight on his soul the likes of which he had not experienced in a great while. Not since the death of his own mother many years ago. Even though Charlie hadn't died in battle, his death occurred in pursuit of a greater, national goal, and he would get all the honors and dignity at his funeral that such a man required.

The men spent the next day preparing the body for burial, and digging a suitable grave set on top of a bluff overlooking the Missouri River below. He ordered the hole dug deep enough that predators wouldn't get to his body. Clark and Lewis jointly conducted the ceremony. Prayers were said and the flag was raised, as each man saluted in turn. Rocks were placed over the area and Nathaniel fixed a small cross into the ground, his cousin's name carved on it. "Sgt. Charles Floyd. Feb 22, 1782 – Aug 20, 1804."

"Never was a better man, there," Nathaniel announced to the contingent of men who bowed. After a pause, Clark dismissed the group and everyone left slowly, leaving Pryor to mourn his cousin in private.

Two days after the funeral, Clark called his remaining two sergeants together and asked them to assemble the men. They sat in a semi-circle around the boats, with the captains and sergeants standing under the tarp. Clark called the meeting to order.

"We have witnessed the passing of one of our own recently, a sergeant whose duty it was to help us guide this expedition into unknown territory. We need to replace his position and elect a new sergeant to fulfill his duties. Sergeants Ordway and Pryor have submitted three names to us and Captain Lewis and I have reviewed them. Will the following men step forward:

William Bratton, Patrick Gass, and Joseph Field." The three came forward, a little surprised at the honor of their nomination.

"You know these men," Lewis stated. "You have worked side by side with them for several weeks, and you must now choose one of them to be your new sergeant. Now we will conduct an election from among the assembled group. To do this, we will have you form a line and I will record your vote. The new sergeant will be elected by majority decision."

Within ten minutes, the votes were in and the captains conferred briefly with each other. Nodding their heads, they turned once again to face the men under their command. "Will the three candidates rise?" Bratton, his coonskin cap not able to fully contain his flowing red hair, looked like he belonged in the woods, with his soft leather garments covering his tall frame. Shy in nature, but wielding an impressive knowledge of the outdoor, he was an expert in survival and hunting.

Gass, by comparison, stood half a foot shorter, with a simple cotton shirt and trousers covering his stocky frame. He had cemented his place in the expedition with his role of carpenter and medic, and could lead men at all levels if necessary.

Joe Field, the third candidate, was a younger man, with short blond hair, and medium build – he looked just as adaptable tending cows in the pasture as leading men in battle against the Comanches. His agreeable nature made him well liked by all the men.

"The choice was not an easy one, and by the registry of the votes, it was very close," Lewis announced. "But the winner has been agreed on. Without further ado, your newly elected sergeant is…Patrick Gass! Congratulations!"

A slight smile briefly crossed the features of the newly elected sergeant, but he quickly deterred any more celebrations on his behalf. "Thank you for the honor, and I will perform my duties with justice. But let us always remember Sergeant Charlie Floyd – it was his assignment and I will never forget that. Rest in peace, Charlie." Then, almost inaudibly, he said, "I'm sorry I couldn't do more for you."

That evening, the captains met with their three officers and went over the plans for their departure in the morning. "Make sure everything is tied down tight, and the sails are ready to go. Any last minute things must be attended to tonight. Assign the men to their boats in the morning and we will be off before eight of the hour."

Morning came swiftly to the small group, and, true to their word, the first boat was launched at just before the appointed time. Clark led the first boat, together with Ordway overseeing the men, while Lewis and Gass led in the second, and Pryor bringing up the rear. Each pirogue carried several tons of food, supplies and men, and the sails were set out fully. With favorable currents, they could expect to make several miles before the sun was completely beating down its summer heat.

The Missouri River was narrow at the initial juncture, which had made it ideally suitable for establishing their camp several weeks back, but it soon opened up as more tributaries sent several tons of water each hour into the open channel. The pirogues, as large as vessels dared to get on these waters, was soon dwarfed by size of the river that surrounded it.

By afternoon, Clark was pleased with their progress. The forest on both shorelines was heavy and thick, and often he wondered who, if anyone, was watching them from behind the tall trees. They would encounter Indian tribes no white man had ever seen before, and they had no way of gauging how friendly or hostile they might be. For protection, each man was outfitted with a rifle but was under orders not to fire it unless absolutely necessary.

The day was long but fruitful and they covered a lot of ground. By evening, the river narrowed a bit as they came around a sharp bend. Clark was discussing the Indian border treaty with John Colter, when he heard a shout from the front.

"Captain!" exclaimed Ordway, his voice rising an octave. "You'd better take a look, sir. You're not gonna believe this."

All eyes in the first pirogue turned towards the shore line and Clark had to hold onto the side to keep from falling in, so great was his surprise.

A white man sat on the shoreline, his clothes ripped and dirty, his body thin and malnourished. Two horses were tied to overhanging branches a short distance away. When the man saw them, he raised his own rifle over his head and tried to shout, but Clark was unable to hear him. He rubbed his eyes and looked once more, afraid he was seeing a ghost.

He was still there. *Shannon.*

Chapter 19

October 24, 1804
Dakota Territory

The first rays of the new dawn peaked around tops of the nearest poplar trees, not quite ready to make its appearance known just yet. The sunlight retreated for a moment, and then came out once again, its orange glow radiating from the dewy grass in the grove. The smell of the cool dampness was pungent upon the air. The soft leather door set in the square earthen hut opened without a sound and a figure appeared, letting it fall softly back into place.

The woman was medium height, with her long, black hair braided in a single ponytail that reached halfway down her back. Her dark brown leather dress had a bead pattern woven into the top, forming an intricate design of two birds soaring. She knelt beside the remains of a small cooking fire, stirring up the coals and putting a few additional sticks on it. She blew on it gently until the briefest of flames appeared and began to lick the new wood.

The woman stopped briefly to pick up a small, empty, iron pot and walked down to the river's edge. There was no one else moving outside just yet and she smiled. She enjoyed these early mornings, which afforded her a chance to be alone and contemplate. She patted her belly and thought for a moment she could feel the baby kick inside her. But she knew it was too early for that, just yet. Still it was a nice feeling.

A few more months and Touissant will be a father! And it will be I who gave him his first-born, not Otter Woman. Touissant may have two wives, she thought, but only one first-born child. She had no wish for personal prestige or glory, but there was a part of her that was satisfied in giving her husband what no one else could. Otter Woman may be my dearest friend, but this baby is all mine to give.

The young woman carried the pot back to her living quarters, stopping outside to place it on a hook overhanging the small fire, now growing nicely. She removed a small leather satchel from her waist belt and picked out of it some of the better tea leaves. After a while the water in the pot began to boil and she removed it from the flames. Taking a fat wooden cup, she scooped a good deal of water in it, placing the tea leaves within to seep for a while. Touissant liked his tea warm and rich.

Just then she stopped, sensing a presence in the village, eyes looking at her. She stood still and looked cautiously around until she spotted the newcomer. He was about 100 feet away at the edge of the clearing. She let her breath out slowly and looked up at him with awe.

The buck was large, with a rack of six antlers rising out of its majestic head. Standing almost as tall as a horse, it looked at her but made no move to run away. After a time, he lowered his head and nibbled some grass before darting away from the river, heading deeper into the woods.

The Indian woman remained rooted in front of the small fire, her thoughts leading her back several years to another place, another time. She was a little girl and was riding one of the smaller horses her people had recently roped, and she was laughing while she held on tight to the short mane. It was almost the same size as that deer, she thought. She hadn't been on a horse in such a long time – she missed it.

She remembered her brother, a year younger and half a foot taller. She hadn't seen the boy in years. How was he now? Surely his path had led to a more successful future than her own. But with the birth of this baby, she thought, rubbing her belly, things might look up for her. The village women would have to treat her with more respect – after all, she was more than someone's servant – she was a first wife, and about to be the mother of an important child.

Important. Touissant was certainly important to the village, and by association, his son would be as well. But if they left? What would happen to them? Men like her husband never stayed for long in any one place. They were nomadic by nature. But no matter where they went as a family, the child within her would be important – she would give everything she had to make it happen. For him.

Lost in her own thoughts, the Indian girl turned her gaze back towards the river, and slowly became aware of a strange phenomenon upon the surface of the water, down river just skirting the horizon. A square cloud was slowly making its way upon the river. She stared at it, mesmerized.

Then a second one appeared. Only then did she see the large, long boats that sailed under them. Frightened, she ducked her head and ran off to observe them from behind a grove of trees maybe twenty feet away.

Should she alert the village? She remembered the call signal for danger, and gave off the quick, high-pitched cry of the whippoorwill. Once, twice, the 'caw caw' echoed through the thirty village huts nestled at the edge of the forest grove. It only took a few seconds for the first warriors to emerge, followed swiftly by others. They, too, looked at the new boats with the rectangular clouds helping them along the river.

Chapter 20

It was Captain Lewis in the lead boat who spotted the village first. "Look! To the right!" he called softly, pointing. The morning light was just beginning to grow and they had been on the river for only half an hour or so. He had been working on a drawing in his journal of the beautiful sunrise, when he spotted the close group of mud huts set off about 100 yards from the river's edge.

By this time other men had seen the Indian huts as well, and a call was made to Captain Clark in the second pirogue. Lewis took the sail to half mast, and then lowered it completely as they neared the village. He ordered the men to steer towards shore and they silently edged closer to their destination. "These natives could be the key to us surviving the winter," he said to William Bratton, sitting next to him.

Bratton had met more Indian tribes in his lifetime than most of the expedition members put together, and he always recommended a cautious approach towards them. Aggressive or friendly? Your life could often depend on making the right choice. The white men had strength in number and weapons if it came to that; however it was always best to hold this card in reserve and play it as a last resort.

The second and then the third pirogue followed Lewis' lead and they silently came upon the sheltered Indian village. From the safety of their boats, Lewis could tell about thirty native warriors stood waiting for them, many with weapons pointed down but at the ready. Just in case these strange white men wanted to take more than they give. Lewis understood their apprehension and wanted to be ready to deal with it, use it as leverage for opening negotiations.

He disembarked, carrying a large, soft, leather bag, followed by about ten of his men, with five remaining behind to watch their provisions. Clark's vessel came next with ten more men joining them. Pryor led the last boat, and ordered another ten ashore. All had rifles with them but Lewis knew it was just adding wood to the fire.

"Put your guns down over there," he ordered pointing to a grove of trees not far away. Some of his men gave him an alarming look, but he nodded "it's alright. It's a show of good faith. If we need to, we can get them quick enough." He smiled outwardly. *I hope.*

Several men approached the stand of trees, and one of them gave a yell. "Captain! We have a little visitor!" exclaimed Colter, who had a young woman by the arm. She looked no more than sixteen years of age and had long hair braided down her back.

Lewis looked at her and then at the assembled warriors. They appeared very agitated by this newest development and he grew nervous himself. *The last thing I want to bring is distrust so early in the game.*

"Captain," he said calmly, calling Clark to his side. Then he motioned for Colter to come along with the young woman. Finally he looked around, his eyes searching for someone. His gaze stopped at Drouillard. "Come along, private," he said.

Together the four explorers and the young woman walked unarmed toward their hosts. The woman kept eyeing the white men but made no move to run away. Lewis was impressed with her bravery, and stood in front of the natives taking stock of their situation.

"Greetings," he said smiling. He pointed towards the Indian woman and said "please, go join your tribe," and swept his arm toward them in a gesture he hoped she'd understand. Language might be a big barrier here. But there was something all men understood. Hesitating only slightly, she walked over to join her tribe, but stayed at the front obviously intent on watching the developments.

"We come with gifts," Lewis continued. Showing them his empty hands, he slowly reached into the large bag he carried with him and carefully removed several rabbit pelts and passed them to two of the Indians. They smiled and nodded, accepting the proffered furs. Before he could continue, he noticed some of the Indians moving aside to make room for someone moving toward them. At last he appeared, standing tall and large next to the Indians who held their new gifts.

The middle-aged man wore an artfully beaded and colorful decoration around his neck over a woolen robe, with long, soft leather trousers, and an impressive feathered headrest that adorned his long black hair, braided down the middle of his broad back. Lewis understood from his appearance and demeanor that he was in charge. A gruff expression of clear mistrust was chiseled on his features.

Lewis could make out some sounds but no clear understanding of the exchange that went on between the leader and his men. Fingers pointed first at the long boats and the assembled men who waited apprehensively beside them, then at the young woman who stood stoically facing him. The first warrior held out to the chieftain one of the pelts Lewis had given, but he looked at it critically without touching it. He made a grunting sound that Lewis wasn't sure indicated favor or not.

Suddenly another figure approached from behind the large Indian, and Lewis' eyes widened with amazement. It was another white man, an older gentleman, perhaps in his late forties, with a beaver skin hat and cotton shirt and trousers. On his feet were the soft-soled shoes of the natives. "Ah, visiteurs!"

Lewis smiled as he recognized the language spoken by this white man. He was conversing in French! Obviously a Canadian and probably a fur trader, by the look of it. And if he could communicate with the Indians...

He turned to Drouillard. "George, your moment of truth has arrived. Please act as interpreter for me." One of three interpreters on the expedition, Drouillard was half French and half Shawnee Indian. He was a good man to have on these negotiations.

"Please convey my greetings to their leader," Lewis said. Drouillard then spoke in French to the Canadian, who broke into a big smile and clapped his hands with glee. He replied in rapid-fire French for about a minute, then allowed Drouillard to speak with Lewis.

"He says his name is Touissant Charbonneau and he is a fur trapper living among the Hidatsa tribe for the past four years. He says the chief is named Swift Eagle, and he commands this village, Metaharta. He says they are peaceful and hope we are as well."

Lewis smiled. Everything was going to be ok. Shifting his gaze between the chief and Charbonneau, he introduced himself and his welcome party. He let Drouillard interpret for him, and then waited for the Canadian to speak to Swift Eagle. The large man smiled and nodded his head in understanding.

More introductions were made. "Allow me to introduce my wife," Charbonneau said in French, motioning for the young woman Colter found to step forward. "I believe you have already met my young wife Sacagawea," he said. Drouillard interpreted to the captains as he went along. The woman nodded her head, smiling. "And let me introduce my second wife, Otter Woman," as another young girl of similar age stepped forward. She had two braids framing her small face, and kept her head down without looking at the newcomers. "She can be a little shy," he said almost apologetically.

Lewis just smiled. "Please convey to the chief that I'd like to discuss the idea of formal trade negotiations with him, which I think will be to his liking." Drouillard, then Charbonneau, interpreted and the chief nodded his head. *We're in!*

Chapter 21

In the course of the morning, it was decided that a celebratory party should be held that evening in honor of the newcomers. Outside of dealing with the fur trapper Charbonneau, these Hidatsa Indians had no experience with the white man and Lewis wanted to make first impressions count. To this end, he needed the support of the Canadian. He had also learned of the existence of another Indian tribe, the Mandan, who lived across the river, about a mile from the Hidatsa. Due to the close proximity to each other, the two tribes existed in somewhat peaceful state. It had not always been the case, he had learned, but since Swift Eagle's rise to power several years ago, he had been an advocate for cooperation and fairness among their common resources.

The sun was still high in the sky as both groups got to meet each other but due to the language barrier, they remained a long way off in cultural understanding. Drouillard helped the men with translations as best he could, working alongside Privates Pierre Cruzatte and Francois Labiche, both of whom were half French and half Omaha Indian. Still, without the additional interpreting skills Charbonneau provided, progress was slow going.

As dusk approached that evening, several young Hidatsa maidens busied themselves preparing the elaborate feast, the centerpiece of which were four pheasants roasting over the open fire pit. The birds were turned slowly by trained hands and basked with the delectable juices made for the occasion. Four warriors had erected a large bonfire stretching almost six feet in height. Lewis watched the preparations very carefully, recording the details in his journals which he kept with him at all times.

Once the sunlight dipped behind the trees, one of the warriors stepped forward to light the great woodpile, sending sparks and hot bits of ash in all directions. A group of men emerged from one of the larger tents and the captain noticed the fine detail of their painted bodies as they slowly began a carefully orchestrated dance around the outer rim of the fire. Slowly the warriors elicited a rhythmic chant which brought a feeling of peace and solemnity to the festivities. The air around them seemed to pulse in time to the rhythmic chants.

Next to him, young George Shannon looked intently at the flames slowly licking the logs, his mind a thousand miles away. Lewis smiled. It has been a close call a few weeks ago – we almost lost Shannon as well as Charlie, he reminded himself. "You're fortunate to be here to see this, George," he said quietly.

Shannon looked over at him, his face lean and drawn. "Sir, I'm embarrassed to admit how true you are. I've never been so lost in my life...but I did know enough to find the river, you've got to give me that much." He smiled which made Lewis laugh.

"Yes, well, there are lots of other things that could have found you instead of us, and some of them might have eaten you for dinner. George, you said before that you thought we'd left you behind so you headed upriver to track us down. You know we couldn't wait forever but we certainly gave you a reasonable chance to return. Next time, don't be so quick to think we'd just abandon you. Everyone on this expedition is like family – we care about each and everyone."

"Hopefully there won't be a next time – getting lost in these woods alone is not my idea of fun."

Lewis, Clark and the majority of their party stood around and watched the festivities with interest. The Canadian fur trapper walked over and stood beside them watching the dance quietly. After a few minutes, he said amicably, in halting English, "They are good, no?"

Lewis smiled and nodded.

"Yes, they are quite entertaining," he agreed.

"What your purpose here?" Charbonneau asked in halting English, looking at the captain with an appraised eye. Lewis looked around and spotted Drouillard. He motioned him over with a wave of his hand.

Lewis took this as a chance to make his intentions known and maybe recruit an ally. "Private, will you interpret for me?" he asked Drouillard, who nodded his consent.

"We are explorers, Touissant, trying to get as far up the river as possible and hopefully reach to the oceans beyond. We want to open up trade agreements with various tribes – and I will admit that the Hidatsa are one of the first we've encountered past the Mississippi. We need to find out from them what we're going to be facing in the coming months ahead." He paused before adding, almost under his breath, "We also want to make winter lodging nearby, and I'd like to know how receptive the chief would be to that idea." Drouillard conveyed the captain's message to the Canadian.

The trapper smiled and leaned in closer to the explorer. He spoke rapidly. "I get you what you want." He tapped his chest proudly, adding "I know something of this land. There are things you need. Horses, supplies. And me. You need me to guide you and to interpret for you."

"We already have several interpreters, Touissant," Lewis replied.

"No one has what I have," said the trapper, his voice dropping conspiratorially. Drouillard conveyed this to the captain. The trapper snapped his fingers and, in a few moments, two women were at his side. Lewis recognized them as Touissant's wives. *What were their names? Oh, yes. Sacagawea and...Otter Woman. Yes, that was it.*

"You see, once you get to the mountains, you need horses to cross," the trapper explained in French. "There is a tribe there, the Shoshone, that has horses, but they will not trust you – you will get nowhere with them."

Lewis' eyes narrowed slightly. "The Shoshone? What do you know of them?"

Charbonneau laughed heartily at this, drawing looks from a few people nearby. "Why," he replied, "I have married two of them!"

As Drouillard continued to interpret, the trapper explained the story of the Shoshone. "They live at the base of the big mountains, several weeks journey from here. Five years ago, a band of Hidatsa warriors out on a hunting party came across a small encampment of Shoshone gatherers, and after a quick skirmish, ended up capturing several of the locals. Several of their men were killed in the fight as well. Two of the maidens they brought back stand before you now." He held up his hands and smiled.

"I took Sacagawea as my wife, and later took Otter Woman as well. They are young, but obedient and hard-working," he said. "They know that territory and the language. I will allow Sacagawea to accompany me if you put us in your employ. Think about it. She is your way beyond the mountains."

The captain thought for a moment. "An interesting proposition. I will bring it up with Captain Clark and get back to you soon. But we also need to winter for the next few months. Can you help us discuss this with Chief Swift Eagle?"

The Canadian nodded his head briefly, then stood up and walked away towards the chief, who was sitting before the great fire, drinking a cup of Italian spirits that Clark had given him earlier that day. A smile seemed etched on the chief's face and Lewis doubted whether they'd have any difficulty getting anything from him tonight.

Out of the corner of his eye, Lewis spotted an unusually large gathering of native children perhaps fifty feet away to his left. They had formed a circle with someone – an adult kneeling down, he thought - in the middle. "Oohs" and "Aahs" could be heard even from this distance. He got up to see who was doing the entertaining.

As he approached, he was startled to see the cause of this great gathering. York, Captain Clark's African slave, was telling stories to the kids around him. Frequently one or two would come up to touch his skin, and it occurred to Lewis that these Indians had never seen a black man before. Maybe they thought he was painted or something and were trying to rub it off.

He smiled as he stood off a distance from them and listened to York, and for the first time, really looked at him – not as a slave, but as a man. His words were not important – the natives certainly couldn't understand his English tongue anyway – but it was the way in which he interacted with them that made the captain take note. York, probably for the first time in many years, was being treated as an equal, as someone that people could look up to. Here he was no longer a black slave, a second-class citizen. Here he was special, accepted for who he was – a fascination of mystery and wonderment, a source of happiness for these children, and it was a role he seemed to cherish with every fiber of his being. Maybe we should all take a lesson from these children, he thought.

Chapter 22

Three days later a swatch of land across the river and downstream about a mile was cleared for the construction of their new winter lodgings. Sergeant Gass, the expedition's carpenter, created several pages detailing the plans for the new building. He had presented the final drawings to the captains for their approval.

"It needs to have a stronger outer wall," Sergeant Pryor said as he looked over Clark's shoulder. The captain didn't reply as he carefully studied the new drawings. Gass stood off to one side, nervous and excited by the new project he was to undertake. If the captains approved it, he was to start right away. To that end, he already had enlisted the help of thirty of the men who were, at this moment, cutting trees in the back country and carting them back to the site.

"What say you, Meriwether?" Clark asked, removing his spectacles and rubbing the bridge of his nose. He hated wearing the glasses but he reminded himself it was only for reading. *Just wait 'til I get older.*

"Three buildings for crew living quarters, one for the captains, two buildings for supplies, one more for stables, two buildings for meeting and dining halls, all surrounded by an ten-foot high wall, with a single main gate," Lewis replied. "On paper it looks practical and solid. Perhaps the only questions in my mind is the close proximity of the buildings to the outer wall – if any natives get over the wall, it's an easy drop onto the rooftops."

Gass stepped forward. "If I may say so, sir, given the spatial constraints we have to work with as outlined by both tribes, I have managed to fit a lot of buildings and necessities into a small area. The walls are ample high enough to discourage unwanted visitors. And we will have removed all trees

96

surrounding the walls, so they will not have the ability to shoot at us from above. It's a good plan, sir."

Clark smiled and sat back. "Yes, Patrick, a sound plan. I put my recommendation on it. You, Meriwether?"

Lewis looked at Clark for a moment then shifted his gaze over to their chief carpenter. "I put my trust in you Patrick, as well. Begin the preparations."

Gass smiled broadly. "Already started sir."

The Indians looked on with curious interest as the scene developed over the next two weeks. Wooden logs were cut and laid down across each other; mortar was made with mud and stone and placed between the slats to dry. The rooftops were made of planks and overlapping shingles to keep the occupants dry inside. These feats of engineering were wonders to behold for the natives who often asked questions about various techniques. But Clark had instructed his crew not to tell too much to either Indian tribe, lest such knowledge later be used against them.

The last part of the winter lodgings, and perhaps the most important, was the outer wall. For this defensive barrier, the crew spent many days cutting trees and preparing them for their proper shape and size. Each outer plank had been carved into a pointed tip, making it more difficult to climb over. There were four sides to the wall, the longest being on the north side facing the river. A large stout gate had been set in the middle, with a thick cross beam locking it from within.

On December 2, 1804, the men were ready to move into their new winter lodgings. "Gentlemen," Clark said loudly at precisely 9am, "I give you your new home...Fort Mandan!" A cheer went up from the assembled men.

The Hidatsa Indians who gathered on the far side of the river could only sit and watch them, perplexed with the culture of their neighbors. The Mandan warriors, while sharing the south side of the Missouri River with the white man, made a point to catch their fish further downstream. They kept their distance from the newcomers and Lewis and his men rarely saw them.

Later that day, as Lewis was recording the new details of the captain's quarters in his journal, he heard his name called.

"Captain Lewis!" It was the Canadian. He came over, with his wife Sacagawea behind him. She was carrying a large bundle in her arms and Lewis motioned for her to put them on the nearby stump. She had been looking larger the last week or so, and he wondered if indeed, she might be with child. Charbonneau had not made mention of it yet, but perhaps it was time to address it with him soon.

"What can I do for you, Touissant?" he asked amicably.

"Where I put my things?" he said looking around.

"Your things?"

"Ya. I work for you. I live here. Where I put my things?"

Lewis suddenly felt caught unprepared. "Uh...I didn't plan...I mean...we didn't develop the plans with you in mind."

The trapper's eyes narrowed in consternation for a moment, than his eyes lit up again. "You! We move in with you!"

Lewis' eyes widened in surprise. "No, that will not do. The lodgings for Captain Clark and me are not big enough to handle any guests. But perhaps we can make other arrangements for you." He looked around, catching Clark as he emerged from the supply hut near the back corner. He politely invited his guests to look around the fort as he conferred with his partner.

"Move in with us?" Clark asked dumbstruck, after Lewis had explained the Canadian's request. "Where are we to put them? Can't they stay with the Hidatsa?"

"He told me since we are hiring them for the expedition, we should pay them and house them accordingly. Hard to blame him for trying to get the most out of us, but it does present a problem."

Clark thought for a moment, then snapped his fingers as an idea occurred to him. "If we shift the supplies into one building, we can make accommodations in the second one. We'll have to store some supplies – the non-perishables – elsewhere, but it should work."

"There is one more thing – something he neglected to inform us of beforehand. His wife, Sacagawea I believe is expecting a child. He has not told us so officially, but it's something I picked up – the glow of her face, and how she holds herself. It's the little things that catch my attention. From the looks of things, she's probably not ready to deliver for a few months yet, but the timing might cause a problem when we are looking to embark in the spring."

Clark rolled his eyes in annoyance and looked at the ceiling. "What other surprises does that crafty Canadian have in store for us?"

Within two days, Charbonneau and Sacagawea had moved into the supply hut, the men having cleared it out as fast as it had been stocked. Otter Woman remained behind in the Indian village. There was no need for two Shoshone guides, the trapper had explained.

At the insistence of Captain Clark, Charbonneau also came clean about his wife's condition. Yes, she is pregnant he stated, but not due for several weeks. He assured everyone they'll be ready to travel westward when the winter breaks.

"Well, that should be everything for now," Clark said to him, with Drouillard interpreting. Then he handed him a piece of paper as he stood to leave. "Here is a list of the new duty roster for the two of you now that you're a part of the team…"

"Duty rosters!" roared Charbonneau. "You mean like…cleaning and…lifting things? That is something your men can do – it's not for us!"

When Drouillard explained the outburst of his guest, Clark blinked his eyes in surprise. "It was your idea to live in the Fort and be part of our team. Now that you are, everyone on the expedition – yourselves included – must do his part to keep the place running."

"I shall not, good sir. I am an interpreter and a guide. You need me, so you will do as I say! And I say we are not going to do anymore than our official duties. Give me a map and a destination and I will lead you there. Give me a load of wood, and I will dump it at your feet."

Clark's normally even temperament was tested in full that afternoon, and it was only after having both the trapper and his wife thrown off the premises that he began to settle down again.

Chapter 23

“The nerve of that man!” he said. “We will get by just fine – we have Drouillard, Cruzatte, and Labiche to interpret for us, and they’ll have to do. I will not put up with such insolence again.” Lewis nodded in agreement but remained silent as his partner seethed in frustration. “And let’s have the men resupply the hut – we won’t have a need for a guest quarters anyhow.”

A knock came at the door. “Yes?” Lewis said.

Sergeant Ordway stood tall in the door, holding someone in his tight grip. Lewis recognized the man as Private Thomas Howard. “What seems to be the problem, Sergeant?”

“I caught this man aiding the enemy,” Ordway said, the anger in his voice apparent.

Both captains rose to their feet and approached the men. “That is a serious charge, John. Please explain what happened,” Clark said.

“I saw him showing some of the Hidatsa how to scale the perimeter wall. They would go in the corner where the walls meet and use each side to brace against. If they learn how to get over the walls, sir, our fort will be defenseless!”

“I was just having some fun with them,” Howard said, his voice rising an octave. “Just sport, you know. See who can get up faster.”

Clark turned to the accused soldier, the tone in his voice clearly showing which side of the wall he was on. “Listen closely, private. While we may be living among the Indians, and we might even share some meals or trade goods with them, make no mistake – they are still to be treated as outsiders within our fort. Our only defense is these four walls, and if we allow ourselves to let down our guard, we will be at their mercy.”

Turning to Ordway, he ordered. "Please place formal charges against him. I want everyone to know the ramifications of sharing secrets with the enemy. We shall take up the matter ourselves. The punishment for such offense, private, is fifty lashes."

Howard's eyes widened in abject fear. "Fifty lashes...!"

"Do you wish me to give you the maximum penalty, as given to me by law? That would put you in a body bag with a bullet in your head. I'm trying to be reasonable here. Fifty. Now go."

Ordway nodded, and escorted the miserable man from their quarters, leaving the two captains alone again.

"It's a shame," Lewis said. "Now, while I acknowledge his actions could cause harm to us, it was not his intention to do so, nor did he exercise wanton negligence. Rather an inappropriate use of uncommon sense. I know you are upset about the Canadian and I am too – but don't let your anger influence your attitudes towards your own men. I recommend mercy, and his punishment be forgiven."

Clark mused for a time, and finally lamented, "Agreed. We need to instruct these fellows on the proper safeguards around here, starting tomorrow."

Lewis walked over to a short desk that Gass had constructed for him the other morning. On it was a bound journal, and he opened it up, looking for a particular page. He found the page marked 'Offenses' and detailed the name, crime and punishment of the man. "Setting such a pernicious example to the Savages," he wrote. Next to it, he wrote "Forgiven." It was the fourth entry on this page, and he hoped it would be the last. He closed it with a sigh.

Clark said evenly, "It's the price of freedom, my friend. While we all enjoy fun and games, we need to be vigilant in our duties and responsible in our actions. Next time, I sincerely hope all the men will take a lesson in this. All it takes is one miscommunication, one breakdown in our negotiations and we could find a horde of natives at our doorstep, looking for our scalps. No sir, that is not how I envision my end."

The Investigation Continues

Chapter 24

The dry leaves crunched under the large hoofs of the lead horse, the sound echoing in the stillness of the great forest. The air was stifling hot and humid, and mosquitoes were out in great force, driving to great irritation both man and beast. The sun was high in the sky, but the four men knew they couldn't wait. Time was of the essence.

The trail was narrower here, allowing only one rider through at a time. They were approximately five miles from Grinder's Stand on the edge of the Cherokee Nation. The mood was quiet and somber. If what Ordway believed was true, that Priscella had sent a warning to a member of the Cherokee, then they needed to act quickly to prevent the perpetrators from escaping. While they were all experienced with Indians and their cultures throughout much of the country, none of them had ever visited the Cherokee in Tennessee. However, that did not stop them from trying to uncover the truth about the stories they had heard along the way.

"Didn't you once tell me, John, that you actually met that Cherokee fella – the one that was writing the Indian alphabet or something? What was his name?" Gass asked.

Colter swatted at a large flying insect, cursing under his breath. "His name is Sequoya and, yeah, I was introduced to him last year, down near Georgia territory. I was passing through, joined up with a Cherokee hunting party I ran across, and bagged a four-point buck on top of a ridge. Just dumb luck, really. I offered it to them and they invited me back for the feast.

Sequoya was wintering with them, and he did try to explain his system of letters to me, but…forget most of it."

"Well, maybe we'll have luck on our side, this time," Gass said. "We've gotten part of the story, and maybe we'll finish up in time to get back by week's end."

Bratton, who was in the lead, stopped suddenly, holding up his hand for silence. Ordway stopped behind him, followed by Gass and Colter bringing up the rear. "We are being watched," he said quietly. "Show your weapons, but don't look to use them yet. We want them to see us…and to know we are not to be attacked."

Ordway slowly unbuttoned his overcoat, exposing his long, ivory handled colt revolver holstered at his waist, while Colter unslung his twin barrel carbine and laid it across his lap. Only Gass chose not to listen to his friend's advice. "Firearms beget firearms," he said. "We're only four men against what…a thousand? Let's show them we come in peace, fellas."

Another hour passed slowly by, without seeing another soul along the road or in the forest. However the feeling of being watched never went away. After a while, a break in the dense tree line revealed another, smaller path that veered to the left, and they took this trail without hesitation. The trees were even thicker now, but the air was a little cooler as the sun failed to find purchase. Thank God for small favors, Colter thought to himself.

All at once, just as they rounded a sharp bend in the road, Bratton signaled a hard stop. Two Cherokee warriors stood in the road, rifles slung across their backs, but neither made an aggressive move toward the newcomers. They stared at the four men for a few moments before the one on the left spoke.

"You are in Cherokee territory," he said, "Go back." His English was broken but understandable.

Bratton said evenly, "We must see your chief. We will not turn around. It is official government business. No harm will come if you let us talk."

The warrior evidently had been prepared for this for his reply was immediate. "If you wish to talk, leave your weapons with us. We will guide you the rest of the way."

Ordway interjected, "This is official business, and we will keep our firearms with us. Make no mistake – we come to see your chief and we will see him. We come in peace and wish to leave in peace. No harm will come to you. Please lead the way."

The pair conferred briefly and finally the one of the left simply nodded his head, then turned and led them down the path. The deputies followed behind them single file, more than a little apprehensive about what they might find – or do once they got there.

After a half hour of traveling, the party emerged into a large clearing, with long huts and small shelters set up around a common area. Native men, women, and children could be seen working at various tasks, from preparing food and gathering water, to making clothes and tanning hides. The smell of the roasted meat assailed their senses, mixed with the almost imperceptible fragrance of lilac and honeydew. Little children played games running and jumping. But as they emerged from the woods, the activity seemed to grind to a halt, as all eyes fell upon them. The silence that surrounded them was more stifling than the humidity.

The four horsemen looked back at them, observing but not challenging, confident in their reason for coming but careful not to overstep their bounds.

Their guides led them to the largest shelter, almost center stage behind a great fire pit. Holding up his hand, the lead warrior said "Stop. Wait," before entering alone.

The men looked around at their surroundings. The huts, both large and small, were canvassed with tanned leather, obtained by years of fruitful hunting in these parts. Evidently they had access to bison and deer, as they noticed several such hides standing out drying in the warm sun. The frames of the buildings were supported by wooden beams.

After a moment or two, the man emerged and beckoned them to dismount. Two men stepped forward to take the reins of their horses. Colter though refused to give the horses to the natives. "If you don't mind, Sarge, I'll stay right here and keep an eye on things."

Gass looked at Ordway, who shrugged. "That sounds like a prudent suggestion." Then, with one last look around, he lifted up the large flap of tanned hide that served as a doorway, and entered the spacious shelter. Gass and Bratton followed him close behind.

The room was lit by carefully opened flaps in the ceiling, serving as a makeshift skylight, allowing the natural rays of the sun to filter in unabated. Several men of various ages were in the room, sitting in a semi-circle around a single, older man, who was adorned with the longest headdress Gass had ever seen. He was smoking a pipe and his eyes were closed. *Was he meditating?*

"Welcome, strangers," the older Indian said, his eyes remaining closed. The other men around him simply nodded their heads in acknowledgement of their presence. Gass looked at his partners, then spoke up.

"My name is Sergeant Gass, federal marshal from the Missouri Territory. We are authorities of the Federal government, on official business," he began. "We are looking for information regarding the death of Governor Meriwether Lewis, at the Grinder's Stand right up the Natchez, back in October of 1809. We were told some Cherokee were involved and we are in need of your assistance."

A moment of silence passed, and then another. The chief continued to puff away at his pipe, his eyes closed. After what seemed an eternity, he opened his eyes and nimbly rose to his feet. Gass tried to estimate his age, but he realized it would be hard to gauge accurately. Perhaps somewhere in his sixties, but he could be ten years younger or older. His hair, already thinning, was a salt and pepper mixture running loosely down his back, and his shirtless chest, while still muscular, was tanned and weathered. His face was long and haggard and, despite his fondness for pipes, his teeth were as white as newly fallen snow.

"Allow me to introduce myself, Sergeant," he said slowly and evenly. "I am Chief Reddox, and these are my people. If one of them has done something dishonorable, it reflects badly for us all, and therefore on me. I will do what I can to assist you." The chief nodded graciously to his guests, but Gass felt an underlying current of hostility just below the surface. *He might placate us with words but we must watch his actions carefully.*

Chapter 25

"Ihave heard about the incident you mention," Chief Reddox continued. "Most regrettable. However I have not heard, until this moment, that any of my people may be involved." He glanced imperceptivity to his left at a younger man standing next to him, who looked slightly afraid. The lad looked at Gass but remained silent.

"Would you allow us to ask some questions to your council or others in the village?" Bratton asked, stepping forward.

"And you are...?" the chief asked politely.

"The name's Bratton. This here is Marshal Ordway. Now please answer our question."

The chief remained impassive as he spread his arms wide. "We have nothing to hide. I'm not sure who will talk with you but I won't stop you from asking questions."

Bratton started to ask the council some introductory questions, when one of the members excused himself, saying a backhanded remark about getting food for the guests, and left the great hall by a rear exit. Gass recognized him as the young man who caught the chief's eye a short time ago. Curious, he followed the man out of the tent, but went out by the front.

The sergeant emerged from the entrance and looked around, but the young man was already gone. He noticed Colter talking with a younger boy off to his left still holding the horses, so he walked quickly to his right. Just around the side of the building, he picked the lad up again. He quickened his pace, while trying to appear casual. He didn't want to warn the young man that he was being followed, or cause anyone else to interfere. The man reached the edge of the woods and entered silently and quickly, without looking back.

Gass paused. He knew he was at a crossroads – if he entered the woods, it would be almost impossible to track him without being heard, but if he didn't, they risked missing something that possibly could be important. Was this guy trying to warn someone? If he didn't go after him, that chance would be lost forever. He decided to risk it.

Looking about cautiously, he proceeded into the forest and tried to look in the direction his quarry had taken. He could not see him at this point, but forged on ahead as quietly and quickly as possible. After about ten minutes, he heard the flow of water up ahead – a river most likely – and stopped briefly to assess the situation. He had still not sighted the man but knew in his heart that – as long as the Indian felt he was safe – he would continue in a straight line. But if the man knew someone was after him, he would disappear. If he had done his job correctly, the Indian was headed here. *What was ahead of him?*

He approached cautiously as he came to the bank of a strong river, running east to west. On the other side were more woods, but there was about ten feet of open space around the river's edge. He saw nothing to his left, but when he looked to his right, he spotted it. A traditional tepee stood no more than six feet wide at the base, its tanned, leather skins pulled across converging wooden posts. He looked around quickly before he spotted a man out of the corner of his eye. It was the young man and he held a knife in his hand, washing it in the water's edge. Gass stood up, deciding it was time to make his presence known.

"What's going on?" Gass bellowed.

The man was so startled, he jumped up and almost toppled into the river. Quickly regaining his footing, he gazed at Gass with an intensity that belied his youthful appearance. A wild look of cornered desperation came over his features as the reality of his predicament hit him and he turned quickly, diving into the water.

The flowing river was perhaps twenty feet across and Gass was hesitant about going in after him. He had lived off the land for his entire life, but unfortunately had never learned to swim very well. He doubted he would be able to keep up with him at best. At worst, he would drown. The man reached the far side in moments, pulling himself up onto the banks and ran into the woods again. He was gone. *Damn!*

Gass looked back at the tepee. Why was the Indian here? Was this were he lived? He approached the hut when he noticed something odd. A foot was sticking out from the far side of the structure, attached to a form he hadn't noticed before. He ran up to it, and suddenly stopped short. An Indian, perhaps no more than late twenties, lay before him, his throat cut. Blood had pooled around his head and chest, but it was evidently very fresh.

The Indian he had followed must have done this killing just moments ago. He looked at the tepee once more. The leather flap of a door was closed, and he gently pushed it aside. Another Indian male lay within, apparently sleeping. His body was curled in a fetal position, his back to the door. But the rivulets of blood that curled around the head indicated that he too had met a violent end. Gass breathed slowly, trying to make sense of the situation.

The perpetrator was gone, so he had no choice but to return to the tribal encampment. But with the knowledge he now possessed, perhaps he could extract more information from the chief and elders.

"Where did you run off to?" Colter asked as he saw him return.

"Are the others still inside?" Gass replied.

Informed that they were, he stepped within the hut quickly. Bratton was asking a question, but the assembled elders weren't jumping to offer very much. Ordway turned and gave him a questioning look. *Is everything alright?*

Shaking his head slowly, Gass walked to stand beside Bratton, who stopped and looked at him expectantly.

Struggling to remain calm and impassive, the Sergeant addressed the chief directly. "Chief Reddox," he said, "may I ask the identity of the young man who was sitting with us a while ago and left suddenly?"

The chief gave a momentary look of disapproval – or was it alarm? – before his face softened into a wide smile. "That was my son, WindStorm. He is capable leader, but doesn't bring home many buffalo anymore. I believe he went to order some food for our distinguished guests."

"He's not coming back anytime soon. And neither are the two men in the woods whose throats he cut just now."

The chief's face grew hard and cold. "It is not polite – or smart – to come into our camp and accuse my son of murder." The other elders stood up and silently stood beside their leader.

The three deputies automatically grew closer as well. "Where did you find this out, Sergeant?" Ordway wanted to know, his eyes still locked on the Cherokee chieftain.

"I followed our friend into the woods, and came across the deed moments after it was done. I caught him washing off the bloody knife in the river. When he saw me, he dove in and got away. Nice handiwork, though." Gass replied, his voice strong and steadfast.

"Perhaps he was sent there to silence the real guilty party," Bratton chimed in.

"Or he was the real killer of Mr. Lewis," Ordway replied.

"Tell me, chief - and don't start with the lies anymore – who were these men and why did your son kill them?" Gass asked. "Are they related to the murder of Governor Lewis?"

Chapter 26

"You have no authority over crimes committed on Cherokee soil that involve Cherokee nationals," said an elder standing to the left of Chief Reddox. His old face was tanned and weathered, his small eyes sunken into his skull. Despite his fragile appearance, his voice was surprisingly strong.

"WindStorm acted to defend the honor of the tribe. It was long suspected by us that these two men were involved but it has never come to light before now. With your arrival, our suspicions have been confirmed and justice was meted out. There will be no trial in your justice system – our tribe has its own way of dealing with those who bring dishonor upon us."

"We still have more questions to ask – why did they kill him – and why have you covered it up for so long?" Gass explained.

Chief Reddox spoke up. "We do not know the answers as to why the act of murder was committed against the white governor, but..." He stopped, apparently debating within himself whether to explain more.

"Please, Chief, if you know the reason for all this, we can complete our investigation and leave your tribe in peace," Bratton said.

"There was no reason I know of for them to target the governor. Perhaps it was a simple case of thievery...or perhaps they were doing the act for someone else. Someone perhaps outside the tribe. We do not know which."

"And now we'll never know because you had them killed!" Ordway said, getting agitated. "That's what American justice is all about – getting to the truth and sending them to jail – not executions, vigilante-style."

"There are other ways to pursue this, John," Gass said. He thanked the tribal elders for their time, and led the deputies out into the prairie once more. It was early evening, but the sun remained hot and the air was still, the sweat

111

rolling off them as soon as they emerged. Colter stood off to one side holding the four horses while talking with some of the local tribe's people who had gathered around him. When he saw his partners, he excused himself and led the horses over.

"How did it go?" he asked. "I heard quite a bit of shouting going on, but no gunshots, so I guess you must have handled it."

Gass and the others took the reins and swiftly mounted their steeds. Colter did likewise and together they turned around and re-entered the deep woods. They proceeded in a single file for several miles until they reached the Natchez Trace once again, and then Gass turned them to the right, back towards Grinders Stand.

They remained silent throughout the journey for they were all too aware of the eyes that constantly followed them. After another hour of travel, they came upon a wider stretch of the trail and Gass stopped and turned around.

"I think it's safe enough at this point to discuss what happened," he said. Looking at Colter, he explained briefly "It seems our arrival at the Cherokee Nation prompted them to execute the two perpetrators to the murder before we had a chance to talk with them. Whether it was indeed a cover up for something else, or if they really were into honorable justice, we don't know right now. But I believe we all agree on one fact. Governor Lewis was in fact murdered, and this act was committed by two tribesmen from the Cherokee Nation."

Ordway spoke up. "It seems in some way to be orchestrated at some higher level though. If it was a simple case of robbery, what did they take? What did Mr. Lewis have of value and what was missing? His papers – government documents, his journal that he had not yet published. Perhaps some money, timepiece, and the like, but it doesn't add up to killing a man for."

"Priscella Grinder said – at whatever degree of assurance we want to accept it – that his papers were with him when he arrived but then went missing sometime after."

"I think you are all forgetting one important fact," Colter interjected. "Mrs. Grinder said the room was locked from the inside – and that the Indians who fired the shots never entered the room at all. So, how can it be a robbery?"

"And how about the marshals who came right afterwards?" Gass said, his voice growing in excitement as he spoke. "Grinder said after Captain Neelly rode back to Fort Pickering to summon the authorities. They showed up and buried the body – and most likely removed any paperwork he had with him.

Supposedly they asked the Grinders to tell everyone it was a suicide. But why do that if it's all on the up-and-up?"

"So the army paid the Cherokee to kill the governor?" Bratton asked skeptically. "But why?"

"He was heading to Washington to answer questions about some illegalities as governor," Gass said. He retrieved a small notepad from his inner jacket pocket and opened it. "He was to meet with the House Treasury committee – specifically with a man named Gallatin. Maxwell."

"Could be someone didn't want them looking too closely at his affairs," Ordway added.

"Or the illegalities were actually committed by some branch of the government, and they wanted to hide any official inquiries," Colter said.

"We should also consider the possibilities that the Cherokee were paid for the hit by someone with a more personal agenda against Mr. Lewis," Gass said. "Working along those lines, who would have a personal grudge against him? He was well liked by all, to my recollection."

"Well, not to all, Patrick," Ordway said. "While on the expedition, we had several people who might have reason to feel resentment towards him. Not the least of which were the Blackfoot tribe. Remember how they waylaid us and Drouillard killed two of them? I heard a few years ago they finally got their revenge on poor George. Caught him while fur trapping up north and killed him. And I also heard they were looking for more blood. Perhaps Mr. Lewis was on that list."

"Let's not forget the saps who received punishments on the expedition too – anyone of which might want to get their revenge on their former captain," said Colter. "We must have a record somewhere of all of them. I remember a few like Reed, Newman…"

"And yourself, you louse," Ordway said half-heartily. "But you're right; we had to dole out pretty severe punishments to a few members, including a few court-martials, whippings, and the like. I think being as isolated as we were ten years ago, depending on each other for survival, made every infraction much more serious, and therefore we had to make sure they were properly discouraged."

"But any one of them could have paid off the Indians to do the hit. You never know," Colter continued. "I remember our first week into it, Sarge," he said looking at Ordway. "You were as green as a frog in heat and thought you were so important – you needed taking down a peg. I served my time for decking you, but it was worth it. You got better over time and I got over it, but…I know of others who never did. Reed deserted – couldn't handle it, not what he signed up for. I can understand that. But when you brought him back, Bratton," he said, glancing to his partner, "he wasn't the same person. He was sullen and angry. The captains organized a formal court martial and all, and sent him back east when they could. But he very well might want to get back at Captain – I mean Governor – Lewis for that incident."

Gass cleared his throat quietly. Everyone looked at him expectantly. "You might very well be on to something, John. Before we finalize our next move, I have one more thing we need to consider, and it relates to the expedition. As you all know, Mr. Lewis kept a very detailed journal of everything that went on during those two years, every person or tribe we came across, every command decision – either formal or not. Even describing with words and pictures, the very trees, foliage, and animals we came across.

"And for all the years after we returned, he never published it. I, personally, put out my own memoirs – even coined the phrase 'Corps of Discovery'! – but the most prolific writer of all never told the public what went on. Never offered his thoughts – his written word – for everyone to see and witness. Perhaps there was something within his journal – a secret he cared not to share with the world – that someone wanted to kill him for. The diary was gone, along with his papers. Do we truly know what happened to it, and if it might have been deemed so valuable to someone that he risked killing for it? Maybe someone within the expedition itself?"

The men were thoughtful for a while, contemplating all the various scenarios that had been thrown out into the open. "My head hurts," complained Colter. "We'll be doing this till the end of the century tracking down all these notions."

"Not necessarily," Gass said. "We just need to be organized. Since there are four of us, we can break down into two teams. Get things worked out twice as fast. I propose Bratton and myself head north to St. Louis, and find out what we can about Lewis and the affairs he ran there as governor. Then we'll head to the capital. We can talk with the treasury secretary – Gallatin, I believe his name is. If Lewis was heading to meet him when he was killed, it would be a good place to start. Find out if there was a government involvement, if we can."

"What about us, Sarge?" asked Colter, pointing at Ordway. "You really trust us alone together?"

"I hope you have sufficient fear in your heart not to lay a hand on my person again – private," Ordway said. "Or it will be the last time you and your hand will be joined together." He smiled thinly.

"Gentlemen," Gass said, with a tone he reserved for impatient children. "I recommend you talk with the local sheriff and find out from him where the soldiers who found Lewis came from and where the papers they took went to. They must have checked in with him before coming down here. If we can trace the papers, perhaps we'll find his journal as well. Also stop in and pay a visit to Captain Neelly – he was the one who found Mr. Lewis and was his traveling companion. Maybe he can help shed more light on what went down that night and maybe rule him out as a potential suspect. It's now September 5. Let's plan on meeting back with Governor Clark on November 1 and go over everything we've found. That gives us several weeks to get a lot accomplished. Agreed?"

The other three deputies looked at each other and nodded slowly. A plan was forming and now it was time to execute.

Chapter 27

T he rolling hills of the Virginia countryside were majestic and tranquil, unbridled by the confines of tall buildings or deep forests. Acres of wheat, corn, and oats covered the area as far as their eyes could see deep into the valley below, while tall trees of white pine and hemlock gave them a canopy of green, red, and yellow above them. The two men rode their mounts along North Road, which traversed the highest ridge of this 850-ft hill, nestled in the Southwest Mountains of northern Virginia. The mid-afternoon sun was high but not overpowering, and the gentle breeze that cascaded over the hills gave the men a much needed respite from their hot summer.

"It's gorgeous country out here, John," Ordway said, breathing in deeply the sweet fragrance that assailed his senses. Having crossed the Rivanna River a short while ago, the two deputies were almost at their destination. He wasn't sure he ever wanted to leave.

"What is the name of his estate again?" Colter asked, looking around with hearty skepticism at the beauty that surrounded him. "We never had names for our houses, that's for damn sure. Not sure I can take all this high-classed livin'."

"You haven't even seen the place, man. Just you wait. Monticello is everything they say about it. And more."

"And you have? What's it like to live among the high and mighty? Please tell me, I really want to know," Colter replied, his voice dripping with sarcasm.

"Really, you should put a rein on your little jealousies. I haven't even seen the place myself yet but I've spent a good deal of time the last few days learning about the estate. And the man who built it. You should consider it an honor to be here."

The road wound gradually along the upper slope then dipped at a nice even pace for a time until it merged with a road coming from the south. Before they knew it, the large mansion came into view. Four white marble pillars set atop wide stone steps gave a grand entrance to the three story brick estate. A black, single chain fence with low white pillars formed a semi-circle around the perimeter.

Ordway led their horses along the walkway leading up to the mansion. To his left, steeping down the hillside was a large orchard with what looked like fruit trees, mainly apple and peach, surrounded by a wooden fence. In front of that he could see other large areas of botanical cultivation and neat rows of ordered vegetation. Quite an impressive establishment.

"So this is where Jefferson lives, eh?" Colter said, a new sense of admiration in his voice.

They dismounted and handed the reins to a stable boy who waited nearby. A manservant opened the double glass doors at the top of the stairs as they walked up slowly, taking it all in. There were side windows on the portico entrance, the likes of which Colter had never seen before. The window was separated into three sections, and it appeared that each one could open individually, sliding down or up. It was so unique that he stared at it, until he heard his partner call his name. The manservant, a tall, middle aged black man, dressed in formal attire, stood patiently waiting, his arm holding the door open for him.

Noticing a clock mounted high just above the double doors, Colter addressed the manservant, pointing upwards. "Now I don't know much about fancy houses and things", he said, "but I think your clock is broken. It's only got an hour hand." He smiled as he realized that even former presidents weren't perfect.

Without missing a beat, the servant said, "Mr. Jefferson feels that such a clock is sufficient for outdoor laborers. You will see other unique instruments in your visit, I am certain. Please keep an open mind."

Holding the door aside, he said smiling, "Welcome gentlemen. The master is expecting you." The warmth in his voice caught the guests off guard.

"Thank you," Ordway said as he entered the estate of the former president, Thomas Jefferson. The parlor area was sublime, as his gaze drifted over artifacts from Native American cultures, and to his surprise, several pieces he recognized from his days on the Expedition. *No doubt, gifts from Clark and Lewis.* The parlor ceiling stretched to the top of the second story with a balcony overlooking the main floor in front of them. There were rooms that branched off the parlor, with arched entranceways and tight wooden tile flooring.

"Please wait here and look around if you like. I will inform Mr. Jefferson of your arrival," the manservant said and quietly exited through a door behind him.

"Can you believe this?" Colter asked when they were alone. "I think he must of robbed a museum or somethin', cause there's just about anything you'd want to see right here." Walking around to a wall on his left, he pointed out several artifacts of interest. "Look! It's the Indian pipe that Chief Swift Eagle gave Mr. Lewis – you know, from the Hidatsa tribe where we met..."

"I know, I know," Ordway replied, joining him. "And a barrel we used for preserving meat. Even has the expedition name burned into it. And buffalo hides, deer antlers, some documents – oh these were..."

"Good afternoon, gentlemen. Sorry to keep you waiting," a deep voice said behind them. The two men whirled around, slow to detach themselves from their reflective thoughts.

Chapter 28

The man before them was tall, just a touch over six feet, and ramrod straight. His red hair was peppered with white and cut to shoulder length but it had probably been shorter during his political years in office, Ordway surmised. His clothing was fine but casual, not the formal attire he expected. He smiled at his host.

"Thank you for allowing us to visit. I am Marshal John Ordway and this is my partner, John Colter. We come from the office of Governor William Clark, from the Missouri Territory."

"Ah yes, you said in your missive that this affair concerned Clark and my dear friend, Meriwether Lewis. It's a shame about his suicide. He was a man of unique gifts, but as so often is the case, there is a darker side to such a personality, and he had his own demons to contend with. The world is still in mourning for losing such a man as he."

"Yes, sir. But that's why we're here. We do not believe his death was a suicide."

The tall man looked at him hard, deep emotions that had been suppressed and dormant for years suddenly brought to the surface. "But that would mean... only murder!" he said, his voice rising an octave.

"That about sums it up," Colter replied.

"Preposterous," Jefferson said, his voice slowly returning to normal. He took a moment to regain his composure, standing up straighter as a smile returned to his face.

"I am seventy-one years old, Mr. Ordway. I thought that nothing could surprise me anymore. I guess I was wrong. If you would allow, I'd like to escort you on a tour of the estate. It gives this old man pleasure to get outside more often. We can discuss things as we walk."

"What is that, if I may ask, sir?" Colter addressed him, pointing to a round metal disk mounted into the ceiling. It was decorated with lines, and he could see something moving. *Curious, indeed.*

Jefferson smiled. "That, Mr. Colter, is a compass rose, the twin of which you will never see in this country. I had it made just for Monticello. You see, it is attached to a weather vane on the roof of the building and tells me instantly the wind direction at any given moment."

"I just lick my finger and hold it up," Colter deadpanned. "Works for me and seems much less expensive."

The former president burst out laughing, bending over with his hands on his stomach. In a few moments, he rose up again, an admirable expression on his face. "Mr. Colter, I do believe you are the first person who addressed my compass rose in such a manner. No one else would have the balls for it."

"Don't get him started, Mr. President," Ordway said.

They walked farther into the mansion, while Jefferson explained the details of the Italian and French neoclassical architecture, and the layout of the large building.

"The beauty isn't just in what you see…but what you don't see," he said, smiling. "I designed the estate with hidden dependency chambers on both sides, which furnish the house with a full kitchen, smoke house, dairy, washrooms, ice house, stalls for horses and a full garage for carriages."

"What do you mean hidden? They are underground?" Colter asked incredulously.

"They open only towards the rear entrances and are not visible from the front. But we do have an all-weather passageway to them on both sides," he said. The trio passed into a large, very sunny parlor which had additional tall, sectional windows looking out onto the back of the house. Ordway pointed towards the windows, and asked their host about them.

"Those are very special windows, designed by my own craftsmen." Jefferson explained. "They can slide open at the bottom to allow air to circulate. They operate on a counterweight system. When I want them closed, we can secure them with spring latches."

"Impressive, Mr. President. You have certainly thought of everything a house can want," Ordway said.

"Well, at my age, I have a lot of time to think and contemplate new ideas. I love to visit new places and pick up different concepts as well. But I want to show you my pride and joy." He smiled and led the way through another set of double glass doors out onto the southwest portico. From here the men could see a beautiful oval flower walkway that extended to the edge of the grove about 300 yards away. Along the walkway, there were groups of flowers divided into stations ten feet in length, each uniquely distinct from each other.

"I have gathered these flowers from across the country, and around the world," Jefferson said, his voice showing the pride he felt. "It was originally designed with shrubs in mind in '08, but I expanded it just two years ago into what you see today."

"It's quite something to look at, sir," Ordway said, his eyes roaming appreciatively over the mountaintop in front of him. Beyond the walkway, the hillside started descending and the tops of many large trees could be seen.

"In addition to my garden, I also have groves dedicated to berries and vineyards. I am still trying to grow just the right kind of grapes that will give me a lush, full-bodied wine. Emphasis on the word *trying*," he chuckled.

"If I may, sir," Ordway began. "I'd like to discuss Governor Lewis."

Jefferson nodded, but remained silent.

"In the pursuit of our investigation," Ordway began, "at the request of Governor Clark, we found it important to account for documents, including his Expedition journal, which he had in his possession when he died. We speculated that someone might want to bring harm to his person because of the documents, or even his journal. In an attempt to rule out a connection between the missing documents and his death, we traced them to the local sheriff, then to Washington, Internal Affairs. We were met with some resistance in the capital, but they did conclude that some items were shipped to you, at your request, Mr. President. With your permission, we would like a list of items belonging to Mr. Lewis that you received after his death, and we'll try and verify them."

"An interesting supposition, Mr. Ordway," the former president said. "But that presumes that he was in fact murdered. I hold true to the belief that his death was a suicide, as does the federal investigative council that looked into the matter, back in 1809. What new evidence supports your unique hypothesis?"

Over the course of the next hour, Ordway and Jefferson passionately exchanged theories and facts about the case, with Colter able to interject only the occasional comment between the pair until, at precisely 5 of the hour, they were interrupted by the presence of the manservant. "Dinner is ready, sir," he announced.

"Thanks, Joseph. We will take it in the dinning room."

"Very good, sir. Are your guests staying for dinner?"

Jefferson looked at Ordway and then to Colter and back again. "Gentlemen, I invite you to dine with me. Afterwards I will show you what I can of Mr. Lewis' possessions."

"We wouldn't want to impose..." Ordway started to say but Colter cut him off in a hurry.

"Sure! I'm starved!"

Jefferson smiled. "Fine, it's settled then. Gentlemen, if you will follow me."

Ordway shot a look of disapproval at his partner, who simply grinned back at him. The marshal rolled his eyes and followed the former president back into the mansion before turning left into an adjacent room through a set of glass doors. The room was bright and spacious, painted a light yellow, with full length windows overlooking the flower walkway, and an ornate fireplace set in the wall to the left.

In the center of the room sat a long wooden table with ten chairs and place settings. Colter stood in his tracks. "Are you expecting anymore company?"

Chapter 29

Jefferson just smiled and nodded towards the large entranceway on the right as three boys rushed into the room. They appeared to be between five and ten years old and were dressed casually in slacks and cotton button down shirts. Their hard soled shoes made a loud tapping noise as they ran past. When they saw Jefferson and his invited guests, all three stopped dead in their tracks, looking a bit off-guard.

"Gentlemen," Jefferson said smiling, "allow me to introduce some of my grandchildren. James Madison Randolph – he's eight, first child ever born in the Executive Mansion! Then there's Benjamin Franklin Randolph – six, and my youngest one – Meriwether Lewis Randolph."

"I'm four!" the little boy shouted for all to hear.

Ordway smiled back. "It's a pleasure to meet you, Meriwether. And you also, James, and Benjamin."

"You can call me Ben," said the one next to Meriwether.

At that moment, more people began entering through the same door. A woman, tall and graceful with short red hair, emerged first followed slowly by several young women who looked to be in their teens. The ladies were dressed in simple cotton dresses and comfortable shoes. They smiled pleasantly at the newcomers.

"Permit me to introduce my daughter, Martha," Jefferson said. "And behind her are my granddaughters, Cornelia, Virginia, and Mary." Turning to the ladies, he then made introductions with his invited guests.

"It's a pleasure to have you dine with us, Mr. Ordway. Mr. Colter," Martha said, as Jefferson held her chair out for her. The two deputies helped the three young women sit down, while the young boys sat together along the opposite side. Jefferson took his place at the head of the table facing the windows, and Martha sat opposite. The guests took a chair on either side next to Jefferson.

Two black servant girls stood off to one side of a great entranceway set into right wall, awaiting instructions. When the guests were seated at the table, Jefferson nodded to them and they quietly exited. Within minutes they returned, pushing a cart laden with roasted chicken, sliced potatoes, and a bowl of steamed peas. They put a basket of bread on the table and filled their glasses with a red wine.

Raising his glass in a toast, Jefferson said loudly, "To Meriwether Lewis. One of the finest men I've ever known. Leader of an extraordinary journey that has reaped unprecedented discoveries for all of mankind. May he rest in peace."

All heads bowed for the blessing that he delivered with grace, and sat back to enjoy the feast. The three boys dug in first, with a little cajoling from their mother. Jefferson chuckled, amused. The young women took just a sampling from each dish before proceeding to eat. Jefferson encouraged his guests to eat heartily.

"You have quite a family here, Jefferson," Colter said as he wrestled with a chicken leg. "Where is your husband, may I ask?" he said, nodding to Martha at the end of the table. "He's not joining us?"

"No, I'm afraid not," she said simply. "Thomas is in Richmond these days. He's a colonel in the 12th infantry now, but served in the Ninth Congress up until a few years ago."

"Martha – we call her Patsy - is my oldest child." Jefferson explained. "But I did father six myself. Unfortunately most of them did not possess my healthy countenance and tended to die young. Much to my regret, she's the last one left, actually."

"My apologies, Mr. President," Colter said. "I was aware your wife had died young also, but I was not given the state of your children."

"No need. No need," he said with a wave of his hand. "That was a long time ago. What I'd like to learn from you is your take on the current state of affairs. Ever since my retirement a few years ago, I feel as if I've lost touch sometimes."

"Now father, that's not true," Martha scolded. "Why just last week, President Madison paid his respects. And the week before, it was John Adams. You get more visitors here than any man alive!"

"True, but hearing it from the men on the line themselves is quite a different perspective, indeed, than the rhetoric from Washington bureaucrats."

"Well, sir," Ordway said, "the war is difficult at times, of course, but we are hitting them hard. Making inroads. Several of my compatriots have served in the militia in the north, against the likes of Proctor and Tecumseh, and one even captured Riall at Lundy's Lane."

"Well, this conflict with the British and the redmen has been a difficult one for me to grasp. Once we gained our independence during the revolution of the late '70's, I had hoped we would never again feel the need to bring arms against another man. It's those "War Hawks" in Congress that pushed for this – Henry Clay and that Calhoun fellow from South Carolina. They were instrumental in getting approval back in '11 for the surge into Canada. If they want to remove the British blockage, or stop them from arming the natives against us, we should have found a peaceful resolution. Now it's our own brothers and sons once again spilling blood for a much more political cause. We're not fighting for freedom anymore. Let diplomacy do its work!"

Discussion during dinner turned from politics to his frequent trips abroad, most notably to his last visit to Paris. "We brought back with us many varieties of flowers and trees to populate in our garden. While I'm no expert, I do fancy myself a bit of horticulturalist. Perhaps it's something that will run in the family," he said looking at James with a wink.

"No, I don't think I want to plant flowers when I get older," the boy said with some conviction. "I'm gonna join the army! I hear they have the Redcoats in their cross hairs!" He used his arms and hands to form an imaginary rifle. "Pow!"

Colter looked at him. "Son, from your end, I know the war sounds all fun and games – but the reality of it is something quite different. We've been there. We know. Trust me; you are much better off here. Learn a trade. Go into politics. But don't go jumping into battle for the glory of it. You won't find any."

As the servants were clearing the table, Colter spoke up. "Jefferson, I have a question. It was my impression you were against slavery. You spoke during your time in Congress and in the Executive Mansion against it, and yet you have many here on your estate. Aren't you being a bit hypocritical?" This time he endured the disapproving look from his partner without a smile.

"My, such direct questions. Well, I'm not the sort of man to discuss personal issues, but I will say this. Yes, I am against slavery, and yes, I do own many. At this moment, about 150 black men and women are working as laborers in my wheat and corn fields. With that being said, I wish I could free them all right now. Just let them leave. But, personally, I can't afford to.

"My father-in-law left me quite a financial burden when he died that I don't have the resources to pay off myself. I need Monticello running and operating in order to keep money coming in. My fields and grain mills produce a generous income as well as my dams and canals along the Rivanna. Without the help of the slaves, none of that would be possible."

"Then what makes you different than the plantation owners you railed against in Congress?"

The president sighed heavily. "In terms of black and white, there is no difference, I suppose. But I have allowed – even encouraged – my house slaves to learn a trade and get a semblance of an education. I have freed several myself, and made sure they are treated right. I do not want to send these people off being unable to fend for themselves. I hope I offer them a better life than they would get elsewhere."

"Mr. President, it's time we should be taking our leave of you," Ordway said. "But first, would it be possible to review the documents you received?"

"Oh, yes. Yes," he said, and he started to rise. The boys had already excused themselves and run outside, while his daughters were in quiet discussion with their mother. "Patsy, girls." They nodded to him smiling as he and his two guests took their leave.

He led the way back into the entranceway and through a sitting room, before finally entering his study. Bookshelves lined three walls from floor to ceiling and Colter whistled slowly. A large desk stood against the fourth wall overlooking the front window, its rounded top molded with intricate designs.

Jefferson stopped, surveyed the shelves, and with swift determination, walked to the one of the far left, pulling out a black leather book from a middle shelf. He held it between his hands and closed his eyes in thought. Then he opened them, and brought it forward, holding it out to Ordway.

The marshal looked at the book, and even before taking it, knew instantly what it was. The black leather cover was worn with use and many of the pages were water stained or faded from the sun. He turned the front cover over, allowing the pages to breathe. The owner's name was written in blocked calligraphy, just as he had seen it ten years ago. It was the journal of his former captain, Meriwether Lewis.

"I had it sent here because, well, he was not just a friend and colleague, but someone who I admired. And as much as I had pushed him to publish it – to share his discoveries with the world – he held back. In part I think he was too modest to think of his work as being that important, but I also think there was a bit of perfectionist in him. As long as he had it, he continued to write in it. It was never quite finished, never quite ready to put it out there for

126

everyone to see. It was – and still is – my hope that his family will permit me to get it published on his behalf. I hold it here for safekeeping, until that time comes."

Colter said, 'Well, that is one mystery solved. If he wasn't killed for the journal, or what was in it, that closes down one area of our investigation."

"Indeed," Jefferson said, accepting it back from Ordway and replacing it on the shelf. "If it is true the Cherokee committed the act – and I'm still not convinced you will ever get your motive – I don't believe it will be linked to the good captain's journal. At least not from my perspective."

Chapter 30

T he carriage whisked briskly along the cobbled stones of the city, amidst the hustle and bustle of a people accustomed to getting someplace quickly. The sky was overcast and looked like rain but the people walking along the sidewalk barely seemed to register their surroundings. The driver slowed the horse after a time and stopped in front of a large Victorian house, nestled on a narrow road, next to two smaller residences on either side.

"So this is civilization," Bratton said. "Not saying much."

Gass smiled. "You're back among the people now, William. Get used to it."

They climbed down and paid the driver, before proceeding up the stone stairs to the large white door. They knocked and stepped back to wait. It wasn't long before it was opened by a tall, distinguished looking man, dressed formally in black coat, white shirt and tie, and top hat. "Good evening, gentlemen."

Gass explained their presence. "We're here to see Mr. Frederick Bates. I believe he was the former Lt. Governor a few years back. I am Sergeant Gass and this is my partner, William Bratton." He opened his jacket pocket and flashed the badge Clark had given him several weeks ago.

The man studied the faces of the guests a moment, his own features impossible to read. "Mr. Bates is in. Please follow me."

They stepped inside and followed the man through a narrow passageway into a waiting area, furnished with a luxurious snow white couch and two upholstered, maroon chairs. Gass eyed the thick oriental carpet and whistled softly. "This must have set him back a bundle."

Bratton smiled, but the servant remained impassive. "Please wait here while I inform Mr. Bates of your arrival." He turned and exited through a small door in the back.

The light was poor in the room with the heavy drapes covering the only window, but that was not uncommon with the wealthy, Gass mused. Light can tend to fade expensive furnishings rather quickly, and open windows invite unwanted guests.

It was twenty minutes before the door opened, and both deputies were getting antsy. They quickly rose, as the man entered. "My apology for the delay. I am Frederick Bates. How may I serve you?"

The man was on the shorter side, and had probably not missed many meals in his day, Gass thought with a smile. His short black hair had a slight curl to it, while a few individual white strands tried to peak through. The man's youthful round face expressed only a couple of light lines belying his true age, which the marshal guessed as early forties. His mannerisms were a bit stiff and he was dressed formally, as if he was about to step out for the evening.

"I hope we did not catch you at a bad time," Bratton said. "We would have called but..."

"No need." Bates held up his hand, smiling. "I was about to head over to see "Tancredi" by that new Italian composer Rossini at the opera house – just opened last year. It's only a few blocks away. Would you care to walk with me? It starts at 7 and I'd hate to be late."

"Certainly, sir," Gass said. They made their introductions, and then the servant opened the front door for the trio into the cool evening air. The streets were busy and the sounds of carriages and horses over the cobblestone, the clip clap of hard soled shoes, and the unbridled voices from dozens of conversations invaded their senses once more.

"I'll never get used to this," Bratton said, shaking his head. Bates quickly took the lead, the two marshals close on his heels. Turning right at the first corner, he heading into the downtown section. The noise level seemed to rise the closer they got, making conversation more difficult. But Gass was determined to get the information they had come for.

"Mr. Bates," he said, jogging to catch up with his host. "We are looking into the death of Governor Lewis, who you served under for several years, prior to his death in '09. You were Lt. Governor back then. We know Lewis was traveling to the capital to answer questions before the Treasury department about illegalities here at home. We know he had documents in his possession at the time of his death, the whereabouts we are trying to track down as well. Would you be able to shed any light on your dealings with Mr. Lewis or the exact nature of the inquiries he was being investigated for?"

Bates stopped for a moment, looking at him sharply. "First off Sergeant, Meriwether Lewis, while a great explorer I'm sure, was a terrible manager of money, and an inept leader. I know not the current whereabouts of the documents he carried – I assumed they went to some Washington bureaucrats when he died. I do remember the governor's office was audited in the spring of '08 and that we were informed by that fall that money was found to be missing. I think the figures we were given were in the thousands." He turned his attention back to the streets and hurriedly crossed them, in front of several fast moving carriages. Gass and Bratton had to hold up to let them pass before running after him.

"But do you know where the money was? What was happening to this money?" Gass asked. "Why did no one know about it until the audit?"

"Sergeant, the federal government was looking into several questionable financial transactions that Governor Lewis had undertaken, including using government money to help fund the St. Louis-Missouri River Fur Company. He liked to oversee much of the financial affairs of the Missouri – I'm sorry the Louisiana – Territory, as it was still called back then. I often asked to see the books or to help – we did in fact have a financial secretary whose job it was to record taxes, handle outgoing payments, bills of notice, payroll, that sort of thing, but when Mr. Tutman died in '07, Lewis failed to replace him. Lewis was a bit forgetful and, frankly, I was not surprised by the audit's findings."

"But Mr. Bates, I've known Mr. Lewis myself for quite a while." Bratton chimed in. "I've never seen that side of him before."

They arrived on the steps of the Elgin Opera House, a large monumental building with more than a dozen steps leading up to the main doors, a pair of stone lions standing guard outside. Several carriages were already in front, their passengers disembarking with the assistance of several footmen and attendants.

Bates stopped and turned back to them, his voice suddenly becoming softer. "Gentlemen, I understand you want to get to the bottom of this. I truly do. However, the man the world knew as the great explorer was...different behind closed doors. Did you know how many times I found him drunk, inebriated with his favorite bottle of scotch? Do you know the financial troubles he was in, on a personal level? No, sir, it is no surprise to me that money was found to be missing, that financial management was nonexistent. No oversights were in place to prevent it. He made the situation what it was, stole the money to help feed his own ills, got caught, and in the end, took his own life when his guilty conscious got the better of him." He nodded to his guests, turned his back and went up the stairs to the opera house without looking back.

The Expedition Continues

Chapter 31

February 11, 1805
Fort Mandan, Montana Territory

The snow covered trees glistened in the first rays of dawn, while the three feet of soft white powder covered the ground in all directions. The brutal storm from the previous two days was finally over and neither man nor beast had yet to mar the complexion of the virgin landscape. The log cabins of the white men were shut tight against the elements, with only the faint whispers of the morning breeze echoing through the fort.

Suddenly a door sprang open, slamming hard against the wall. A figure appeared in the doorway, disheveled and uncertain, a hint of fear radiating from his person. Dressed in only his woolen undergarments and his boots, he quickly stepped out into the snow. He sank in the soft powder up to mid shin, almost toppling over before catching himself. Standing up straight, he shivered as the temperature of the morning found its way in the very marrow of his bones, then headed straight for his destination.

He knocked quickly then entered without preamble. "Captain! It's time!"

Meriwether Lewis had a stag in his sights – large and straight, at least 14 points. He had his rifle raised to his shoulder, his breath coming softly as his heart rate slowed. He had been following this one all week, always getting close, but never close enough to make a try at it. Until now. His eyes focused on the task at hand, his finger gently squeezing the trigger… A loud sound from somewhere distant startled both man and beast, the later running off unscathed deep into the wood.

"What the...?" he exclaimed loudly. Then his focus shifted and he awoke, his fuzzy thoughts slowly giving way to clarity. He opened his eyes and saw Charbonneau standing in the doorway, wearing only his....

"Il est temps! Il est temps!" the trapper spoke rapidly in French.

Sensing the urgency of the man, Lewis quickly dressed, kicked the prone form of Clark lying in his bed nearby, and yelled as he left, "Get Gass right now, William! Let's get a move on!"

Stepping out into the frigid air, Lewis felt his breath catch in his throat. Pushing past the desire to crawl back into his warm bed, the captain got to the door of the trapper's quarters in ten big strides, the Canadian close on his heels. Charbonneau held the door open for him as he quickly entered, letting it slam shut behind them. The room was small, but there were several lanterns set around the room, giving off adequate light for which he would have to work by.

On the bed lay the very pregnant Sacagawea, perspiring and panting every few seconds, her eyes locking on him from the moment he entered the room. He smiled warmly at her as he knelt down beside the bed. "It's going to be okay, now just listen to me. I've done this before many times back east, so I know what I'm doing. I only wish you could understand what I'm saying."

Turning to the woman's husband, Lewis said simply "Labiche. Go get Labiche."

The trapper, hearing the name, nodded in understanding and hurried from the room. Lewis turned his attention back to the woman, who was in obvious pain from contractions, but had yet to utter a sound. *Brave woman.*

Within a few minutes, the room got more crowded as Charbonneau returned with the interpreter, and Captain Clark arrived, his overcoat forgotten and his boots still untied. Two native girls arrived as well, their ages close to that of Sacagawea. They looked nervous but ready to help. Clark knew their elders wouldn't step inside the fort, but these girls were not afraid. *The new generation.* Gass arrived soon after that, carrying a small bag of instruments. Lewis sat beside the bed, counting contractions.

He looked up when he saw Labiche, and asked him to help communicate some questions to Charbonneau in French, and then to his wife. When did contractions start? How far apart are they? Is she in distress?

The men spoke rapidly, and then the trapper turned to his wife. He spoke to her in the Hidatsa tongue, and she nodded quickly. "Luetza. Luetza," she said, a hint of fear just barely detectable in her voice.

"Un minute!" the trapper said excitedly.

"The contractions are one minute apart, captain," Labiche replied.

"Captain, would you like me to take over?" Gass said.

Lewis didn't move, keeping his focus on the woman. "Sergeant, how many babies have you delivered?"

"Well, to be honest, just one. My wife's sister had a daughter about five years ago. Things went fairly…"

"I've delivered four, myself," Lewis replied. "So I think I will remain here for now. But you can assist me, sergeant. We'll need warm water, several blankets, and an apple."

Gass turned to leave, but stopped suddenly, turning towards his commanding officer questioningly. "Sir?"

"I've not eaten breakfast yet. Most important meal of the day."

After clearing the room of non-essential people, Lewis and Gass set about delivering the baby of their new guide, Sacagawea. Only the two girls were allowed to remain and help give moral support to their friend.

The woman was in visible pain and more than a wee bit scared, Lewis noted by her facial expressions. But she steadfastly refused to give in to it, a trait that he admired. A strong woman. He patted her hand and spoke to her softly. Even if she couldn't understand him, he wanted her to feel comfortable with what was happening. He checked the placement of the baby's head and it had descended, but he noted a lot of pressure towards the back of Sacagawea's spine.

He had garnered enough knowledge delivering his sister's children to know the baby's head should be face down, and that the pressure he was feeling might be an indication of the baby facing the wrong way. With the back of its head pressing against the mother's spine, she would be in excruciating pain with little relief available.

He explained his thoughts to Gass who nodded. "I haven't delivered too many myself, Captain, but I have heard some plains Indians would sometimes grind up the tail of the rattlesnake into a drink, and this would often be a worthwhile pain remedy. If you want to, I'd be willing to make it up."

"Do we have the rattles of the snake?" Lewis asked.

"No," Gass said slowly, "but I bet I know who does."

He took a few steps towards the two young women and used rudimentary sign language to explain what he wanted. He thought about having Charbonneau and Labiche come in to interpret for him, but he didn't want to worry the husband any more than he was. In the end, he thought he was successful, as the two girls went out in a hurry, nodding and speaking rapidly in Hidatsa.

The contractions were coming fast, and as he held her hand, Sacagawea squeezed so tight he wondered for a moment which of them was in more pain. Then it passed and she relaxed slightly. She was exhausted and couldn't take much more. Gass felt frustrated at his inability to do more for her, but he reminded himself that childbirth was nature's design and he was just a bystander. No, he was more than that. He was a man whose limited training might make it possible to ease her suffering. He wished the girls would return with the essential ingredient he needed.

Lewis stroked her hair and spoke softly over and over. She seemed relaxed until the contractions started once again. She was sweating profusely and her legs were restless, but she never screamed or spoke out loud. Was this an Indian custom, a show of strength among the women of their tribe? He felt, in some ways, it was. Time passed slowly. He offered her sips of water and wiped her brow, all the time talking with her.

Before the hour was halfway gone the girls had returned, a small bundle under them arms. They each wore a long-sleeve, soft, hide dress, and a smaller fur-lined wrap to cover them against the elements. They offered the bundle to Gass, who took it. Carefully shaking out the contents of the pouch onto a small table, he held up the stacked, rounded rings that had once graced the tail of the poisonous snake. He smiled, and then got to work.

The carpenter turned doctor started to prepare the mixture, placing it in a small bowl and crushing it with a wooden mallet. When it was of the desired consistency of fine powder, he dumped the contents into a cup of wine which he had already set aside. Using a wooden spoon, he stirred the contents thoroughly.

"It's ready, captain," he said, holding it out to Lewis.

Taking the cup, the captain put it to the lips of the laboring woman, who, noticing the strong smell of the alcohol, briefly looked up in surprise. But she had learned to trust this man who helped her and drank a little of the concoction. She put her head back and closed her eyes, just before another stronger pain wracked her body once again. Lewis held her hand this time, willing the pain to abate, hoping she was strong enough to survive the ordeal. When he last checked on the baby ten minutes ago, the head was still very low, and she was more dilated, but the pressure on her spine was preventing the baby from going any further.

They waited through one, two, then three more contractions, each time, watching the poor woman grimace in silent agony. The two women who had watched stood near the head of the bed, and spoke softly to her in words only the three of them understood.

Chapter 32

When the fourth contraction hit her, Lewis did notice a difference in her body's response – not so tight, not quite as rigid as before. Her face, while still registering pain, was not as severe as it has been just minutes ago. He took that as a positive sign. Perhaps the elixir was doing what they hoped it would.

The next few minutes brought remarkable progress in both mother and baby; with her relaxed state, the baby's head began to crown and within another few moments, the little child was out and crying loudly. Gass immediately wrapped it in a soft hide blanket and placed it on Sacagawea's stomach. She was crying now, but it was tears of joy and Lewis felt so happy for her, he could barely contain himself.

Still there was work to be done. He stepped away, allowing Gass to bring out the placenta, and cut the umbilical cord, while he dealt with making sure the baby was breathing on his own. He had witnessed first-hand some of the difficulties a birth can present to newborns, and he was quick to take action. He was a good, light tan in color, with a remarkable thick head of black hair for someone only minutes old. He was a fine baby and very healthy too.

Charbonneau, forced to wait in the officer's quarters, sat in a chair, a blanket wrapped around his long underwear. His boots were perched next to the fireplace drying out but he was restless. He would get up periodically, march around the room, muttering unintelligible words in French, and then sit down again. Labiche had given up trying to translate to Clark long ago. "He's speaking nonsense, sir", was all he had to say.

By late-morning, the door opened and Lewis stepped inside, closing it quickly behind him. Charbonneau leapt to his feet immediately, his eyes searching the captain's face for any clues on the health of his family. Lewis looked tired but happy and he smiled at the Frenchman. "It's a boy, Touissant. Sacagawea is doing great. She's a real trooper, that one. You can go see her now."

The trapper gave a big hoot and bounded through the door in a split second, his blanket and boots abandoned for the moment. Lewis sat down on the available chair and rubbed his eyes. "Well done, my friend, well done!" Clark said warmly.

"I'm glad we allowed them to come back to live with us." Lewis said. "I think she benefited from living at the fort these last few months, and especially today, being so close to us and all."

"Well, that husband of hers is a pig-headed fool," Clark retorted, "but he did finally apologize and help out as we asked him to. Besides, we will benefit from their presence as well, helping with translation and navigation and such."

"Now we just have to factor into our expedition one new member."

Clark looked at him quizzically. "What?"

"Well, we can't exactly expect Sacagawea to leave the baby behind, now can we?"

"Charbonneau does have another wife here in the village. She can leave the baby with her," Clark said.

"I don't think either of them will go for that," Lewis replied. "This is Sacagawea's baby, and the expedition could easily take a year, perhaps more. But if we wait till spring, the child might be just big enough for her to travel with."

Clark sighed heavily. This was something he hadn't factored in and it could be an obstacle to the success of the trip. But they would gain the benefit of a strong guide and translation team and that was a great addition, easily offsetting the difficulties of traveling with the new baby.

Later that day, Clark paid the new parents a visit. When he entered the room, he saw the woman sitting up in bed, holding the newborn. He was wrapped in a blanket, with only a few strands of dark hair emerging from the top. Charbonneau, now fully dressed and dried out, got up from his chair beside the bed to greet him as he entered. He was beaming with pride over his new son, and it was easy to see.

Translation was difficult, but Clark did his best. Looking delicately over the folds of the blanket holding the baby, the captain just caught a glimpse of a small round face, light tan in color, with eyes closed and contented. His jet black hair was fairly thick for a newborn, he noted. He seemed content to sleep in his mothers arms and Sacagawea looked happy.

"What have you named him?"

"Name?" Charbonneau pondered this English word for a moment, before coming up with the proper answer. 'Yes, name!" In halting English, he said "He name is… Jean-Baptiste." He smiled broadly once again.

"A handsome name, a handsome name," Clark said agreeably. Soon he bade them farewell and stepped outside into the cold once again. The fort was alive with activity now, and the snow had stopped falling. The weather was bitterly cold and he pulled his jacket around his body a little closer, anything to stave off the chill.

He made his way to the storeroom, checked on supplies and made an inventory on what needed to be restocked. As always, food was at the top of the list. He could hear the high pitched pings of metal on metal and was reminded of the sweet deal they made with both Hidatsa and Mandan Indians.

The explorers would make or repair any metalwork the natives required, with the exception of firearms, and in return they would be supplied with corn and other foodstuffs they needed. It was Lewis who helped settle on the agreed exchange rate of one piece of metal work for eight barrels of corn. With so many people to feed, even this supply kept falling short, but it was certainly better than the alternative.

Clark had given the job of smithing to Private John Shields, who had learned the trade during his apprenticeship in Kentucky. Their supplies would also be replenished after Drouillard and his men return. He had sent George as well as Bratton, Gibson, and Private Hugh McNeil, two days ago to pickup a cache of buffalo meat they had stored the week before during a hunting party. They had two pack horses with them, as well as several rifles. Clark expected them back soon and he would be glad for it.

Two more days went by, and there was still no word from the party. Clark busied himself with organizing repairs and fortifications on their winter lodgings, and making occasional visits to see their newest addition, Sacagawea's son Jean-Baptiste, whom Lewis had begun to affectionately call "Pomp". Lewis told Clark that the lad looked so regal and pompous, he just couldn't help but give him that nickname.

It wasn't until four days had past that he got the advanced word from a scout that all four men were returning, sans buffalo meat. Or horses. By the time they were seated in the captain's office, Clark was fuming.

He started off by saying, "Ok, now what happened? We needed that meat for our winter stores!" He tried to stay calm but the situation was maddening.

"Well, sir, we got there fine," Drouillard started to explain. "Took us the better part of the day to arrive on site and find where we hid it behind the rock formation. The next morning we loaded up the horses and were on our way back. Billy and I," he explained, nodding his head in Bratton's direction, "led the first horse, and George and Hugh were behind us with the second."

Bratton chimed in. "But as we winded our way through the valley, and headed for the shelter of some woods, I heard the cry that I'll never forget. It sounded like they were coming from all over! Sioux; must have been a hundred or so, coming down out of the woods towards us. I knew we were outnumbered, and it was best to try and run for it. I cut the bundles of meat from the pack horses, threw them into some bushes, and then tried to make our escape. I was trying to lighten our load and give us a chance. But those horses weren't meant for speed, I can tell you that… After a time, we had to turn and make our stand. I had my rifle out and squared away at one of the nearest ones, and I think Gibson and Hugh did too. But then George said…"

Drouillard picked up the tale again. "I told everyone in the group to hold their fire. This wasn't a shootout we could win. I knew it and so did they. The Sioux had us outnumbered 100 to 4. What odds are they? None. So we held our fire. They came around, grabbing the horses and our guns as well. We stared each other down for a time - I don't think they knew what to do next. They coulda killed us, but they didn't. Eventually they ran back the way they had come, with our horses and guns. We took a roundabout way home, 'cause, with no weapons, we didn't want to meet up with them, or anyone, again."

Clark rubbed the spot between his eyes, where a headache had started to form an hour ago. He was tired, and this news disheartened him. He was glad they hadn't gotten themselves killed, and if anyone had started firing their rifles that day, he was certain all four of them would have been. However they had worked hard to get that meat, and had cached it only because they couldn't get it all back in one trip. Now it was gone for good.

Bratton spoke softly, as if sensing his captain's poor spirits. "If I may say, captain, I don't think all is quite lost. At least not if we move fast. After the incident, we walked up out of the valley and from the top of the hill looking down, I could see the spot where I had thrown the meat. I don't think the savages found it, sir. They all appeared to retreat back into the woods, not giving much thought to what we were carrying. If…"

Clark picked up on this thread, his headache lessoning by the second. "So if we go back, with more men and more horses…"

Drouillard finished the enticing thought. "We might be able to retrieve the meat after all! But we need to act before the Sioux realize what they passed up, or before it spoils. The snow and ice will keep it for a time, but we need to get it back. Captain, with your permission, may I head this venture? I'll need more men, weapons, and horses, but I think we'll be able to get it back. Plus, I'd like to make it up to you."

Clark said, "George, it wasn't your fault. Outnumbered like that, I would have done the same as you. Yes, gather what you need and return as fast as you can. Go!"

Maybe, just maybe, he thought, we might get those stores replenished soon after all. He smiled, then left the building and headed off to find Lewis and make his report.

Chapter 33

June 2, 1805
Along the Missouri river, Montana

The hawk flew high in the evening sky, a mere speck to the eyes of the men in the boats. They watched it soar through the air on its mighty wings, making a large circle as it sought out its next meal. Within a few minutes, it came down fast and straight, but disappeared from view among the treetops lining both sides of the Missouri River.

The large red pirogue was making good time, as eight men pulled their oars against the weak current. The sails were helping, but the calm wind didn't employ them to good use. Traveling with them were six smaller canoes obtained from the Mandan tribe when they left their winter lodgings in April, and a second, but smaller, pirogue. Bratton stood at the head of the first boat, when he saw something unexpected. He turned to direct his attention to Captain Lewis, who was writing in his journal next to him.

"Captain, I think you better see this. I'm not sure what to make of it."

Lewis looked up, squinting as the sun set in the far distant horizon. "What's the matter, Will? I don't..."

He stopped and stared, then quickly looked through his journal. After a few minutes, he closed it and stood up. "It definitely shouldn't be there. At least not from what the Hidatsa told us. Let's pull over and sort it out."

Bratton ordered the men to head to the south shore, as the other boats followed their lead. He heard Lewis muttering to himself, searching through his journals over and again. "No, there is no record of this," he said in frustration.

The captain looked up and viewed the situation. The westward river they had been traveling suddenly forked up ahead into two distinct halves, the current of both waterways heading against them, as it had been all along their journey. One river seemed to come from the north and one from the south. The mouths of each looked about the same, which begged the question. Which river was the real Missouri and which one was not? The Indians had told them to follow the Missouri all the way into the Bitterroot Mountains but they made no mention of this second offspring. Lewis made detailed notes in his journals and he was convinced there had been no discussion about it.

Without further information, it would be foolhardy to risk everyone going down the wrong path. By the time Clark had joined him on shore, Lewis had already made up his mind.

"William, do you see it?" Lewis asked, pointing to the mouth of the southern river. "Is that the right one? I think perhaps, in the morning, we ought to send out two parties on foot up a distance and see if we can make a distinction. We have to know."

"There is nothing in your books about this?" Clark said evenly. "You keep records on everything!"

"No, no, I looked. Maybe the Hidatsa overlooked it, or something, I don't know. But it was not mentioned, I can assure you."

"Well then, Meriwether, your idea is a sound one. Let's take this opportunity to make camp and we'll see where we stand in the morning."

Sacagawea and Charbonneau approached the captains. On her back, she carried little Pomp in a makeshift harness, his five month old frame already beginning to outgrow the constraints. He was asleep at the moment and his mother was trying not to jostle him too much as they walked.

When Drouillard saw them coming, he approached the men as well. For the past several months, communication between the leaders and his new interpreters had required the services of either Labiche or himself.

Charbonneau asked in French what the problem was and Drouillard explained his question to Clark and Lewis. They told them of the issue of the two rivers and asked if they had any thoughts.

Quickly, the trapper pointed north, saying in a firm voice what which Drouillard interpreted as "Head north into the Bitterroot!"

But Lewis was looking at his wife, who was slowly shaking her head. She began to speak softly and slowly, and when she stopped, her husband looked at her, a quizzical look on his face. He spoke to Drouillard who suppressed a small laugh.

"It seems Sacagawea is of the opinion that the southward river is the proper route to take to the Bitterroot. She has some memory, she says, of being south in the mountains when she lived with the Shoshone."

"Hmm, even among our guides, we are of a divided opinion," Clark mused.

By morning, the day brought a clear sky and a clear course of action. On Lewis' orders, Sgt. Gass prepared to travel the southern river on foot, accompanied by Shannon and Joseph Field. Sgt. Pryor set off on the northern fork with Drouillard and Private Alexander Willard.

"I'll give you each the day to go as far as you can and return. Learn what you need to and give me your report. We need to have a decision soon."

By the afternoon, Clark had decided to make a supply camp at the land between the two rivers. They would need it for the return trip home and it would be essential to have a cache of goods ready for them. He ordered several large holes dug into the soft ground, as the men unloaded two kegs of parched corn, a keg of salt, a handful of rifles, several bear skins, and essential tools such as axes, chisels, files, and blacksmith bellows. All of it went into the holes, and were covered up by rocks and brush. They built a temporary wooden shelter over it, and referred to this as Camp Deposit. Clark silently prayed they all survived the trip to make use of these goods on the return journey.

Clark observed Bratton standing off on the side, as the men worked all around them. He walked over and joined him.

"How's the hand, William?"

Bratton smiled ruefully, flexing his fingers and wincing in pain. "It's been better, sir. To tell the truth, I've had more ills on this trip than I've ever had in my life."

"I know," Clark replied. "But I'm grateful for all you have done, even if you are limited in certain duties."

"I'm a decent lookout," Bratton said. "But if I'm not doing that, I prefer to walk along the shore. I feel if I can't use the oars because of my hand, I don't want to take up space in the canoe."

"You know, that kind of thinking almost got you killed, son," Clark replied laughing. "When you come running out of the woods back in May, I thought you was gonna jump right over the water into the boat. That grizzly you hit must have scared the bejesus out of you."

"Yeah, well it did. I hit it square in the chest with two shots – must of hit it in the lungs – but it never stopped and just came after me like it was possessed or something. I seriously thought I was a goner."

"I have never seen Captain Lewis so mad before," Clark commented, but quickly added. "At the bear, not you! He tracked it down and put two bullets in its head before the day was out."

"You know who surprised me the most, so far?" Bratton said.

"I shan't say it was our new Canadian interpreter friend," Clark replied.

"No, actually, I'm thinking of his wife. Remember back in May, right after the affair with the grizzly, that storm hit and the pirogue tipped over? We lost lots of items, most of it floating away. Charbonneau panicked but it was Sacagawea who calmly got most of it back for us. Documents and maps, most importantly. She was incredible."

Clark smiled at the incident. But he remembered it was no laughing matter at the time. The storm had come upon them suddenly, and the Frenchmen had been in charge of the rudder during that leg of the trip. Despite orders to the contrary, he steered the large boat sideways against the wind, causing it to capsize almost immediately. It was also the last time he was put in charge of anything on the pirogue.

Chapter 34

As night fell on the new establishment, they heard a shout off towards the south entrance of the forked river. Gass and his group had returned.

Within the hour, Pryor too had completed his journey and both men stood with the captains making their report.

Unfortunately the outcome wasn't as decisive as Lewis had hoped for.

"We traveled some fifteen miles, captain, down the south entrance," Gass explained. "We didn't encounter anything of real importance that would indicate it was the Missouri. However the river never really got much smaller either, which might have shown us it was a smaller tributary."

"I know the Hidatsa had indicated we would run into a series of waterfalls along the Missouri. Did either of you come across something like that?" Clark asked.

Both Pryor and Gass replied no, they had not. It was Gass' opinion that the Missouri led south, but Pryor still felt, without anything concrete, that the Missouri was up the way he had traveled in the north. Which left the two captains essentially back where they started.

"Well," Clark said. "The only thing left to do is take your idea one step farther, Meriwether. We'll divide again, taking a larger party in a canoe each, and travel further than before, and find the waterfall."

The next morning Lewis headed up the party going north, taking along Pryor, Drouillard, Shields, and two other privates while Clark headed south with Gass, Shannon, his servant York, as well as Reubin and Joe Field. Their plan was to meet back at the new camp here in two days time.

The further along the northward journey he went, Lewis was more and more convinced this river was just too far north to be correct. But not having seen the south river, he couldn't be completely convinced. He hoped to find the waterfall and have a definite answer.

By that evening, he had estimated they had covered dozens of miles over the open river, but there was still no sign of a waterfall. Knowing they would have to return to camp the next day without a clear sign, the captain felt frustrated.

When everyone met once more the following day, the majority consensus was that the northward waterway was the proper route to take – all except for Lewis and Pryor. Both men voiced their strong opinion that if that route was indeed the Missouri, its course was running too far to the north. Based on information from the Hidatsa before they left, they should be on a straighter course. However, Clark insisted the southern course grew slightly smaller as it went along, indicating a smaller headway.

Despite the majority opinion against him, the men in the expedition were willing to trust Lewis' judgment and decided to explore the southward passage together. He was happy with their faith in him, but privately apprehensive.

"What if I'm wrong?" he asked Clark when they were alone, sitting by the fire that night. "It's just my own opinion, but I really think the north…"

"Meriwether," Clark said gently. "That's all anyone has to go on. We'll give it a go. If we're wrong, we only lose a few days. By the way, no matter which way we end up, we have discovered a new waterway. I propose you be the first to name it, just as we've been doing."

Lewis was silent for a long time, looking at the fire. Clark was beginning to think perhaps he hadn't heard the question, when he finally spoke up. "I'd like to name it after someone special. You know I've always enjoyed the company of Maria Woods, my cousin? I'd like to name it after her."

"Maria's River! A splendid name!" Clark said emphatically.

On June 10th, the expedition headed down the southward passage with the full contingent of canoes and pirogues, hoping it would lead them to the Bitterroot Mountains. Lewis hoped that he was not leading them astray.

The next day, Lewis decided to take a scouting party ahead of the main group, hoping to find the waterfall or any further evidence he could that they were heading in the right direction. The indecision nagged at him and he felt better being able to do something to alleviate the anxiety.

Lewis took with him Drouillard, Joseph Field, Gibson, and a private named Silas Goodrich. They headed down river in a fast canoe and spent the next three days on their own. By their fourth day out alone, Lewis heard a sound that was welcoming to his ears.

It was only mid-morning, yet the sun was high and scorching hot. Mosquitoes were abundant on the water's surface, and the men in the canoes were sitting ducks for the biting insects. The far off sound of a waterfall began gradually and after an hour or so, it had become very loud.

"I told you!" Lewis said, clapping Drouillard on the back in delight. "We're on course!"

The private smiled at his captain. "Yes, sir! It's about time!"

The current of the river pushed stronger against them, and they had to work harder to make decent progress. But soon the tiring work had paid off, as they witnessed a remarkable sight. As they rounded a bend in the river, they found themselves at the bottom of a huge fall, which sheared off a cliff face at least 500 feet high. As the column of water hit the surface of the river, large plumes of spray and mist rose up and spread out across the surface, causing the men in the boat to get soaked through after only a few minutes.

"Let's pull over and make camp, gentlemen. We'll do some fishing and hunting so we'll have some food prepared when the rest of the party joins up with us."

"I wish Richard had been able to see this sight, sir," Goodrich said.

"I understand, Silas. He was a good fellow, and a friend. But he was the best person to make the journey back to St. Louis with the prisoners and the letters. That was an important job and I trusted Private Warfington with the task. People, particularly President Jefferson, have to know what's going on."

When winter had broken in April, Lewis and Clark had sent Warfington back home to St. Louis. He carried letters to President Jefferson from the explorers as well as trinkets and parcels, and items of interest. He also brought home two expedition members who, for various crimes, had been summarily court-martialed by the captains. These included Moses Reed, who had deserted early in the expedition and was brought back by Bratton, and John Newman, who was charged for disorderly conduct. No longer part of the traveling party, they deemed these two suitable to transport home.

The men made camp on the north side of the falls basin, and gathered together a makeshift shelter. Trees were in abundance and large foliage was growing everywhere, making their task pretty easy. They made bindings using vines and after an hour had a decent enclosure, big enough for three people.

Lewis understood the problem they now faced. Once the rest of the boats arrived, their task would really begin. Each boat would need to be completed unloaded, and one at a time, carried up to the top of the falls. The goods would also need to be transported up and then repacked into the boat. This would require a thorough mapping of the area in order to find the proper land route to the top. Not too steep, but not one that was terribly out of their way. The pirogues would be extremely large and heavy.

Goodrich offered to catch some fish. He was very skilled at this task and Lewis readily agreed. He ordered Drouillard, Field, and Gibson to finish building their camp with enough shelters for everyone, and in the morning they planned to do some hunting. The transporting of their boats and equipment would likely last a week. It was better to have the men eat fresh food now and save their stores of food on the boat for later.

"Where are you going, Capt'n?" Goodrich asked.

"I'd like to have a land route mapped out to the top of the falls. By the time they come tomorrow, I'll be ready to show them."

He took a rifle and a water sack and headed off northwest. He thought the land sloped slightly more gently on the west side, but he would have to see. His clothes were a little damp from the continual mist put out by the falls, but the sun dried them almost as fast.

As he traversed the falls, he made notes in his journal that would be helpful in recreating the path again. He walked for a good while, trying to stay north and up hill, through areas not too dense with trees that would cause hindrance for the boats and equipment. He came out onto a large steep bluff overlooking a small valley below, no more than 100 feet away. He was surprised by the sight before him.

Four large bison stood in the valley, grazing casually, unaware of his presence. A thin layer of trees surrounded the small open area. The roar of the falls could be heard off to their right. He looked at his rifle and smiled. *This will be a good catch, if I'm successful.*

He took careful aim at the nearest one, standing fifteen hands in height at the shoulder, its curved horns protruding from its large shaggy head. He looked down the barrel of his specially-made, repeating air rifle, and gently squeezed the trigger. The rifle made a loud bang, and the group of animals looked up sharply and began to run towards the right. He saw an opening in the tree line that they headed for and knew he would not be able to get off another shot. He stood up from his hiding place, and looked after the animals. Three had almost made the tree line but one… was faltering, missing a step…

"I hit it!" he said loudly. Quickly, he put a new cartridge in his rifle, and set off the short path into the valley to catch up with his prey.

He ran down the hill towards the valley, dodging trees and underbrush until he was standing on the valley floor, no more than twenty feet from the beast. It was still upright but no longer moving forward. He could see a patch of red on its chest and thought about finishing it off or waiting until it died. Frugality with his ammunition won out and he sat down to wait.

Over the course of the next twenty minutes, the great beast slowly sank to its knees, then rolled over on its side. Its chest continued to expand and contract, but even this became less significant over time.

Without warning, Lewis heard a giant roar from his left side, and turned quickly, startled. A great bear, its fur as white as snow, had just come through the tree line, no more than ten feet from Lewis. The bear noticed him and rose on its hind legs, lifting its head a good eight feet off the ground!

Chapter 35

Lewis stood stock still, not willing to risk any sudden movement. Maybe it will leave me alone, he thought, and satisfy himself on the bison's carcass. The bear fell on its four legs again, moving slowly, sniffing the air with great fanfare. The rifle was in Lewis' right hand, but it would take several seconds to move it into position, aim and get off a shot. He doubted the bear would give him that much time. He had engaged bears in the past, but fortunately they had never been quite this close before. *How could I not have heard him coming?*

Evidently deciding the fallen bison was his to feast on, the great white bear walked over to the animal, pawing at it, making sure it was dead. Lewis also made a decision. With the bear momentarily distracted, Lewis raised his rifle slowly and tried to take aim at the large target in front of him. The bear stopped pawing his meal, and stood still, then looked over at the man standing there. Lewis swallowed hard, then squeezed the trigger for the second time that morning.

There was no loud crack of the rifle as he had expected. No startled look from the white bear as he was hit by the bullet. The gun had misfired! Damn!

The bear was not in the forgiving mood. With a roar of his own, he ran at the man who stood against him. Lewis desperately flung his firearm at the beast and ran as fast as he could towards the tree line.

Once Lewis started running in the woods, the cover worked in his favor, giving his pursuer more obstacles in his path. But there were not enough trees to really give the great beast a reason to stop or call off the chase. Lewis ran hard, swerving erratically so the bear could not build up momentum in any direction. He was a fit man, built for endurance, but this was the run of his life. He looked back only twice and the bear showed no signs of stopping on either occasion. If it was a track race, the bear would have eaten him for sure. But the uneven terrain worked in limited part in the man's favor as he neared the river once again.

Without looking back, he headed for the water of the mighty Missouri, jumping in off a low hanging bank. The bear came to a standstill at the edge, roaring in anger. Lewis stood, dripping wet in water up to his waist, wondering what to do. The bear would have no fear of joining him in the water, he knew that, and if that were to happen, his life would be over quickly. His rifle was gone, discarded on the valley floor. His only weapon still left on his person, was his espontoon, a short metal pike with a handle blade, which he carried tied across his back. It was Clark's idea to bring them along on the expedition, precisely for this purpose. Lewis reminded himself to thank his partner later.

Quickly reaching his arm around his back, he brought the weapon in front of him, the dangerous blade facing the menace standing on the riverbank. He gave the pike a few thrusts in the air, for effect, yelling at the bear as he did so. He was no longer running, but a viable threat, and the bear seemed to suddenly understand the dynamics of the new situation. Snarling loudly, the bear turned around and headed off into the underbrush, leaving the captain alone in the water.

When the bear was gone, Lewis planted the pike in the water and leaned heavily on it, trying to catch his breath. He must have covered a mile or so, he estimated, running at a speed he had not reached in twenty years. He looked up at the sun, and thought the time to be around high noon. There were few shadows cast on the ground and the sun was hot.

Looking at the river and the banks on each side, he guessed that he was probably half a mile north of the waterfall, having passed through this way yesterday. He climbed out of the water, his pants and shoes soaking wet, but his shirt relatively dry under the circumstances. He assessed the situation. He still had not achieved the purpose of mapping a land route above the falls, and his rifle was missing. He opted to retrieve his firearm and then continue his excursion.

Making his way back the way he had come, he was careful to listen for any signs of the white bear. He saw a deer come out of the trees to his right, followed quickly by two more as they bounded away from him. He smiled at their grace and beauty. If he had his rifle...well, they might have eaten well tonight. And if George and the others have a successful hunt this afternoon, we still might, he thought.

Within the hour he was back in the valley once again, having found the trail back easy to follow. All he had to do was look for the smashed trees and crushed undergrowth that the bear had left in its wake. He peered into the valley first, trying to ascertain if the bear was nearby. There was a large chance he had come back to eat the bison carcass, or carry it away.

The first thing he saw was his rifle, lying in the open where it had fallen. He glanced over towards where the great bison had laid, but it was gone now, a matted trail of grass marking where the bear had dragged it off to the north. The area was peaceful and quiet, a far cry from an hour ago when all hell broke loose.

He walked slowly into the valley, still on the defensive in case the bear decided to return, and picked up his rifle. He opened it, ejected the bad cartridge and pushed in a new one. He hefted it on his shoulder, and then proceeded to walk up the hill once more. With luck, he'd have the trail marked by tonight.

Over the next hour, he made his way to higher ground, keeping the roar of the waterfall to his right. He avoided areas that were too steep or too densely wooded. When he finally reached the top of the hill, he could see a beautiful sight. The Missouri River extended south before him for a long ways, the northern end making a cascading descent over the cliffs of the falls, no more than 500 feet to his right. The hill was covered in trees but the banks near the river were manageable and he thought he could see a good clear place to repack and launch the pirogues in the next few days.

He finished making his notations in his journal, drawing maps of the area in great detail. When he was finished and closed the book, he looked up, and saw, to his surprise, a tiger cat perched on a rocky outcrop about twenty feet below him. The animal was medium size with sharp teeth and a quick, fluid body. For the moment, the animal had not yet seen or smelled him, the waterfall helping to mask his presence.

Having lost the bison earlier, he thought nabbing this cat would be a good consolation prize. He got himself in position, raised the rifle to his shoulder, took aim at its head, and, breathing out slowly, squeezed the trigger. The rifle rewarded him with a satisfying crack but the tiger cat jumped off the ledger, bounding away unscathed.

Lewis couldn't believe he had missed him. Missed at twenty feet! Twice he had been thwarted and he was frustrated with himself. But at least he had accomplished the task he had set out to do. Picking up his rifle, he started making his way back down the hillside.

When he reached level ground again, he opted to do some exploring around the hillside. He was now very familiar with the valley where he had felled the bison, so he made his way north of it, picking his way through the tree line. Within half an hour, he came out to a prairie, with tall grasses and a few scattered bushes. He smiled as he noticed the three bison standing tall before him, grazing. They were close, perhaps thirty feet away, but one of them looked up as he came into view.

The great beast snorted which brought the attention of the other two. Lewis estimated each one weighed over a thousand pounds or more, their pointed horns a formidable weapon. He raised his rifle towards the nearest one, took aim and pressed the trigger slowly.

But alas, this day is not to be mine, he thought, as the rifle's hammer came down with a dull thud. Again, nothing happened. But instead of turning and fleeing as they had done earlier in the day, they moved towards him menacingly, giving him alarm. Backing up slowly and keeping a wary eye on the trio, he attempted to discharge his faulty cartridge and reload.

But when his left foot hit a large rock, he fell backwards, losing the new cartridge in the tall grass. Cursing, he struggled to get up, just as the first beast took a run at him. Lewis gripped his rifle and ran hard across the prairie, aiming for the tree line about fifty feet away. He looked back only once, the sight of the three great beasts giving him cause to once again run for his life.

When he reached the safety of the tree line, he afforded a look back. The three large animals had stopped no more than ten feet away, but they wouldn't leave the area. Lewis decided that enough was enough, and walked through the trees back to their camp at the base of the waterfalls.

It was evening by the time he returned, and his three traveling companions were all there, with a roaring fire going and some small game roasting on some makeshift spits.

Goodrich had succeeded in catching several large fish, each one a good ten to twenty pounds. Drouillard, Field, and Gibson had finished building ten shelters, each one capable of housing three people, and had done a little hunting, catching two rabbits and a groundhog.

"How was your trip?" Drouillard asked the captain while they ate one of the cooked rabbits.

"Not bad," he replied simply. "Killed a bison, got chased by a great white bear, lost the bison to the bear, found the land route I was looking for, missed a tiger cat – lord only knew how – and got almost trampled by three more bison. All in all, quite an eventful day."

Lewis retired for the night early, determined to rise in the morning and prepare to receive the rest of the group's arrival. He took one of the new shelters his companions had built, a rudimentary structure that resembled a lean-to. Its roof was made simply of large-leaf foliage that was bound to poles, strong enough to minimize the effects from a light rain.

The night was cool and the sky clear as he settled down. He had no covering, nor did he need one. In moments he was asleep, dreaming of the white bear. He had encounters with bears before, most recently chasing after the one that had attacked Bratton last month. He was a sure shot and the bear was no match for the anger he felt that day. But today his firearm had turned against him; maybe due to wetness or something else, he knew not what. Two targets he should have had, two targets escaped him. One almost killed him as a result. *Gotta be careful.*

"Captain." The voice sounded hesitant and soft. He opened his eyes and noticed dawn was just beginning, the red glow of the sun barely peaking over the tops of the trees to the east. But the something in the voice seemed wrong.

"Captain, hold still." The voice came again. It was Goodrich, the young private who had caught the fish yesterday. What was going on? He tried to sit up and right away felt a weight on his lower legs. He looked down and groaned inwardly. The new day was starting no better than yesterday had ended.

A rattlesnake lay curled up on his legs, evidently attracted to his body's warmth on a cool evening. He did not want to disturb it and risk being bitten by its poisonous venom, but the idea of leaving it was even worse. "Hang on, Captain." Goodrich answered his silent call.

The private was making his way around towards the reptile, a long stick outstretched before him. Gingerly he placed the tip of it beneath a section of the snake near its head, and lifted it off Lewis' leg. As its head rose with the stick, the rest of it moved off of Lewis, and when the snake was clear Goodrich gave a heave and tossed the creature into the bushes nearby. Lewis got up quickly, rubbing his pants down absently.

"Thank you, Silas. That was good work," Lewis said. "I do think the animals around here are seriously out for my blood."

The Investigation Continues

Chapter 36

September 15, 1814
St. Louis, Missouri

T he little wooden sign next to the old oak door was worn and faded but John Colter could just make out the lettering, "Indian Affairs". The building was small and tucked away in the seedier side of St. Louis, off the main drag, sandwiched between a butcher selling meats that were questionable at the best of times, and a brothel whose clientele numbered in the dozens even at this early morning hour. The woodsman turned up his nose at the pungent smell emanating from the meat market, and pushed his way inside the building. His partner, John Ordway followed on his heels.

It was cleaner inside than he anticipated, and the furniture, what little there was, was uncluttered and in good condition. Rolls of maps and parchment lay on two neat shelves against the back wall and a small safe sat in the corner. There was only one window in the place, looking out at the narrow street outside.

A man sat behind a small wooden desk, his feet propped up and a hat pulled down low over his face. He appeared to be asleep and Colter came over and banged on the desk loudly to get his attention. Before he could even straighten up again, Colter was looking into the business end of a small bore pistol and the eyes behind the deadly weapon gleaned brightly.

"It ain't polite to cause a ruckus when someone is sleepin', mister," the man said slowly.

Colter looked at the man and remained where he was, his own hand fingering the pistol at his belt. The man looked from Colter's face to the gun in his holster and smiled. "You're not a man accustomed to backing down. I take that as a good thing. We're cut from the same cloth." He released the hammer slowly and pulled back his gun, pausing a moment before putting it on the desk in front of him.

"Bad part of town, you know? Gotta be careful 'round here." The man had dark black hair, cut short, and a face hardened by weather and violence. A small scar on his chin rose halfway up the right side of his face, while another deeper cut gave his forehead an extra crease. He looked to be in his forties but could be younger. But it was his dark blue eyes that seemed to be his most startling feature. Colter could almost feel them boring into his skull, searching his soul for answers he didn't know the questions to.

John Colter introduced himself and Ordway, stating they was here looking for James Neelly, an agent that worked for Indian Affairs. Could this man be the one who led Mr. Lewis on his trek through the Natchez Trace?

"Well, well. It seems you've caught me on a good day. I'm the one and only agent in town," the man said, grinning wide. "Captain James Neelly at your service."

Ordway stepped forward. "We're U. S. marshals investigating the death of Governor Meriwether Lewis back in October '09. I'm told you accompanied him on his trip down the Trace and identified the body."

Neelly sat back in his desk, not looking away from the men standing across from him. His face looked grim and he responded soberly. "Nasty business, that was. But I thought the investigation they did was over years ago. Why are you reopening the case now?"

"Some new evidence has come to light that indicate he might not have died by his own hand," Ordway said. "It leads us to look into…other causes of death."

"Us? There are more of you looking into this?"

"Governor Clark has assembled a team and we are working through the possible scenarios, interviewing witnesses, reexamining the facts. We don't want to jump to conclusions, you understand. The evidence will point us in the right direction."

"Is that a fact? Well, if you ask me, it's a waste of time. I was there after it happened and I seen it with my own eyes. He was shot, twice. Lay on his back, dead as a possum out in the sun too long." He grinned at his own joke.

Ordway just looked at him with distain. "The man's dead and you laugh at his expense?"

"Listen," Neelly said, moving forward, closing the distance between himself and his guest. "I'll tell what I know, if it'll help your…investigation.

But I won't hide the fact that I think Lewis was…not quite right in the head, if you know what I mean. I wasn't cryin' when I came to know what happened to 'im."

"Just start from the beginning, if you would," Ordway said. "You started out on the trip from St. Louis down the river?"

"That's right, son. Lewis and his servant, a fellow named Pernier, wanted to travel to the capital for some business – something about a meeting with some treasury guys. He wanted me to come along and smooth the way with the Indian tribes we'd be dealing with. Hire guides along the Trace when the time came. He was willing to pay my usual rate so I accepted. I hired along another man to help with the bags, a fellow named…Raincliff, I believe. Haven't seen him in ages now."

"So what happened next?"

"I got us chartered on a ferry heading downriver. But no sooner had we gotten started on the boat, than the ferry captain came to me complaining about Lewis. The first night, one of the crew had to fish him out of the water – Captain said Lewis jumped overboard!"

"Jumped overboard?" Colter replied, shocked. "This was the first I'd heard of it. I doubt Mr. Lewis was one to harm himself."

"Well, Lewis started behaving oddly, that much I can tell you. Thought someone was out to get 'im. The trip downriver was only three days but soon after the jumpin' incident, I caught him trying to shoot himself with the rifle! I stopped him, of course, and told the captain right away. Didn't want him dying on my watch, you know."

Colter looked at the man coolly. *But he did die on your watch, Neelly.*

"When you arrived at Fort Pickering outside Memphis, had his behavior improved any?"

"No, no," Neelly said, shaking his head. "The boat captain told the fort commander about Lewis and he had him on a constant round-the-clock watch for a week, just to make sure he wouldn't try anything again."

"Who was commanding the fort at the time, Neelly?"

"Man, you're asking an awful lot today, aren't you?" the Indian agent remarked laughing. "Well, that's several years ago, but I think it was…." he rose to his feet and walked towards the back wall, turned around and came back. Suddenly he snapped his fingers, "I remember now! Russell! Captain Gilbert Russell was commanding Fort Pickering back then. I knew it now 'cause I had to ride fast back to the fort to tell them what happened to Lewis."

"Ok, so after you left the fort, the four of you headed down the Trace…"

"No, not just the four of us. Once we got to Fort Pickering, I hired two Chicksaw natives to guide us along the trails. It's a dangerous place to be – filled with thieves, and other terrible creatures on both two and four legs." He grinned again and Colter stared back at him.

"You also had horses – I read you lost them at some point just before you reached the Grinders."

"Yeah, there was a storm come up one night, the wind and rain was very strong. But we were okay until a big bolt of lightning came cracking down not more than a hundred feet away, and scared those horses somethin' fierce! They took off into the night and we were all alone then. The Chicksaw told us they'd round them up, but I could tell we weren't gonna see these fellas again if we let them out of our sight, so I told Lewis I'd stay behind and help them find the animals."

"And Mr. Lewis agreed?"

"Well, it was raining hard and I wanted to get him as fast as I could to the next inn owned by a white man, so I insisted he start off. But remember this was night time and we had already unpacked the horses. Pernier and Raincliff were left in charge of bringing the bags along behind Lewis. I'm sure he musta gotten to the inn well ahead of 'em."

"So the last time you saw Mr. Lewis, he was walking towards the Grinders Stand?" Ordway asked.

"Yep, never saw him again after that – until I arrived the next day with the horses. The Chicksaw ran off, as I thought – worthless guides they turned out to be. But that's what you get, down there."

"And what was the scene when you arrived the next day?"

"Well, I came across them in the morning – took me most of the night to find those horses I tell you – and I see Raincliff standing outside. At first I didn't see anyone else. He sees me and runs over, saying Lewis is dead – killed himself, he says."

"I give him the reins to the horses, and rush into the building – the door was standing open and I see the innkeeper's wife and Lewis' man standing inside, looking at the body. They didn't seem to know what to do, so I kinda took charge of the situation. The woman said she heard two gunshots, waited a while, then ran to tell our two men who she had put up for the night in the barn when they arrived after midnight. She said the door was locked and Pernier crawled in through the window to unlock it. They hadn't moved anything, she said."

"Well, we've interviewed her again and she paints a slightly different take on things now."

"Is that right?" Neelly said with obvious interest.

"She claims it was a hit by the Cherokee, who had a settlement down along the Trace. Someone paid her and her husband off to look the other way and not say anything. Which leads us to the all important question...Who hired the Cherokee to take the shot? And why?"

"Well, if you're looking for suspects, there are plenty to be had. It wasn't a secret the governor was not well liked in St. Louis. He had many political enemies, I've no doubt."

Colter walked over to stand eye to eye with the Indian agent. "I've one question for you, Mr. Neelly. Were you involved in hiring them Cherokee to kill Mr. Lewis? You had the time, when you went lookin' for them horses."

James Neelly looked stern and his eyes grew narrow. "I don't take kindly to anyone accusin' me of murder, Colter. I've no beef with the man. He was crazy, I know that much. He was suicidal, he surely was. And he did have enemies. But, kill him? Or hire anyone to do it? No, sir. That's not in my play book. I act for the best interests of my clients and Mr. Lewis was my client. I was entrusted to get him from St. Louis to Washington. I failed, but through no fault of my own. If you want to find out who killed your precious Mr. Lewis, you'd best turn your sights elsewhere."

Chapter 37

October 22, 1814
Alberta, Canadian territory

The large, grassy area of the Porcupine Hills was brown this morning. Dozens of buffalo were grazing lazily, old bulls and young cows together in one place. They had traveled northward from their summer prairies as the hot sun had gradually dried their food supply. The hills provided them shelter from the elements as well as a good source of food. They would eat until their reserves were full and then migrate north again.

The men who watched from the shadows of the trees smiled at the sheer number of animals they saw this morning. It was going to go well. Dozens of natives, wearing the soft leather robes and shirts that the cool weather dictated, squinted in the sun, the bright morning rays reflecting off the black paint that adorned their faces.

At the appointed time, dozens of men leapt out of their hiding places to the west of the herd, some on horses, some on foot, all shouting at the top of their lungs, driving the animals off the hills to the east. At first only the nearby bulls responded to the distraction, and then, as if a tidal wave had washed over them, the rest of the herd responded in kind. Braying and bleating in response to the intrusion, they began to panic.

Another group of men suddenly emerged from the north, shouting alike, running alongside the great beasts as they attempted to drive them south, through the large opening leading into the valley below.

Gradually the herd moved, slowly at first, their size and number hindering their progress. But as they cleared the opening, the large animals began to run harder, their fear multiplied by those around them. They ran for a mile in a gradual slope downhill, while the men on horseback continued to run alongside, shouting all the while. Those few men who had guns fired into the air, and the cows near them bleating in response.

As the animals approached the flat grassy valley at a full run, they tried to spread out but ran into another obstacle. Tall stone piles, or cairns, were stacked up along each side of the valley, in an ever narrowing fashion, constricting the path the bison were forced to take. Those who couldn't maneuver the narrow passage either slammed into the stone piles or fell down where they were, causing a violent pileup for those following them. The men, following on horseback, ran outside the cairns encouraging the herd as best they could, forcing them further and faster through the valley.

The animals continued on this pace for another two miles of prairie, the stone piles now only twenty feet across. The buffalo, once driven by panic and discourse, could see no problems up ahead and their anxiety levels eased accordingly. The men had fallen behind, and the herd was able to keep a steady rhythm in their strides.

Then the world seemed to drop from under them, quite literally. The first of the herd stepped out into open air and fell with a thickening thud 10 yards below. The next one, then two, ran off the sheer cliff, their eyes showing their surprise before they too dropped into a heap of broken legs and crushed bodies. Loud cries erupted from both sides of the even increasing pile as the Blackfoot Indians danced in celebration.

As more bodies of buffalo piled up at the foot of the blind cliff, those behind them tried to jump down or drive around the narrow drop. The cliff itself, while steep, was narrow in width, no more than twenty feet across. Those who could get through the cairns had a good chance of making it successfully around the melee and those than couldn't took their leap of faith and hoped for the best. By the time the herd had passed, about twenty bodies of the great beasts lay at the bottom of the cliff face, the rest having passed unmolested.

The Indians ran out, finishing off those animals not yet dead with spears or rifles. It was not their intention of making them suffer, but this communal buffalo jump was a very effective and quick way of getting meat and clothing for their tribes before their trek to winter lodgings in a few weeks.

"Estipah-skikikini-kots," some of the boys chanted excitedly. *Heads-Smashed-In.* For some of the boys, it was their first buffalo jump and this location was one of the oldest and most effective jumps in Blackfoot culture.

A tall, middle-aged man stood off to one side, his head adorned with a full war bonnet of feathers that draped halfway down his back. Despite the cool temperatures, he was shirtless, save for the ornamental beads that hung low around his neck. Soft leather pants and worn shoes completed his look. Several men, aged in their years, surrounded him in quiet contemplation as they reviewed the success of the buffalo jump.

Another man rode up on horseback, and dismounted near the small group. He was dressed in soft leathers as well, but evidently preferred to ward off the chill with a complete long sleeve outfit. His headpiece contained two feathers, both white as ivory. He held a rolled parchment in his hand.

"It is time, Chief Tukamansha," he said simply. "They have arrived."

Tukamansha nodded once, his face in a perpetual frown, his black eyes seeming to stare through the young warrior. The messenger turned quickly around, remounted his horse and rode away at a good clip.

The man and his aged followers turned and walked slowly, retiring to a permanent structure about a quarter of a mile distant. It had four walls made from earth and stone, with a single doorway in front. Its entrance was covered by a large bearskin, white and shaggy, and worn with age. The men entered solemnly, with only four young men standing guard outside. The four each carried a rifle, their half naked bodies covered in tattoos and decorations for war. It was a sign of intimidation, meant for the eyes of the white man. Newcomers were rarely seen in these parts, and those few that were found quickly wished they had stayed home.

Within ten minutes of their arrival, the same man on horseback approached the small building, this time leading two other men with mounts of their own. One of them was tall with black hair, his back straight as an arrow. The other was slightly shorter but solidly built, and kept looking around, evidently not happy to be here.

Together they dismounted, as one of the natives came forward to take the reins. He led the horses away to secure them to a small tree. Two of the other guards stood before the door. One spoke a quick command and held out his hand. His partner raised his own rifle in case there was any argument from the newcomers.

But they had been briefed well beforehand and handed over their rifles without an issue. If they wanted to conduct this interview, this was the only way to do it. They were no longer on American soil, a condition that played well into the hands of the Blackfoot. These ambassadors of the U.S. government had no official jurisdiction here.

"Please tell our host of our arrival," Ordway said amicably. His interpreter, the young warrior who had guided them here, Prancing Bear, conveyed the message to one of the guards. He nodded and stepped inside to announce them.

Prancing Bear stepped inside, and indicated to Ordway and his partner to do the same. The sergeant pushed aside the giant bearskin and entered, but when Colter tried to enter one of the guards put his hand on his shoulder, stopping him. Looking the white man in the eyes, the young warrior spoke quickly and with extreme anger, spitting on the ground at his feet.

Colter had been nervous about coming to meet with the Blackfoot from the beginning. Ordway had assured him that, as government officials, they would be protected. Now he was beginning to have doubts all over again.

He understood the young man's anger. It had been only two years since Colter had killed the chief's son and escaped the hundreds of pursuers that were out for his scalp that day he and John Potts were canoeing along one of the Missouri tributaries, checking their traps. He knew he was not at fault, but at the same time, he had come to realize the embarrassment the Indians must have felt in allowing him to escape. He had heard through other trappers soon afterwards, how much the Blackfoot still wanted him, dead or alive.

When Ordway made arrangements for this little rendezvous up north, through government tribal contacts such as Prancing Bear, he was careful never to mention the names of those coming. He wasn't sure if they would recognize Colter by name or not, or if the natives he would meet would even recognize him, but he took no chances.

"Look," Colter said but then realized that he need not waste his efforts on lowly guards. If he needed to address anyone, it would be the chief himself. Knocking away the hand that held him, he shot the guard a dirty stare and entered with a confidence he sure didn't feel.

Chapter 38

As he entered, all eyes turned on him. There was no furniture of any kind in the room. Five elders sat cross legged on the floor in two rows. Colter recognized the chief immediately, sitting in the middle front row. He was looking at Ordway and shifted his gaze to the newcomer when he crossed the threshold. The guard that had given him trouble did not follow him in.

Their eyes met and locked for a moment, but Colter did not look away. This was their territory and he wanted to show them he felt no fear. He remembered he was here on official government business and they would be foolish to try something. Not that he or Ordway would stand a chance if it came to violence, but hopefully they understood this time any incidents would be followed up by the U.S. army, whether they happened to be in Canada or not.

The chief spoke slowly in his native tongue, and Prancing Bear interpreted his response when he was finished. "Chief Tukamansha would like to welcome you both to the traditional Blackfoot buffalo jump. He says he would like to help representatives of the U.S. government."

The eyes of the chief never left Colter, who felt the room getting smaller by the minute. Ordway spoke to the chief, explaining the purpose of their visit and expressing the hope of getting answers that only he could provide. He stressed that they were not here to arrest anyone, but to gather more information regarding this important murder investigation of a prominent American.

The chief spoke sharply, his voice suddenly rift with anger. He rose to his feet with astonishing speed. Prancing Bear stepped back, a little off

166

balance. He had dealt with this adversarial tribal leader on one other occasion, but this behavior was uncharacteristic even for him.

Prancing Bear replied back to Tukamansha for a few moments, before reluctantly starting to translate. "He asks who from the government will investigate the murder of his own son. He says the killer is here among us and nothing is being done." He seemed almost apologetic when he spoke next, turning to Colter, "Sir, from what he said, I think he meant you."

Ordway spoke up. "Tell him that Marshal Colter is not on trial and the incident he is referring to is not considered part of this or any other investigation. Tell him we need a few direct responses to our questions, and we will be on our way. Tell him…"

"Tell him," Colter said, "that I am sorry for how things turned out. But even a man such as he must understand the difficulty of my situation. He knows. He was there."

Prancing Bear paused for a moment, thinking about the heated exchange of words, and then began to speak once again to the tribal chieftain. When he finished, the chief came forward slowly, looking hard at the man who had killed his son. He spoke again slowly, and waited for Prancing Bear to interpret for him.

"He says you trespassed on tribal land, and deserved your fate." Prancing Bear said. "He said his son was named Running River and was destined to be chief himself one day. You took that from him and he feels the pain every day. He says that the Blackfoot will never forget."

Then the chief closed his eyes and began to chant loudly, then softly, his body moving in small fluid motions with the rhythms of the words. After a few minutes of this, he stopped, his eyes opening and looking around as if seeing them for the first time. He smiled slightly and returned to his seat. He looked at Ordway, ignoring Colter for the moment.

The chief spoke and Prancing Bear smiled. "He says he asked the spirit of his son for forgiveness on your behalf. For the moment, he is at peace. He expresses that he is ready for your questions." The interpreter looked at Ordway. "I personally recommend you get your answers and get out as fast as possible. With him, there is no telling what he is willing to do at any moment."

The marshal nodded his understanding and carefully asked the most important question. "We know that Governor Lewis was killed by Cherokee Indians, in the southern state of Tennessee. But while that is far from here, we are looking into a possible connection between them and who might have hired them. There are many motives for murder. We know there was an incident between your tribe and Mr. Lewis ten years ago, the very first time your people ever encountered a white man. Two of your tribe were killed in the encounter. We also know the Blackfoot have recently killed another man who was there at the time, a Private George Drouillard, so we have probable cause. Did you or someone in the Blackfoot community order the death of Governor Lewis to satisfy your personal vendettas?"

Prancing Bear looked at him for a moment, unsure how to word the question this man posed. Accusing the tribal leader of murder? Was he signing his own death warrant right now by putting the question to the chief? He gulped and started slowly.

As the Indian interpreted his partner's loaded question, Colter saw the chief's eyes widen in surprise and could feel the tension in the air. When he finished speaking at last, all was deathly quiet. Colter looked around, not sure if they were going to be killed on the spot, or captured and eaten for dinner later on. Personally, he thought, the former would be quick and altogether the better way to go.

But the one thing he did not expect was to hear laughter. The chief let loose a roar that surprised everyone in the house, especially Prancing Bear who took a step back in response to this most unexpected behavior. The tribal leader, one of the most feared in all of the northern territories, continued for awhile unabated, while even his fellow council elders looked on in shock. Then the chief grew serious again, his mood gradually returning to a steady calm, and he began talking in earnest.

Prancing Bear listened and, when the chief was finished, turned and addressed the two white men. "Chief Tukamansha wants me to convey that Mr. Drouillard was killed because he was found trapping on Blackfoot territory. That crime determined his fate, which was his to bear. The chief says the fact that he was involved in the unprovoked attack from years past, just added a harsher sentence for him."

"What was he laughing about?" Colter asked.

"And what of his motive for killing Governor Lewis?" added Ordway.

Prancing Bear put his hands on his hips, looking at the two men directly. "He said the white men do not understand the ways of the Blackfoot. If he wanted Mr. Lewis killed, he would have done it himself, or instructed his own tribe to do so. Involving outsiders, especially rivals such as the Cherokee, is not their way. It is amusing to him that anyone gives credence to your suggestion."

He turned back to the chief, but stopped and faced Colter one last time. "He also wanted me to convey to you that, as representatives of the U.S.

government, you are guests of the Blackfoot. That is why you are still alive. But if he catches your hide on Blackfoot territory again, he will personally hang you upside down over a fire pit, put a dagger through your heart, and feed your entrails to the birds. And please believe him. I have given witness to such an affair myself."

Chapter 39

October 24, 1814
Washington, D.C.

T he streets were deserted at this early hour, the smell of smoke upon the land still lingering three months after the attack by British troops. The two men on horseback had passed small one-room hovels miles back and had not seen much until now. The landscape of the nation's capital, populated with slightly more than 8,000 souls, was dense woods and a multitude of swampy marshes, all leading up to the Chesapeake Bay a few miles to the east.

There were a few mosquitoes this morning, but most had died off after the hot summer, giving the residents a welcome respite. They passed a stately manor house on a small hill overlooking the narrow dirt road and further up, another slightly larger house on the right. These had remained unmolested by the ravages of the invading army, and they were beautiful to look at.

Sergeant Gass reined in his horse as they overtook an older black man walking down the road, his clothes slightly tattered but standing the passage of time. He had no shoes, but carried a pole over his shoulder and a straw hat on his head. "Hello there, sir. Can you give us direction?"

The man stopped and looked up at the newcomers on their horses. "Sure, I can try. Where ya headed?"

"Which is the road to the capital?" Gass replied.

"You looking to see someone important?" the man asked, drawing out the words as if they could go on forever.

"Yes, in a manner of speaking," Bratton said, "but it would be helpful if you could…"

"Say no more, say no more," the man said. "Old Ferguson will do ya right. Ya see this here road? Well, if you're on it, you're not heading to no capital."

Gass lifted an eyebrow, but said nothing.

"About a mile back, there was a turnoff, ya see, going across a covered bridge – take that across and go about thirty minutes, then when ya get to a fork, go to the left – that'll take you into the important sections of town. If there are any left. I heard tell the British folks didn't leave any public buildings standing when they came in August. But fortunately for my masta, they left the people's houses right where they are at. But I ain't been there myself, you hear. But I pick up things, you know?"

Bratton looked at his partner, and nodded silently. "Much obliged."

When the two men had turned around and began following the old man's advice, Gass posed the question they both felt. "What do you think is left? If the Treasury building is burnt out, where do you think we'll find Campbell? It's too bad that Albert Gallatin died a few months ago. As Treasury secretary, he would be a great person to talk with regarding the federal inquiry into Lewis' money matters. That's who Lewis was to meet here when he was killed."

"Well, maybe they moved to another manor house or something," Bratton said. "I heard talk in St. Louis about the burning of Washington, but I wasn't sure how widespread it was. Maybe it's not as bad as we think."

Over the course of the next hour, the pair realized the situation in the capital was far graver than they had imagined. The smoke continued to linger over the countryside and as they crossed the Potomac River and headed inland, they came across several burnt out structures and damaged buildings. But they were surprised at how many private houses were still intact. "I guess British honor does extend to some degree," Gass remarked dryly.

When they reached the downtown section of the city, about a mile from the Executive Mansion, they saw for themselves the widespread destruction the army of 4,000 did on that fateful day. The capital building, which used to house the Senate and the House of Representatives, was gutted as was the Executive Mansion where First Lady Dolly Madison had fled for her life along with a cadre of servants and guards. One man told them the only thing she had saved was a full-sized painting of the nation's first president, George Washington. She considered the Landsdowne Portrait to be very valuable and she didn't want to part with it.

Her husband at the time was leading the defense in a vain attempt to stop the marauders. Fortunately, neither she nor the President were captured or hurt that night, although rumor had it that the British had planned to parade the first lady as a prisoner of war, if they had succeeded in finding her.

The treasury building, as it turned out, had also been burnt to the ground, together with the Library of Congress, and the Washington Navel Yard. It took about an hour more to discover the whereabouts of the Treasury secretary, who was using the nearby house of a close friend as his temporary office. Together the pair of deputies proceeded to their new destination, about a mile through the woods along a well worn path. Out of the way, yet conveniently close to the city, the house served as an ideal location for several federal officers.

When they arrived at the house, they noticed it sat alone on a small hill, its front porch overlooking the Potomac a mile away. There were no other houses within sight but fields extended on all sides, with dozens of people, both black and white, working diligently in them.

The house was a large, three story structure, painted blue with white trim, and had the appearance of a kept and orderly estate. When they knocked on the door, a man opened it cautiously. "May I help you, gentlemen?"

"We're here to see the Secretary of the Treasury, Mr. George Campbell," Gass said.

The man's eyes narrowed slightly and shook his head. "I'm afraid Mr. Campbell has passed on. He was killed in the attack with the British troops in August. President Madison has just recently appointed Mr. Alexander Dallas as the new secretary. He is in his office, and I will alert him to your presence. May I ask who is calling for him?"

Bratton told him their names and explained they were federal marshals on a murder investigation. The man asked to see their paperwork and, once satisfied, handed them back. He led them into the foyer and left them alone.

Soon after, a large man, dressed in a newly purchased suit and a silk tie, arrived. He introduced himself as Dallas and had a smile as big as Missouri, shaking hands all around.

"What can I do you for, gentlemen?" he asked gamely.

"We're investigating the death of Governor Meriwether Lewis," Gass explained, "who, as you might know, was killed on October 11, '09, along the Natchez Trace in Tennessee. He was on his way here to meet the former Treasury Secretary Gallatin on questions regarding some financial matters of the Louisiana Territories."

Dallas frowned a bit at this news, standing up to pace for a few moments. "That is a shame about Lewis. I had read all about his exploits in the west several years ago. Never met the man, but respected him. I don't know a lot about the charges that Gallatin was discussing with him, and unfortunately, most of the records were burned along with the rest of the city. But I'll try and recollect what happened."

"What do you have here – just yourself?" Bratton asked. "Were any records saved at all?"

"Well, sir, you have to understand what happened that night. It was August the twenty-fourth, a hot night, when the British troops rowed ashore. They came from their ships on the Chesapeake – I guess the lure of destroying the capital of Washington won out against attacking the Baltimore port and destroying it instead. They were here only a single day before a fortuitous hurricane swept through and made them retreat back to their ships. But their numbers were such that they couldn't hope to hold the city. I think they merely wanted to strike at our heart – demoralize us, hit us hard and leave."

"And they seemed to have done just that." Bratton observed. "The city was burnt pretty badly. I'm amazed how thick the smoke still is after three whole months."

"You should have seen it that night. The British general in charge, I think his name was Cockburn, hit all the government buildings and we had no viable defenses. President Madison had tried to help the men at the front but we had nothing that could stand up to them, and we got him out of the city soon after they broke through. The first lady had to make a run for it though."

"We heard about her escape," Gass replied. "Must have been a scary time."

"Actually she was setting up for a dinner party that night, and all the food was laid out when we got the word to evacuate. It was only minutes later that the redcoats came in. They ate all the food and then burned down the Executive Mansion. I was working at the time heading the National Mint, under Secretary Campbell, when we got the word for us to leave as well. Mr. Campbell wasn't a particularly healthy man to start with, and as we were leaving, I think the stress got too much for him. He had a heart attack soon after we got the orders to evacuate the building and I carried him out myself."

"So you were not in a position to bring any records out?" Bratton asked.

"Unfortunately no," he replied. "The country was, and still is, very fiscally poor, and we had very little staff to help us with such a task. There was no way to bring out boxes of documents in any large quantities."

"Where is the president now?" Gass asked.

"Well, we set him up at the Octagon House."

"The Octagon House? What is that?" Bratton asked.

"Oh, sorry. That is the house of Colonel John Tayloe – it has eight sides to it, so everyone calls it the Octagon House. He offered it to the Madison's after they returned to the capital. There is some talk about moving the capital to Cincinnati, Ohio to make it more defensible against British attack, but we may just rebuild here. Hard to say right now."

Chapter 40

"Is there any way we can get information on Governor Lewis' charges or the root of the federal inquiry on him?" asked Bratton. "That may lead us to who killed him."

"Well, from what I know of the subject – and I don't proclaim to know the whole story, mind you – he had some discrepancies in his tax ledgers where almost $20,000 was unaccounted for. The government gives a certain amount of federal monies to states and territorial governors, and expects them to raise money on their own through taxes, fees, and such, to balance their budget. They need to give the federal government their fair share of tax dollars accrued from the citizens and businesses in their territories."

"Of course," Gass said patiently.

"But on two separate years – in '07 and again in '08, I believe the money his office provided fell shorter than what we expected from them. Our records indicated they should have provided a certain amount of tax dollars, but I believe their record books showed considerably less. This raises to us in Treasury a red flag which we have to investigate. I believe that is the crux of Mr. Gallatin's original inquiry into Governor Lewis' office."

It was Bratton who spoke first. "But surely there are other possibilities as to the missing money – less business produces fewer tax dollars, and that expansive territory is extremely rural – it's not easy to map out or get a good picture of who has claim there."

"We always try and take factors such as those into consideration but we base our predictions on past reports – what you produced last year should be close to this year – and we must have noticed a significant drop-off from before '08. The numbers that accompanied the payment didn't quite add up to what we had. Now, I have considerable respect for the man, and he might not have been intentional in his shortchanging the federal treasury, but..."

"Mr. Dallas," Gass said emphatically, "I am quite certain Governor Lewis did not shortchange anyone on purpose. He was a meticulous man who paid attention to detail like no one else. But there must be another rational explanation."

"Well, really the person - whether it was him or someone else - who prepared the tax books and accounted for the collections of the taxes in the territory would be the responsible party. As I recollect, he liked to do most of it himself, did he not?"

"But surely the books can be altered – changed in some way. Or not reported to him correctly," replied Gass.

Bratton was thoughtful for a time listening to the conversation. "But that does not really go to the heart of the issue. We're not here to assert his innocence or guilt. We're here to see if the federal inquiry played any role in his murder, or gave anyone cause to have him killed. And if someone else had altered the books, or miscounted the number or scope of the taxable assets in the territory, and was trying to cover up his tracks - that might provide a viable reason for murder."

Dallas smiled at him. "You know, son, you might be a good trial lawyer. Frankly, I hope he was not guilty of embezzlement. That would put a serious mark on his record. The evidence, such as is, provides no solid conclusion one way or the other. To the best of my knowledge, the books never arrived here at all. If they did, they were probably destroyed in the fire. Perhaps they were taken or lost after his death. But the inquiry was dropped after that."

Gass paused for a moment. "You never got them? I thought the soldiers who initially went to investigate brought them back. There is evidence they did. One of the items found its way to President Jefferson, although how, he did not divulge."

"When did you – or the Treasury department – hear of Governor Lewis' death?" Bratton inquired. "Governor Clark was able to track down a Major Theodore Higgins who signed the official investigative report on the death, but he said the documents Mr. Lewis had on him at the time were sent here. I assumed the Treasury received them shortly after."

Dallas shook his head. "Now, it's quite possible Mr. Gallatin received them, but the information in the documents has been lost and, consequently cannot be of any use to your investigation right now. I don't know when Mr. Gallatin found out about his death, but it was not public knowledge in the department for probably two weeks or more since the date he was found. You know, they say he killed himself. Suicide."

"Well, don't believe everything you hear," Gass said dryly.

As they made their way outside, the two men looked at the sky. It was mid-afternoon now and they would need to find lodging for the night, and consider their next step. Dallas had told them of a place about two miles to the west that put visitors up for a decent price. The day was becoming chilly and they pulled their coats around them tightly.

A man peered through the bushes in their direction, his body well concealed by the dense foliage all around him. He wore a warm black coat as well, and he was grateful for it. Standing outside for the past two hours watching the visitors, wary of being seen, sapped his energy and he was happy they had come out at last. After they rode past his location, he left the spot he had been standing and ran down a narrow dirt trail, deeper into the forest.

Chapter 41

Gass and Bratton rode slowly along the path, then made their way through the burnt-out downtown district. They looked across the fields at what remained of the Executive Mansion, the central building gutted and blackened within. Its white exterior still shown in spots but it was tarnished with soot. The annexes on each side had survived to some extent but the rebuilding effort would be massive. Such a waste. It had been built, Gass knew, in 1798, and only Adams, Jefferson, and Madison had lived in it. He wondered if anyone would live here again.

They made their exit from the city along the path they had come, heading to the only bridge spanning the Potomac for a mile in each direction. The area was heavily wooded and the trail was so narrow that they could barely ride two abreast without having branches brush against them. They had another few miles to go before they would reach the house of Colonel Henry Noth, who they were told routinely took in visiting dignitaries to the Capital.

As they approached the bridge, the woods parted into a small clearing and they could see the water about 200 feet away. The two men were discussing the British attacks, when a shot rang out, reverberating through the trees and startling them both. Bratton's horse reared and, unprepared, the rider fell off to the right near the trees. Gass held the reins tight on his horse, withdrawing his revolver, and looking carefully up and down the path for the source of the shot.

Just then, two men emerged from the woods off to Gass' left, rifles pointing at each deputy. They were dressed in peasant clothes, the thin fabric of their shirts providing little protection from the cold. They wore boots routinely seen on soldiers, so Gass surmised they were ex-military, but they could have just stolen them. Outnumbered, he raised his hands, but refused to let go of his weapon. He heard Bratton moaning on the ground next to him and wondered if he had been shot. *There is no way I'll let our lives end like this.*

"Drop 'em, sergeant," one of the men said, his voice rising with excitement.

Gass did as he was told and his pistol fell to the dirt below.

"You don't want to do this. We're federal marshals..." Gass began.

"I know who you are," the man said. "Now drop your weapon. And him too," he added, pointing his rifle at Bratton who was quiet now. The second man started to walk over towards the fallen figure, partly hidden behind the horses, looking to see if he had any weapons. Bratton lay prone on his back, his body twisted in a strange, unnatural contortion. His head was tilted slightly and his eyes were closed. His left arm lay outstretched by his head, while his right was caught under his body. The man saw him, and walked closer to check him out.

"Earl, is he dead?" the man pointing his rifle at Gass called out, shooting him a sideways glance.

"He looks dead. I didn't even shoot at him, though. Must have been a hell of a fall from his..."

In a split second, Bratton's right arm came up holding his pistol, and fired point blank into the man's chest above him. Earl's body was dead before his mind registered the fact, and his eyes widened in surprise. His rifle fell from his lifeless hands as a large red stain spread out across his shirt. He hit the ground hard, first on his knees, then falling onto his back. Bratton's horse reared again, and galloped out forward into the clearing where it stopped.

When Bratton fired his shot, the man holding the gun on Gass spun around in his friend's direction, his attention momentarily taken off the deputy. Gass took immediate advantage of this lapse, spurring his horse and swinging it right into the man, using his steed as a battering ram. The man fell hard on the ground, dropping the gun, as Gass jumped down on top of him. The sergeant hit him hard in the jaw once, twice, three times before he was certain the man wasn't getting up again soon.

Gass checked the man's pockets, satisfying himself that he had no weapon remaining on him, then stood up, looked around him, and spotted the man's fallen rifle. Gass picked it up, then retrieved his own firearm which lay in the road next to his horse. He heard a moan from Bratton and came over to his aid.

"Aren't you done playing around yet?" he asked the fallen man.

"Look, doc, I think I really did twist my back again when I fell," Bratton said through clenched teeth. He lay on his back, looking up at the blue sky, the body of his attacker at his feet. "You remember how bad it was before, don't you?"

Gass nodded, saying "Yeah, I remember. You were laid up for weeks on the expedition. We had to carry your sorry ass over the Blue Ridge Mountains. Just don't think I'm carrying you all the way back to St. Louis."

Bratton laughed and Gass smiled. "Let me help you up." Grabbing hold of his arm, he gingerly got Bratton into a standing position, where he leaned his tall frame against a tree. While Gass went to retrieve his partner's skittish horse, Bratton stared at the man he had killed. This appeared to be a simple robbery, he thought, but if you look at it a little deeper, there was nothing simple about it.

When Gass returned, Bratton addressed his concerns. "That first guy knew who we were, do you remember?" Bratton said. "He called you 'sergeant' and when you told him we were deputies, he said he knew us. What ordinary thief in the woods would know who we were?"

"Let's ask him," Gass said, turning towards the unconscious man on the ground. He kicked at the man's legs and called down to him. "Wake up, you swine. Time to talk."

Holding his pistol on the man, Bratton knelt down about ten feet away. His back hurt like hell and it was all he could do to keep from crumpling to the ground. He steeled himself to keep going. This was no place to fall to pieces.

After a while the man regained his senses, but refused to talk to either one of them. Undeterred, Gass got some rope from his saddle, and tied up the man's hands, then secured them to his horse. "Let's go visit the sheriff, William. I'm sure he'd be thankful to have one less perp off the street – or out of the woods in this case. I think the going rate for attempted murder is hangin'. Nice day for it." He swung himself into the saddle.

"You know," Bratton said. "Why bother going all the way back? I mean, we can just try him here ourselves and do our own hangin'. There's a good branch right there." He pointed to a strong branch hanging over the road, ten feet in front of them.

"Hey, that's not a bad idea. Then we can get to the inn by dinner time and still get some food!" Gass paused, as if thinking it over. Finally he jumped down off his horse.

"Now wait a minute!" the man cried out. "You can't do that!"

"We're federal marshals," Gass said. "You acknowledged so yourself, when you accosted us like that. We can certainly do it."

His eyes widened in terror as Gass proceeded to undo the ropes binding him to the horse. When Gass was finally holding the rope, and tried to pull him toward the tree, the man broke.

"Ok, ok, I'll tell you whatever you want! Just don't hang me!"

Gass smiled thinly, sneaking a sideways glance at Bratton. The ploy had worked.

Over the next half hour, the two men learned about the plot to kill them, disguised as a robbery. They questioned him further on a third man who allegedly paid them twenty dollars each to commit the act, and how they were given the signal to tell them when the deputies were coming. It was supposed to go smoothly, with no one aware of the real motives in the death of the two lawmen.

He repeatedly told them he did not know the identity of the third man, the one who found them yesterday at a local bar, and convinced them everything would go without a hitch. "Yeah, like that's ever happened in my life," the man lamented to his captors. In the end, he could give them no more to go on than to say the third man was an outsider.

"Never seen him around these parts. If he lived anywhere around, I'd have known it. He had a bit of an English accent, but dressed casually. Not shabby mind you, but not too high off the horse like them Washington aristocrats."

As evening crept on them, the two deputies left the man tied to a tree along the road, telling him someone will come along eventually and let him go. Or send him to jail. One or the other. As to the dead man, they left him in the road, and told the man to start coming up with a good story to explain it.

As the men crossed the bridge, a pair of eyes looked at them from behind a large brush across the field. Cursing his luck, the man retreated from his hiding spot and walked slowly back through the tree line the way he had come. It had been a hastily crafted plan but there would be other opportunities. He just had to be patient.

The Expedition Continues

Chapter 42

August 15, 1805
Lemhi Pass, Present day Idaho

The hot sun blazed down upon the winding river, the green leafy foliage on each bank extending out upon the surface of the water, searching for relief. The bow of the canoe cut a small, almost imperceptible, path through the waterline as two men worked paddles on both sides. The wind had a deathly calm about it, unwilling to aid the men in their struggle against what little current they encountered. But the men said nothing in protest, carrying on with the task at hand, stroke after stroke.

"I hope we see them soon, Capt'n," Shannon said. "We've been searching for days and days. Maybe they heard we were coming and ran off."

Meriwether Lewis, sitting in the front of the little dugout canoe, merely nodded. "We'll find them – they're here somewhere."

"But if we don't?" asked Colter. "There's no magic river that runs all the way east to west. From what we've heard, I think that old theory can be put to bed. We're gonna hafta cross the mountains sometime, and we need horses. We've got to find the Shoshone."

The three men were scouting ahead of the expedition party, hoping to do some exploration ahead of the slower, heavily laden pirogue.

It had taken them two months working the Missouri River upstream, since they had crossed the Great Falls. They were behind schedule, and Lewis felt the burden with each passing day. If they didn't meet up soon with the Indians and secure the much needed horses, they would never be able to cross the mountains before winter set in. If an early snow caught them exposed on the mountains, they would all perish. Everything they had worked for had come down to this.

Perhaps if they had not wasted two weeks of their time trying to build their fabled iron framed canoe, they wouldn't be quite so pressed. But Clark had wanted to build it, to replace the red pirogue with a more sturdy boat held together with iron bands. It has almost worked too – until it leaked. And then more time was spent fixing it, but none of it mattered in the end. Two weeks wasted, the boat now scuttled at the bottom of the river.

He had hoped to be crossing the Bitterroot Mountains by now. Then into the larger mountain range beyond that. What lay on the other side, God only knew. But God would not be able to protect them from the snow if they didn't finish the crossing in time.

He spent the rest of the day detailing notes in his journal, describing the river and the trees around him. Occasionally they would pull over if he saw something of interest, whether it was animal or floral, and he'd record it for posterity. His journal, already getting worn with use, was his most prized possession, and he gathered much satisfaction from it each day. Clark and the others were several hours behind him and he had wanted to make the most use of their time by doing some scouting with John and George. He liked to be prepared for anything.

The next morning saw much of the same, as they advanced a few miles in the morning's early haze. The foliage along the banks had thinned to where some clear fields could be seen. Lewis did not know if this was a good or bad omen. But as the fog began to lift, something new and unexpected was revealed. A group of natives stood along the shoreline, about ten in all, a mixture of men and women. The maidens worn dresses of soft buffalo hide and carried baskets of fruit. Many of the men had no shirts on, their chests painted decoratively with red and black dye, figures and patterns crisscrossing their bodies.

They remained where they were as Lewis instructed Colter and Shannon to paddle to shore. The natives seemed unafraid and most curious of the newcomers. Lewis thought it could well be the first time these natives had ever seen a white man. He chided himself on not including Sacagawea and her husband in their scouting party, but they didn't have the room. Now translating their intentions would prove a challenge.

Lewis got out first, helping to drag the dugout canoe onto the shore. The natives remained where they were, and did not move. They did not attack either, so Lewis considered it a positive thing. When all three men had disembarked, leaving their firearms in the boat, Lewis cautiously approached them. He tried to use hand signals, as he had many times before on their expedition to convey his thoughts to the natives, but after a while he realized it didn't seem to be working.

"Horses," he said slowly, trying to pretend to ride a mount in the air. The Indians looked at him and then at each other. Once or twice someone spoke, but the meaning was lost on the newcomers. But they did not leave. In fact, the natives could not keep their eyes off of Lewis or the others, reinforcing his opinion that white men were indeed brand new to this tribe.

Finally he walked back to his canoe, sat down and waited. Colter and Shannon followed suit, understanding that only with their interpreters could they make any progress. The Indians waited too, as if sensing something would happen that they did not want to miss.

An hour passed, then two, and several of the Indian women had left and returned with empty baskets which they proceeded to fill from trees and bushes around them. Lewis watched with a fascination as the women continued their gathering. Even the native men watched for a time, talking quietly amongst themselves.

After what seemed an eternity, Lewis heard the faint sound of the boats approaching, the paddles pulling hard at the water to get the single large pirogue they had left to move further upriver. He stood up and approached the water's edge. The sun was hot once again, and he shielded his eyes as the sun beat down. Clark directed their crew of five canoes and the pirogue to the shore line. Most of the men stayed on board, while he, Sacagawea, Touissant, and Drouillard disembarked. Together they formed a sophisticated interpreting troupe and Clark considered them an indispensable part of the team.

Sacagawea stood on the shoreline for a few moments taking in the sight, baby Pomp sleeping soundly on her back in a makeshift sling. A large smile spread across her face and she gave a squeal of delight before rushing over to the group. One of the women stopped gathering fruit, and ran over to meet her, jumping into Sacagawea's outstretched arms, crying out in happiness.

The jostling woke Pomp who gave a small cry of his own. Sacagawea laughed joyfully, taking the baby and showing him to her friend. The two women talked rapidly for many minutes until finally Clark spoke tentatively. "Can you introduce us?"

Chapter 43

Sacagawea turned to face them, not letting go of her friend. Her smile was contagious and soon everyone was in a spirited mood. She began to speak rapidly, not waiting for her husband to translate to Drouillard and then to the captains. But finally her story came out.

"This is my friend, Jumping Fish," she said. "We were best friends until the day I was taken away by the Hidatsa five years ago. In fact she tells me that she received her name right after that incident, because she jumped into the river to escape the men who came after us. Before that she was known as White Meadow." She looked around at the Indians who stood around her, smiling. "These are my people. These are the Shoshone. Just over the hill are their summer lodges."

"Tell them I'd like to arrange a meeting with their chief to negotiate the purchase of horses," Lewis said, "and, Sacagawea? Welcome home!"

She indicated their camp was about half a mile inland, so the Indians helped bring the canoes and pirogue into a shallow inlet a short distance down river. The canoes were beached and the pirogue was secured to a large tree, which Lewis estimated to exceed one hundred years in age.

The two women continued their spirited dialogue all the way back to their village. The area was nestled in the foothills of the Bitterroot Mountains, a small range which led to even steeper and rockier terrain further west. The trees were tall, but sparse, allowing plenty of open distance for horses to roam free. The Hidatsa had told the explorers the Shoshone were the horse brokers of the area, frequently capturing, domesticating, and trading the large animals with neighboring tribes. It was this skill that had led the Hidatsa to the area that fateful day five years earlier.

As they walked, Touissant explained what details he knew of the event, as told to him years ago. His English had gotten a bit better over the last few months, but Drouillard still did most of the interpreting. He explained how a group of approximately twenty Hidatsa warriors were hoping to sneak in and steal some horses that the Shoshone had, a ploy made necessary because of the hostility between the two tribes. "They had tried to trade with the Shoshone peacefully in the past, I was told," he said without much conviction, "but there was too much animosity. So they resorted to brute force to take what they needed."

"The Hidatsa made their way down here, over 500 miles distant, and surprised a group of Shoshone who were camped along the river. I think you named it Jefferson's River, when we passed it. I think that was the one. From what I'm told, the Shoshone ran off, covering about three miles of wooded territory, and the Hidatsa chased them. In the end, I believe, four Shoshone men were killed, along with four women, and a number of boys as well. They fought to the end, though, from what I'm told. The Hidatsa got the horses, ten in all, along with six girls and two women."

"What happened to the others, besides Sacagawea and Otter Woman?" Lewis asked.

"Well, I don't know the whereabouts of all of them," the Frenchman replied, "but a few were sold to others tribes, and one woman was kept with us, but she died about three years later."

"A sad story," the captain acknowledged, "but at least Sacagawea is home again and, hopefully, she'll be able to help secure the horses we need."

"Ever the practical one, you are, captain," Charbonneau remarked dryly. "Now mind you, I had nothing to do with the attacks, myself," he assured Lewis, "but I felt it an honorable gesture to accept the girls into my home."

The captain smiled at him. "They just gave the girls to you? Are you sure it wasn't payment for a gambling debt they owed you, or something of that nature? I've seen you gamble with them on a few occasions and you tend to win more than you lose. How much of your winnings is due to a subterfuge on your part or just plain luck, I have no idea, not being a betting man myself. But honorable isn't exactly the word I would use to describe it."

The Frenchmen grew red in the face, but did not deny the accusation. After a minute of silence, he shrugged his shoulders, and replied, "Hey, I treat them well and they keep good house with me. Prepare my meals, mend my clothes, whatever I require of them. Everyone is happy."

"Why don't you ask Sacagawea if she's happy," Lewis said.

"I may not be the best husband in the world, but she can do a lot worse. Besides, I think the baby means everything to her. If that makes her happy, I will consider myself having done my part."

Before Lewis could reply, there was a commotion in front of them. Dozens more of the natives came up to them from the village to greet them, curious about the newcomers with white skin. And of York, the large, dark skinned man of the group, they simply stared and kept their distance. A few daring boys tried to get close enough to touch his skin then ran off. The big man smiled an even larger grin. He enjoyed being the center of attention, a far cry from his days back east.

As the group crested the hill, Lewis saw the village nestled below them, a scattering of earthen huts and gardens that took up a good amount of space. There was one that was larger than any of the others, and he assumed it was the lodging of the tribal leader. If he could get some time with him...

As they approached, Lewis noticed a Shoshone man standing tall and erect off to one side. He smiled but did not approach the newcomers. His eyes seemed to stare intently on Sacagawea who was still deep in conversation with her friend. She cradled little Pomp in her arms as she walked by him, not seeming to notice his presence at all. But then she stopped in midstride, turning to him with a look of startling clarity. She smiled and took a hesitant step toward him.

She said a few gentle words to him in her native tongue, the meaning of which were lost on the captain, but when the man turned and walked away slowly, his head bowed low, Lewis couldn't help but see a tear appear in the woman's eye.

She stood looking after his departing form for a minute or two, then slowly continued her short journey into the village proper. Jumping Fish was waiting for her in front of the large hut, a look that mirrored both sorrow for her friend and a suppressed happiness she could hardly contain. Lewis hurried down after them.

"Who was that man?" he asked Sacagawea when he had caught up with the small group in a small courtyard just outside the chief's hut. It was frustrating for him to wait for the translation between her husband and his able interpreter, but he was a patient man and it was a day that promised good fortune. Or so he hoped.

As Charbonneau asked her the captain's question, she seemed to hesitate, not sure of her words. For a moment, he wasn't sure she even wanted to tell him, and this made him all the more curious. Was that the chief? He hadn't been decorated as such, wearing a simple garment of leather that covered his legs and chest, and his head bonnet showed only a single feather, hardly the accoutrements he would have expected from a tribal leader.

But finally she spoke, and her voice was soft, even timid, as she told a story of a boy she had loved years ago. They had been betrothed for marriage, at the tender age of twelve, until that day five years ago that ended her life here as she knew it. The boy's name was Striking Spear, and after five passings of the seasons he still pined for her, hoping for her return after all these years.

And when she did appear on the river today, and he received word of her arrival, his heart had gone out to her! But alas, cruel fate, that lays waste to love and hope. She was married, and even more, had a child with this new white husband! She was not his, would never be his, and he had to walk away, letting her go once more. There would be no tearful reunion, no rekindled romance, and, most poignant of all, no future together. Only a path that split in two, forcing each other in separate directions.

Lewis heard the tale and his heart reached out to her. Her husband, interpreting his wife's story of love lost, seemed amused by the whole thing, laughing when the captain had expected compassion, indifference where there should be love. The captain knew a thing or two about love. And how fragile the heart can be.

Chapter 44

Clark stood behind him and put a hand on his shoulder. "It's time," he said. "Let her put this affair behind her and let's move forward. We'll get the horses secured. Then I'll feel better at least."

They let Sacagawea talk to the elders and try to arrange a meeting with the tribal leader. It wasn't long before she returned smiling. "Come," she said in halting English. She, too, had started to pick up some of the white man's strange language during the last few months together.

She led the way into the lodge, accompanied by the two captains, her husband, infant son, and Drouillard. The interior of the hut seemed slightly larger than expected, with ample room for everyone to seat themselves on the dirt floor. A man sat before them, youthful in face, and dressed in soft, leather garments, festooned with beads of black and white. On his head he wore a bonnet with several feathers, indicating an exalted position despite his years.

Behind the man sat four elders, native men who ages could not have been any younger than fifty, but who looked slim and able bodied nonetheless. The chief stood and smiled warmly. "You come into our village in peace. In peace we receive…"

But his introduction was cut short by Sacagawea who cried out and ran towards the chief, embracing him, almost knocking him over in her zeal. Everyone was taken aback, but no one intervened. The woman was happy and ecstatic, not one bent on harming her tribal leader.

Finally, she got up and talking rapidly to the chief, who simply stared at her, a shocked expression on his face. But it was quickly replaced by a broad smile and he gave her a hug back that was just as feverish as the one he had received.

"If I may ask," Clark said tentatively, "what is going on?"

The woman turned to him, as if seeing him here for the first time. Then she broke out laughing, and spoke more slowly, allowing her interpreters time to get the message across.

"Captain Clark and Captain Lewis, allow me the pleasure of introducing the leader of the Shoshone, Chief Cameahwait. He is my brother!" she squealed with delight once more.

"I had not seen him, of course, for five years and I did not recognize him at first. He was but eleven years of age, and now he is sixteen, and the leader of our people."

Cameahwait spoke to the captains, and his sister proudly interpreted for him. It was an important role she had waited all these months to fulfill, and the fact that this man who commanded this tribe was her own brother, made the arrangement all the sweeter.

"Chief Cameahwait said that he is very happy to have us in his land, and that he will do anything he can to help us. Especially for a people who have returned his sister to him." She beamed at him, and he smiled back.

Sacagawea held out her son to his uncle for the first time, who took the baby in his arms proudly. She spoke to him in her native tongue, and they talked for a while before getting down to the business at hand.

"Please tell the chief – your brother – that we will pay for the horses we need, in order to cross the mountain range." Clark said. "According to my calculations, we would be in need of about 29 horses, if they can be spared. In return, we are willing to pay you handsomely for them."

They struck the deal, and with both parties in full merriment, settled down to a festive evening. The Shoshone were generous in their hospitality and nothing was spared for their honored guests. When word had spread that the chief's long-lost sister had returned to them, everyone welcomed the white-skinned newcomers warmly.

The horses were gathered and readied for the trip that week, while the pirogue was unpacked and stripped of essentials. Traveling overland for the first time, the explorers had to severely limit what they carried with them. Even with horses, they could only expect to carry food, water, firearms and ammunition, some essential equipment and a scant assortment of clothing and non-perishable items.

"Tomorrow we leave," Clark said to the assembled expedition party, "and let's pray we get across the mountains before the first snow."

The group of men nodded in unison – they understood the consequences if they failed.

"Now before I give the floor over to our venerable host, I want to take a moment and congratulate our very own Captain Meriwether Lewis on making it to the start of his 35th year! We don't often remember anniversaries of our birth, but Captain Lewis deserves the recognition, for the long journey we have already taken, and the more miles yet to come. Here's to a long life!"

At this, the journeymen erupted in cheers, while the Indians looked surprised and a little taken aback. Even when the translations came through, they didn't quite understand the significance of the celebration, but shrugged it off to one of a growing number of white man's customs they were beginning to learn about.

Chief Cameahwait stood off to his right side, listening to the white man discuss the long, difficult journey ahead. He could not understand the captain's words but recognized the respect he was given by the assembled men, and knew they were in good hands. Cameahwait loved his younger sister and was grateful to these men for returning her to him. He had made a promise earlier that day, and now he was going to keep it. He watched her translate the words of the white man into his native tongue and was impressed with her remarkable ability. He was proud of her.

When Clark stood back and nodded his head in his direction, the chief stepped forward to speak. It was the first time he addressed both his own tribe and the newcomers at the same time, but what he had to say would impact them all. He enjoyed leading the great people of the Shoshone nation. Why did he feel a growing sense of dread in his stomach now?

He spoke carefully, allowing the required small group of interpreter's time to tell his story. Sacagawea translated her brother's words to her husband, who in turn spoke to Drouillard, who gave a running commentary to the white men listening.

"You are a most honorable men, bringing my sister back among us, and we of the Shoshone nation are in your debt. We freely trade with you for the horses that you will need, and for the food that will sustain you over the mountains." He turned and looked at his sister who smiled back.

"As much as I tried to persuade her to stay with us, Sacagawea is determined to see your journey through to its end. She will accompany you, and I gave her my blessing. However, I realize her knowledge of the Bitterroot Mountains and beyond are limited, so I am providing a Shoshone guide in whom I trust. His name is Toby, and he will help you find your way."

When Drouillard had finished translating the final line, Clark came up to the chief and shook his hand warmly. "Thank you," he said. Cameahwait acknowledged the sentiment with a simple nod of his head. A new stage of the journey was about to unfold, and Clark was grateful for the young Indian maiden and her chieftain brother for giving them all the best chance at succeeding. Now it was all up to him and the others to make sure their efforts were not in vain.

Chapter 45

November 13, 1805
Along the Columbia River, Oregon

The rain came down on the backs of the hapless men thick as flies, unrelenting in its persistence, flooding the canoes, and spoiling the food supply. For two straight days the rain vented from the heavens, with only a brief respite of a few hours the night before. The river on which they traveled had swollen in size and the waves upon it threatened to overturn the boats with each swell. The baby cried in misery as its mother tried in vain to offer him comfort from the cold and the wet conditions.

The 33 explorers made camp again that night along the shore of the Columbia River, in an area clear of trees and brush. They had to walk a ways inland to avoid the rising water line that crept ever upwards toward them. Unable to build or maintain a fire, the men huddled together for warmth, as the stinging bite of the freezing rain continued to cut deeply into the men's bodies and mind.

The following morning brought a temporary halt to the rain, and the men awoke to a few rays of the sun peaking through the gray clouds. Captain Lewis had already been up before the others making a small fire to boil water for tea. He looked at the rising sun with happy anticipation. *A day without rain would be a good day.*

Taking a sip of the hot brew, he looked westward towards the direction they would continue to travel that morning. They were high on a large hill with the valley floor spread out before them. He saw it for a moment, but then squinted harder, not quite believing what his eyes were telling him. When at last he was sure, he set down his mug, and walked casually over to his partner, who was just now rousing himself in his wet tent.

"William," Lewis said without preamble, "I think we have arrived at the coast. I suggest you come and see what we've journeyed so long for."

Clark turned over and stared at Lewis, who just smiled. His first thought was his partner was joking, for there was no hint of the ocean last night when they slept, but he acknowledged the fog, darkness, and rain made it nearly impossible to see very far at that late hour. Was it true? Could it possibly be?

Bolting out of the small enclosure, the captain stood up and looked out across the expansive rolling hills to the west. The gray skies still loomed overhead, and a thin fog lay upon the earth, but the unmistakable vastness of the sea lay many miles distant, its foaming whitecaps showing severe turbulence. The remaining miles of river before them winded down towards their inevitable collision with the mighty ocean.

The thinning trees that caressed the shores of the mighty river were still losing their leaves and their various colors seemed to shift from deep umber to blustering lilac. Captain Clark announced, then and there, that this was the 'best morning of the entire year' and roused everyone up that they shall give witness to the end of their long journey.

Within the next three days, the men continued their journey down river, anticipation evident on the faces of everyone involved. Now that they had seen the end of their journey, the wait to get there was sometimes difficult. More rain continued the next day but the sky cleared once again after that. The trees gave way to stark plains and even firewood became scarce at times.

"I think this weather is the worst I've ever dealt with," Captain Lewis said as he navigated the wide river, with the clouds threatening once again. "Even the 100 mile trek through the mountains wasn't this bad."

Sergeant John Ordway looked at his captain and chuckled. "I think you have forgotten already how difficult that was, Capt'n. Granted we didn't have rain, but the mountains, especially once we got higher than the Bitterroot – were rocky and treacherous. If it weren't for the Nez Perce natives who were generous with their food, we would have surely starved. As it was, we ended up shooting our own horses for food. Heck, we even ate our candles. If we can survive that, we can deal with a little rain."

Lewis only grunted in reply. Ordway remembered vividly how debilitating the starvation made him and most of the others in their brutal trek through the various mountain passes. He also remembered how Lewis had constantly pushed and cajoled them to maintain their pace. The captain never let it show how close he was to losing it out there, Ordway thought. He was stoic in his defiance of the elements. *He was our rock out there.*

The first snow came two days after they left the large mountains behind and encountered the Nez Perce. With the assistance of the Indians, the explorers ate and rested, grateful for their survival on such a difficult journey. Although fed a good amount of local salmon, berries, and roots, the explorers struggled with a bout of sickness before being rested enough to continue. They branded their remaining horses and left them with the natives for use on their return journey. They quartered for a few more days in the huts of their native hosts while weathering out the snow. Then Clark and Lewis directed them to actively prepare for the next leg of their trip.

"We didn't do a half bad job on these canoes, Captain." Ordway said, trying to lighten the mood. "Carved them out real smooth like." They set five wooden boats out on the Clearwater River on which the Nez Perce lived, which soon merged with the Snake River, before finally feeding into the mighty Columbia. It was as wide as the Missouri and going downstream was, by and large, much easier than the upstream legwork they had been required to do before.

Lewis finally acknowledged his sergeant, nodding in agreement. "Yes, the boats are quite adequate for our uses. The boat took in more water from the rain than from leaks of any kind. Though the canoe we got from the Chinook has certainly proved lighter and stronger than ours. Your men did a good job, John. Even got us through the falls alive."

Ordway smiled broadly. "Never seen anything quite like that, Capt'n. Not sure which was the hardest to get through – the Celilo Falls or the Dalles. And don't forget the rapids we encountered in the Cascades – shot through them like buckshot! Those natives were certainly impressed! I saw 'em watching us, probably expecting us to drown. They almost fell over when we roared past 'em!"

"Yes, that was successful – but risky." Lewis said. "I'm glad I sent the valuables and those who could not swim around by land. You never want to put all your eggs in one basket, especially when it's racing through white capped rapids at breakneck speed. But I'd still take the difficulties there over this constant rain any day."

Ordway worried about his captain because, for some reason, this weather seemed to affect Lewis' disposition more than most of the men. Sure, he thought, it rained, but they were alive and relatively healthy despite the best the elements could throw at them. He tried to coax Lewis from his doldrums.

"Do you remember last month when we passed that large, snowcapped mountain that rose up out of nowhere? That must have been Mount Hood that General Vancouver found back in 1792 when they traveled up the Columbia. Capt'n Clark thought it was Falls Mountain, but now that I think about it, it must have been Mount Hood. If that was true, that makes us the first Americans to see it. Vancouver, being British, doesn't really count in my book. Don't you think?"

Lewis, despite the misery he felt from the rain, tried to wrestle with the question put before him. The pair discussed it at length, while the boat made its way along the large river look into the evening's twilight. By midnight, the rain had ceased once again and the morning brought forth a renewed feeling for everyone.

Chapter 46

Clark recorded the time that the first boat passed the shoreline of the Columbia and ventured into the great Pacific Ocean, completing the odyssey that began a long time ago. 10:05am, November 15, 1805. "This will go down in history, my boy," he said to George Shannon, who sat beside him in the large canoe, trying his best to handle the paddle in the large swells that now buffeted the boat.

"Can we beach somewhere, sir?" he asked earnestly. "I don't want to capsize and drown now that we've made it!" Clark spotted a large, treeless peninsula that emerged from the mouth of the Columbia, indicating they should head there. Shannon and the men with him needed no further urging. Within twenty minutes, all five canoes were beached on the rocky shoreline.

It had taken 554 days, and a journey of 4,132 miles to reach the Pacific Ocean, after their departure from Wood River in St. Louis in the middle of '04. They had successfully navigated their way across the continent, traveled over the great Missouri and the Columbia Rivers, trekked through the freezing mountain passes, and negotiated countless encounters with the natives of this land.

And, although it would disappoint the president to hear, they also proved that the fabled Northwest Passage was nonexistent. Their journey proved that no pure waterway existed from east coast to west coast that ships could successfully pass through. The mountains, and even the difficult rapids and falls of the Columbia, would prove insurmountable obstacles to such ships.

Clark looked out over the ocean before him, but not a vessel was to be seen, British, American, or any other kind. "We'll keep an eye out," he told Lewis in passing, but truth be told, he was not in favor of the president's plan. He reached into the inner lining of his jacket and produced a faded letter, which had been folded and partially wet. He opened it carefully so not to tear the fragile paper. It had the seal of the president and he read it to himself quietly. Dated March 1804, and signed by Thomas Jefferson himself, it offered guaranteed payment for any American or foreign vessel found at the mouth of the Columbia, who could return the explorers home. But although it was an option, it was not one Clark wanted to partake in. They made it over land and river this far - he fully intended on returning the same way.

With the assembled crew gathered around him, breathing in the salty ocean air and the waves breaking all around him, William Clark felt alive and refreshed. They had made it across the entire continent, their only casualty being poor Charlie Floyd early on in the voyage. He would have enjoyed this moment and should have been here with them today.

"Gentlemen, I stand before you, a humbled man," Clark began. "You have done the impossible and completed it with determination and fortitude. The country owes you a debt of gratitude. But first, I want to remember someone who really wanted to be here with us today and will always be with us in spirit. Let's give a prayer up to you, Charlie." Bowing his head, Clark offered up a silent prayer to remember the sergeant, while the company followed suit, each in their own way.

Realizing how exposed this peninsula was, they immediately set out to find a more suitable base camp in the area. They turned their attention to an abandoned Indian fishing village they had passed a short way back on the Columbia. The captains and the crew of the five canoes assembled there later that afternoon, grateful for the shelter the wooden huts provided them from the intermittent rain.

Lewis and a few men set out on a small reconnaissance mission and returned a few hours later with some information they shared. The huts, 36 counted in all, were scattered around the area in a semi circular pattern, some along the shore line and some intermingled with the dense forest that marked the coastal plains. No natives were found as of yet, but Lewis noted that they had found food stores and tools that indicated recent activity.

"At least since the summer, perhaps," the captain said. "It's most likely a fishing village, since we found nets and the like. Don't know where the natives are but maybe they'll be back. In the meantime, we should spread out and take advantage of the opportunity."

Clark agreed, and the men set to work unloading their boats into a few of the nearby huts. The cold high winds coming off the ocean chilled them more than they had anticipated, and the next day a few men brought up the idea of moving further inland.

"We will give the idea some thought," Clark agreed, "but for now we should look to fortify our winter food supply. The cold is just beginning, I'm afraid."

Two days later, the two captains were roused during the early morning by Ordway, who was stationed on guard duty. "We have visitors, sir."

Chapter 47

The sun was just coming over the horizon, the sky still uncertain as to its intent whether to drown the newcomers with more rain or give them a reprieve. Lewis silently hoped this visit would be a sign of favorable weather.

When Clark and Lewis were dressed and had stepped outside, they were greeted by a group of ten natives, and a ragged circle of his own men, some having dressed rather quickly due to the unannounced visit. The Indians, to their credit, were clothed rather lightly with only a few using any sort of heavier wrappings to ward off the chilly morning air. One of the visitors caught the attention of Captain Clark immediately, his robe of unusual blue pelts very distinctive to the eye.

"Welcome, my friends," Clark began, using his interpreter Drouillard to translate into French. He recognized the dress of the natives as common among the Chinook tribe, which they had encountered a few times traveling down the Columbia River. These natives were familiar with the French language, living so close to the Canadian border. But this encounter seemed to be different. This group was more formal, the people before him holding themselves with more importance than the tribal Indians they had run into before.

The exchange of dialogue continued for a time, each side trying to find a common ground. The captains learned their visitors were two chiefs in high accord among the Chinook, whom they understood to be Shelathwell and Comcomly. "They've come to trade," Drouillard explained after a time.

Clark, eager for contact with natives and hungry for information, invited the newcomers to sit with them as they prepared a light morning meal. It was evident that these men had some experience trading with Europeans, undoubtedly from English merchant vessels that came by. One warrior even carried a British canteen under his cloak, while another wore a metal hunting knife on his belt.

They also had perfected the art of hard bargaining. Lewis parted with two hunting knives in exchange for four barrels of newly caught fish. He hated to part with them, but his men needed food and they were in desperate need to replenish their stores.

Over the course of the next two hours, the captain learned a great deal about the area from their visitors, including the whereabouts of the former inhabitants of their camp. This was a Chinook fishing village, used only during the spring and summer months. Now that winter was upon them, the villagers headed south for warmer weather and to follow the game trails. They were due to return after the last of the snow melted in a few months.

As Comcomly got up to leave, satisfied with the success of their first meeting, Clark spoke rapidly to Drouillard. "Private, please ask him for one last trade. It's important." Somewhat confused, his translator did as he was asked. The Chinook leader waited patiently, his arms folded across his chest.

"I want the fine cloak that fellow has." Clark said, "I believe he works for Comcomly. That looks like it's made from sea otters and it would be a wonderful prize to bring back home to show everyone just what treasures the Pacific can offer. Tell him I'll give him three blankets and two more knives if he'll agree."

When the message was relayed, the only response was a loud laugh from the chief. He snorted and turned to take his leave once again. This time, Clark gripped the chief by his arm, stopping him. "Please, let's talk a little more. I'm sure there is something you want for it." Drouillard quickly translated his captain's request.

Comcomly was tall and stately, his body well muscled and reserved in movement. He stopped for a moment, his face registering shock at Clark's touch. Another warrior yelled at the captain as he tried to place himself between the two leaders, but the chief quickly waved him off. He smiled thinly, and faced the captain once more. As tall as Clark was, the Chinook leader still looked down on him by several inches, a fact that he seemed to enjoy playing up.

The chief remained in place, but allowed his eyes to look around the captain's hut, and the people who were assembled, including Lewis and Sacagawea. He looked hard at the Shoshone woman for a moment and then moved on, his gaze settling on one item or another, before returning to look at Clark once more.

He spoke in calm, measured French to Drouillard, who then relayed the leader's demand. "It seems, captain, that he has his eyes set on the blue beaded belt that Sacagawea has. He will give us the sea otter belt for that."

Clark smiled broadly. "Done!"

Of all the trading that had gone before, the captain was most proud of acquiring such a cloak. One as soft as this one, with a distinctive light blue hue, made from the skins of sea otters, will surely convince the powers that be at home that a permanent outpost should be established and these tribal connections should be well greased.

He turned towards his Shoshone interpreter and pointed towards her prized belt, making a gesture that she should take it off. Reluctantly she did so. He took it from her, then turned and presented it to his tribal guest with a formal bow.

Lewis looked at Sacagawea and saw the hurt in her eyes, but to her credit she did not say anything about it. *William may be a little too focused on making this trade work,* he thought, *but what's done is done. I'll have to think of a way to make it up to her.*

After their guests had departed, Lewis watched as Clark carefully wrapped the new cloak in between two pieces of beaver hide, and stored it in his hut. That will look nice to the folks back home, he thought, but despite his happiness for his partner's newly acquired prize, the captain realized, maybe more than anyone else, how quickly winter was coming upon them and how little time they had left to prepare for it. If we don't have proper shelter and food, that little fur coat is not going to keep anyone alive.

Lewis had done his own reconnaissance survey the previous day and had yet to share his findings with the rest. With the departure of their guests, he decided it was time to have a meeting. He briefed Clark on what he wanted to say and then gathered the rest around the central square in the middle of the native village.

When everyone was assembled, Lewis explained their situation and stressed the dire predicament in which they now found themselves. "The facts are clear, gentlemen. While this village may be fine for warmer weather, it was never meant to keep out the cold or the forces of nature that present themselves in the winter months. And as we saw today, there is also no protection against hostile natives or wild animals." As he waved his arm around in a circular arc, he said "Anyone can walk in here and who are we to stop them? No, we need to establish our own buildings with a high wall for protection. We need to have strong lodgings to keep us warm."

"What 'bout food, capt'n?" asked young George Shannon. "Do you want us to get a huntin' party together?"

Lewis smiled at the young man. "Yes, George, I was just getting to that. For food is just as essential to survival as shelter. But just as important as food is keeping it preserved for the next few months. For that, we will need salt. And God, in His wisdom, has given us an ocean to use at our disposal."

Bratton spoke up for the first time. "I've had some experience with sifting salt, captain. I did it a few times on the eastern seaboard up near Maine many years back. I'll volunteer to head up a small group to tackle that task."

The Field brothers, Reubin and Joseph, volunteered to lead the hunting party. Lewis thanked them all for their assistance and explained those tasks would be needed very soon. But there was one more thing to do before that began.

"Now, since this is a group effort, Captain Clark and I have decided to put the direction of our future to a group vote. Having said that, the group vote will include everyone who has traveled with us and helped us along the journey. That includes our interpreters Monsieur Charbonneau and his wife Sacagawea, and York, Captain Clark's man."

At this announcement, a small murmur of voices could be heard, and someone stepped forward, the assembled men parting on each side to allow him passage. It was Private Hugh McNeil, his face suddenly red and blustering. "But Captain, surely you can't mean to include a woman and a slave in such a vote! They are incapable of understanding the realities... the facts that we need to address..."

"Private, that is quite enough," Lewis said sternly. "And this goes for all of you who may believe as he does. While our government may not grant the vote to women or to slaves as of yet, it is a captain's decision, and ours alone, who gets to decide all matters in the field. It is our opinion that both Sacagawea and York have proven themselves time after time that they are important, some might say essential, members of this expedition. And in so proving, they have earned their right to help decide our next steps. They both have as much, if not more, intelligence than some assembled here. Any more questions, private?"

McNeil remained silent. Gradually, Lewis could see a nodding of heads, of a quiet acceptance to his decree. He smiled, yet his voice was strong. "Here are our choices. We can decide to stay here in the village, although I strongly advise against it. We can decide to return to the mouth of the Columbia River and build a new fort there. It will border the ocean, allowing access to the waters, but provide little protection from the elements. Or we can decide to move our operations somewhere south of the Columbia and find a suitable location for a new fort. We can try to find another location that is more protected."

The following vote went the way he expected, with an almost unanimous decision looking to relocate south of their position. Only a small minority voted to remain here and take advantage of the current huts and proximity to hunting and watering grounds.

Chapter 48

Over the course of the next two days, both captains led canoe expeditions into the lands south of the Columbia, searching for the right locations to winter for the next several months. Traveling back to the Columbia, they immediately set off down the coastal waterways, and on the second day, found a suitable inlet with a navigable river that led back into the interior of the Oregon coast. They met with a native Indian group that was known as the Clatsop, who offered to guide them in their search.

About a mile up the smaller river, which they called the Netul River, they found a location to their liking. It was a wooded area with plenty of resources for building, close to the river to provide a good watering source, but far enough away from the ocean to protect them from the strong winter wind. In addition, the Clatsop Indians indicated good hunting grounds nearby. The captains had found the location for their permanent winter quarters.

Once the entire group reconvened on the spot two days later, the real work began in earnest. Every able bodied man pitched in cutting down trees, clearing the land, and began erecting the buildings. They built according to new design plans that Sergeant Gass has developed at the captain's request. The plans included the placement and layout of each building and the wall around it.

"We need two long buildings," he explained to Lewis and Clark. "They should be situated parallel to each other. One building, on the left, should have three rooms. This will be for the expedition men. Each room should have a central fire pit for warmth. We can erect bunks for sleeping."

The second building should have four rooms. One for storing meat with a locking door, one for the sergeants – which will have a fire pit, one for the captains with a more elaborate fireplace and exterior chimney, and one for Charbonneau and his wife, which will have a fire pit as well."

For the outside walls, we should have two gates, one a main gate which is locked, and the second smaller gate for access to the spring and such. The entire fort itself will not take up any more than fifty foot square." The captains liked the plans and agreed, hoping they would be able to finish before the first snow fell.

The foundations for the two buildings were laid by December 10th, and over the course of the next four days, the walls went up and roofing had begun. This took the longest time to complete but by Christmas Eve, they were finished. Finally, mud was packed into the walls to make a tight seal, essential to keep the cold drafts out and the heat from the fire pits in.

The captains moved into their rooms first, on December 24th. As Christmas morning came, rain fell and the temperature dropped. The rest of the party finished moving in later that day, grateful to finally have a warm place to stay.

"Merry Christmas, William!" a jovial Meriwether Lewis exclaimed. The coals that glowed red in their new fireplace drove out the chill that had seemed to permanently settle in his bones. "It feels good to have a place to call home. At least for now."

"You too, my old friend." Clark replied warmly. "I think it is time to show the men a little Christmas thanks. I'm glad we were able to make use of those two hunting knives on our last bartering trip."

Lewis smiled and opened the door outside. There was a break in the rain for the moment and they wanted to take advantage of it for now. They assembled the group before them, a look of relief and happiness on all their faces.

"I want to wish you all a Merry Christmas!" Lewis said loudly and a cheer went up from everyone around them. He noticed Sacagawea smiling and knew, even if she didn't understand everything about the Christian culture, she was enjoying the merriment of the white men today. He has taken some time of late to express to her some of the important aspects of their beliefs and the meaning behind this important celebration. He hoped she was able to glean some moderate understanding and share in the celebration as well.

Clark approached, carrying a parcel under his jacket. "I know we don't have spirits to drink on this fine Christmas Day, gentlemen, however I want you to have something from both of us, which show you our appreciation for getting here safely and in one piece!" He unwrapped the cloth and revealed a bundle of silk handkerchiefs. Lewis helped him pass them out until all the men had one.

"And for the lady in our midst, the one whom we cannot seem to do without," Lewis added, smiling at Sacagawea, "I want to give you this token of the Christmas season." He handed her a larger silk cloth the color of ivory. She reached for it tentatively, carefully touching the smooth material and her smile broadened until she seemed ready to burst. She took it and hugged it close to her, then, taking her baby, Jean-Baptiste, wrapped him in it snuggly.

"Even little Pomp gets a gift!" Clark said laughing. Just then Sergeant Ordway stepped forward.

"Captains, we'd like to formally christen the new Fort Clatsop, on the holiest day of the year. With your permission?"

Clark nodded his head. Ordway turned to a group of men on his left, nodding in turn. The seven of them raised their rifles to their shoulders, aiming up into the air, away from the gathering. "Fire!"

A single shot was fired from seven rifles, but it seemed to Lewis as if one small cannon had gone off. The sound reverberated off the surrounding walls and echoed back into the compound. It was as if the fort was giving its own statement. I am here to stay.

Rain continued to fall, with intermittent snow showers over the next several days, but by New Years Eve, the captains were ready to initiate their winter food storage plans, on two fronts. As he had volunteered earlier, they assigned Private Bratton to head the salt shifting process, together with privates George Gibson, Alexander Willard, and Sergeant Nathaniel Pryor.

They would set out the next day towards the ocean and prepare to separate salt from the ocean's water and store it in barrels they would make on site. These salt barrels would be used to store and preserve the meat for the winter.

In order to get the meat, the Field brothers would head the hunting party, joined by private George Shannon, John Shields, and John Colter. They would also set out in a southerly direction in the morning and plan to return within three days.

As the dawn broke on the start of the new year 1806, Captains Meriwether Lewis and William Clark wished the men Godspeed. Their rations were dangerously low as it was, and both of their missions would be crucial for their survival.

Bratton set the pace, the only equipment he carried being a large brass cooking pot, three hammers, two hand saws, and a single change of clothes.

The rest of his party carried only what they needed. They made the ocean by mid-morning and began setting up.

Gibson built a fire while Bratton and Willard began cutting trees to make thin strips for barrels. They would then rub oil on the planks to make them more flexible for bending. Pryor waded into the cold ocean waters to get a good pot full of saltwater with as little sand mixed into it as possible. Once the water was boiled off, the remaining salt would be stored in the barrels. The process was simple enough but very time consuming for all the men.

If they wanted to preserve the meat the hunters would provide, this was the only way to keep it from spoiling. Once the real snow hit, they would lose any opportunity to hunt again until spring. Would they have enough meat to survive until then? It was a question Bratton asked himself time and again during these short winter days.

The Investigation Continues

Chapter 49

The unseasonably cold autumn wind ripped across the cobbled streets, driving people along in a hurried walk. A lone carriage approached from the east, the horse making clear, rhythmic tapping on the hard stones as it approached. The driver, bundled against the cold, stopped in front of the stately manor house. He jumped to the ground and held the door open for his traveling guests.

The two men descended quickly and made their way to the large white double doors, giving the brass knocker two good strikes. After what seemed a long time coming, the door finally opened and a large black man looked out upon their faces.

"Welcome, good sirs! The master is expecting you!"

"I'm sure he is, York," Sergeant Gass replied, smiling pleasantly. John Colter followed behind him as the men were led down the long corridor. Strains of music could be heard throughout the house, maybe from a piano, he thought, though he knew not where it originated.

Had it been only two and half months since they had been here last? Gass thought, as he looked around. So much has happened since then. And there was still so much to do.

Instead of meeting in the office of Governor Clark as he had presumed, the sergeant was surprised when York led them into a large living room, where the source of the music became evident. A large grand piano sat square in the room, with a boy seated in front, playing his best for his assembled guests. William Clark stood off to his left, while two more visitors sat at a long couch to his right.

A young girl in a frilly white dress sat beside them, trying her best not to fidget too much. Gass noticed the girl's skin tone was a shade darker than usual, perhaps of some mixed heritage, but she was as prim and proper a young lady he had ever seen at her age. He smiled at her as he walked in.

As they entered the room, all eyes turned toward them. "Ah, you have arrived!" Clark said, smiling broadly, "How wonderful! You are just in time to hear from our little protégée. But I know you've met before, albeit it's been a long time. Patrick, John, this young lad here is Jean-Baptiste. I still call him Pomp occasionally though."

Gass blinked several times, his mind trying to understand how the little boy that Sacagawea had given birth to on that fateful expedition nine years ago could end up here playing piano for William Clark. "Captain? How did he...?"

"Well," Clark said, "I guess the last time we met, I was a little preoccupied with getting you gentlemen started on your investigation - which I promise we will get to shortly – but I have to say that, sadly, Sacagawea died two years ago. She had fallen ill with fever and never recovered, poor thing. For the past four years, at my insistence, Pomp has been attending boarding school here in St. Louis, receiving a fine education.

"His sister Lisette, who is 4 now, was left without a mother, so I took her in as well from Fort Mandan. Her father, Charbonneau, couldn't care for her himself, so he signed over adoption papers to me for both children. I am lucky to have them both – they are great kids and fill the house with light and music again."

"Well, that's terrific, governor, it really is," Gass said. "It's not much of a life without one's parents to care for you and they can receive so much here. They are fortunate to have you in their lives."

"I agree," said Ordway, as he rose from the coach. "Lisette, here, has shone a great maturity for one so young."

"Anyone who sits next to you for any length of time has got to have rocks for brains," Colter replied laughing.

"Knock it off, John," Clark said coolly. "This is not the place for this."

"Hey, I was just...um, yeah, sorry," he said contritely. Colter bent down next to Lisette, smiling at her. "You sure are a pretty one...just like your mother."

She smiled and gave a little giggle.

"Unfortunately, she really doesn't remember her mother. She was too young when Sacagawea passed on." Clark said. "But as long as we remember her, and what she was like, Sacagawea's legacy will live on. Maybe for a long time to come. We can only wait and see how history paints us in the years ahead."

Clark turned to his attendant. "York, can you please take the children to work on their studies? I promised to have Pomp back to his dorm by tomorrow morning."

The large man bowed slightly and then held Lisette's hand while the three of them left for another part of the house. Clark waved his hand around the room. "Please have a seat. I appreciate you all coming. I'm sure we have a lot to talk about."

Ordway and Bratton remained sitting on the couch, while Gass took possession of a large, soft chair slightly opposite. Colter sat at the piano, running his hand over the ivory keys. Clark sat in wooden chair next to the couch. "Can you play, John?" Clark asked.

"Me? No, I just like to stab at it," the woodsman laughed. "Only in my dreams, am I any better than little Pomp here."

Chapter 50

Over the course of the next hour, they shared stories of the events at Grinders Stand and the run-in they had with the Cherokee, emphasizing their belief one or more of them probably carried out the killing. Ordway and Colter explained more of the background they gleaned from their conversation with Captain Neelly, the Indian agent who reported back to the authorities after finding Lewis' body.

"I just don't see any motivation for their attack on Mr. Lewis, unless it was for money or retribution," Gass said.

"The Cherokee as a tribe have no conflicts that I am aware of with Mr. Lewis personally or with his position as Governor. They don't reside in his jurisdiction even. However, it may be a simple case of robbery and he was just at the wrong place at the wrong time," Clark responded.

"But nothing was taken!" Colter said loudly, jumping up from the sofa. "He was shot through the window and they ran off."

"You're forgetting about the missing diary and papers, John," Ordway said. "While the Indians might not have taken them, they were removed, most probably by the soldiers who came to investigate."

"Which leads us back to where we started," Gass said. "If he was killed by the Cherokee because of the diary or papers, why didn't the Indians take them when it first happened? Why let the authorities confiscate them?"

"They might have been scared off by the innkeeper's wife," suggested Bratton.

"Scared off by Mrs. Grinder?" Gass replied. "Not bloody likely, unless she had them in the sights of her rifle. And remember it was still dark out. She wouldn't have been able to raise a weapon against them. There was some uneasy alliance between them to be sure, but the Grinders were afraid of them. If they were bent on retrieving the diary or papers, they wouldn't let Priscella stand in their way."

"Now I'm trying to wrap my head around another possibility. One that doesn't bode too well." Clark said, more to himself than anyone. "What if the authorities were behind it from the very start? After Captain Neelly rode back to Fort Pickering, they show up at Grinder's Stand the next day. They take the diary and papers with them, which seems perfectly acceptable from the outside, but what if that were the real motivation all along? From my findings, there was some cover-up on the death report indicating the grazing of his head wound, leading everyone to believe he could have reasonably shot himself again in the chest. This led people to a false conclusion of suicide. We've already shown that to be incorrect."

"But if the killing was politically motivated, who could benefit from his death?" Ordway asked. "Staging the attack to look like a simple Indian robbery while taking care of the real business by protecting those in power."

"Tell me about your visit to Jefferson in more detail." Clark asked. "The fact that he now possesses the very diary which was missing is very suggestive."

Ordway and Colter proceeded to explain how they followed the trail of the diary to former President Jefferson, and ended with their journey into Canada to rule out any connection to the Blackfoot.

"If Jefferson received the diary after the fact, with no supposed link to the attack itself, that might rule him out," Clark said. "The diary itself might be a factor but maybe it was a coincidence. But it bears keeping in mind."

"I don't think the Blackfoot are involved in it either," Colter said. "Granted, they'd like nothing better than to get their hands on me and cut the very skin off my body over a slow roasting fire, but getting someone else to do their dirty work is not exactly their style."

"I accept that, John," Clark said. "But you were brave to go back there, especially since you killed the chief's son a few years back."

"Hey, it was him or me, and I'm glad it's him," Colter replied. "When you're running for your life, nothing gives you greater motivation."

Then it was Gass and Bratton's turn, as they described their meeting with Lewis' former Lt. Governor Frederick Bates, stressing his strong animosity towards his old boss, and then their escape from attackers while calling upon the treasury secretary in the Washington capital.

Clark interrupted only to ask a question here or there, but allowed the narration to take its own path. He was quiet for a short while, trying to process all the new facts.

"You were fortunate to get out of Washington alive, gentlemen. I also think, while it's possible the attack on you was a simple robbery, it could also be a move by someone to silence questions being asked that they'd rather not have brought up. If that is the case, the stakes have been raised very high. Such people are not above killing to protect their secrets. And such secrets must be extremely important, possibly on a large, even national scale."

"I don't think there's any question we were targeted, Governor," Bratton spoke up. "The bad ass we questioned told us about another man who recruited them to attack us – told them where we'd be and the time we'd be there. Unfortunately, we don't have any idea who he is or why he wanted to target us. The guy just said he spoke with a slight English accent and was not dressed like a Washington regular – appeared to be from out-of-town."

"Well, that description narrows it down to about 50,000 suspects between here and Washington," Colter remarked dryly.

"Something else intrigues me," Clark said. "When you spoke with Bates, he seemed to distrust Lewis – went so far as to suggest he mishandled territorial money. He knew Lewis was traveling to Washington to address that very charge to the treasury secretary. Meriwether was always fastidious – looking at every detail and nuance that others frequently ignored. That doesn't sound like the same man I knew."

"Well, you also need to bear in mind how time can change a person," Gass replied. "Bates had mentioned Mr. Lewis had taken a bit to the bottle the last few years of his life, and had some personal issues. We have all known someone who has wrecked his life with excessive drink. It can happen to the best of us. Mind you, I liked Mr. Lewis as much as any man, but I am also realistic. Maybe he had a vice that he couldn't control and the charge may have had some volition."

"I'm not saying he was a saint, or couldn't do any wrong," Clark said. "But it just doesn't seem in his character to let such details get so out of control. Money matters are a serious business and he, of all people, should have known that."

"So where does that leave us, Mr. Clark?" Ordway asked. "Where do we go from here?"

"It's always been my philosophy that in order to find a needle in a haystack, we first need to reduce the size of the haystack," Clark said. "In other words, gentlemen, we rule out all other possibilities and carefully comb through what is left. The answer is before us – we just need to find it."

"Well, let's put political motivation on a back burner for the moment. What is left?" asked Gass.

"Retribution. There are a number of possibilities here," Colter chimed in. "We already addressed the Blackfoot and I believe ruled them out. The few others I can think of go back ten years or so."

"The four men we court-martialed?" Clark said. "That's an interesting theory, assuming any one of them had ties with the Cherokee and paid them to make the hit on Mr. Lewis."

"I wouldn't put it past Reed," Colter said. "He probably got drunk somewheres, thinkin' about how he was wronged by everyone, especially during the expedition, and focused the blame on Capt. Lewis. Found out he was traveling through and decided to settle an old score."

"What's he up to now, does anyone know?" Gass replied.

"Not at the moment, but I will damn sure find out. The same with the other gents who may have felt we did them a disservice to the Corps," Clark said. "I want you to split up, find them and interview them. See what bugs crawl out from under them. If any of these varmints played a part in this, they won't see the inside of a jail cell. Meriwether Lewis was my partner and my friend. If they are guilty, we'll serve justice ourselves."

Chapter 51

T he man closed his eyes and breathed in deeply the sweet scent of pine and lilac. No one was around and he wanted to enjoy this moment, make it last forever. He had been too long in St. Louis. When this investigation is completed, one way or another, he was going to finish his house in Kentucky and settle down on a small farm. Maybe it was time to make a decent woman of Rachel – maybe…

A branch snapped near him, and William Bratton started from his daydreaming. His horse, an older nag he rented from the local constable, didn't flinch. Bratton looked around warily, certain he was being watched. The trees were large but spaced sporadically around the flat Tennessee landscape. Bushes dotted the ground, not many large enough to hide a grown man. There was a farm about a mile distant where he hoped to find the person he was looking for. Still, the feeling of unease refused to leave.

He unholstered his .45 and kept it in his right hand, his left holding the reins loosely. He hoped to make his visit unannounced, but word might have reached the wrong ears anyway. The boy at the stagecoach station, he thought. The way he looked at me, when I asked him for directions to the Reed farm. Damn!

He decided to quicken his pace, and soon the trees stopped all together. A small plot of tilled earth was visible over the next hill but the plant stakes were empty this time of year. The short rows of corn stalks were cut deeply but would no doubt return to full height by the summer, looking nice and full once again. The small house that sat adjacent looked old and decrepit, lacking the touch that a wife normally provides. If Moses Reed indeed lived here, he did so alone.

Suddenly, as he approached, a man stepped out from behind the house, a rifle leveled straight at him. "Drop it!" the man ordered. He was a tall man, wearing loose fitting clothes that seemed to hang on his thin frame. A wide brim hat kept the bright sun off his weathered face.

Bratton smiled thinly. His long red hair whipped around his face as a strong gust of wind picked up along the flat land. "Nice to see you, Moses."

"Heard you was lookin' for me," Reed said evenly. "Now drop the pistol or I'll put a bullet through your head." He moved the cock back on the rifle to emphasize his point.

"Hey, sure, no problem," Bratton said as he carefully dropped his gun on the dirt beside his horse. "Just want to ask you some questions is all. No harm in that now is there?"

"If I see the constable, I talk with him. With you showin' your face 'round here, that only means one thing to me. And I left that disaster behind me ten years ago! I told you I wanted no part of that expedition. Now leave me be!"

"Listen, I understand completely," Bratton said. "Told you so a long time ago, didn't I? You left the group, wanted no part of the traveling. I was under orders to get you back. Me, George, Reubin, and Francois. And we did, sending you right back to St. Louis within a short time. Just like you wanted."

"And if I didn't go back with you, you had orders to kill me! That crazy Lewis told me so!" Reed screamed at him. "What I wanted was to get away from those mixed-up people – both captains were bent on a suicide mission! They actually thought we was gonna go all the ways cross the country and make friends with the indians! I told 'em they was crazy but no one listened to me. I only signed on 'cause I owed that Pryor fella money."

Bratton slid off his mount, keeping the nag between himself and his adversary. Carefully he removed his hunting knife from his belt and hid it down his sleeve point first. He came around the horse from the rear, hands held up slightly.

"Look, you have the rifle - I can't do anything, understand?" Bratton replied. "I just wanna talk."

"Damn right you can't do nothin'!" Reed cackled. "The great frontiersman, William Bratton, can track anything in the woods, even find little ol' me, but he can't..."

In the time it took to blink, Bratton swung his arms down, the knife slipping into his palm in one smooth motion. Before his arm had finished its downward trajectory, the knife was already in the air, cutting through the emptiness with astonishing speed. It struck the man high up in the shoulder, forcing him to drop the rifle with a clatter in the dusty earth. Reed screamed and clutched his shoulder, falling to his knees in surprise and shock.

Bratton was upon him in an instant, kicking the gun away and knocking the man down to the ground. He looked at the shoulder wound and was satisfied it was not life-threatening.

"Stand up, you old fool," Bratton said tersely. "You should know better than to go around pointin' guns at people." The knife was on the ground and he picked it up, using Reed's shirt to wipe away the blood, before replacing it back in its sheath on his belt. He got Reed to his feet and half dragged him inside, where he found a rag and made a field dressing over the wound.

"It's not deep – just put pressure on it for now and the bleeding will stop," Bratton said. "Now where was I before you accosted me? Oh, yeah, I came to pay you a little friendly visit. It's so nice to meet up with old friends, isn't it?" His voice was harsh, all trace of sympathy gone.

"Well... what brings you back to little Moses Reed?" the man stammered, his voice rising an octave. His bravado was as broken as his two-bit rifle that lay on the ground outside.

"Funny you should speak so unkindly of Captain Lewis...he is why I'm here. Ya see, Moses, he was murdered some time ago – four years last month to be exact. And I think you know something about it. You and him weren't exactly friends now, were ya?"

"Mur...murdered?" Reed stammered again. He appeared thoroughly confused. "I didn't know nothing 'bout that!"

"Listen, you hated him from the moment we took off from St. Louis! Thought he was about to kill us all! Well, you know what? We made it to the Pacific and back, and I'm standing here in front of you as living proof! You ran off like a coward, and I tracked you down and dragged your sorry ass back! You got four trips through the gauntlet as punishment and a swift court martial, and if it were up to me, you'd still be runnin' through the switches."

"Look," Reed said, "I don't know nothin' of what happened to Capt'n Lewis. Really, I don't. When I got back to St. Louis, I wanted nothin' more to do with the party, so help me God. Just to be left alone here, mindin' my own business. That's all, honest!"

"Before I came down here, I did some checking around. The local sheriff seems to have taken a shinin' to you, considerin' all the time you've spent in his jail cell the last few years. Seems not a week goes by you're not knockin' down more whiskey than is good for any living soul, and causing a ruckus to boot. He even told me of a little tirade you pulled a while back in the local pub, about poor Capt'n Lewis. Now tell me the truth, Moses. Did the knife in his back belong to you?"

"Knife? What knife? I heard he was shot! It wasn't my knife at all!" His eyes opened wide suddenly, as a cold sweat broke out all over his face.

Bratton smiled thinly. "I thought you didn't know what happened to Capt. Lewis, Moses. Now, you had motive. You had time to make the plans, and the connections to do it. The only thing I don't yet know is where you got the money to pay off them Cherokee."

Suddenly Reed squinted his eyes and tears began to stream down his cheeks uncontrollably. He face screwed up tight and he cried out. "No! I'm not gonna go to jail for this! I may not have liked the man – God knows, I hated him, you, and Capt. Clark something awful – but I didn't kill the man. That doesn't mean I wasn't glad to see him go, but I wasn't the one who did it. I live off the land; I got no money to pay nobody nothing! You gotta believe me, Bratton!"

The deputy sat back, and smiled again, this time a look of satisfaction on his face. "You know, Moses, for the first time today, I do. The fact of the matter is, you ain't got the brains to orchestrate something like this, or the money to make it happen. You're a small time drunk with a chip on your shoulder the size of Louisiana. But carry out a murder-for-hire with the Cherokee against one of the most important figures of our time?" He shook his head slowly back and forth.

Bratton got up, and put on his wide brim hat, before turning to take his leave. "You best to wash that out and clean it right," he said pointing to Reed's shoulder. "And next time I come around, don't go pointing anything at me again."

Chapter 52

November 12, 1814
Dakota Territory

The cold, running creek ran strong through the dense wilderness following last night's heavy rain. The trees overhead were a bright multitude of browns, reds, yellows, and greens, and John Ordway was enjoying himself. Born and raised in the mountains of New Hampshire, he enjoyed the changes the autumn brought to the forests and the cold, refreshing breath that winter brings. Snow wouldn't come to these parts for a few more weeks, he surmised, but when it does, it will pack quite a punch.

He looked again at the map in his hands, and then glanced ahead to the small hut that lay just to the north side of the creek up ahead, no more than a thousand yards. No one seemed to be around, so he took a deep breath, and strolled carefully forward.

"John! John Newman!" he spoke sharply but not loud enough to carry beyond a few yards. *If Newman was indeed trapping beavers in this part of the county, as Clark had been told, then he should return soon. And if Blackfoot are nearby, it was best to not advertise too much. And they are one of the most territorial tribes I've ever known.*

The journey from St. Louis to the shores of Beaver Creek, an offshoot of the Missouri River deep in Dakota territory, took two days by stage, followed by another two days of overland navigation along the shoreline. Ordway knew the general terrain well enough – it hadn't changed considerably since he last navigated it by boat ten years before. The creek itself had been small and unexplored at the time, but it hadn't taken too long to find the right branch in the river that would lead him to his quarry.

Hey, he's not guilty of anything right now, remember that, John. Newman may have been a scoundrel, he might have bristled at authority, and showed contempt early on towards the captains and the expedition as a whole, but he got what he deserved, and maybe that's all it comes down to. Unless the man has decided lately to take personal grievances into his own hands, the connection between him and the death of Capt. Lewis might not exist at all. *Give him the benefit of the doubt, John. Easy words to say, if you didn't know the man. But I did. I did.*

He went back a ways into the thick woods to give his horse some water. The rented black mare was fit enough for navigating the difficult terrain and Ordway loved horses. Nature's gift to the traveler. They take a man and his belongings places he could never go on his own, and only ask for food, water, and shelter in return. He gave the thick coat of ebony hair a coarse brushing for what seems a long time, speaking with him gently, as if he were a trusted confidant and ally. Out here in the harshest wilderness, the mare was all he had.

From his vantage point, John could see the small hut through a grove of overgrown bushes and long-dead trees while remaining essentially undetected. *I'd rather approach him on my terms than on his. Let's see if he's got anyone with him. Trappers hardly ever go alone.*

Towards late afternoon, he heard the sound of approaching footfalls breaking through the crisp underbrush. He looked cautiously out and saw a balding man, medium height and thick beard, wearing a cotton shirt, pants, and a coat of animal pelts that was dirty and old. He wore a cap over his head that resembled beaver skin that had seen better days ten years ago. The beard hid his face somewhat, but even from this distance, Ordway knew he had found his man. He waited a little longer to see if anyone else would come unannounced down the path as well, but no one did.

It was time to get reacquainted. Ordway unhooked his pistol from his hostler but kept it in place for now. He might not need it, but there was a decent chance the man might not want company.

The balding man had slipped inside the hut, and Ordway waited for him to come outside. After a few moments, he did and gave a cry of surprise at the sight of the visitor before him.

"Evening, Newman," Ordway said evenly.

"Who the bloody he…" the man started to say, before his eyes widened in shock. "Is that…you, John? John Ordway? Man, that brings me a long ways back."

"Yeah, it's me," Ordway said, letting his guard down just a hair. "Governor Clark sends his best wishes to you."

"Clark?" the man replied. "He's a governor now, is he? Sure as shootin', I figured he'd been in politics after all this time. Not Capt. Lewis though - I figure him bein' a professor at some high falutin' university or somethin'. You know he always had the head for it." Suddenly his eyes grew a shade darker and his voice lower slightly. "But you didn't come all this way to say hello. What purpose brings you to these woods, my friend?"

"Well, for starters, I'm doing some investigating for the governor – and I need some information from you before I decide what to do next."

"Is that a fact?" Newman replied. "You sure look all official like in your fancy getup and little bronze star and all. Whatever brings you here ain't likely good news for me." His eyes suddenly shifted to his left, and Ordway followed him, only realizing too late that Newman was one step ahead the whole time.

The heavy branch was swung hard at his head from someone behind him, and he turned away from it at the last second, feeling a glancing blow strike him hard across his right shoulder. Ordway struggled to stay on his feet, turning around to face his attacker. A large, young man was standing there, dressed in similar fashion as his partner, his hair long and braided down his back. He held a large, heavy branch in his two meaty hands and hesitated for a moment, the element of surprise now gone. His target had not gone down immediately and he was unsure what to do.

Newman shouted at him. "Take him down, Max! Do it! Now!"

But it was too late. His brief hesitation gave the deputy the short time he needed to draw his pistol and level it at the young man's chest. "Drop it. Do it now or I'll drop you." Ordway said through clenched teeth.

The young man looked questioningly at Newman who simply sighed and nodded his head. The wood hit the ground with a heavy thud, then both men looked at the newcomer. Ordway was visibly upset and he had a hard time concealing his anger.

"I ought to arrest you both right now for assaulting an officer. Or shoot you now where you stand," he said sternly. He tried moving his shoulder some, feeling some pain. "There was no need for that, boy. I just came by to ask some questions of your partner here."

224

"That boy is my son, John," Newman said. "He's only 16 but look at him – he's bigger than me already. He was just protecting his old man – he won't give you any more trouble. I promise."

"Promises from you are laughable," Ordway replied. "But if you answer some questions for me, and be honest with me, I may look to forgo any…official disciplinary action here."

He explained briefly the death of Meriwether Lewis and the known connection to the Cherokee and the possibility of a retribution plot against him. Did Newman know anything about that, given his own court martial ten years by the same Capt Lewis who now lay dead?

"Listen, I was a different person back then," Newman said. "I was loud, crass, and not afraid to say what I felt. I wasn't as careful with the booze as I should have, I guess, and said things to the captains that I later regretted." He was sober now and looked almost apologetic. "I even tried to make up for it after my court-martial. How many people do that?"

"You received your seventy-five lashes at the discretion of Capt. Lewis and Capt. Clark. Can you honestly tell me you felt no animosity toward them? That you weren't looking for a chance to get even?"

Newman looked down at his feet for a few moments, then looked up, straight into the eyes of his interrogator. "Listen, at the time, of course I was upset. Who wouldn't be? But I did try to redeem myself afterwards. It was just that they didn't want to trust me again. As soon as we built Fort Mandan, I was sent back to St. Louis, along with the other rejects. But I tell you, desertion like Reed did – sure, that's a court martial offense in my book. All I did was say some things the captains didn't much like. I regret it now, and wish I hadn't said it. But all the same, it wasn't worth the punishment I took. That's all I'm saying."

"What 'bout Max here?" Ordway said, shoving his thumb in the young man's direction. "You teach him to coldcock any stranger that walks by? Is this the new 'John Newman' you're telling me about? One who uses violence at the drop of a hat?"

"Now John, you know how it is out here," Newman replied spreading his arms out to take in the forest and camp around him. "When strangers come by, nine out of ten it's not good for my body or soul. Thieves, Indians, crooked sheriffs – I've seen 'em all, and I've taught my boy to protect 'imself - and me. Now when you comes along, he had no idea if you was looking out for my interests…or not. Surely, you can see that?"

Ordway looked around the camp, appreciating for the first time how remote they were up here in the north country. Even he didn't feel completely safe as he traveled the shores of the creek to locate Newman. He remembered the headstrong kid John Newman was ten years ago. He didn't see that same man now – just a protective father and a cautious trapper, savvy in the ways of the forest and all its dangers. Upset with the past he had carved out himself, but responsible enough now not to engage in murder for the sake of revenge. He looked at Max and understood. There was his reason for keeping out of trouble. Newman loved his son. It was really that simple.

Chapter 53

November 13, 1814
Little Rock, Arkansas

The four horses trotted through the growing town of Little Rock, the dust from their wake making lazy, swirling circles in the air before settling down again. The stagecoach they pulled behind them was medium size, its passengers numbering only two this morning. The driver, a short, portly man with a small mustache that curled at the edges of his face hurried them along to the station platform. Taking out his pocket watch, he checked the time. Two minutes early, he noted with satisfaction as he pulled up on the reins and carefully steered the horses alongside the wooden dock. A station handler stood outside waiting for them, and quickly held the door for their passengers.

John Colter looked out and jumped lightly to the platform below. He only carried one piece of luggage and took it from the station handler before walking briskly inside the stage office.

A man sat behind a small booth, his shirt showing several sweat stains despite the cool weather. His suspenders took great exception to holding up his clothes over his immense girth and his hat did little to hide the perspiration on his brow. He didn't speak as Colter approached him.

"Mornin', sir," Colter said genteelly. "I'm looking for a fellow named John Collins – I know he's holed up in Little Rock, but not sure of his exact whereabouts. Perhaps you know him?"

The man looked up at Colter with a quizzical expression, then took off his hat and wiped his brow with his sleeve, before replacing it again. "Collins. Sure I know him. You'll find him down at the jail today."

Colter sighed inwardly. *John Collins seems to have fallen quite far since we were partnered together during the expedition. He was a good man too – and a good hunter. But too much drink can corrupt even the best of men.*

He thanked the man and headed back into the street, towards the building marked simply 'Jail'. He found it not more than 400 yards away. It was a small wooden structure, like many of its kind - non-descript yet functional. On the door a small sign read 'Sheriff' and a crude symbol of a five star badge etched next to it. He knocked and went in. There was no officer anywhere in the jail room – most likely he was out on a short errand.

There were three tiny, holding cells next to each other, buttressed against the back stone wall with a single, small, barred window in each. The bars of the cells looked thick and rusted, and a thin cot was chained to the wall. The first one was empty but the middle one had an occupant, who was sleeping away the demons of the previous night. The third had a man in it who looked curiously at him as he entered. One look from him told Colter this was not Collins. He turned his attention to the man in the middle.

He slept with his hat over his face, and his clothes were dirty and ragged. He was skinny but tall, and he looked like a ghost from ages past. Colter felt a pang of sympathy for his former hunting partner.

He walked over to the cell, grabbing a stout wooden stick from the sheriff's desk as he went. He rapped gently on the bars of the cell and when that got no response, he rapped louder. "Collins!" he said loudly.

The sleeping man stirred but still did not wake up. Colter grew a little impatient. He rapped it again, this time louder still. "John Collins, I need to speak with you!"

A voice from behind him made him turn with a start. "And who may I say is looking for him?"

A tall man stood before him, the silver star on his lapel indicating to the entire world his role in this town. His boots were polished and his hat was fixed solidly on his head. He had a small thin beard that he kept neatly groomed. His facial expression was stern and unfriendly.

Colter turned to face him, saying "I need to speak to this prisoner, sheriff. He might have information vital to my investigation."

"And who might you be?" the sheriff growled. "I ain't seen you 'round these parts before."

"The name is John Colter. I am a federal deputy…" but then he stopped and simply stared at the man before him. Then his eyes widened in shock. "John…?"

The sheriff smiled thinly. "You don't recognize me, Colter? Thought I was some lowlife drunk wasting my life away? Look whose laughing now, partner." He sneered wickedly as he spat out these last words.

"Well, all I heard was you were in Little Rock and then down at the jail," Colter said quietly. "Guess I didn't expect you to be so… civil-minded, I guess."

"I've come a long way since our journeyman days, John," Collins retorted.

"We all know you had your share of problems," Colter said evenly. "Getting drunk no more than a month into our expedition and suffering Private Hall to do the same – you had a problem not too many men would have recovered from."

"But I did my penance with Clark and Lewis – 100 lashes on my bare back for my libations, my dear sir. And I was still forced to row that day in the hot summer sun. Oh, yes, I did my penance, I tell you."

"And you were not removed from the expedition – you finished it along with all of us, and that's a credit to you." Colter looked at the man coldly. "But I've come here to see if your disciplinary problems caused you to seek a personal vengeance against Capt. Lewis a few years back."

Collins' eyes narrowed. "What are you talkin' bout, John? I ain't got myself mixed up in any affairs and you know it."

"What I know is that Capt. Lewis was killed by Cherokee Indians back in '09 while traveling from St. Louis to the capital. Recent evidence we've been able to uncover points to a murder-for-hire plot. You, along with others that might hold a personal grudge against the man, must be ruled out as suspects. Right now, I'm not accusing you of anything, but it would be to your advantage to talk with me about it."

Collins' face turned a shade redder and he practically pounced from where he stood next to the door. "How dare you come in here and think I had anything to do with that! I tell you I did my time, finished the expedition, and let bygones be bygones. I am an officer of the law now, John – like it or not, you have to accept that. I wouldn't jeopardize my job now or my freedom for want of some petty revenge. Now you get your ass out of my jail, or I'll lock you up myself!"

Colter looked at the sheriff but didn't move a muscle. "You are forgetting that I too am an officer of the law – a fantastic twist of fate on both our parts. I will not be badgered or intimidated by the likes of you. I am on a fact finding mission right now – if you are lying to me, I will be back and with more men than you can muster, I assure you."

"I got nothin' to hide and you have your work cut out for you, Colter. That man Lewis crossed a lot of people and, while I'm not saying he deserved what he got, he had more than enough detractors who would like to see him brought down. Cherokee, you say? Why don't you try the natives or their friendly allies, the British? There are lots of suspects, my dear sir. Go and find a real killer and leave me the hell alone."

Chapter 54

November 14, 1814
Baltimore, Maryland

The stately inn was small but homey and Patrick Gass took a liking to it immediately. Only a block off the main road leading into Baltimore, it was an ideal setting for putting travelers up for a night or two. Its picturesque view overlooking the Inner Harbor made it a must-see for those who could afford its high prices.

Having settled his single overnight bag in his room and taken a short nap, Gass felt refreshed. At the stroke of six on the hour, he heard a knock on his door.

"Come," he said.

The door opened halfway and his host, an older gent by the name of Malloy, said from the doorway, "Dinner is ready, Mr. Gass."

Patrick followed the man down the single flight of stairs into the dining room. Before the table stood another gentleman, wearing a dinner jacket, creased slacks, and polished shoes. He wore no hat and his collar bore no evidence of a tie tonight.

Gass nodded to him and took his place opposite, while their host came around to the head of the table. As if on cue, a woman emerged from the kitchen carrying a large bowl of steaming liquid and set it on the table. A young black servant came out carrying a plate of freshly made biscuits and set them aside the bowl, then proceeded to help the hostess into her seat. Only when Mr. Malloy pulled out his chair to sit, did Patrick and the other man do the same.

"It's nice to have company on this pleasant, crisp autumn night," Mr. Malloy said.

Mrs. Malloy looked at her husband sternly. "Donald, have you introduced our guests?" She turned to Patrick and said apologetically "I'm sorry; ever since the British attack my husband hasn't been quite himself."

"Make no apologies, kind woman," said the man across the table. "War is not for the faint of heart." He turned to face Patrick and held out his hand. "The name is Key. Francis Scott Key, at your service."

Gass nodded, and introduced himself as well. "Patrick Gass. On federal business out of St. Louis."

Key smiled. "St. Louis, you say? Ah, the gateway to the undiscovered territory!"

"Well, I've had the pleasure of doing some discovery myself out beyond the borderland during the last ten years."

"Is that a fact?" Key answered, and he poured a ladle of the brown onion soup into his small bowl before passing it to his host.

Gass took a biscuit and broke off a large piece, before dipping it into his own soup bowl. "Yes, in fact I was part of the Corps of Discovery that was undertaken by William Clark and Meriwether Lewis back in '04. Walked all the way to the Pacific and made it back within two year time."

"Lordly be, that sounds excitin'!" their hostess exclaimed. "You must have had some fine adventurin', I do declare!"

Gass smiled. "Sure enough."

"We have been fortunate to have Mr. Key here staying with us for a fortnight," their host spoke up.

"Indeed," Gass replied. "I believe I heard of a poem of yours that was receiving national attention of late. Something having to do with the Battle of Fort McHenry, if I'm not mistaken."

Key smiled. "I am a lawyer by trade, Mr. Gass, but I do like to dabble in poetry from time to time. Yes, the little bit you must have heard was one I titled "Defense of Fort McHenry". I was able to view the actual battle from a very unique vantage point and felt a strong urge to put pen to paper that night. I printed it on a handbill and distributed copies – it wasn't long before the Baltimore American newspaper picked it up and it became more widespread. I just didn't realize it had reached St. Louis as yet."

Having finished his soup, Gass put down his spoon and took a small drink of the red wine. He swirled the smooth liquid in his glass a bit before replying.

"Actually, I read it while I was visiting the capital last month." Gass said. "I went out to see the treasury secretary and got a first hand look at the devastation the British has caused. Terrible, just terrible."

Key nodded in understanding. "Yes, quite. After they retreated from Washington, the British fleet turned their attention northward, apparently trying to overrun the American defenses along the Chesapeake Bay."

"But you were in the battle itself? In Baltimore?" asked Gass, now more curious than before.

"Not exactly IN Baltimore, my good man. Just a few days before, this must have been around September 10th or so, I received a visitor who told me some devastating news. My good friend, Dr. William Beanes, had been taken prisoner by the British. As I was well known in Georgetown – having spoken before the Supreme Court a handful of times and did a stint as U.S. District Attorney – this chap wanted to know if I could help the government negotiate for his release. He told me about the fleet heading towards Baltimore, so I immediately took a stage here."

"Most kind of you to intervene like that," Gass said sincerely. "Not many would have put his neck on the line for someone else."

"Beanes was a friend of mine," Key said. "If I could help get him freed, I felt honor bound to make the attempt. When the British fleet arrived in the Bay, I rowed out to meet them, along with Colonel John Skinner, who normally handles prisoner exchanges for the government."

"My word!" Mrs. Malloy said, "You might have been taken prisoner yourself!"

Key smiled. "No worries, my dear. The British were very courteous. I met with the captain and two of his officers in his stateroom. I had brought with me a few letters that I felt might help the cause – mainly from British prisoners we held that Dr. Beanes had treated, demonstrating his kindness to them. After a time, they agreed to release him, for which I was most eternally grateful."

"They let you return to Baltimore before the attack?" Gass questioned him.

"Now there's the rub, my good sir," Key said, warming up to his favorite material. "It was already growing dark by this time and the British had sent a ground force to skirmish around the Fort. They also began to bombard the fort from their gun ships in the harbor. They knew we lay privy to their plans, so they decided not to allow us to return until the battle was over. For our safety, they put us back in our boat but sent us eight miles behind their fleet. We remained there for the duration of the attack, but bore witness to the events that transpired. It was quite a..." Key smiled, "unique vantage point."

"What could you see from eight miles out?" Mr. Malloy interjected.

"Against the night sky, we could see the flashes of bombs and Congreve rockets that lit the sky like it was noonday in August," Key replied. "As the dawn approached, the shelling never let up. There were about a half dozen ships in the harbor that kept firing cannon fire and rockets into the fort. But the British were smart in their defense as well. They made sure to keep their ships back just beyond the range of the fort's cannons. They kept up the assault for over a day.

"As night began to fall again, we wondered how much punishment the fort could withstand. After all, the military had abandoned Washington to the British, and the towns along the Chesapeake had surrendered without a shot fired. Clearly the Americans were demoralized by this time. What lay within them to keep up the fight in Baltimore? It was something that I thought about a lot during our time on the bay watching the bombardment. And when night turned back into daylight once more, and I saw the huge American Stars and Stripes waving from the top of the Fort, I knew we had won. And so, too, did the British. It wasn't long before they pulled up anchor and left the bay for good. By the time we rowed back to dry land, we were exhausted and happy... and proud. Very, very proud."

"That must have been quite a large flag to be seen from that far away," Gass said.

"You betcha," Mr. Malloy said. "My second cousin's friend and her daughter made that flag just a few months ago." Addressing his wife, he asked "What was it dear, twenty feet by fifty?"

"No, I'm pretty sure Mary made it thirty feet by forty-two feet. She wanted to make sure everyone coming into the bay could see it. The old one the fort had was torn and ratty, so they loved this one."

"I wrote the little poem that very night and even set it to a tune – an old British drinking ditty called the 'Anacreontic Song'. Maybe, if you'd like, I could sing a few bars..."

"Oh, my, yes!" said Mrs. Malloy.

He cleared his throat once, smiled at his audience graciously, and began to sing softly.

"Oh, say can you see by the dawn's early light.
What so proudly we hailed at the twilight's last gleaming?
Whose broad stripes and bright stars thru the perilous fight,
O'er the ramparts we watched were so gallantly streaming?

And the rocket's red glare, the bombs bursting in air,
Gave proof through the night that our flag was still there.
Oh, say does that star-spangled banner yet wave.
O'er the land of the free and the home of the brave?"

"Magnificent!" cried Mrs. Malloy. "Oh, my dear Francis, you have touched on something…it certainly tugged at my heart strings, if I may say so. I'm just glad Mary's flag was big enough for you to see!"

That brought a laugh from Gass, who responded in kind. "Yes, that tune does set the lyrics in context quite nicely. Stately, yet lively, for all to enjoy."

"My dear sir," addressed Key to his fellow guest, "I think we have heard quite enough about my little poetic fancy. I'd like to hear what brings one of the legendary Corps of Discovery journeymen to Baltimore. What say you, Patrick?"

Gass smiled ruefully, as he allowed the servant girl to collect his plate. When she had departed, he turned his attention to his new found friend. "Murder," he said evenly.

"My word!" declared Mrs. Malloy.

"Indeed," said her husband, "are you investigating? And who was the poor chap who met his foul end?"

Gass gave a general highlight of the investigation, but did not go into great detail. "It's still ongoing," he said almost apologetically.

"Who have you come to see in Baltimore?" Key asked. "Someone you suspect may have played a hand in Mr. Lewis' death?"

"Well, actually I've taken today to do some investigating to that end," he said. "Turns out the fellow in question, a one Mr. Hugh Hall, met his own end during the battle of Baltimore last month. I discovered recently that he was assigned to Fort McHenry and it was just poor timing that I arrived a few weeks too late. From what I gleaned from the commander at the fort, the poor chap was cut down by British field artillery when they tried to storm the ramparts. He was a good man, really – I didn't know him well, but I did serve with him on the Corps of Discovery and he deserved a better end than he got."

"Why did you suspect him in Mr. Lewis' death," Key asked with interest. "If he was a nice guy…"

"Nice guys who kill are worse than bad ones who don't," replied Gass. "You can never judge a man just by looking at superficial things. I've seen nice guys do awful things when it came during the course of war. In this case, the motive might have been revenge. A way of getting back at Mr. Lewis for a court martial against him some ten years ago. But while we can not rule him out completely, I do not believe he played a hand in this messy affair after all."

"And why is that?" Mr. Malloy asked.

"I've spoken with his commanding officer and have learned a few more things about him… his character, his motivations – things that define a person. Now while he wasn't stationed here during the period of time the murder was committed, I have discovered from his fellows at the barracks that he was home with his family in Kentucky during the year 1809. He has a daughter, who is now five years – that put her as a newborn in the year in question. Most fathers I know who have little ones at home are not thinking of committing acts of murder and revenge. Just trying to put food on the table is difficult enough. In my mind, it's not one thing that stands out to make me reject him as a killer – rather a series of small, but significant details."

"Interesting, Sergeant Gass," replied Key, "but as you say, unfortunately, we'll never know for sure."

"If we catch the right individual – we'll know Hugh Hall had nothing to do with it," countered Gass.

"If you are looking for motivation, my friend… money, greed, revenge, lust… are all worthy candidates for murder," Key said smiling. "That may be the writer in me… or the lawyer. I've seen a lot during this war to never rule out anything. Maybe even look to the British. They were in the process of building up their armies back in '09 and '10 and money is a strong motivator. War is a crazy business."

The Expedition Continues

Chapter 55

June 30, 1806
Montana territory

The afternoon sky was bright blue, with not a cloud to be seen for miles in any direction. Tall mountains surrounded them on each side, as the line of horsemen followed the swollen banks of a large river, its icy cold water fresh from the snow capped mountains behind them. Despite the arrival of summer, the weather was still cool in the mountains and most of the men had their jackets on, not yet ready to accept that summer was already here.

"Halt!" Captain Lewis called out, as he crested the next hill. Slowly, the line of horses and men converged on the spot, most of them dismounting and allowing the animals to graze nearby.

"What do you see, Capt'n?" Gass asked, as he joined his commanding officer. Together they looked out beyond the rise of the hill and took in the grand sight before them. The river system split into three branches ahead, one going south, one east, and another sending its icy waters between them both.

"This is where we head to the south, if our guides are indicating correctly," Clark said, as he motioned to two Nez Perce natives, who were attempting sign language with their white guests.

"Indeed, we need to get out of the mountains by the quickest – and safest route," Lewis agreed. "But it would be good to do some exploring while we have the chance."

"Meriwether, I already have a plan I've been formulating – we never did fully explore the Yellow Stone River on our initial trip on the Missouri. Once we are free of the mountains, I'd love the opportunity to cross overland and check it out more closely. Remember why the Minnetaree natives called it the Yellow Stone River? They claim there are actual yellow rocks somewhere along its coast, and it's something I'd love to investigate further."

"Well then," replied Lewis, "let us do some exploring. But it is not the Yellow Stone that hold an interest for me." Clark turned around and smiled at his friend.

"Pray tell, Meriwether, do you not have a desire to map out a new river on the frontier?"

"Indeed, but it is one to the north I have a fancy in. If you recall, I named it after my dear cousin last year and I want to see for myself if Maria's River may indeed lay the northern boundary of the Louisiana Territory. If it does, I think we can redirect a good deal of fur trading from the Canadian territory into our own."

Patrick Gass laughed as he came upon the pair, "You are always the practical one, Captain Lewis. But why don't I propose a solution? Perhaps we should divide and conquer? We are approximately on an even latitude with the upper half of the Missouri River, near the Great Falls, if you go overland for a few days. You can explore your river while Captain Clark can take a party and head south to explore the Yellow Stone. We know from our first travels down that the Missouri and Yellow Stone meet up at a conflux some 500 miles east of us. We can meet up then and compare notes."

Clark looked at the sergeant thoughtfully. "You know, Patrick, that's not bad, not bad at all. We shall give it some consideration."

That evening, Lewis sat on a stout log under a makeshift canopy that served as his shelter for the evening. He took out his diary and began making notes of the trip, including the wildlife and vegetation they found, along with their traveling progress so far.

"Evening, sir," Sergeant Pryor said, as he stood outside the canopy. "Just wanted you to know we'll be ready to move out first thing in the morning."

"Thank you, Nathaniel," Lewis said. "I dare say we have had a hell of a winter, haven't we? Hard to believe it's actually July."

"The winter was a bad one, yes sir, but you got us through that, and I dare say it was quite a fight with the devil for all our lives," Pryor remarked earnestly.

"We thank God for getting us through, sergeant. And all of us were instrumental as well – each man doing his part for the sake of the whole – that, by definition, is what makes us successful. The hunting, the salting, the building, negotiations with the native tribes – all came together with God's grace."

"Amen to that, captain." Pryor said, before taking his leave.

Lewis continued to write in his journal, expanding on the descriptions of all the animals, and flora around him, as well as the details of the freezing trip across the Bitterroot Mountains, and the larger mountains behind them. They sure were rocky and steep. Maybe I ought to name them…

"Hey Meriwether," Clark poked his head in. "You gotta come see this for yourself, my friend!"

Lewis looked down at his journal and sighed. One day, he'll be able to finish an entry without being interrupted. He got up and walked outside. Several of the men were waiting for their commanding officers, along with two of their Nez Perce guides, who seemed quite animated tonight. They communicated in sign language and instructed everyone to follow them.

The party of ten men made their way by moonlight several miles south following a small creek. When they reached a certain spot, one of the guides indicated for them to stop, then pointed to a series of large stones set in a circular pattern in the middle of the creek. The air was cool in this summer weather, but he knew the water from the creek came from the snowy mountains and would be quite cold. He walked closer to the stones and stopped suddenly.

"Is that…steam coming off the water?" Lewis asked.

Without looking back, the native quickly removed his garments and jumped feet first into the water inside the circle. The other men grinned and quickly followed suit. Only Lewis and Clark remained on the shore, still fully dressed.

"Captain, it's…hot!" Colter said excitedly. Just then the native jumped out and ran a few yards back upstream before plunging into the icy waters of the creek once more. He cried out with a high pitched yelp as the frozen fingers of the creek scalded his warm body. When he could stand it no longer, he ran back to the circle of stones and jumped in once more. Several men were getting out now, the heat from the springs beginning to take its toll on them. Only a few men, Colter included, decided to duplicate the actions of the native, and brave it out in the icy waters, before returning for another dip in the hot water.

"It's a natural hot spring," Lewis decided. "Marvelous, I will say! Indeed."

"Are you going in, Meriwether?" Clark asked, standing next to him. "After all the cold weather we've been through, it will feel nice on the body, I'm sure."

Lewis looked at his partner, not quite sure. When Clark grinned, Lewis smiled back. "We have come a long way…"

William Bratton emerged from the water, put on his trousers and shirt, and came over next to Lewis. "Trust me, sir, it's very…therapeutic. I should know."

Lewis laughed. "You and your confounded back problems. I trust your hot steam treatment the Nez Perce gave you was sufficient?"

Bratton gamely twisted his torso right then left, declaring he was pain free. "It was all in my lower back. Really started this winter and I just couldn't shake it. Once we left our winter camp, it just got worse the further we traveled east. I felt bad when I was the only one riding horseback when everyone was walking, but my legs felt so weak…"

"Well, what exactly did they do for you? I wasn't around camp for the whole thing."

Bratton thought for a moment. "Well, the natives – they heated up rocks and poured water over them to generate steam. I soaked that up while they gave me a drink – it was an herbal tea of some mint variety. We followed it up with a few cold dips in the river and then repeated the process a few times. Now I feel great! Believe me, those hot springs do wonders for you!"

As the men rested that night, the captains were busy planning their next step in their tent. Taking the advice of Sergeant Gass, Lewis and Clark agree to part ways as a means of exploring more territory than they could together. Lewis was eager to find the northern boundary of the Louisiana territory, and was certain Maria's River could be the source. His intention was to head overland and find the Missouri near the Great Falls and then take Maria's River upward to where it originated. Once he was satisfied, his party would continue along the Missouri.

Clark maintained his desire to explore the Yellow Stone River to the south. He wanted to follow a trail through the Continental divide that would bring them close to the Yellow Stone and then travel overland to meet it. He intended to explore it all the way until it met the Missouri and reconnect with Lewis. They divided the men into teams, split the supplies, and made arrangements to meet in mid August at the point where the two river systems converge.

Chapter 56

On the morning of July 3rd, the two companies parted ways. Captain Lewis took Sergeant Gass, William Bratton, George Drouillard, the Field brothers, and several others, while Captain Clark's group included Sergeant Pryor, John Ordway, John Colter, George Shannon, Sacagawea and her family, and the rest of the company.

"Meet you on the other side, Meriwether," Clark said, shaking hands with Lewis. "And good hunting!"

Over the next several days, Clark and his men traveled through the mountains, and, while not freezing as they had been, the going over the steep terrain proved difficult. However, this time around Clark made use of information he obtained from the Nez Perce, who suggested an alternate route that should give them safe passage deep to the south. On July 6, following a route that he named Gibbon's Pass, Clark and his party ended up in the flat prairie lands that stretched beyond the horizons. They met up with a river they named after their president, and continued on for two more days.

The weather continued to stay nice and dry, with only an occasional midsummer warm shower that never lasted very long. Jefferson's River was large, at least 75 yards across and fast moving, as it made its icy way from the mountains behind them into the distant lands in front.

On the evening of July 12, they reached a fork in the river, a single location that converged not just two rivers but three. On their first journey down, Clark and Lewis had named these three rivers after their president, Thomas Jefferson, their Secretary of State, James Madison, and the Treasury Secretary Albert Gallatin. The merging of the rivers at this point started one of the major headways of the Missouri.

"This is where we made a cache of supplies last year, if you recall – one of several along the journey." Clark said. "The Missouri heads north, right into the Great Falls."

"But first things first I'm afraid," Clark said. "Let's open up our supplies we left here and see how they've weathered over the course of the year. If water got to them, we may not have all that we had hoped for."

He sent several men to unearth the supplies of food and equipment that they had left hidden at the base of a nearby hill last year, and was not surprised when they discovered much of the food spoiled. But there was some good news – the pots, pans, axes, knifes, and other supplies weathered their stay in far better shape.

"Captain Clark," said Sergeant Ordway, a few hours later, "we've also retrieved the iron frame boat we sank in the water last year, several miles upstream. The iron is still in good shape if we want to think about reusing it."

"Aye, that debacle," Clark said dryly. "The idea was sound but it leaked too much – cost us two weeks of time and effort when we could least afford it. We missed the mountain snow by a handful of days on that one. No, I think we can salvage some of the metal, but the boat can stay where it is."

"Captain," Ordway said, "Have you settled on a name for this place, yet? With such a distinctive location, it will surely have a future as a trading post in later years."

"No, Sergeant, I haven't. I've named lots of things on this trip and frankly am running out of ideas!" joked Clark. "I'll let you name this one. What do you suggest, son?"

Ordway smiled as he looked around. The conflux of the river system seemed to indicate a significant name. "I'm more practical, I guess, when it comes to naming. Since it's a fork, where three rivers merge in this one area, I suggest... Three Forks. How does that sound, sir?"

"Sounds like you just named your own future town, Sergeant." Clark said smiling.

"I guess so," Ordway replied. "Maybe I'll come back here one day with my grandson and tell him how it all started..."

"Quite right, John."

Clark was quiet for a time before turning to his sergeant, his tone becoming serious. "I have a quest for you to undertake. Right now, we are at the crossroads – I will take the party overland to the east and hope to connect with the Yellow Stone, but I'd like you to take three men and head north from this point up the Missouri and rendezvous with Captain Lewis at the Great Falls. Please organize what you need and be prepared to set out in the morning. You'll be able to bring their party more supplies than they were able to carry themselves."

"Aye sir," Ordway replied. "And may I say…good luck to you."

The men were met the next day with a surprising treat. Sacagawea's brother, Chief Cameahwait of the Shoshone tribe, and a band of six warriors rode through their camp as the morning sun began to break out over the mountain tops. Behind them were forty horses, brought up by two more natives in the rear. The sight was a wonder to behold! Sacagawea emerged from her tent and flung herself into her brother's arms.

Through his interpreters, Clark understood the horses were a gift from the chief, who was grateful to him for bringing his sister back safely from the "wonders in the west". Apparently, the Shoshone had been looking for the foreigners for some time, and were happy to see them return.

That afternoon Clark approached Sacagawea and her husband and, through the use of his interpreter, Private Labiche, asked what her intentions were. "Now that we are back among your people… are you going to stay here with them or continue with us back to Fort Mandan?" Clark had come to value her navigational instincts and level-headedness and hoped she intended to stay on… but was ready to be understanding if she chose to remain with her brother. After all, these are her true people…

After talking with the husband and wife, Labiche turned and address his captain. "She chooses to stay…" he said. "With you and the expedition!" Labiche broke out in a grin and the captain realized he was not the only one who had a great appreciation of this native woman. Little Pomp was adorable too. When it came to dealing with other tribes, the two of them were actually the best defense in the world. No natives ever believed their intentions would be warlike if they had a woman and child with them. The mother and son had helped them in so many ways, he realized at that moment.

"Well good, that's settled!" Clark said happily. His voice grew softer as he began to understand the sacrifice she was making. "Tell her…thank you." Labiche nodded.

The next morning, as the first rays of the sun broke over the horizon, four men on horseback left camp and headed out, striking a path up the Missouri. An hour later, Clark and his remaining company of fourteen men along with Sacagawea and her family, and fifty-five horses, set off to parts east.

Three more days passed as Clark and his smaller company forged their way across more steep mountains hoping to find the start of Yellow Stone River. The men were beginning to complain that the mountains would go on forever – with hunting near impossible and water scarce, it was critical they find their way out, and soon.

Clark called a halt at noon on the third day out from Three Forks, and the men immediately set about gathering wood for a fire and to scrounge up what food they could find. It was slim pickings. The captain wondered, not for the first time, how Meriwether was doing and if he had fared any better on finding his beloved Maria's River far to the north.

"Captain? Sacagawea would like a word with you – says it's important," said Labiche. "She and Charbonneau came to me and asked me to interpret for you."

Clark turned and faced his guests, nodding his assent. "Yes, go on please."

The Shoshone woman, cradling sixteen month old Jean-Baptiste in her arms, spoke quickly and animatedly to her husband. The fur trapper spoke to Labiche in French, who nodded in understanding.

"Captain, Sacagawea as you know grew up in the area around what we call Three Forks – she knows much of the land around here. She says she knows a way through the mountains – a gap that we can pass through to the great plains beyond. It is south of here and slightly eastward."

As he spoke, the woman handed Jean-Baptiste to her husband, picked up a stick, and began drawing on the cold packed mountain earth. She indicated the mountains and the pass the explorers must cross. When she was done, she stabbed the stick into the dirt at the location of the pass.

Clark squatted down beside her and looked at the map, then up at the mountainous landscape before them. His face began to light up and he smiled for the first time in several days. The path was clear to him now, and he realized they would make it after all, thanks to this remarkable woman, who gave up her own chance to go home, in order to stay and help him. Clark turned towards his Indian guide and thanked her profusely, not needing the talents of Labiche, to convey his sentiments this time.

Chapter 57

By the evening of the fourth day, the journeymen had traveled through the pass, a narrow gap that separated two larger hills on each side. With a brand new horizon to behold, the men celebrated with whoops and hollers! The way before them lay flat and clear, with only an occasional grove of trees to break up the view. The Yellow Stone still could not be seen from here, but Clark knew where they had to travel.

"The headways of the Yellow Stone must bleed off the mountains to the north, and flow eastward that way," Clark said, pointing into the distant horizon. By the morning of the next day they had found a creek, replenishing both their water supply and refreshing their spirits. The mood in camp was jovial once more, and Clark was glad for it. "Only a few more days, I reckon."

True to his prediction, Clark emerged onto the Yellow Stone River before the end of the second night, on July 15. The river was wide at this point, perhaps 40 yards across, and continued its winding path through the plains and valley of the Midwest. The snowcaps of these rocky mountains, he thought, must be what starts the whole cavalcade, he thought smiling. *And now we're here.*

Now that the river was before them and flowing in a direction that was favorable, the captain immediately set the men out to create canoes. They cut down two large trees and hollowed them out by setting them on fire. They proceeded to take axes to them and carved out suitable interiors for sitting, while allowing for strong enough hulls to keep them afloat.

Once this was accomplished, they tied them together for greater stability in the water. It was a tiring day and Clark and his men rested the night, with thoughts of an eventful journey ahead.

The first day on the river was a good one – they made remarkable headway, using the river's current to aid them in their journey. Four men rode bareback alongside the river, transporting the forty horses carrying the equipment, food and supplies their party would need on the journey.

Once their new camp was established for the night, Clark sent five men hunting, who brought back several deer. He even allowed his French Canadian interpreter Pierre Cruzatte to join them, despite the fact that he was blind in one eye. Cruzatte had been asking to join the hunt for some time, but Clark always refused, citing his vision problems. However, he was inclined to grant his request today.

"I've seen the elk in such abundance, I doubt even you could miss them! Go with the others and get dinner for us, Pierre," the captain responded to his latest plea. That night, the men had an enjoyable evening, using two fire pits to cook their first good meal in weeks.

Clark awoke the next morning to angry shouts from some of the men. He stood up and looked around wondering what the problem was. It didn't take him long to find out. John Colter ran up to him, shaking his fist in the air.

"They're gone, captain!" he said angrily. "Half the bloody horses are gone!"

Clark's face grew slightly paler as he realized the implications. The horses were the backbone of their transportation efforts, as well as being excellent assets for future trading – without them, it would be very difficult to continue their journey. They would have to make do with less, or find another way of shipping the equipment and food.

"What do you make of it, Colter?" Clark said. "Were they secured and watched last night?"

"Of course!" he said exasperated. "All the horses were roaming in the field just west of our camp and we had two men keep watch through the night – looking out for both the horses and our camp. But the men said they didn't see or hear anything. When dawn came, we realized we had been robbed."

"Who do you suspect? The Crow natives?"

"Who else? The Crow are notorious for horse stealin'…" said Colter. "We shoulda kept a closer eye on 'em."

"We had two men – didn't think more would have been needed." Clark said, disappointment creeping into his voice. "Well, what's done is done – let's regroup and come with a plan for finishing our journey."

With twenty-two horses left, they divided the equipment and food between them, but everyone was upset at the loss of so many. Despite hearing about the Crow, none of the men under Captain Clark had ever seen one, which only inflamed their notoriety. As the day progressed, stories of ghosts and evil spirits were mingled among the chatter of the men. Clark himself didn't believe such nonsense, but it was hard to convince men who grew up in the back country not to pay it any mind.

The following evening as they ate dinner at their next camp, Clark approached Sergeant Pryor. "Nathaniel, I have a need of your services. We are getting closer each day to our arrival home, and I would like to be able to bring with me some representation from several of the native tribes in the midwest. As a gesture of future trade and closer relations."

"I agree, sir. That is sound thinking. But what part am I to play, captain?"

"I have drafted a letter," Clark said, handing over a parchment, "addressed to the fur trader, Hugh Heney. I have asked him to try and convince many of the Sioux tribal leaders to accompany me to Washington."

"Heney, sir? He's up in Dakota territory, am I right?"

"That's him, sergeant. He's just east of Fort Mandan. It's important that you get there before us and solidify the arrangements. I want you to set out tomorrow. You'll be on your own, but I know you can do it. You're resourceful. If anyone can accomplish this task, it's you, sergeant."

As Pryor turned to leave, Clark put a hand on his shoulder. "Nathaniel, there is one more point I want to emphasize. My letter to Heney also states that, as much as he is able, to try and change the tribes favor away from trading with the British. I'd like him to encourage the various tribes to trade with the Americans who will soon be coming to the area. It's a delicate balance, as we don't want to come across as heavy handed, but we need their business in order to justify expansion into the area. I need you to help convince Heney to use his influence."

"Aye, captain," Pryor said. "I'll convince Heney – just trust me on that."

"That's what I want to hear – thank you, Sergeant. Take five horses and present them to Heney, so he may use them to negotiate with the Sioux."

Pryor set out the following morning riding a sturdy mount, one of the Shoshone steeds he had become attached to. He led five additional horses across the northern plain, carrying a small amount of equipment and food he would require for the journey. Clark wished him well and silently hoped he would be able to convince the fur trapper. He had met the man only a handful of times two winters ago but hoped Heney would understand the importance of what Clark was asking.

Soon afterwards, the rest of the company started out on their twin canoes, with four men leading the remaining horses across the plains after them. The hills were smaller and the wide open, grassy plains were worn along paths frequented by herds of animals, both large and small; a far cry from the conditions they had experienced for the past several months. They had a constant source of water and the numerous bison, deer, and elk made for easy hunting.

Four days out, they camped along the Yellow Stone, the winding river skirting several hills in front of them. They were making great progress and were hoping to do some exploring tomorrow. They had already passed one other east flowing river that merged into the Yellow Stone. They had named it Clark's Fork, as an honor to their captain.

It was George Shannon who spotted the canoe first. Arriving in camp at a dead run, he approached his captain quickly. "Sir, I was on lookout and spotted a canoe coming downriver. Looks like a small boat sir – one, maybe two people."

"Thank you, private. Let's take a look, and see to our guest."

Fifteen minutes later, the small craft came around the bend, with the assembled party waiting anxiously to see the newcomer. It could only be a native – but whose tribe, and with what intention? Did they know we are here? Clark felt a flurry of thoughts as he waited to see.

Chapter 58

William Clark gasped as the canoe turned towards them, and he got a good look at the figure paddling. It was Pryor!

The craft he maneuvered was a bullboat, and Clark could see it was cleverly made – quick and light for carrying one person in a hurry. Framed with tree branches, an animal skin was stretched around the bottom and sides, making a waterproof but fragile craft. Handled the right way, it would make for a quick and safe transport – provided you didn't carry too heavily.

Pryor looked tired and dirty, but he was alive and Clark was grateful for that. He remained quiet as he beached the craft and emerged, helped ashore by many hands. The sergeant walked towards his commander, his head held slightly down. "Sir, I must report I was…unsuccessful," he began. "I was only gone two days, when I was besieged by the Crow – they robbed me of all my horses and equipment – I barely managed to get away. I had my rifle but didn't fire – I realized it would be suicide if I tried. There were just too many and most of them were armed themselves."

"Nathaniel," Clark said, putting his hand on his friend's shoulder. "I am just glad you made it back alive. I guess my ambitions got the best of me, and I put your life in danger. For that, I accept the responsibility for what happened out there. Get cleaned up and have a good night's rest. There is more of this river that I intend to see tomorrow."

Clark assigned Pryor to horse detail the next day, giving him the stallion he himself prized the most. It was a beauty, sleek and black all over, standing over 17 hands at the shoulder. Pryor took a liking to it immediately and was grateful for the kindness his captain bestowed on him.

"It's not every man who is honored with his captain's stallion after failing a mission," he quipped.

"The mission was mine in the failing – not yours. Remember that, Nathaniel," Clark said. "There is more ahead of us and we need to be ready to meet it head on!"

The next week saw the men witness breathtaking sights on or near the water of the Yellow Stone River, as it carved a path through the heartland of the Montana territory. On the late afternoon of July 25, Clark saw something that forced him to call an abrupt halt to their travels.

"Look at that! It's remarkable!" he exclaimed.

Along the south side of the wide river stood a tall sandstone butte, at least 150 feet in height. It appeared square in shape, perhaps covering two acres of land. They had encountered other sandstone shapes before, much smaller, along the river but this was the largest by far and several miles distant from any other.

Clark told the men to beach the craft near the structure. "I want to check this out – it's not something you see everyday!"

As it was already late, they setup camp for the night at the base of the structure, while several men went on a short hunting party. Clark took four men as well as Sacagawea and her family to explore the huge stone block.

As he walked around the base of the structure, he found a clear flat face, and taking a sharp stone, carved his name and the date into the sandstone. "W. Clark July 25, 1806". Standing back to admire his handiwork, he noticed his Indian guide put Jean-Baptiste on the ground.

"Little Pomp is getting bigger everyday," he said. The child had thick black hair, and a complexion slightly lighter than his mother. His eyes were an ocean blue, a rarity among Indian children. This trait must somehow have started from his Canadian father, he mused. How else to explain it? He gathered the boy in his arms and together they walked a path up to a flat ledge that jutted a third of the way up the butte. There was grass on the ledge, and from this view, they could see a fair distance.

As they continued to walk around this ledge, they came to the front of the butte, with a deep indentation that extended almost all the way to the top. They continued the walk up, finding purchase on a rocky path from the back until they stood on top of the butte, 150 feet in the air. There was nothing around them nearly as tall as far as they could see in any direction. Clark breathed in the fresh air deeply, watching the little boy in his arms try to imitate him. Clark laughed.

"I know what I'm going to name this place," he said. "I will give it a name worthy of greatness. This is your tower, little Pomp. Pompey's Tower!" As Sacagawea skirted the last few stones to arrive on the top beside him, he smiled at her and repeated the new name for the boy's mother. She smiled and nodded, understanding crossing her face. This man was honoring her son, and she was happy.

They left the next morning and continued their travels down the Yellow Stone, stopping for the night near a fork, with a river that merged in from the south. A large herd of bison grazed peacefully nearby to the north. Clark and his company made camp and ate well that night.

Darkness was already upon them several hours, and Clark turned in for the night. For the first time in a long while, sleep eluded him. He tossed and turned, not understanding what the problem was. This had not happened before since spending several cold nights at Fort Clatsop. But at least then, there had been a reason. He was frustrated and sat up trying to understand the problem. But he couldn't think with all the noise the buffalo herd kept making.

"There must be over a thousand head out there!" he growled to himself. "The noise just won't stop....", but then a smile creased his face as he realized the source of his sleeplessness. Never had he slept this close to so numerous a herd before and it took him most of the night to realize the downfalls. He laughed to himself as he lay back down and tried once more to find the elusive slumber.

He must have dosed part of the night at least, because he woke up with a start in his tent. If Meriwether had been there with him, as he usually was, he surely would have woken him earlier. The sound of the herd continued unabated, but with daylight, the noise was a little easier to manage.

He got dressed and stepped outside to help the men prepare their morning meal. But his thoughts drifted to the frustrations of last night.

He walked over to Sergeant Pryor who was gathering firewood. The man looked tired and had seemed to have lost a step or two. "You had trouble sleeping as well, Nathaniel?"

"Damn buffalo," he said.

"Well, in honor of their attempt to deprive us all of sleep, I think it only fitting we name this river yonder," he said pointing across to the south, "the Bighorn River. Wherever the Yellow Stone and the Bighorn meet, the buffalo will surely make its presence known."

Pryor stood for a moment, his arms full of wood, and he smiled for the first time that morning. "Right fine name, captain. Just thankful it was buffalo and not geese or something else bothering us. Have a hard time naming it 'Honking River' or some such nonsense – just doesn't sound as nice."

Chapter 59

The midday sun was warm upon the grass, yet the great beast took no notice. It stood on all fours upon the top of the hill, shaded by several ancient spruce trees as it took in the river below. Hunger was foremost on its mind and the berries he had eaten a short while ago were not enough to satisfy his huge appetite. The brown fur on his back bristled as his nose suddenly picked up a new scent. It was not one that he noticed in these parts before; it was somehow…different.

The grizzly bear sniffed the air again, thoughts of the river trout momentarily forgotten. It shook its 1,500 pound frame vigorously and let out a growl that made smaller animals run for shelter. The scent was behind him… he turned…

The shot rang out, scattering a flock of birds nestled in the trees around the great beast. It felt a stinging pain in its side, but brushed the thought off. It growled again at the unseen smell, the source of which still eluded him. He tried to advance down the hill when another sharp noise filled the air. This time the bear felt the pain more acutely in his strong chest, suddenly realizing there was a problem. His legs felt suddenly weak, the weight of his body forcing him down. Determined as he was to find the source of the scent, his defensive intuition took over, and he looked for a way to get off the hill top.

Surprisingly, his front legs failed to lift his great weight any longer, and he couldn't understand it. He needed to move and he could not. Frustrated, he let out one more growl, crying out to the unseen enemy, hoping to scare him away.

One final shot rang out and the great beast thought no more.

"Got him, captain!" Bratton said excitedly.

A handful of men rose from the bushes 400 yards away, Bratton in the lead, as he carefully made his way through the tall grass to his fallen prey. The beast was huge, larger than any he could remember in a long while. It would make quite a meal tonight!

As he crested the hill and leaned over the giant bear, he stopped suddenly, staring at the river beyond. This must be it! The Missouri River at last!

"Captain! Captain Lewis!" he called back to the eight men coming up behind him. Patrick Gass and Meriwether Lewis were the first to reach him. Several others led horses burdened with equipment and food as they began to cover the remaining distance between them.

"I see it, William," Lewis said smiling. "Good shot, too. We'll eat well tonight as we celebrate our good fortune."

It took four men several hours to dress the carcass, while the rest prepared their camp. Lewis took this opportunity to explore the river on horseback with Hugh McNeil and Silas Goodrich. It was perhaps two miles distant, the way between gently sloped with forested greens and several open fields. Both bison and elk were frequently seen all around these parts and the trio marveled at the beauty that surrounded them.

"Yes, sir, captain, I'd sure like to come back here one day and build me a little cabin…do some trappin'…all the food I could ever want," Goodrich said smiling.

"We haven't seen many Indians in this area as of late, but the Blackfoot have been known to frequent the parts north of the Missouri. I'd best be careful if I was planning on staying near here," Lewis replied.

"Don't you worry, captain", McNeil said laughing, "Silas is more comfortable in the east – I doubt he'd ever really make a move out here. This is a nice place to look at, but…"

"Hey don't sell me short," Goodrich said, a little too sharply. "I've grown to love the great western frontier…"

"Alright, gentlemen," Lewis intervened. "Whether you want to come back west is up to you – it's wonderful country, there is no denying that. But for now, I want you, Goodrich, to head south and see if you can spot any signs of the Great Falls. I'd like to know where we are at the moment. McNeil, you take the north. I'll stay and explore this region some more."

The three men split up, agreeing to reunite back at the camp in no more than four hours time. The sky was clear and it was still mid afternoon. Lewis calculated they should be back well before sunset.

Hugh McNeil was a careful man, an aptitude that had kept him alive in some difficult situations throughout his life. Born and raised in Pennsylvania, the 29 year old hunter was comfortable in the outdoors, but regarded the great beasts of the wild with high regard and a safe distance. His own cousin had met an unfortunate end several years ago at the hands of a rogue bear and he was always on the alert for whatever might be out there.

Hugh bent down and gave his horse, a white and brown mare, a gentle pat on his neck and talked to it from time to time. He enjoyed bonding with his mounts – it made him feel less alone in the untamed wilderness. He rode along the western side of the Missouri heading north, winding his way between trees, bushes, and rocks. The mare's footing was solid and he felt confident with her.

After a few hours, he heard the sound of rushing water, and knew what he had found. The river water was rushing at a faster pace than it had previously, although the width of the river was not quite as wide as he remembered from last year. He continued to skirt the river until at last he saw the cascading spray of water hit rocks in the river before disappearing into a huge abyss. Nothing lay on the other side. He had found the Great Falls!

Excited, he turned the mare around and started heading back, his mind anxious to report his findings to Captain Lewis. The company had come upon the Missouri at a spot much closer to the falls than many had thought they would. He knew the mouth of Maria's River was just a couple days distant.

Without warning, the mare reared onto its hind legs, and a tremendous growl came from bushes to his left. Too late, McNeil saw a large white shape, huge against the setting sun. The horse turned away from the enormous bear, twisting at the same time. McNeil, caught off guard, felt his body leave the horse's back, his hands grabbing vainly for anything, something… He hit the ground hard, his head snapping back forcibly against solid rock. He was shaken, his vision momentarily blurred.

A giant roar from directly overhead roused him, and his mind snapped back into the moment. His rifle had fallen with him, laying only a foot away to his right. The white giant had risen on its hind legs, showing the man its full height of seven feet – but to McNeil lying on the ground, the beast looked more like ten feet. Desperate for anything to use against him, McNeil rolled towards the fallen rifle, away from the huge beast and its sharp claws. Adrenaline surged through his body as his fingers curved around the barrel of the weapon, swinging it like a club against the bear's side.

The beast shook with fury, but the action saved McNeil – for the moment. The animal crashed down with his fore paws in the spot the man had just vacated, giving him a split second. Scrabbling to his feet he swung again, bringing the stock of rifle down on the bear's head like a giant wooden club. This time he heard a satisfying crunch as the bear's skull took the full weight of the blow.

The beast fell to the ground, rolled onto its side momentarily stunned. McNeil thought for a brief second about finishing him off with a shot to the head but sadly realized the force of the blow had damaged the rifle beyond repair. The stock lay broken and cracked in several places and the metal barrel had bent slightly in the middle. It had saved McNeil's life, but its use as a hunting weapon was over. Throwing it down, he looked quickly around. The bear would recover soon enough and be after him yet again. The mare was long gone. Where was he to go?

Looking around, he spotted a tall willow tree. An idea came to mind and he ran over and grasped the lower branches, pulling himself up. Quickly, he began climbing as high as he dared, hoping he would remain out of reach of a beast as large as this one.

It only took less than half a minute until the bear was back on its feet, growling and more upset than ever. If McNeil knew anything about bears, it was their keen sense of smell. The willow tree wasn't going to hide him forever. The bear grew quiet for a few moments as it failed to quickly see his adversary, and his other senses took over. His nose, as expected, quickly revealed McNeil's hidden location.

Through the leaves of the trees, McNeil momentarily lost sight of the bear as it walked around, but after a few seconds, he felt the earth shake below him. The great beast was directly under the tree, throwing his full weight against the trunk. If he fell now, he was as good as dead. McNeil clung to the branches above him, while wrapping his legs around the branch he sat on. The sun was going to set soon and he would be in total darkness. McNeil never felt so alone in his life.

Chapter 60

Captain Lewis stood against the tree that had shaded the great brown bear just hours ago. They had cooked a portion of its meat for their dinner, and packed as much of the rest as they could carry. Goodrich had returned an hour before sunset with nothing remarkable to report. But now that darkness had set, he was worried about McNeil. It had been hours since he had departed for a look north, and he had failed to return.

It wasn't the first time one of his men had gotten lost in the woods, but McNeil should have been able to find his way home. Had he found something? Or worse, had something, or someone, found him? Lewis realized he could not launch a rescue party until dawn, as his own men risked getting lost in the darkness as well. There was no moonlight tonight – a late easterly wind had pushed clouds into the area. Maybe it would rain tomorrow – it was hard to tell. Rain would make tracking harder than ever…

Suddenly he heard something – a voice in the night. It didn't last long – perhaps it was just an animal, he really couldn't be sure. Then he heard it again. Slightly louder but still far away. Could it be Hugh? Could he hope for a miraculous return so deep into the night?

Lewis called out, hoping his voice would be heard. Several of his men came over to his side, listening as well. The fire was behind him, acting as a beacon high into the dead of night. Gass, Bratton, and Drouillard quickly grabbed small logs and lit them in the fire. Using these torches to light their way, the trio quickly set out into the night looking for their friend. If he was close, maybe they could find him.

Within the hour, Lewis' hope had been realized as the men came back with their prize. Hugh McNeil walked into camp exhausted, dirty… but alive. He told his story long into the night, until he finally fell asleep.

The next day the company retraced McNeil's path towards the Great Falls, finding it by mid-afternoon. There was no sign of the bear but pieces of his rifle were located near a large and mangled bush, only 100 yards from the waters edge.

"It was fortunate you outlasted the varmint, Hugh," Gass said as he surveyed the trampled area. "He musta had quite the headache to give you up."

"Well, I won't say I'm not grateful," McNeil declared. "That tree saved my life. I only hope I find that mare again – she was a beauty."

"I hope to give you some time for that, Hugh," Lewis said as he came around. The rest of the group gathered around him, as he addressed them all.

"I'm organizing a smaller, separate party to explore up Maria's River. The rest of you should proceed to portage the horses and equipment around the falls. If all goes well, we will meet you at the mouth of the river in ten days time."

"Who's going with you, Capt'n?" Gass asked.

"Patrick, I need you to stay and lead the men around the falls – all the horses and equipment will go with you. That's the most crucial part – without which, none of us will make it back to Fort Mandan. My little party will go overland from here with just our mounts and find Maria's River in a few days time. I will keep our group simple – myself, George Drouillard, and Joe and Reubin Field. That's all. With so few in number and equipment, we'll travel much faster."

"Understood, sir. It will take time anyway for us to navigate the horses around all the falls – you best do your business and have at it. We'll catch up with you in ten days."

The party packed some food and cooking supplies on their horses and the four men set out in the morning, heading overland in a northeasterly direction. Gass stood to watch them go. "May you find the northern border, Captain," he said softly.

After traveling for three full days and most of a fourth, the small group of Americans came upon a wide river in a pouring rain, with fast running water heading down to their right, in the direction of the Missouri. "This must be it, captain," Drouillard said.

"If the direction of the river north of here reaches the 50th parallel as I hope, we'll have found the northern boundary of these Louisiana Territories. It would be a wondrous thing to bring back news to President Jefferson that we have reached the top…"

"And an even bigger thing if we can divert trading away from the British," declared Reubin Field.

"Captain Clark and I talked about that. It was his intention to send someone with a letter ahead of him to parts near Fort Mandan. He would like to get some tribal representation to come back with us to Washington. And if, at the same time, they can bargain with the natives to do business with us instead of those English, so much the better."

"Amen to that," said John. "Those Brits are taking away a good deal of the fur trade. If we can get a piece of the action…"

"Well, first things first, gentlemen," Lewis said. "It's time to find the answers we've come all this way for. I just hope the rain doesn't stay with us for the duration."

But hope as they might, the rain continued on and off, for another two days. The quartet saw not a single Indian in that time, despite the fact that they were getting deeper into Blackfoot territory. The abundant game they had encountered along the Missouri began to grow scarcer the further up the river they traveled.

By July 22, they had traveled dozens of miles up the Maria's River continuing in a northerly route. They had hoped it would deviate to the east around the 50th parallel, the extent of the northern boundary of the new territory. But the further they traveled, the more convinced Lewis became that they had been wrong about the direction of the river.

They rode in silence as the rain continued to soak through their clothing and chill their bodies. The territory was very open here – fields far and wide, with only occasional forested areas scattered about. It seemed desolate to the explorers, with scarcely an animal anywhere to be found.

That afternoon, Reubin Field who rode in front, stopped the horse in his tracks. He waited for the others to catch up before pointing silently towards the northwest. Lewis could tell what the private meant him to see, and he sighed loudly. The river they were following headed off into mountains visible in the distance…to the west, not the east. The end of their journey on the Maria's was at hand.

"It's official, captain…I'm sorry to say. Maria's river does not seem to be any type of northern boundary…it just ends in the mountains to the northwest." Reubin said quietly.

"Gentlemen," Lewis said. "You have allowed me to pursue my dream, and I appreciate it. I wished for a different ending…I think President Jefferson would have to agree with me on that…but it is what it is. I can't change geography, as much as I'd really like to."

"May I suggest we make camp then, sir?" Drouillard asked. "We can stay here and recoup before heading back."

"I wouldn't want to stay too long though," Joe Field added. "Did you notice the lack of game on the way up? It's a definite sign we are in Indian territory. They are keeping a low profile for now, but they must know we're here."

"Agreed," Lewis said. "Let's make camp tonight and see what we can do."

Chapter 61

Together, the men built a small three-walled shelter from logs and mud, leaves and brush. While not the Taj Mahal, it was adept at keeping the rain off their heads during the night. Lewis chose to name this Camp Disappointment, in light of their mood and the futility of their search for their northern boundary.

But one night turned into a second, as Reubin came down with a fever. Lewis didn't want to risk traveling with a sick man, so he waited another day. Joseph stayed by his brother's side, giving him water and warm blankets as best they could. They kept the fire going round the clock, both for warmth and from protection against… whatever was out there. Wild animals, desperate for food, might wander into camp and try and take what doesn't belong to them.

"Reubin, I believe your fever's broken," Joe said, relief in his voice, mid-afternoon on the third day. "With any luck, we can start to head back in the morning."

Reubin still looked pale, but he was able to sit up and take in water and a little food. He lay back down inside the small shelter, exhausted from this brief exercise. Joe came outside, and met up with his partners. "He's beginning to feel somewhat better, sir…"

"That's wonderful news, Joe," Lewis said. "We'll take our leave of Camp Disappointment tomorrow if he…" but he stopped, as he looked at Field. Joseph was looking beyond the shoulder of Lewis, his eyes fixed on something. Lewis turned around to see what had befuddled his friend.

Four Indians stood there, guns aimed at Lewis, Drouillard, and Field. They were dressed in leather and beads, the hair braided in two long tails on each side of their head. One of the four, farthest on the left, wore a lone feather in his hair, held by a leather strap.

Lewis immediately put his hands up, and his fellow travelers did the same. "We are here in peace," he said in English, but the Blackfoot just looked at him. He asked Drouillard to repeat his sentiment in French but this produced the same result.

Four more Indians similarly attired walked up behind them, but they had no guns in their possession. The eight warriors made no immediate move on the explorers but they weren't leaving either.

"It appears to be a standstill," Lewis said to his compatriots. "Let's try a little peace offering instead."

"I want to offer you something," he said calmly, as he slowly walked around to the front of the shelter, knelt down and picked up his satchel. From their vantage point, the Indians could not see inside the lean-to where Reubin lay. When Lewis peaked inside, he noticed the man had a grip on his own rifle, ready to charge out if needed. Lewis gave him a quick shake of his head. Not now. But he was glad to know his backup was ready if he needed it. It instilled in him a little more confidence.

But Lewis was a man built on negotiation and peace, not violence. In all their travels, they had never fired a shot in anger, and if they could avoid it this time he felt they should. The Indians seemed more curious about him than afraid and the captain took this as a good sign. He reached his hand in the bag and removed a silk handkerchief, one given to him last winter by the Clatsop natives. He held it out to the group assembled before him. After a moment one of the men with a rifle came forward to take it. They all looked at it with excitement in their voices.

Lewis felt better – grateful for a chance to defuse the situation. He reached into his satchel again and brought out two more handkerchiefs, as well as some small American flags that he had brought with him from St. Louis. Another man, who was not armed, came forward to accept these gifts and bowed slightly in acknowledgment.

Lewis decided it was time for a truce. He sat down upon a log that lay next to the fire, and motioned for Drouillard and Joseph to do likewise. Reubin remained in the shelter for the moment, still undetected. Lewis didn't feel he needed the backup now, but it would confuse and perhaps frighten the Indians if he emerged without warning.

The Indians grouped together, each man reaching out to touch one of the objects. After a few minutes, they turned their attention back to the white men. They collectively placed their guns on the ground to one side, and sat down facing Lewis. He smiled warmly.

"Reubin," Lewis called out, "I want you to put your rifle down and come out slowly – don't make any sudden movements that might cause our guests to panic. Now is the time to talk."

Field did as instructed and sat down next to him. His presence drew a slight surprise from the natives but the fact that he was unarmed gave them no reason to confront him. Lewis had one more item to show and he waited until he had everyone's attention. He stood up slowly, and reached once more into his bag. He removed a medallion that was attached to a looped string.

He had worked with sign language before on natives of other tribes and thought he was able to communicate rather effectively in most cases. He used his gestures and occasional rudimentary drawings in the dirt, to indicate where they came from and how they traveled up the river.

He pointed to the flag he had given them, and told them how it represented a much larger area and a culture of people like his own. Lewis indicated the items he had given them and attempted to convey a sense of trade between their two groups of people. Many of the Blackfoot were nodding in understanding. Lewis knew the rifles these natives were outfitted with came from trading with the British, so he explained how he wanted to open trading posts throughout the area.

Sometimes he talked as he gestured, a measure to himself and his friends of what he was trying to say.

"We will trade with all the tribes of nations," he said. "We have rifles and more ammunition, food, and medicine…lots of things of value."

Two of the Blackfoot suddenly seemed agitated and Lewis couldn't quite put his finger on the reason. What had he said that bothered them? Surely they would stand to profit from trade. Any tribe in the area would. Why would they object to that?

He tried to ask what was wrong, but the natives were getting more restless. Lewis decided to defuse the situation a bit by offering the medallion. He held it out as he explained its significance.

"This is a peace medal," he began. "You can put it around your neck, like so," as he draped it around his own neck. "On one side," he pointed out, "is an engraving of President Jefferson, and on the other," he turned it over in his hand, "is a handshake, symbolizing friendship and peace." He removed it from his own neck and held it out to the natives.

The tall native, whose hair was adorned with a single feather, came forward and took the proffered medal. He turned it up and down, apparently fascinated by the markings. He smiled and they all began talking at once in a language Lewis couldn't begin to understand.

Finally, Lewis stood up and pointed towards the fire, and gestured that he wanted them to eat dinner with them. More nods all around. Lewis smiled. This actually wasn't going half bad, he thought.

Two of the Indians indicated they would procure some game, and left immediately, each carrying a rifle. The rest helped the four Americans build a hefty fire, gather fruits and edible roots, and wait for the hunters' return. Within an hour and half, the men had come back to the camp, carrying three rabbits and a beaver, which they promptly dressed and prepared over the roasting fire.

Everyone ate well and Lewis was pleased. Their trip might not have resulted is discovering the northern boundary of Jefferson's large purchase of land, but they had made successful contact with the Blackfoot and perhaps, if all goes well, cemented a new trading partner.

At dusk, the Indians retired for the night, heading back towards the west in the direction of their tribal grounds, carrying with them the symbols of peace and trade they had acquired that day. Lewis and his men likewise turned in for the night, prepared to start their return journey in the morning.

Their horses were left untied outside, as they would retrieve them in the morning. The rifle for each man was stacked just inside the shelter.

As they had everyday since they began their journey, they took turns standing watch during the night, sitting by the fire and watching for animals or other dangers. The first man to remain on duty was George. Lewis was due to relieve him at midnight.

The shelter was small for three men sleeping lengthwise but it was sufficient enough for their purposes. Lewis slept fitfully, his dreams often returning to the Blackfoot. A trading establishment along the southern portion of Maria's River would be a coup for them, as they could easily meet up with members of different tribes in the area...Blackfoot, Crow, Sioux, Hidatsa, Mandan, Cheyenne... we could outfit them all with whatever they needed...

A loud cry woke him from his sleep and Lewis sat up, eyes and ears searching for the source. The light of the fire danced before him and he could see shadows of numerous figures outside. Another cry! He turned and saw John next to him, roused from his own sleep. There was no sign of Reubin or George. Quickly he leaned over to grab a rifle. He stopped suddenly. They were gone! All of 'em. He ran outside and into chaos.

Chapter 62

The Blackfoot had returned, and Lewis could see Drouillard struggling with one, the tall native with the feather in his hair. Lewis' peace necklace still hung suspended from his neck. A knife was in the hand of the native, poised over George as he struggled for his life. Reubin was fighting two more Indians, one of whom had the reins to Lewis' own horse. Reubin had his own knife out, as did the second Indian. Together they moved like agile dancers, taking large swipes at each other with their menacing weapons.

Another native had the company's four rifles as he too looked at the dancing pair, but his attention was not on the shelter. Lewis made a quick run at him, hitting him low around the legs. The man buckled immediately as the firearms flew from his hands.

Joseph followed his captain out of the shelter and was the first to retrieve one of the precious weapons. Quickly he fired into the air. The noise startled the Indians, and Reubin used the distraction to lean in and deliver a stabbing blow to the chest of his adversary. The other Indian holding Lewis' horse screamed, dropping the reins and ran back in the direction of their tribal village. Reubin looked at the man whose stomach now oozed red blood. The Indian's bone handled knife dropped from his fingers a second before his body collapsed in a heap on top of it.

The tall Indian battling George seemed clearly focused on skewering the American alive, and the stronger native appeared to be winning the contest. Both of George's hands gripped the arms holding the knife above him, but the Indian was stronger and taller, and the arm descended lower and lower every second. Suddenly, a third Indian came from behind and knocked George's right leg with a hefty stick, forcing him to the ground.

Lewis grabbed a rifle that lay at his feet, held it to his shoulder and pointed it at the Indian holding the knife over his friend. It was now or never. He squeezed the trigger. The sound of the rifle shot reverberated through the night, and the Indian seemed to freeze in his tracks. A red stain could be seen on his upper right side, and the small river of blood quickly spread out and down the length of his body. Still he refused to go down. George used the time to suddenly twist the knife away from the weakened arm, pushing him over in the process. The Indian fell without a word, his face still etched in anger and surprise, even in death.

The rest of the natives suddenly scattered to the wind, their cries punctuating the darkness that seemed to grow more menacing to the Americans left behind. Lewis ran over to Drouillard who was kneeling on the ground, catching his breath. He appeared to be unhurt – for now.

"We've got to go, captain! Right now!" Reubin said as he ran over. "Them Blackfoot will be back with more warriors than anyone can count before the hour is up. We dare not let them catch us!"

Lewis looked around, shaking his head slowly. What had happened tonight? What has sparked this... violence? "Yes, yes, you're right Reubin. Round up the horses and pack only what we need. Leave the rest."

The three men got to work, while Lewis began walking through the camp, retrieving objects from the Indians. He took back the small flags that the feathered Blackfoot warrior still had on him, but declined to take the peace medal. He wanted them to know who they were – perhaps someday another peace could be established with these people. Someday.

He placed four arrows in a square near the fire, together with two shields he found in the grass outside their camp. Within ten minutes, the four men were mounted and were making a hasty retreat back towards the Missouri.

They pushed their horses all night, never stopping to rest even for a minute, as they covered the dozens of miles in a blur. They passed the point on which they had found Maria's River from their trek overland and galloped by without looking. It was only when they reached the headway of the Missouri did they finally stop. The rising sun was just coming over the treetops. They had traveled the entire night.

The horses were led to the water as the men took a long deserved breather. Drouillard came over to Lewis as he replenished his canteen.

"Captain, I...I want to thank you for saving my life last night. I...wouldn't be here if you hadn't intervened."

"George, I just can't understand what happened. I can't wrap my mind around it – we had a peaceful meeting, a good dinner, and we parted on agreeable terms. And then they come back in the night to attack us?"

"I can tell you what I know, and some of which I've speculated on since we left. I was standing watch, sitting by the fire. I had my rifle in my lap – the rest, as you know, were just inside the shelter. I heard a rustling noise at one point just outside the firelight, and suddenly they were there – one jumped me from behind and others came from…everywhere. They were after the horses – I could hear them in the field around us – and I think someone headed for the shelter – he was probably after our rifles."

"I'm just thankful that not one of you was killed in that fight. It was something out of Dante, I tell you."

"Captain, I think…" Drouillard said hesitatingly, "I think I may have a possible… motive, if you will. Remember how they acted when you told them you expected the Americans to open a trading post and exchange goods, food, and firearms to all tribes in the region?"

"Yes – I thought they'd appreciate…"

"Think about it, captain! The Blackfoot control this entire region – they must also control the flow of firearms through the British. Such a powerful tribe must have a slew of enemies as well. The Crow, the Sioux, just to name a few. What if, suddenly, the Americans come in and start giving rifles and ammunition to all these other tribes – what do you think will happen?"

"A power struggle…" Lewis closed his eyes as he realized the implications. "One the Blackfoot might not win. They would feel threatened by our presence – not for what we can give them, but what we can give their enemies. My word, what have I done?"

"Nothing you could have foreseen, captain, I assure you." Drouillard said, smiling. "Believe me, you only wanted to share and share alike. But sometimes things…are not interpreted the same as you and me."

Suddenly, a cry went up from their left and both men rose to their feet in a flash. Was it the Blackfoot? Had they found them already? Lewis felt emptiness in the pit of his stomach, which he just couldn't shake.

Chapter 63

“Captain Lewis! I found them!” Joseph Field called out. He was downstream trying to spear a fish with a long thin pole.

Suddenly from around the bend, Lewis saw a sight that brought a smile to his face. Patrick Gass strode into view, followed by William Bratton and…John Ordway.

“When did John get here?” Lewis asked an equally puzzled Drouillard. “I swear I left him with Captain Clark heading for the Yellow Stone…”

The men of the Corps of Discovery regrouped once again, with Ordway filling the men in on the tales from Captain Clark navigating his way down south. “If all goes well, he plans to meet you where the rivers merge again in the east – in about two week’s time, I reckon.”

Lewis was pleased to see that Sergeant Gass had used his time wisely, having already burned and hollowed out four new canoes for their trip down the Missouri. With the Blackfoot to the north and the Crow to the south, the explorers knew that a large presence was crucial to averting any attackers. Still, they wasted no time in heading out, with seven men leading the horses while the rest continued unabated downriver.

The members of Lewis’ expedition continued down the Missouri without further encounters from the natives until, on August 11, they came within sight of the Yellow Stone River, which branched off to the right. There was no sign of Clark yet, so Lewis directed his men to set up camp for the night along the south side. He took Gass and McNeil and tried to scrounge up some much needed game for dinner. There had been an abundance of elk in the region, so he told Ordway to expect him back soon. The trio, each armed with a rifle, set off through the tall grass.

A half hour later, as they approached a wooded area, Lewis heard a loud gunshot, and immediately collapsed on the ground. His right thigh felt as if it was on fire, and he clutched it tightly. He called out to his friends who came running out, confused.

"Which one of you shot me!?" Lewis called out between clenched teeth. But both Gass and McNeil shook their heads.

"Wasn't me, sir," Gass stated, and he tore off a strip of cloth and tied it around the wound.

"I never saw an elk, let alone shoot at it," McNeil replied.

But the trio looked up unexpectedly when they heard a shout from the woods. "I got it, I know I did!"

A figure emerged from the woods in a hurry, but came up short as he saw the trio, and the man lying on the ground.

Gass recognized him immediately. "Pierre Cruzatte! You blind fool! You didn't hit an elk – you shot Captain Lewis!"

"Captain... Lewis?" The Frenchman replied. "But... you're not supposed to be here yet! Captain Clark said you weren't to be expected for another few days..."

"I can't believe Captain Clark gave a rifle to a man who can't see in one eye!" Gass exploded on him.

"It wasn't his fault, sir," the Frenchman said apologetically. "He didn't even know I was out here – I wanted to surprise him with a good catch today."

"Are you ever gonna catch it for this! Go fetch Captain Clark and bring him here on the double..." Gass said as the man ran off.

He turned to Lewis, who was still clutching his leg. "Well, we made contact with them...in more ways than one, I suppose."

The Investigation Continues

Chapter 64

T he stage pulled up along the raised, wooden station platform, the dust it kicked up refusing to settle amid the strong autumn winds. The air was cool this afternoon and the driver jumped down, drawing his coat closer to his body for warmth. The hat was pulled down lower on the driver's face as he secured the reins of the horses to the stage post.

As the first passenger disembarked, another man walked quickly from the station house, dressed in a maroon vest sporting the name of the stage coach company, St. Louis Express, and climbed up on top of the carriage. He fumbled a bit with the lines holding the luggage in place. When he had them freed, he proceeded to drop them down, one by one, to the station manager below.

"Welcome to St. Louis!" announced the station manager warmly to the arriving guests. A man stood before him, his hat in his hands, his face showing obvious displeasure. Another man disembarked from the coach, wearing an expensive black jacket, and sporting a bowler hat and green bow tie. His briefcase indicated he might be a banker of some sort. The manager had seen all kinds of passengers arrive in this big city, and he enjoyed trying to guess what they did for a living. A woman accompanying the 'banker' was dressed in a white frock and long sleeve jacket, her parasol twirling aimlessly between her fingers.

The last man was a bit of an enigma. He wore the badge on his coat, which showed he was a federal marshal, yet he looked like no lawman he had ever laid eyes on. He looked at the paperwork in his hands, indicating the stage had originated in Little Rock, Arkansas. What type of deputy travels so far out of his jurisdiction?

John Colter was in a mood – it was evident the moment Ordway spotted him. As he made his way through the crowd and out in the street, Colter showed no hint of civility or graceful demeanor. But then Ordway had never known him to be anything but gruff even in the best of times.

"What's eatin' you, John?"

Colter just growled as he walked, then stopped suddenly in the street and turned around in the direction he had come from, pointing his finger accusingly in that direction. "That man…!"

The horse and carriage traveling down the street just managed to turn at the last minute and avoid running over Colter standing there, his rider swearing angrily. The marshal paid no mind to either.

"He said I was a fraud!" Colter said angrily. "We traveled ten hours on that god-forsaken stage, and I was telling him all about the things I discovered seven years ago, along the Yellow Stone River. Back in '07, you remember, when I went there myself to do some huntin' and explorin'? I told you all about it. How I discovered that water jet that erupted like clock work – right out of the ground! And how the great lake – I figure it's the largest lake higher than 7,000 feet by far - led out on that incredible water fall and then how it poured through this grand canyon, and down through this valley that looked like paradise – and he said I was full of shit! Can you believe that?"

"Well, the nickname going around about it is "Colter's Hell", so I think it's fair to say not everyone is a believer. Maybe someday when more people move out there and see it for themselves…"

"I was the first one to see all those things – the first white man anyway – and all I get from people is disbelief. Lewis and Captain Clark never got told "You're full of crock!" when they returned. Just makes me mad as hell, is all."

"That's the nature of exploration, John. Wherever you go, you need witnesses, and documentation – you know that."

The baggage handler watched them go as he stood on the raised platform. Then he went inside the station house, left his company vest on a chair, retrieved a long black overcoat, and hurried out a side exit. Leaping on a waiting horse held by a young boy, he turned and galloped away, tossing the lad a penny for his help.

Things were moving quickly now – there was no going back. The damn marshals of Clark had seen to that. It won't be long before they pick up the pieces left behind. The rider smiled to himself. Who'll be left to find them?

Within a few moments he heard the blast originating from the downtown area, as he anticipated. His smile grew broader as his horse slowed to a prance, maneuvering the cobbled stone streets leading to his master's residence.

Patrick Gass and William Bratton waited in the office of Governor Clark. Ordway had been dispatched to bring the final member of the team back from the stage, but neither man had returned in over an hour. Finally, Clark stood up and said impatiently, "I don't think we have time to wait any longer on this. Knowing Colter, they probably stopped for a pint or two at the pub."

"I think you're selling John a little short, sir, if I may say." Gass replied. "He knows what's at stake here – besides, that is why I sent Ordway to look after him. Just in case he gets lost."

Clark was agitated and couldn't sit for very long. He walked around to stand in front of his two marshals. "As I've told you this morning when you arrived, my office was broken into sometime in the last week. No idea on the culprits, but all my instincts are telling me it's related to the investigation. First, I got a letter in the post, instructing me to meet someone at a remote location – I was to come alone. The location was a cave, five miles west of here, out towards the old mine that closed last year. I did as instructed but no one ever showed. Evidently a ruse of some sort. In the meantime, someone entered my house and went through my office – desk, cabinets, files, everything."

"You never told us if they actually took anything, captain. Did they?" Bratton asked.

"Well, fortunately, I had left York in charge until my return. I had been instructed to come alone, but perhaps the perpetrators didn't know – or count on – my house staff. York heard a noise and came to check on it. From what he said, there was one man, dressed in a black overcoat, boots, and a wide brimmed hat pulled low on his head. When he saw York, the man pulled out a knife and tried to fillet my manservant."

"As York answered the door this morning, I take it he survived the ordeal," Gass said.

"Indeed," Clark smiled for the first time this afternoon. "York said he took a candle stand – the iron one standing in that corner - and swung it at the man's arm holding the knife. He hit pay dirt. He must have seen me play cricket – dare say, I may include him on the team next season, if the others will allow it. The knife fell out of his hand and the man ran out the door."

"Then did York recover the knife used? And did you find anything taken?" Bratton asked.

"Yes – to both questions." Clark walked to a painting mounted on the wall, removed it, revealing a small safe. Quickly he turned the knob once to the left, around to the right, then back again. The door swung open on silent hinges. Clark reached in and extracted a long knife with an ivory handle, its metal shaft measuring at least 6 inches in length. It was a deadly weapon belonging to a man of wealth – and power. Whoever they were dealing with were no ordinary street criminals.

"And they did find and manage to take several documents I had in my desk drawers – documents from Washington detailing some of the legal challenges pending against Mr. Lewis. It is a blow though – without them, I will be hard pressed to delve into the financial matters that might have led us somewhere. It was one of the last remaining areas we hadn't covered."

"Perhaps the killer – or whoever was behind the attack on Mr. Lewis – knew it was only a matter of time until we got close. Perhaps they tried to get rid of evidence they knew would be damaging." Bratton chimed in.

"If the attack on Bratton and I while we returned from Washington was led by the same man, it could be that they are scared of us finding a financial connection to the crime," Gass said.

"Meriwether Lewis was a detailed man in many respects, as we know," Clark said. "If there were problems with the finances, he would be the first to find them. Unless…"

"Someone else was manipulating the books – taking money without his knowledge and covering up to mask the losses. Allowing Mr. Lewis to take the heat for the missing money…and then killing him to eliminate the evidence."

Clark snapped his fingers, an idea flashing into his head. "But what if the evidence didn't die with Meriwether Lewis? The papers he had – most of them anyway – came back here or to Washington. But President Jefferson had heard the news of his death and was able to divert Lewis' diary to the one place on earth the killer couldn't reach. His own home in Monticello. Maybe the killer was looking for that diary – uncertain what Lewis has written about him and anything that might lead authorities to investigate him."

"The diary itself, from what the President said, didn't seem to contain anything related to the financial mess he was in. But the killer could not have known that. Maybe we can use that to our advantage…somehow flush him out."

The double doors open suddenly and York came in quickly. "Sir, you are needed immediately. There has been an explosion."

Chapter 65

The three men looked at each other and quickly rose as one, following the manservant outside on a dead run. When they emerged into the sunlight, they could see a thin waif of smoke trailing into the sky about a half mile distant, towards the downtown district. Where the stage was located, Clark realized suddenly.

"It must be Colter and Ordway in this somehow – let's go!" Clark started to run in the direction of the smoke, but Gass and Bratton quickly overtook him. He would love a horse right now, but in the slick cobble streets, winding through the district, it would actually be faster on foot. It took ten more minutes until he reached the heart of the downtown area.

Smoke was thicker here, as he made his way towards the center, hoping against hope that he wouldn't find his friends. He looked around, carefully scanning faces and body types – until his eyes fell on Gass and Bratton, already at the scene and tending to the wounded.

Clark ran over, bending down over two forms that lay stretched on the ground. Gass stood and rose up to meet him. "It's them, sir. They are alive, thanks be to God. Colter is conscious but Ordway is still out cold. Apparently, he struck his head as the force knocked him into that brick wall." He pointed to the bloody stone wall behind them.

"How was it...?" Clark started to ask, but Gass cut him off.

"Don't have all the details yet. Looks like some sort of explosive device. Possibly carried with them in a bag of some sort. John said he had an overnight case with him when he got off the stage. If they had been holding it when it went off, they'd be literally all over this street. But John told me he wanted to go into this pub over there," he nodded towards a local bar with a sign 'Pints and Ales' hanging from a sign above the door. The blast had knocked the sign off the hook on one side so it swung to and fro in the breeze.

"He must have put it down and gone to check it out, when the two of them started arguing about him going in. I haven't gotten Ordway's side obviously, but the next thing Colter said he knew he was picked up in the air and tossed hard on the ground by the force of the blast. I hope Ordway will recover – his head hit the wall pretty hard."

"Someone wants to silence us," Clark said. "And they are getting bolder by the minute. That also means we are getting closer than ever. We need to find them, and fast – before we lose our own lives in the process."

Clark had both men transported to his estate at once, and paid the best doctor in St. Louis to do a thorough check up on them. Colter was fine, outside of a headache that he insisted could be cured with a shot of whiskey. Ordway, meanwhile, had awoken but could not remember anything about the explosion.

"The last thing I remember, Governor, was picking John up from the stage. We were walking and talking – he was mad about something, I forget what exactly – and then I woke up here. The rest is just...gone."

"I was afraid of that," the doctor said. Frances O'Toole was a physician in St. Louis, going on twenty years next month, and he had seen men injured in explosions often enough, most all of them in mining accidents. "A loss of memory is not unusual, but I think it means the brain has been damaged. The man needs rest and lots of it. My prescription is two weeks strict bed rest, Governor. I'll be back in that time to check on the patient." He walked towards the door, passing Colter in the hall.

"As for you..." he said, but after taking one look at Colter's wide grin, he just shook his head and headed out the door.

"The man don't like me," Colter said, still smiling. "Maybe it's my breath."

The four men stood around Ordway's bed, on the second story of Clark's large mansion. They were silent for a while, each deep in his own thoughts. It was Ordway who spoke up first.

"I think...we need to focus on who had access to the financials, when Mr. Lewis was in charge here," he said. "If it was indeed a theft of money and a cover-up, as you say, who would be the most likely suspect?"

"The staff wasn't that large five years ago," Clark said. "Even now, it's mainly a handful of people. When I took over last year, I brought with me my own people, individuals I knew I could count on. But Meriwether was a trusting fellow – he would not have felt the need to do that. Maybe someone exploited him. Used him. Framed him. Then killed him when it was... convenient." Clark almost spat out the last sentence in disgust.

"We spoke with Lewis' former Lt. Governor, a man named Bates. Frederick Bates. He has an estate several blocks back up into the hills." Bratton said. "Bates said Lewis was an inept manager, and claims he was a...drunkard. Said he quite likely stole the money himself, though I never believed him."

"I suggest you look a little deeper into this man," Clark said. "Find out his background, and if he had anyone else on staff who might have had a red hand in the financials."

Chapter 66

T he house was as they remembered it, a large white mansion with a cobbled walkway, set halfway up a gradually sloping hill covered with grass and small trees. From the wide porch, they could see the layout of the city of St. Louis below. Sergeant Gass looked at Bratton and Colter, nodding towards the back of the house. The two men took up their prearranged stations, one in rear of the mansion, and one by a servant's door halfway down the right side.

The sun was just rising above the housetops below as Gass knocked loudly on the stout oak door. A few minutes passed and there was no response from inside the house. He knocked again, this time declaring in a loud voice. "Mr. Frederick Bates, sir. It's urgent that I speak with you. My name is Sergeant Patrick Gass, and I'm a federal marshal. Please answer the door."

Another minute passed, and finally he heard footsteps shuffling in the hallway. The door opened and a man stood before him in a formal suit and bowler hat. "I'm sorry to inform you, sir; Mr. Bates is not at home at present. If you were to try back in a few…"

But Gass would not be denied. He flashed his badge and put his foot firmly between the frame and the door. He placed his shoulder against the solid wood and pushed his way in. "I am here on official business and you will allow me entry."

The manservant tried to protest, but Gass ignored him, walking further into the house as if it were his own. "I have a warrant to search the premises immediately," he said turning around to face the man. The servant's eye grew wider at the news, and he stammered. "This is highly improper... highly irregular... I will have to inform Mr. Bates..."

"Please do. I'd love to hear what he has to say," Gass replied. He remembered the layout of the mansion from his initial visit. The study must be upstairs, he reasoned. It would be the safest place in the house to shield against prying eyes.

He took the stairs two at a time, the manservant on his heels loudly protesting the intrusion. When he reached the door of the study, he stopped, turned and faced the man. "You will show me the key to access this room, or I will have it broken down immediately."

The man looked like he was trapped and, gritting his teeth, reached into his pocket, producing a key. He inserted it slowly, and turned the handle. The door opened with a slight creak.

Before Gass could enter, he heard a commotion downstairs. He turned and called out to his friends. "I'm upstairs! What's with all the racket?"

Colter came up the stairs, holding the sleeve of a young lad. "I found him trying to bolt out the back door. Wouldn't say a word when I asked him who he was."

The boy, who looked no more than eight or nine years old, was dressed in dirty overalls and worn shoes – not the sort of child anyone would expect to be living in such a pricey mansion. The boy looked at the manservant, his eyes wide in fright. The man returned the look with a hard stare.

"I've never seen this lad in my life," the manservant declared. "Must be a runaway. We get them from time to time. You know the sort, always looking to steal what they can from those of us who work for a living."

The boy looked at the floor, crestfallen. He shook his head dejectedly, but still refused to speak. Colter walked over and told him to sit in a chair against the wall. The lad complied, his eyes still glancing towards the man who had just disowned him.

Gass turned his attention back to the study. He walked in and looked around. It was not quite as nice as Governor Clark's, sacrificing the view for privacy. There was a stout mahogany desk against the far wall with a straight back chair, two smaller chairs in front, and a large bearskin rug spread out on the hardwood floor. A tall filing cabinet stood next to the large desk. Bates' desk was immaculate, not a paper out of place or a piece of dust to be seen. The sergeant went immediately to the filing cabinets, opening the top one, and began perusing them.

"What do you think you are looking for, if I may ask?" the manservant said defensively.

"You may not ask," Gass said. But then he turned his head, thinking better of it. "Actually, maybe you can be of assistance. I know Mr. Bates would hate to see his house invaded, his study dissected and torn up. It's such a waste of time and it will be such a mess when he returns."

The man nodded, "Yes, yes it would! I'll tell you what I can if you will just leave at once! He'll have a heart attack if he knew anyone was in his study!"

Gass smiled. "Good, I'm glad you are willing to help. But first let me tell you what we have found out as of late. Perhaps it would be a little eye opener for you to see who you are actually protecting."

"Mr. Bates is a noble man – an important man in St. Louis. He is also a good employer and I will not hear his name slandered," the manservant said defiantly.

"I'm sure he treats you well, as he should." Gass replied. "Good help is always hard to find these days. Especially when he wants things done quietly and without drawing the wrong kind of attention to himself. Someone such as you would prove a worthy accomplice."

"Accomplice? For what purpose?" the man's voice cracked slightly.

"Mr. Frederick Bates, Lt. Governor 1805-1810, formerly on the staff of Mr. Meriwether Lewis. Discharged upon new governor, Mr. Benjamin Howard, taking the oath of office, January 1810. Led a quiet retirement in the foothills of St. Louis ever since." Gass recited from memory. "However we have dug quite a bit into his past over the last few days and have come across some startling information."

The manservant remained quiet, his face a mask. The boy looked at him with a frightened expression.

"Mr. Bates was born in 1769 and raised in Boston, Massachusetts, the oldest of three siblings. Mother, a woman from a wealthy Colonial family. Father, an officer of his majesty's army, stationed in Boston in 1768. Whether the union was arranged as a matter of course to influence the king's council in Massachusetts, or if it was love at first sight, we do not really know. But it doesn't truly matter. Frederick, being the son of an English officer, was reared in the finest Boston schools, even after the revolution was over. I'm sure a little extra money in the pockets of the school's chancellors saw to that."

"That doesn't prove a thing. Many people grew up in Boston," the man said.

"True, but allow me to continue," Gass said, beginning to enjoy himself. "Upon completion of his law degree at Harvard he headed west, setting up a practice in St. Louis around 1791. Here is where it gets interesting."

"I'm all ears, sir," the man said sarcastically.

"Keeping his public life as a civil servant and a practicing lawyer out in the open for all to see, Bates also maintained close ties with…many loyalists who would like to see the British regain control of the colonies."

Gass watched his reaction and was not surprised by the man's vehement denials. "That is outrageous!" the manservant declared.

The sergeant ignored him for now, dismissing him with a wave of his hand. He wasn't finished yet. "Mr. Bates used his position as Lt. Governor, first under Governor Charles Stanley, and then by Mr. Lewis, to divert money coming from the territorial districts and secretly sending them to loyalists in support of the growing Red Coat presence in the country. He then attempted to cover his tracks by altering the financial statements."

"That…that is absurd!" the man said, but his voice began to waiver slightly. Gass wondered if the man was already suspecting as much himself.

"Finally, perhaps when things began to spiral out of control and the federal government took an interest in the missing funds, Mr. Bates decided to frame an innocent man, his own commander Governor Lewis, for the theft. But even that was not good enough, for you see," Gass turned quickly and walked directly up the man, "Mr. Lewis could deny wrongdoing, perhaps even implicate Bates. No, he had to kill Mr. Lewis, so his misdeeds would never be discovered."

"I…he would never…" the man said, but fell silent as Gass delivered the final coup-de-grace.

Chapter 67

"Coward that he is, Mr. Bates would never commit the murder himself. He arranged through a third party for the hit to take place while Mr. Lewis was traveling en route to Washington. He hired a pair of Cherokee nationals to kill Mr. Lewis, making it look like a simple robbery. Then Mr. Bates retired and lives a quiet life, perhaps attending a meeting of the loyalist club Christmas parties each year, in some remote hovel in the woods."

The man's face was pale, his eyes downcast. He looked as if his world had fallen apart, and perhaps it had. "I just don't believe it…" he started to say, his voice weak.

"Believe it, son," Gass said. "Once we started looking into his past, it wasn't hard to put the pieces together. But at the moment, most of it is just speculation – educated guesswork. It actually took a chance meeting with a poet lawyer from Baltimore who suggested to me to look for British motives. We have already tied Bates to two known loyalists in the St. Louis area and are looking for more connections. What we really need now is some concrete evidence of theft to charge him when he returns."

The man was silent for what seemed a long time, but Gass let him have his thoughts. Perhaps he would decide to cooperate. One can only hope.

"I've worked for Mr. Bates for the last ten years," he said finally. "I've seen things…unusual things…secret meetings, and letters, correspondence to people I've known to be loyalists, but I've always dismissed them…guarded my job and blocked things out to protect my employer – protect Mr. Bates.

"But if what you said is true, that he setup and ordered the murder of Mr. Lewis, to hide behind his stealing, and the funding of the British, I can't help him. My brother was killed fighting against Tecumseh last year – if Bates had a hand in his death..." he looked directly into Gass' eyes.

Gass smiled – he had an ally now.

"Can you tell us about his staff, or someone who might have helped him transfer the funds out? It was probably done as a courier transfer through a third party, perhaps even the Indians as they are aligning themselves with the British these days. Anything to push us out of their territory."

"He keeps his staff small, maybe for fear of trusting too many of the wrong people. The man on the staff closest to him would be his assistant, a man by the name of Richards. Joseph Richards. He's a bit of a strong willed character if you ask me. Quiet, but resourceful."

Gass wrote down the name. As he was talking, he noticed the boy began to fidget in his chair. "Do you have something you'll like to add, boy?" The manservant looked down at his feet sheepishly.

"That's my son," he said quietly. "I didn't mention it earlier..."

"My name is Daniel, sir. My papa thinks I get in trouble too often, so please don't have him fired, ok? But something happened the other day that...well, I just didn't think anyone would get hurt, you know?"

Gass walked over and knelt in front of the boy. The small lad looked down, putting his hand into the pocket of his overalls and slowly pulled out a copper penny. "Mr. Richards paid me to watch his horse for him the other day. To stand by so he can make a quick escape. Said he had to give something to a man coming in off the stage and they might not like what they get. I don't think he saw me peek, but he came onto the platform...and was wearing the stage vest I've seen Rudy wear when he's on duty.

"Then he walked back in to the station, and ran out the back where I was waitin'. I thought nothin' of it, until I heard a loud bang a minute or so later. Thought it was fireworks, maybe. So I ran over to see what was going on. And I see people hurt in the street, blood on them," he looked directly at John Colter standing next to him, "I was scared...I knew it had to be Mr. Richards who done it...when he don't like someone, he gets even one way or another."

Gass looked at Colter. "Well, well. I think we have to pay Mr. Joseph Richards a visit today."

"He left with Mr. Bates...that's what I'm not supposed to tell you, and he'll kill us both if he found out..." the manservant said, a tear coming down his face. "But if you catch up to them, maybe you can...put an end to them, permanent like..."

"We don't plan on killing anyone," Gass said evenly, "But you need to tell us where they are...it's very important we find them."

"Mr. Bates took his travel bag with him, and Mr. Richards drove him to the stage yesterday morning. They said if anyone asked about him, to say he was going up to Indianapolis for a conference. That he'd be back in a few weeks. But I heard them talking the night before – they don't often think people like us have ears you see…but they're headed for New Orleans."

Colter said, snapping his fingers excitedly, "New Orleans! That's where the British are gathering! Some say, they hope to make a last stand there. The war is almost over and they know it. Perhaps Bates knows it too and is hoping to meet up with his own sort there."

Gass nodded his head in agreement. "You have been most helpful. Mr. Bates is not coming back, one way or another. If I were you, I'd take the boy and move on, head somewhere you have family, or can get employment. Let us deal with Mr. Bates."

That night, the four deputies had one final meeting with Governor Clark at his mansion. Ordway refused to stay behind, claiming he felt fine. "Just a little ringing in my ears, sir, but I've suffered far worse. I'm ready to put an end to this."

Clark looked at the men assembled before him. "Go to New Orleans, find Bates and bring him back for trial. If you cannot take him alive, make sure he gets justice meted out to him. Think of Captain Lewis and what he's meant to us all. Give him closure."

"Hear, hear," Gass replied. The four men clinked their glasses, filled to the top with the finest red wine in Mr. Clark's cool basement. Their final toast.

"To Captain Lewis," Bratton said.

"To the Corps. The Corps of Discovery," Ordway added. "And to the friendships that we have forged in the fires of our journey."

"Gentleman, this battle is yours now," Clark addressed them. "I will remain here, and finish going through Mr. Bates' house and papers – I will find the concrete evidence we need to bring him to trial. And keep an eye out for that Richards fellow – he already tried to blow you up, and he may very well have been responsible for your attack in Washington. I've shown the ivory handled knife York took off the man who invaded my estate to Bates' servant, Miles, and he's confirmed that it belongs to Richards. If you do see him, proceed with caution."

"As always," Gass said. "But he probably knows we'll be coming for him. If he's the kind of man who expects trouble, he'll have something up his sleeve."

"I've already alerted the authorities in Memphis to stop the coach when they arrive and take Mr. Bates and Mr. Richards into lockup. I've given them basic charges of theft and attempted murder, which will certainly hold them for now. They will hold them until you arrive to pick up the prisoners."

"Understood, governor," Gass said.

The next morning John Ordway, Patrick Gass, John Colter, and William Bratton mounted the best horses found anywhere in St. Louis, taking off at a fast clip along a well beaten path to the south. Clark stood in front on his estate watching them go, confident in their abilities, but worried all the same. He turned and looked up at the second story window facing the street. A young face peered down at him smiling, and he waved to the lad. Jean-Baptiste was growing up fast and he knew it wouldn't be too long before he was out having adventures all his own. Worrying about those you were responsible for, no matter how old they are, was a part of life. "Good luck, gentlemen," he said softly, taking one last look down the road, wondering if he would see any of them again.

The horses that Clark had procured for the four men ran swiftly along the dirt pathways, carrying their charges without complaint. Over the next several hours they covered dozens of miles, stopping only once to allow their mounts to drink from a creek they had to traverse.

Their spirits were high and they covered the distance quickly over the next few days. The Mississippi River was a constant companion off to their left and they were never far from the sound of its rushing waters. Its twists and turns made slow progress by sea and they were grateful they chose the more direct approach overland.

The stage would have taken its course along a similar path, and by now should have reached Memphis, almost 400 miles along the route to New Orleans. Colter wanted to see the look on the faces of the men when they were stopped by the Memphis sheriff. After the attack on Ordway and himself earlier in the week, he was itching for some payback.

On the fourth day out, they began to see the outlying farms around Memphis, and by that evening had rode into the main district area. Colter wanted to stop for a pint but was voted down by his fellow riders. They rode slowly up the dirt road that constituted the main thoroughfare in the city, shops and saloons decorating both sides of the street. People milled about, often cutting directly across the street, causing riders and horses alike to pull up short.

They found the small office marked simply 'Sheriff' and dismounted at the post outside, where they tied their horses. Gass strode in first then stopped short.

"What's the problem, Patrick?" Ordway asked behind him.

Slowly Gass walked in, his eyes looking around quickly. A lone sheriff deputy sat at a desk, facing three empty cells.

"I'm Marshal Patrick Gass, from St. Louis. I am expecting to transport some prisoners that Governor Clark had telegrammed you about several days ago."

The deputy looked at him, his face questioning. "I remember the message. Problem was your men were not on the stage. It arrived right about noon yesterday but it only held two women, an elderly gentleman, and the driver. I interviewed all of them, and none of them seemed to know this Bates fellow. I had to let them all go."

Gass walked around and pounded his fist on the desk, making the sheriff's deputy jump in surprise. "They might have gotten off before Memphis and switched to a horse or a wagon. They're probably close to New Orleans even as we speak."

"Or perhaps they just fooled you, by dressing up as the driver and an old man – Richards can be devious and I wouldn't put it past him," Ordway said. "Remember how the boy told us he dressed like the baggage handler at the station to slip in the dynamite in John's bag."

Bratton growled, "Well, they ain't here now. So where do we go?"

Colter said what was on all their minds, "I'm afraid we're going to New Orleans, gentlemen. And hope to hell we find him before he meets up with the British."

The Expedition Continues

Chapter 68

August 15, 1806
Fort Mandan, Montana

T he summer sun was high overhead, beating down on the land beneath. The clear water of the Missouri River reflected the heat back onto the people in the three canoes, but they hardly seemed to notice. Several red faces peaked from beneath wide brim hats pulled low over them, but no one complained.

The child had slept most of the morning in the second canoe, and was now looking at the forests and valleys around him as they passed by. His mother soothed him with her quiet words and caressed the back of his head. His black hair was coming in quite full now and he sported several new teeth, which gave his smile a whole new look. Sacagawea said softly to him in Hidatsa, "We're almost home."

John Colter was paddling the lead canoe with Captain Lewis sitting behind him nursing his leg, a strip of white cotton cloth bandaging his thigh. He had not been able to walk since the accidental shooting, and the captain was anxious about the future. Would he recover quickly? How will his injury impact the rest of the voyage home? He wanted to do his share of the work, but the injury hampered his movements. Besides, Clark would have his head if he did anything that caused the bleeding to start up again.

They headed down a straight stretch of river, and Lewis scanned ahead and around them, cataloging things in his journals. Suddenly, he saw a few men camping along the shoreline to their left. At first he thought they were natives, perhaps Mandan, but as they got closer, he saw they were white men – trappers most likely.

As they approached the camp, the two figures waved at them and Lewis told his men to head for shore. They might have news from the civilized world and he wanted to learn what he could. After George Shannon and Hugh McNeil pulled the boat alongside and tied it off to two trees that hugged the water line, Colter and Bratton got out, supporting Lewis between them. They carried him to a fallen tree so he could sit comfortably.

The two men came over, shaking hands all around. "The name's Dixon, sir. Joseph Dixon. This here," he turned to indicate his partner, "is Forrest Hancock. We've spent the summer trappin' along the Missouri. There's some fine pelts to be had in these parts. Beaver, 'coons, and the like."

"Yes, that is true – animals are aplenty," Lewis said. By this time Clark had come ashore and walked over to join them. The third boat was just coming in now.

"Clark," the captain said, shaking hands with the men. "William Clark – we've completed a full exploration of the Louisiana territories all the way to the Pacific Ocean. We're headed back for St. Louis – haven't seen civilization in two years or more. What can you tell us?"

"William Clark? We've heard of you – who hasn't?" Hancock said. He turned to Lewis, "That must make you…"

"Meriwether Lewis, yes. Pardon me for not getting up but I suffered a bit of an accident recently and…"

"Oh, no need to apologize! I can't believe you – any of you - are alive! I must say you've been gone so long, the American people had given you up for dead long ago." Dixon said, a large grin spreading on his face. "I can't wait to see what reception you'll get upon your return to St. Louis!"

Colter came over, fingering some of the pelts that Dixon was carrying. "These aren't half bad. Who's the shearer?"

"I do that, for the most part," Dixon said. "Forrest is the trapper – he knows all about setting the right traps for the right animal. But I'll tell you what we need…"

"I can tell you that," Colter said smiling. "You're in territory you've never laid eyes on before. You don't have any idea what's ahead for you. You need someone to show you where to go and how to find the best furs in the land."

Lewis smiled at him. "Would you know of someone like that, John?"

Dixon looked from one man to the other, "Exactly! We need a guide – and someone who understands about trappin' and…"

Bratton came up, "Sir, should we set up a camp here? It's only midday, but if you'd like to stay, I'll see to it."

"No, William, that won't be necessary. We'll leave in an hour or so. Don't want to delay our return any longer than necessary," Clark said. "Besides, I don't want to impose our large party on these two men for very long."

"You're not imposing at all!" Dixon said loudly. "Why just meeting you has been the best part of the journey so far! We met up with several natives about a day's journey from here," he pointed his thumb back down the river, "and traded several furs. They were very receptive to us. Is that the way you've seen the Indians in these parts?"

Colter said, smiling, "Joseph, you need a guide now more than ever. Believe me when I tell you, there are natives out there who'll skin YOU alive if they catch you. Captain Lewis can attest to that, can't you, sir?"

Lewis just nodded. His encounter with the Blackfoot had left an empty feeling inside him – he hated having to kill those two men, and he wished he could have done something different – anything – that could have prevented it. Now the Blackfoot will be more wary of white men coming into their territory. He hoped he had not set the stage for future conflicts with them. Settlers were sure to come west in the coming years – good relationships with the natives were of utmost importance.

Dixon turned to Colter, "Do you know anyone – perhaps from your group – that would be willing to join us as a guide? We'd pay you of course – and everyone would be better off for it."

Colter looked down, as he mulled it over. Before he answered, he turned to address his commanders. "Captain Lewis, Captain Clark. I'd like to join these men. The expedition is nearly over and this would be a great opportunity to continue exploring these parts. Besides, Dixon and Hancock are in need of someone with my knowledge and experience. Would you be inclined to discharge me early so I can join them?"

Lewis eyed his partner who nodded. "Yes, I think we can grant you that privilege, John. We should be home within the month as it is, and you've more than fulfilled your duties with us. Once you make your arrangements with these gentlemen, we'll give you your payment and your official discharge papers."

"Thank you, Captain Lewis," Colter said. He turned to Dixon and Hancock, who could not seem to believe their good fortune. "You've got yourself a guide, gentlemen."

Before they parted way, Clark paid Colter his salary based on their agreed on rate of five dollars per month, along with papers Lewis had drawn up that granted him an honorable discharge from their service. After shaking hands and wishing him luck, the captains and remaining journeymen returned to their canoes and pushed off downstream, headed for the native villages further along the river.

Colter watched them go, as his new partners Dixon and Hancock chatted on about what they might see up in the Montana wilderness. Colter smiled, as he turned to them. *You've no idea.*

Chapter 69

The three canoes continued down the Missouri throughout the afternoon and camped overnight several miles away. The next morning brought occasional sightings of natives along the bank. They identified one group as Mandan and Clark ordered the crew to come ashore. He alone got out and approached the small group of men. They spoke briefly and Gass noticed the captain pass a piece of parchment to one of the natives. The Indians left quickly, running back into the woods. When Clark returned, he was silent as he wrote in his own journal.

"Excuse me, captain, but what was that about?" Gass asked, as he paddled back into the center of the river.

Clark continued writing for another minute, then closed the book and returned it to his satchel beside him. "I asked them to fetch Rene Jessaume and gave them a missive. We've used Rene a few times when we were camped here for the winter, two years back if you recall. He's a trapper that did some interpreting for us with the Mandan. I wanted him to spread the word among the local tribes and see if we can get someone to come with us to Washington. I know Nathaniel tried his best, but I still cling to hope we can succeed in bringing one or two chiefs with us. That will make a big impact when we try and negotiate for western trading settlements."

"I agree, captain," Gass said. "But he'll need some time to organize that – I hope he can find someone in time. We can't delay long."

The next day brought more good weather and the mood among the journeymen was running high. By noon several Indians could be seen along the banks of the river spearing fish or gathering water. Many heads turned as they passed and several raised their arm in greeting. By the time the small caravan had reached the shores of the Hidatsa village, a large crowd had gathered to greet them.

Meriwether Lewis was the first to disembark from the lead canoe, assisted by Gass and George Shannon, followed by Sacagawea carrying Jean-Baptiste, and then her husband, Touissant Charbonneau. The Canadian looked around and stamped his feet on the ground, as if affirming he was back on familiar soil. He grinned as he saw the large form of Chief Swift Eagle. Walking over, the trapper gave the Indian a bear hug that left the chief speechless.

Clark came up behind Lewis after telling his men to disembark. Rene was there to greet the returning men. He came up to them both, shaking hands all around. "Welcome back, sirs! Most happy for your safe return!"

His voice dropped an octave as he came in closer to state the results of his recent efforts. "I have been around the villages and am confident that the Mandan chief, Big White, will agree to accompany you to Washington. I told him to be ready when you come by later today."

"That's splendid news, Rene! Splendid!" Clark said, his voiced filled with excitement. "That will go a long way in Washington, to have a man of his stature to negotiate with."

Swift Eagle ordered a few men to kill a large pig that had been kept just for this occasion, and had it dressed and ready to cook in short order. Others gathered roots and vegetables, while several older boys gathered wood for a roaring bonfire that evening.

Sacagawea seemed happy as she explained many of their adventures to the assembled audience, allowing her husband's second wife, Otter Woman, to hold her nineteen month old son. The rivalry they once had shared was gone now, as Sacagawea had everything she wanted in life – a son, a husband, and stories to tell until she was an old woman. No one could take that from her.

"Chief, allow me to show you some very handsome silk scarves, all the way from the tribes on the Pacific!" Clark said in a booming voice, as he approached the group mingling around the boats. It was times like these he didn't need any interpretation. He was in his element now, displaying fine wares obtained from his adventures to the newcomers. He wanted to show everyone what could be traded for, if people were willing to invest in establishing a regular route across the land.

Sacagawea and Charbonneau sat together with Jean-Baptiste, watching the bonfire start to burn, as they realized they were finally home after two years away. Clark approached them, holding out his hand to the Canadian.

"It's been a pleasure, Touissant." He didn't need an interpreter for this exchange. Over the months, the trapper had gotten used to his English and Clark himself had learned a little French. *Together, we're almost understandable.* He chuckled at the thought.

"I want to…thank you…for the opportunity," Charbonneau said in halting English. "Sacagawea and Jean-Baptiste…thank you too."

Clark smiled. "Well, I am not quite done yet. There is the matter of the payment for your services." He pulled from his satchel a smaller sack, from which he carefully counted out several bills and some coins totaling the agreed-on rate. He placed them in the Frenchman's hands.

"Before we take our leave tonight, there is one more important matter I wanted to discuss with you. It involves all of you, actually. There is the matter of educating little Pomp, who I must say I have grown more attached to each day. There are schools back east that can teach him all matter of subjects, from math to writing, and who knows? He might want to take advantage of opportunities back in civilization that he just won't find here."

"What exactly are you asking, captain?"

"I'd like permission to bring Pomp back east with me. He would live with me and go to an American school. Money is no object – my estate is large enough to accommodate all his needs. It's a better life for him than he would get living in a native village. You've lived in civilization, Touissant – you alone know the importance of a decent education. Let him come back with me."

The Frenchman looked down at his wife and son, and slowly interpreted the captain's wishes to Sacagawea. At first, she looked fearful, as she realized she might have to give up their only child. But then she stood and faced the captain. She knew him to be honorable, and she trusted him. But she wasn't ready to give up her only son… not yet.

She spoke to her husband and as they discussed the matter, Clark walked around the fire studying the land, thinking about the future. He knew he was right about Pomp's education. What kind of life would the boy have if he remained here? He was already at a disadvantage, being a product of mixed parentage. He deserved a chance to…

"Captain, we have come… to a decision."

Clark turned and walked back, trying to keep his emotions in check. "What do you think of my proposal?"

"Sacagawea…says the boy is not…weaned. She feels in…a year's time…he would be old enough. We want you to…educate him – give him a good start in life. Can you…come back in a year?"

Clark smiled and the men shook hands on it. "I would love nothing more than to return here, Touissant. I will be back in one year's time and I promise you, I will take good care of him then."

They all ate well and drank much of the ale that the explorers had on board their canoes. It was a great feast that lasted until late afternoon.

Finally, it was time to say good-bye to their Hidatsa friends, but Clark reminded them that it was only temporary. He would return in a year and they said they would look for him.

The canoes continued down the Missouri, stopping shortly at the Mandan village to pick up Big White, their excited chief who was ready to accompany them to Washington. Dressed in traditional leather garments, and wearing a full headdress of colorful feathers, he looked every inch the part of Indian chief. Clark welcomed him wholeheartedly aboard.

The following morning, August 17, brought a light, warm rain, but it cleared up within a few hours. The progress was much faster than the trip west, in large part due to the current pushing them along and the wind at their backs. Having fought against the current for the entire trip west to the Bitterroot Mountains, Captain Clark and his men seemed to take an immense pleasure in having nature aid them for once.

With the swift wind helping to clear the cloudy skies to the east, it was Lewis who noticed the man running toward them along the left bank. He was a native, a large man dressed in leather garments, and beads hanging around his neck in a primitive necklace. He waved to the boats, trying to get noticed. Lewis ordered the boats to shore, to find out what he wanted.

The man ignored the first canoe as it approached but looked beyond it to the second canoe. Lewis turned around and could see the Mandan chief, Big White, smiling and waving back at the man. Lewis smiled and wondered just what was going on.

When Big White's canoe came ashore, the man on the beach rushed up to him, talking in Mandan with quick, short bursts. It was clear he was out of breath, evidently having run a great distance. Lewis remained in the boat, as did most of the men. Clark, Gass, and George Shannon accompanied Big White onto the land, and the two Indians talked in earnest. After a few minutes, the pair grew quiet and Big White finally turned to Clark.

In halting English, Big White explained "He... is my brother. His name is...Toscupah." He attempted to use sign language as he explained how his brother was gone on a hunting trip the day Big White took his leave of the village to head east with Clark, and he ran many miles to catch up with them to say his goodbye. Big White's eyes were moist and it was clear that his brother's actions touched him deeply.

"I understand, Chief," Clark said. "Please tell your brother you will return here a hero."

Big White nodded, conveying the sentiment to his brother Toscupah, who broke out in a wide grin.

Chapter 70

T he sun was high in the sky, its light shining through a handful of thin clouds to the west. It had been nearly three weeks since the last rain had fallen, and Lewis found himself treating cases of sunburn on a few of the men. The temperature was unusually high, hovering around 85 degrees.

As they prepared dinner in camp that evening, Hugh McNeil approached Lewis, sitting on a log looking at the fire. "Captain, may I have a word with you?"

"Sure, Hugh," Lewis said. He could tell right away something was amiss. "What's wrong with your eyes? Don't tell me you have the same thing as Shannon and Potts."

"I can hardly see, my eyes are so itchy and crusted over," McNeil lamented.

Lewis stood up, favoring his good leg as he did so. Walking was easier these days, as the wound had been healing for more than a month. But putting much weight on it for too long caused him discomfort, and he sat whenever he could.

The captain brought him over to the firelight, and looked into the private's eyes. They were red and bloodshot, just like the others.

"It appears you all share the same ailment, Mr. McNeil," Lewis announced. "Red irritating eyes, crusted over…the only thing I can think of to treat it with is warm compresses over the area. Maybe the heat and dampness may draw the malady out and away from the eyes."

"What do you think caused it, sir?" McNeil asked as Lewis cut a strip of cloth and soaked it in a kettle of water sitting on some low burning coals.

"When the other two first approached with these symptoms yesterday, I really wasn't sure," Lewis responded. "But I've had some time to think it through. I'm inclined to believe it's not from a sickness in as much as a form of snow blindness."

"Snow blindness? But, captain, it's warm out! It's only mid-September."

"I believe the same principle applies in both cases. The strong sunlight we've been having reflects off the surface of the river almost as efficiently as it would off snow. The reflection of the heat or light must adversely affect the eyes. If someone looks at the water too long with such a strong light reflecting off it, you might experience the same symptoms as you and the others have."

After Lewis had applied the dressing, and told the man to rest for the night, he made his way over to his partner, who was talking with William Bratton. Clark looked up when he heard him.

"Something must be up for you to walk over to see me, Meriwether. How's the leg today?"

"Painful as always but manageable. Next time you want to go hunting, don't send Cruzatte out with you. He might hit you instead."

Clark laughed heartily. "I'll take that under advisement. But just remember it was not I who sent him out in the first place. He took it into his own head to catch an elk that day. You weren't even supposed to be in the area yet."

"The fault is mine alone. I should be more careful with my time and make sure I am suitably late from now on."

"Now that we've established who is to blame, what brings you over? Surely it's not for a spot of my tea?"

"McNeil just came to see me. Same eye condition as Shannon and Potts. That makes three people in two days. None of them can see worth a damn right now. I've given them warm compresses to wear over their eyes, but it won't improve by tomorrow. If they are out of commission, I'm concerned about having enough manpower to support all three canoes."

"We can't delay our return any longer. I even vetoed a hunt that the Field brothers wanted to run this afternoon. The sooner we get back the better. What if we use just two canoes? We can transfer the goods from the third one and redistribute them into the other two. Since they'll be heavier, maybe we'll lash them together to avoid a spill."

"That sounds like a reasonable plan. Let's get the men on it first thing in the morning," Lewis said, happier now that this concern had been addressed.

The next day, using only two canoes, the party continued their journey down the Missouri river. The sky began to fill with clouds by late morning, and the strong rays of the sun seem to be held at bay for the time being. Lewis was pleased to note that there were no more cases of sore eyes, and that perhaps his theory of light blindness might have been correct.

Just before they were to stop for dinner and camp, the explorers came across a few huts scattered about on the far left bank. Another quarter mile brought them to a larger group of small buildings of similar design. They were clearly European in shape and form, and when Lewis saw the first people approach them, he was certain of where he was.

"This must be La Charette, that little French village, which Rene had told me about. Remember, it was little more than a single hut when we crossed here two years ago." People numbering about a dozen came out to greet them, and the weary travelers beached their craft on the far shore.

Clark called out a hearty welcome and asked to speak with their governor. A man dressed in a simple cotton shirt and knickers raised his hand in acknowledgement. "I am he. Sir Frances Youngman. Welcome Captains!"

Several of the party wanted to celebrate the return to the civilized world in a hearty firearm salute, and having been granted permission from Youngman, three men were picked for this duty. Clark chose Sergeant Pryor — having lost his cousin, Charlie Floyd, early on the journey, it was felt he had earned the privilege. Lewis chose Patrick Gass, honoring him for his tremendous leadership and tactical qualities, as well as his skill in designing all their permanent camps. The last person who would do the salute was Lewis himself. Clark insisted on it, feeling he owed it to his partner for being somewhat responsible for his injury. Lewis accepted, though he said Clark was still not off the hook.

Three rifles rose into the air, and three volleys of round ball shot high into the air, one after the other. When the salute was finished, several Canadian trappers who were on shore with the French fired off five rounds of their own; a testament to the courage of the explorers.

Once the Americans had come ashore, they met up with the trappers, learning they were of Scot heritage living in the country to the north for the present. "We're on our way to do some fur trading with the Osage tribe, but we'd love to show you and your men our other wares," one of them said.

The trappers gave freely of some pork and beef to the men of the Corps, and then sold them two gallons of whiskey for eight dollars in cash. Clark and Lewis had the men establish a camp along the shore line, after which they enjoyed an evening of merriment and ale.

"You know, Captain Lewis," Governor Youngman said, as he swallowed a long draft of his own whiskey, "we never expected to see you – any of you – again. Two years is a long time to be lost in the wilderness, and well, most folk had given you up for dead." He flashed a wide grin and he raised his cup once again. "I'm certainly glad to be the one to announce your return!"

"We're not quite done yet – we still need to go to St. Louis. By my calculations given the current speed, we ought to reach it in three days time. We're almost home, governor! If you want to send a wire to the dispatch in St. Louis and announce our return, I'd be much obliged."

Chapter 71

The following day, late in the afternoon, the lights of the port city of St. Charles could be seen in the distance and the group of explorers sent a loud cheer and hurrah. Upon arriving near the shoreline, Clark allowed the men to initiate another firearm salute, as many of its citizens came out to greet them.

They used the opportunity to purchase new clothes for Chief Big White from a local merchant, acquiring for him a few European accessories that he enjoyed. He was in wondrous awe of such a large city, touching things and trying to converse with the people in his own native tongue, or with sign language. For many of the citizens, this was their first contact with a real native, and they were equally curious as well.

"This is the last stop before we arrive in St. Louis, gentlemen," Clark said as they made camp that night. "By afternoon two days hence, we shall be returning heroes! Let us give thanks to God for granting us safe passage home." The men bowed their heads as one, allowing Clark to lead them in prayer.

True to his word, the party approached the last stop on their journey a day and a half later. The hour of their triumphant return was at hand, as the canoes passed the outskirts of St. Louis. Captain William Clark turned and addressed his fellow journeyman as people began lining the shores to watch them come in. "Gentlemen, it gives me great pleasure to welcome you to the end of our passage – the great city of St. Louis!"

The men gave a mighty cheer, clapped each other on the back, and shook hands all around. The rowers dipped their paddles in deeper as they approached the port, eager to set foot firmly on the soil marking their return.

"Captain Lewis, please record it in your journals of the official record – On September 23, 1806, we return to St. Louis, having traveled over 8,000 miles over a span of two years, four months, and two days. We have accomplished for the United States of America what very few thought possible. In honor of our great leader, President Thomas Jefferson, we have returned conquering heroes!"

The people of St. Louis received their guests warmly, inviting many of the men to their own homes for a warm meal and a comfortable bed. Captain Clark arranged lodgings for both Lewis and himself at the home of the local mayor, a short, thin Irish man with spectacles and a generous smile named Kevin O'Grady. His estate was not large, but the three bedroom ranch was sufficient for their needs. Mrs. O'Grady had a large pot of pork stew cooking when the three men entered, and they shared stories of their adventures during the evening meal.

While sitting before a warm fire in the hearth, Captain Lewis penned a personal letter to President Jefferson announcing their joyous return and arranging passage to Washington with their visiting native spokesman, Chief Big White. When he was finished, he put down his quill and sat looking into the fire reflectively.

Clark approached him, and stood by his side for several minutes without saying anything. The fire was warm upon his face and he closed his eyes, taking it all in.

"It's over, Meriwether. It's hard to believe! We've accomplished our mission – and I must say I was quite a skeptic at times, especially through the long winter months. But we had a great crew and God was watching over us the whole time. It's quite a feather in our caps, my good friend. The political ramifications will be extraordinary! I expect a stronger drive to settle in the west, now that we know what's out there. Trading agreements with different native tribes, and so much more!"

Lewis remained thoughtful for a little while longer before he spoke. "Yes, there is all that. But I often wonder what the impact of the white man's constant push into Indian territory will bring. I'm still a bit haunted by my brush with the Blackfoot, I suppose, William. But it made me understand something – our very presence in the territory, trading with everyone – will upset the natural balance these tribes have right now with each other. We could be starting a tribal war, something we won't be able to stop. That's something I believe needs a great deal of attention as our civilization expands westward. Something I intend to bring up with President Jefferson when we see him."

"I don't think anything will stop the natural push west, Meriwether. It's in our nature to explore the unknown. What we like to call Manifest Destiny. The entire country of America running from ocean to ocean."

"William, we've seen the unknown land in the west. It's beautiful, it's dangerous, it's wild and unpredictable. But it's also full of people already, and we should implore the president – in fact anyone who ventures west – to respect their cultures and their ways. It's in the best interests of both us and the native tribes to get along – cooperate and learn about each other."

Lewis looked up at his tall partner, standing beside him. "I'm extremely happy about the success of our journey, William. We've discovered and cataloged a great deal of data about the land, and mapped thousands of miles of passages that will be used for decades to come. I only hope we see fit to look beyond the numbers and see a land that is alive and flourishing, and not be so quick to put our own stamp on it. It's a land of opportunity – let us all share in its riches together."

The Investigation Continues

Chapter 72

L arge, green leaves from the tobacco fields rose high off the ground, spread out through the fifteen acres that belonged to Dilmore Hubard. The tall Creole lifted his long bladed knife high in the air and brought it down cleanly through the plant at the base. Tossing the crop into the wagon behind him, he repeated the process several more times. The plants rose all the way to his chest and he paused a moment as he surveyed the ten rows he had harvested that morning. *Five more to go and I'll be able to move on to the Rosewood fields after high noon.*

Suddenly, Hubard heard voices on the road – English speaking if he were any judge, although it had been several years since he had heard the tongue. Curious, he lifted his head up higher in order to see better over his prized crop. Two men on horseback were traveling along the path, their bags small and light. *Not planning on staying long, I reckon.*

As they approached, he waved his hand and called out in French. The men stopped and looked at him, and for a brief moment, Hubard felt a chill travel up his spine. One of the men looked slightly overweight and on the far side of forty, but it was his companion that gave the farmer pause. The newcomer wore a long, black coat, with a wide-brimmed hat pulled down low, covering his face. He had a thin frame, yet Hubard felt that beneath the coat, he would find a body hardened by years of discipline and hardship. Neither man smiled as the thin one approached him.

"Greetings," the man in the black coat said evenly.

Hubard smiled back at him, wiping the sweat from his brow with the back of his shirtsleeve.

"Bonjour," the farmer said politely. There was something about the man that was unsettling, but he couldn't put his finger on it.

"New Orleans?" the man asked pointing further down the road. "Is this the way to the port of New Orleans?"

Hubard understood that he wanted directions into the city, and he smiled. Nodding his head, he pointed down the path, saying "Suivez la route. Droite de séjour jusqu'à ce que vous veniez au fleuve." *Follow the road. Turn right until you come to the river.*

Joseph Richards nodded his thanks and tipped his hat to the farmer. He rejoined his boss as they continued along the small dirt road into New Orleans. Frederick Bates looked red under the sun, despite the mild temperature. Winter in the south was so much warmer than St. Louis, and he had not accounted for the difference before hurriedly packing his clothes before catching the stage.

He envied Richards – the man never wavered from his tried-and-true overcoat, often claiming it brought him good luck. More over, it was big enough to conceal his identity if needed, or to smuggle in a piece or two when the demands of the job required it.

Frederick Bates had no formal plan in mind where to make the jump, although it shouldn't be too hard. He knew from personal missives the British were massing their forces in Jamaica, in preparation for an overwhelming assault on the meager, yet strategically important port city of New Orleans. Once he had delivered himself to their commander he would share his knowledge of the Americans in exchange for safe haven. He thought for a moment, trying to come up with the British commander's name. *I believe Pakenham is mounting this assault – Major-General Sir Edward Pakenham, if I remember correctly. A hero of the Peninsular War with France, from what I read of him.*

After the recent defeat of Napoleon, the English fleet was finally permitted to set sail for the former colonies and bring them to heel. With my information on the American forces, the English will be in New Orleans by mid-week, he thought. Smiling to himself, Bates kicked his heels in the sides of his brown mount, and caught up to Richards.

That night brought a shower of rain upon the valley and the new dawn did little to clear the subsequent fog. The tobacco fields were covered in mist and the four men who approached the farm didn't see the tall man look out his window as they passed. More travelers – a rough looking bunch. They also seemed to be carrying lightly, he thought, which was good. Hope they won't be stayin' too long.

"Where do you figure we are, Sergeant?" Bratton asked.

Gass smiled. "Well, we've been following this road since leaving Baton Rouge yesterday, so it should be maybe a day, perhaps a little less, until we hit the outskirts of the town. But this fog makes it impossible to see much more than 20 feet in front of you."

"What makes you think we have any chance of finding Bates? There must be many ways of getting in and out of New Orleans," Colter interjected.

Ordway, who led the procession, cocked his head around sideways to see him. "Because, if you looked at the map we found in Jackson, you dirt bag, you'll see the city is blocked from the north and east by lakes. I doubt he'll risk the isolation and slower pace traveling on the river, which makes this his most likely route. Or don't you know how to read?"

Colter was about to launch his own attack when Gass trotted his horse between them. "Cut the crap, Ordway," the sergeant said. "John brings up a valid point. But rest assured, we will get him. We owe it to Mr. Clark…and Mr. Lewis."

By nightfall, they had skirted round to the south side of Lake Pontchartrain, and stared across the flat horizon that led to New Orleans. The area was marshy and wet, a constant reminder of the proximity to the large lake. The mosquitoes were out in force, attacking any exposed skin they could find. This simply gave Colter another excuse to let loose a verbal tirade against the small insects.

They continued along the marshy road and the horses found softer soil on which to tread. Bratton's black and white mare got stuck in the syrupy mess at one point and panicked, almost throwing his rider before Colter was able to coax him to safety. After another hour, they arrived at the headway into New Orleans.

It was the first time any of them had really seen the city and they were startled by its geography. Standing on the north end, they looked down into a deep valley where the city extended. The large lake acted as a natural boundary to the north, while the broad Mississippi River twisted its way below them along a high plain, forming a cup-shaped southern border with the city proper laid out before them. The valley itself was spread out over a dozen square mile area from their vantage point. Even at this late hour, a few ships could be seen making their way down the Mississippi River heading for the Gulf of Mexico 100 miles to the south.

"Sure makes for an interesting town," Ordway said, surveying the land.

"Well, it's almost the late dinner hour, so let's get into town before we totally lose what light we have," Gass said as he gently nudged his white mare forward.

Following single file, the four men made their way down a gradual slope to the bottom of the valley, where they encountered a straight muddy road taking them through more fields, mostly tobacco and indigo. Working the fields were a mixture of French-speaking Creoles, slaves, free blacks, and whites, most of whom didn't bother to look at the newcomers. With the news of the British fleet off their shores, more people were leaving the area. Very few were arriving.

They were looking for the headquarters of the military adjunct in charge of the district and they found him with little difficulty. A large mansion a quarter mile from the riverfront was guarded by several men carrying Springfield muskets. They came to attention as the four men dismounted in front of the house.

Gass introduced themselves as federal marshals, and asked to see the military commander. One of them, a young lad with red hair and freckles that reminded the Irishman of a nephew back home, quickly examined their badges before allowing them entrance.

"I will see if he is available," the lad said. "If you'd kindly wait here, I'll be back shortly."

Chapter 73

The four men waited for ten minutes before the French doors opened upstairs and a tall striking figure stood looking down from a balcony above. He wore the tunic of a high ranking officer, blue with red collar and cuffs, and real brass buttons. His jacket was neatly adorned with several rows of medals to boot. His shoulder-boards with epitaphs marked his rank and the importance of his position. His white shirt was tied at the neck with a white ascot, and his pants were black, pressed and neatly trimmed.

He descended the stairs, examining his guests as he went. At the last step, he paused, and introduced himself. "Gentlemen, I am General Andrew Jackson, commander of the Seventh Military District. Am I to believe you are federal marshals?"

Gass stepped forward. "Yes sir. I am Sergeant Patrick Gass, and these are my men, John Ordway, William Bratton, and John Colter. We are here on official business from Governor William Clark of the Missouri Territory. We are on the trail of a murder suspect, who is believed to be a British loyalist. It is our understanding he is here in New Orleans attempting to rendezvous with the British forces. He was a high-ranking member of the Missouri government and may possess information that will aid the enemy. He has already secretly funneled hundreds, perhaps thousands, of dollars of government money through Indian couriers to those aiding the British cause. Moreover, he has orchestrated the murder of a very important American figure, Governor Meriwether Lewis. "

"What is it you ask of me, Sergeant?"

"Simply your cooperation, at this point. You know the situation with the British and have knowledge of the land and the people. It is important we lay our hands on this man before he gets a chance to make his escape."

"Right now, I need every available man to help solidify our defenses. If this man is a British spy with such a storied past, I will do what I can to assist you, but I can only give you one or two men at most. But first, come with me and I'll acquaint you with the situation."

He led the way back up the circular staircase, before passing through the French doors into a spacious room, complete with a long wooden table and several straight back wooden chairs. Several documents and maps lay spread out over the table.

General Jackson came to the head of the table and indicated to the four men to have a seat. "Let me begin by saying the might of the American military is coming together in this city to defend against one of the largest and best equipped navies the world has ever seen. The English fleet, as we know it, has been sent over directly from the Peninsular War against France, and they are all hardened veterans who will not run from a fight. A large contingent of British ships that attacked the capital in Washington also sailed south to meet them. Late last month, their fleet departed from the island of Jamaica and was headed towards the bay outside New Orleans."

"What is their estimated number, general?" Ordway asked.

"Our sources tell us we are looking at a fleet of fifty vessels, carrying more than 18,000 men, with enough firepower to level the city. The news is grim, gentlemen. If they do take the port of New Orleans, they will control the entire Mississippi River, effectively cutting off the western territories from the Americans. If they get the western settlers – who are mostly French and Spanish as you know – together with the southern slaves, as I heard is their intent, their bargaining position with the Americans will become much stronger when negotiating their peace treaty. Those negotiations started on August the eighth, at Ghent in Belgium."

"What's to stop them at just taking New Orleans?" Bratton responded. "If their numbers are so great, they could just continue north and retake the rest of America. I'm sure they'd love to have their 'little colonies' under their control once more."

"Indeed, that opinion has been bantered about and has merit," Jackson agreed.

"What forces do we have to counter their assault?" Gass asked.

"I have a force under my command consisting of four thousand men. On the sea, our navy forces have five gunboats currently blocking access to the port, a little less than 200 men in all."

The men fell silent for a few moments as they absorbed these startling numbers. It was Gass who broke the silence.

"Where have you gotten your intel, if I may be so bold as to ask, General?"

"It's not widely known, but a privateer who operates around the bay area, a man by the name of Jean Laffite, has informed us that the British attempted to bribe him for information, men, and guns. This was back in late September. For those of us who discussed the matter with Governor Clairborne, it was evenly divided as to whether or not to believe his story and accept his terms."

"Terms, sir?"

"Laffite offered his services to us as well, in exchange for freeing his brother, Pierre, whom Governor Claiborne held in prison here in New Orleans. I had not yet arrived in New Orleans so I did not partake in the vote. I didn't get here until November 30th, so this was a good two months before. Governor Claiborne ended up breaking the stalemate, by siding with Laffite. Claiborne allowed his brother to break out of jail and reunite with Jean at his holdout on the island of Grand Terre. He provided to us numbers and positions of the British fleet as he knew them."

"Have you been able to verify Laffite's information?" Bratton asked.

Jackson smiled. "We have done what we can, but the pirate has vantage points on his island to see things we simply cannot. However, that may be a moot point."

"Why is that, General?" Colter asked,

"Against his better judgment, Governor Claiborne decided to go ahead with a scheduled raid on Laffite's stronghold on Grand Terre a few days later. In return for his information and support, he had granted Laffite a one day warning where he managed to escape to points east of the city, but our forces captured over 500 of his men, as well as gold, guns, and supplies. Since the raid, he has not been able to provide any further intel on the British forces. It's a rather sore spot with me, I'm afraid."

"But surely Governor Clairborne could see the value of Laffite's support? Why did he go ahead with the raid so soon?" Gass asked.

"The raid was scheduled through Commodore Daniel Patterson, who heads the U.S. Navy in this region. Unfortunately, the commodore maintains Laffite's message to us was a ruse, and he strongly advocated his position to the Governor in favor of the raid."

"So where does that leave the four of us?" Colter asked. "We still need to figure out where to find and intercept Bates before he can cross over."

"Perhaps I can help you there," General Jackson said, and he stood and looked down at the maps before him. They showed the general area around

New Orleans and the bay area, and were pockmarked with notations and colored markings.

Chapter 74

"These maps were done last year for surveying purposes but they will be sufficient to aid us." The general pointed towards the east, indicating an opening from the bay into Lake Borgne. From there, there was a smaller opening through a series of islands into the much larger Lake Pontchartrain in the north.

"We have laid out the presumed route of the British fleet. They should skirt east of the Chandeleur islands – the west is too shallow for their large ships – and come around to the mouth of Lake Borgne. That's where Commodore Patterson has set up his blockade with five American gunboats. If the British get past them, we are taking the position they will go through all the way to Lake Pontchartrain and try and march overland from the north. I am presuming we can engage them around the little town of Gentilly, which lies north of New Orleans proper but still well within the marshland, which would be to our advantage in a fight."

"If that is so," Gass said, eyeing the chart, "I would expect Bates to try to make his first contact with the British here, around Lake Borgne, assuming they get past our blockade. That would be the first chance they would have to set foot on American soil. I doubt he'd want to wait much longer. The more time he stays here, the greater risk he takes of getting caught."

"Do you think he knows we're after him?" Ordway asked.

"After that switch off in Jackson, he's playing the game very hard," Gass replied. "He won't want to take any chances. If his man Richards is as good as he seems to be, he'll want to protect his boss at all costs. We need to be ready to meet that challenge."

Over the next few days, the four men led reconnaissance into the areas surrounding Lake Borgne in the hopes of flushing out their elusive prey, but three days of searching yielded no results. They even asked around the waterfront and in the town, but no one could recall seeing two men fitting the descriptions that Bates manservant had provided. Only Gass and Bratton had actually seen Bates, and no one could accurately recall what Richards looked like. It was frustrating work, as they realized if they didn't find them soon, they could lose them forever.

The sun was halfway up in the eastern sky when loud cannon fire could be heard across the bay. Gass and Colter were walking along the northern rim of Lake Borgne, while Bratton and Ordway took the southern route. The British ships had been outside the bay for the last three days, with the five American gunships the only thing blocking their path. Neither side had taken any action... until now.

Gass stopped and looked out. Dozens of small, light, rowboats could be seen leaving the large British ships and making hard and fast for the American gunboats. Cannon mounted in each small boat breathed tongues of hot ball towards the larger, less maneuverable American ships. The U.S. Navy opened fire on them with their cannons, sinking a handful before the 1000 strong British marines and sailors reached their targets.

The battle was taken onboard and the Americans were quickly overwhelmed. After an hour of frantic activity, the battle was over, and all Gass and his companions could do was watch helplessly from shore. The American ships were commandeered and by late afternoon the last of them had been taken out to sea and sunk, opening the channel into Lake Borgne.

The four men returned to General Jackson with the grim news, and he took the information somberly. It was the first engagement between the newly arrived British forces and the thinly stretched Americans, and the battle could not have gone worse.

"Still no sightings of Bates yet," Gass said, "but the British haven't come ashore at this point, so he might wait until he sees company. They're back on board their ships and are probably busy making their preparations."

"I would advise you to keep your vigil around Lake Borgne," Jackson said. "In the meantime, I have taken a fancy to your stories with Captain Lewis and Clark and your adventures out west. You are good entertainment for a cold night, Mr. Gass, I can tell you."

Jackson smiled at the men. "I made it a point to mention your presence to many of my senior staff, and one of them made a connection of sorts, of which I felt was most profound."

"Sir?" Ordway asked, curiously.

General Jackson rose and left the room without saying another word, returning in a few minutes with another man, wearing the blue uniform of a captain in the Forty-fourth Infantry. All four men rose as one, a smile creasing their faces as they recognized the newcomer.

"Nathaniel Pryor!" Colter exclaimed, coming over to shake his friend's hand. "Great to see ya!"

Gass, Bratton, and Ordway also approached, with heartfelt greetings of their own. Pryor looked a bit bewildered himself.

After a minute, Jackson filled in the blanks for them. "One of my lieutenant's knew of Captain Pryor's involvement with the famed Corps of Discovery and we put two and two together. I thought you'd appreciate being reacquainted."

"Thanks for your thoughtfulness, General," Gass said earnestly.

"Oh, one more thing. Until the matter with your man Bates is closed, I am temporarily reassigning Captain Pryor to work under my direct authority, to aid you in your search. Pryor has been here for several months and knows the territory better than most. With the five of you on the case, Bates will have his hands full."

"How long have you been in service?" Ordway asked his old friend.

"It's been two years now, John. I used to do some undercover work up north before this – I even spied on Tecumseh before he was killed. But that ended badly. I and a few others were captured by his men and they took the fire to us. They were gonna kill us but the night before they planned it, I was able to get free of the ropes and escape. I was the only one of the three of us to make it back in one piece. I'll never forget it, I'll tell ya. After that I came to serve under General Jackson and we were stationed here a few months ago."

"I had a similar run in with the Blackfoot a few years ago," Colter replied softly. "I know where you're coming from, my friend."

Over the next week, General Jackson continued building his own defenses as more units entered the city from Baton Rouge. He also commissioned men from the town proper and armed farmers and anyone else who would help aid his small army. The mood in the city was grim, the odds clearly against the weakened Americans. Many who gave up hope of a victory were leaving the city ahead of the conflict, much to Jackson's dismay.

It was at dinner with Gass' men two days later, that the general made public his displeasure with his governor. "You remember those privateers we captured a few weeks ago? Laffite's men? Clairborne actually wants me to release them so they can join us at the battlefront. These men are pirates, for God's sake! They hold loyalty to no one, and it wouldn't surprise me if they end up killing as many Americans as they do British."

Gass looked at the general, as he speared a small piece of chicken with a fork and put it in his mouth, chewing slowly. The idea of freeing privateers was nasty business - anyone on the waterfront can tell you stories of their own encounters with them. But these were desperate times…

"General, if I may be so bold as to respectfully disagree with you on this issue. I know how hard you and your men have been working to secure able-bodied men to guard the city's defenses. But these times are extraordinary indeed and sometimes it might be prudent to look beyond your natural inclinations. You have 500 men sitting in a jail cell who could be used out in the field, or on boats, or doing the biding of your military if you give them amnesty. Pardon them for their past crimes and let them aid you and the city. I imagine most of them are quite adept with a rifle and knowledgeable around boats – put them to use! Use the resources you have!"

Jackson looked at the man sitting across from him, a smile spreading across his face. "It is not often a sergeant disagrees with a general, respectfully or not. But as you say, these are extraordinary times we live in. But your point is well taken. However, since these men are under military jurisdiction, the decision is mine and mine alone. Governor Clairborne is lobbying for me to grant them amnesty, and so apparently are you. I shall continue to give more thought on the matter."

Gass smiled, "It is not often a sergeant gets to dine with a general either. But as we are federal marshals, not under your jurisdiction, I like to think of it as gracious hospitality on your part. We more than appreciate the service you have given us while we're here."

"Let's just hope you get the bastard," Jackson said.

Chapter 75

Three days later, on December 17, an announcement was made in the city proper. Jackson agreed to grant amnesty to the 500 privateers in exchange for their support in fighting the British. Many thought he was crazy, but several, including Sergeant Patrick Gass, smiled when he heard the news.

Christmas was only a week away and many of the fighting men were hoping to be out of the cold before that. But the British put a damper on their plans when a report came in from sentry posts that light rowboats had been spotted leaving the British ships in the bay and were headed towards the inlet of Lake Borgne. With the American gunboats destroyed, there was nothing standing in their way.

Gass, Pryor, Ordway, Colter, and Bratton set out immediately, intending to catch Bates if he used this opportunity to make contact with the British. After an hour's ride with their mounts, they surveyed the situation. Fifteen small boats had already entered the inlet, making a direct approach to an island along the north bank of the lake.

"They're heading for Pea Island," Pryor said. "It would serve as a suitable garrison for them, as they make their way north into Lake Pontchartrain. It's several miles across, giving them ample room, yet provides close access to the shoreline."

"If Bates will make his move here, he'd do it as close to shore near Pea Island as possible," Gass replied. "That's where we need to be. All of us together." He nodded his head and the five men silently walked the northern lip of the lake towards what they hoped marked the end of their journey.

The island lay offshore about 500 yards, with a length close to a mile hugging the coast the whole way. Only in the middle did the island get narrower and the distance from shore increased to almost 800 yards. They decided to cover as much ground as possible by splitting themselves up on the chance Bates decides to head to the island. They could see some British troops already walking on Pea Island from the east. Dozens of light rowboats filled with British marines and sailors were in the water, making their approach. Before too long, the island would be overrun and they would run the risk of discovery.

Gass placed Bratton and Colter along the east end of the shoreline, and Pryor and Ordway along the west end. He patrolled the middle, hoping to give assistance to either side if they needed it. They settled into the bushes or along the high weeds of the lakeshore. Gass himself climbed into a willow tree to see if he could spot anything from a higher vantage point. Now the waiting game was on.

Nothing happened for a long time, as the five men watched the British with growing unease. The number of English soldiers grew steadily until Gass estimated more than two thousand walked upon its shore. Noise from the island increased and they could listen to several conversations going on close to the water's edge. They watched their enemy build a small garrison on the island, from which they planned to base an attack. Still, there was no sighting of Bates or Richards.

It was late afternoon when Gass climbed down from his perch, stretching his legs, careful not to reveal his presence to any prying eyes only a few hundred feet away. He made his way east to check on his men. He kept his body low to the ground, moving from trees to shrubbery to tall grass, his boots caked with mud and slime.

Suddenly he stopped, his ears alive with a different sound, closer to home. He wasn't sure if it was whispered voices, or the wind gently stirring the leaves of the oak and spruce trees that stood tall around him. He was squatting in reeds at the waters edge. He remained perfectly still, not moving a muscle, trying to keep the beat of his heart under control. Despite the chilly air, he found he was perspiring a little. The thought was amusing, and he smiled. Was the sound he heard coming from Bratton or Colter? Had he finally found Bates? Had the British come ashore from the island, perhaps? Or was it just his imagination?

Nothing more came to him and he relaxed slightly. He stepped out lightly into the marshy weeds, but his boot stuck in the muck and he lurched forward off balance. His hands spread out before him to break his fall as he hit the water with a splash. He cursed silently for his clumsiness and quickly got to his feet. But his worst fears were realized as a shout was heard from across the way, and then more cries rose with increasing alarm. It was time to make their getaway or face capture. A shot ricocheted off a tree near him and he ducked down. Death was closer than he realized and he cursed his luck once again.

"Move out!" he cried to his companions who lay a few dozen feet away. Bratton and Colter made for the safety of the tree line behind them, hoping to rendezvous later with the rest. He called out again, this time to Pryor and Ordway to the west, but he couldn't be sure he had been heard. There was no time to second guess. They would hear the outcry soon enough. He stepped back into the woods and made a quick dash for safety.

He failed to notice the depression in the earth near a large bush only a dozen yards away from where he fell, or the small piece of pear that Bates had discarded while he and Richards had waited for the marshals to leave.

The one time Lt. Governor had been upset to see them, frustrated that his arrival had been delayed by their presence. That the marshals had been here in New Orleans at all was disturbing enough – evidently they were better trackers than he had given them credit for. Or perhaps they had persuaded someone to talk more than was good for them. Well, no matter. It was mid-afternoon, when he motioned to Richards that they would take their leave and try again another time. The British were here and would be for a long time. He could wait one more day.

Frederick Bates was a man of resources, both in business and in his personal life. He had cultivated the right friends, silently supporting the patriotic causes of his father's homeland. Even though he was born in the colonies, whose subjects had subsequently revolted against their rightful rulers, he knew where true power lay.

He sat back against the stout tree, on a small hill overlooking the lake now occupied by his father's countrymen. Richards tended to a small fire, preparing a large rabbit he had trapped earlier that evening. The night brought the only safe time that a fire would be acceptable. The darkness masked the smoke that rose like a serpent through the boughs of the trees above. He closed his eyes. *Tomorrow I'll be able to sit before a fire on British soil, where the red coats will tend to my every need. For the amount of money I've provided them, they better be carrying me across the water on their shoulders.*

As daylight approached the following morning, they broke camp, making their way a half mile to the northern edge of the lake. He allowed Richards to run reconnaissance, a task he was always well suited for.

After fifteen minutes of searching, he declared the area safe for now. The marshals had not yet returned. But he knew their time was short, so he told

Richards to uncover a small rowboat they had hidden further along the shoreline. He had purchased it from a local farmer who had seen an opportunity to make an easy sell, before departing for safer lands up north. They had hidden it well several days ago, about 200 yards east of the island, covered in tall weeds. Together, they pushed and dragged it onto the shore.

Richards held it for his boss, who got in and took the oars. As the swarthy mercenary placed his foot inside to join him, Bates rebuffed him.

"No, Joseph. It is not quite time for you to accompany me. I have a special assignment for you."

Ten minutes later, Richards stood among the trees on the lake front, watching his boss tie up his boat on Pea Island. Immediately, Bates was surrounded by a sea of red coated soldiers, who whisked him away unceremoniously. Richards smiled as he heard two marshals silently make their way along the edge, not a dozen yards from his position. He almost laughed as he saw the look of helplessness on their faces as they realized they were too late. Silently, he blended back into the tree line and headed back to their camp. It would be soon time to set Mr. Bates' wonderful plans in motion. *He couldn't wait.*

Chapter 76

The door slammed hard, banging against its wooden frame. The sound echoed off the walls around him and Patrick Gass didn't care. It was over and he had lost. He had gotten to the shoreline just in time to watch helplessly as Frederick Bates was surrounded by British soldiers. The English were up and about early this morning, and there were too many for Gass to even attempt to intervene. There was no sign of Richards but he was probably there with him. It would make the most sense.

Pryor and the rest of the marshals were sitting outside or walking around, waiting for further instructions from him. For the first time since they had begun this investigation, he had no course of action – nothing to pursue, no leads to follow-up with. What was he to tell Governor Clark? He sat alone in the empty parlor room at General Jackson's headquarters. He had no other place to go for now. For the first time in years, he felt despondent and discouraged beyond words.

An hour dragged on, then two. Just before noon, the door opened again and a captain rushed in, a look of worry etched in his face. He looked at Gass.

"Is General Jackson in? It's urgent!"

Gass nodded slowly. Something was happening. Did it have anything to do with Bates' arrival this morning? It was quick work, but sometimes it's good to strike when the iron is hot…If he passed on information, they could be in a lot of trouble…

"I'll get him, captain. Wait here."

In a few minutes, General Jackson appeared at the top of the stairs, Gass by his side as they walked down to greet the captain. By this time Pryor, Ordway, and Bratton had entered the general's mansion, sensing something was going down.

The captain spoke without introduction. "It's the British, sir. They've been spotted advancing eight miles from the city. They've come across Lake Borgne and headed through the swampy marsh west of their position. They are now camped along the eastern side of the Mississippi just south of New Orleans."

Jackson's eyes blazed with intensity. "This is bad news indeed, captain. All our planning was geared to defend the city if they came from the north, through Lake Pontchartrain. That's how our military experts predicted their path. If they've suddenly altered it now, we are all out of position. From their current location, they can swiftly advance upwards and we will not able to stop them."

Gass took in the news and understood one thing. If Bates had been able to get information into the right British hands, he might have persuaded them to take this new approach. Allowing Bates to get away was not enough punishment. Now he would have to pay for helping the British win the battle, and perhaps the whole damn war.

Patrick Gass looked up suddenly, his eyes focused and ablaze with anger and determination. "General, I know your military plans are technically out of my jurisdiction, but if Bates has alerted the British to our strengths and our strategies, then I feel it's my duty to offer my advice on this. We need to hit them now, strong and hard! They don't expect us to offer much resistance. They know our defense is out of position. It's time to change our strategy as well – by becoming unpredictable, we will negate any advantage Bates can offer."

Ordway turned to Jackson, "I understand what Gass is saying, sir, and I concur. It will take time to re-establish our defenses to counter their attack from the south. Too much time if we don't slow them first. But we can take a few thousand men and take the battle to them – that at least will give them pause and buy us the time we need to reestablish our defensive perimeter."

"I understand your advice," Jackson said, "but it goes against conventional warfare strategy. We must make our defense here. We can't allow our men to fight the redcoats without support or a position to fall back too. It's tactical suicide."

"If we need to fall back, we'll retreat to New Orleans, fight street to street, house to house, if need be," Gass replied. "But if we wait any longer, they'll be here before we have a chance to get our defensive line in order. At least it gives us the time we need. It gives us a fighting chance."

"And count us in the festivities, general," Bratton said. "We're gonna love to crash this party!"

Jackson looked around the faces awaiting his decision. The captain who brought the news of the British advance looked nervous. Gass and his men had a concerted look of determination on their faces. "Ok, gentlemen, I'll give you the chance to take the fight to them. It might be our last chance. Now let's get organized."

Within the hour, Jackson's war room was filled with his top advisors and aides, and he permitted Patrick Gass to sit in, representing the federal marshals. "It was your idea, Gass," Jackson said as he extended the invitation. "You should have a say in the strategy."

Within another two hours the plans were solidified, and Commodore Patterson left Jackson's headquarters in a hurry, preparing to initiate step one. Messengers were dispatched to notify positions defending the northern city boundary to reestablish their lines further southeast above the Mississippi River valley. A carriage with two horses stood out front waiting for General John Coffee, who held back for a few moments, talking things out with his commander.

"I want your Tennessee riflemen to come in along their northern flank tonight after dark, and hit them hard and fast," Jackson reminded him. "Shooting should be kept to a minimum since visibility will be almost non-existent, but there will be a partial moon tonight to give you at least a chance to see their positions. But the darkness will also hide your numbers and, if done right, will cause enough confusion and chaos on their part that they will not know where you are or how many you have with you."

Gass stepped outside and walked up to the pair. "If I may add, sir, that in this instance, it would be best to use close combat weapons - hunting knives, tomahawks – whatever the men have that will cause damage inside. It will be brutal, but it's not something the British have much experience with. They'll not suspect it and should give them sufficient pause before coming north at us."

"And you will be joining us, marshal?" Coffee asked. "You and your men?"

"The more the merrier, yes sir," Gass replied smiling. "We put ourselves at your disposal. All of us have experience leading men in battle against the red coats in this war – let us make a contribution to your efforts tonight."

"And what of Commodore Patterson's mission?" Coffee asked. "Will it cause any problems for us? I don't need our own men to get shelled tonight."

"By positioning your men to attack the northern end of the British flank, you will avoid any repercussions the *U. S. Carolina* might make from the bay." Jackson replied. "They will be directing hot shells at their southern flanks near the Mississippi. One advantage we gain with the British moving their men so quickly west was their artillery and guns haven't caught up to them yet. Their hard arsenals are very light right now, and I don't think they'll have any answer for the *Carolina*. Two different attacks, two different approaches. One beleaguered enemy."

"It was fortunate Patterson had the *Carolina* on site," Coffee added. "Normally, it is stationed further north but he had brought it down to attack the privateer base on Grand Terre several weeks ago. Without intending it, Laffite actually did us a favor in that regard."

"Gentlemen, the defense of our city, and indeed our country, awaits your successful mission tonight. Take the battle to the enemy, as Mr. Gass would say." General Jackson smiled. "God speed and may He favor our task tonight."

Chapter 77

Gass and his men, including Nathaniel Pryor who asked to be included in the assault, met four miles to the south, on a large indigo plantation along with over two thousand men under General Coffee's command. General Andrew Jackson was in attendance as well, but left the tactical planning for Coffee. It was eight o'clock in the evening and dusk had settled over the land two hours before. Coffee had instructed them to prepare for hand-to-hand combat, as they walked the remaining four miles to meet the British line.

Shelling from the *U. S. Carolina* in the bay could be heard all afternoon, and it was a sound that brought hope and fortitude for the citizens of New Orleans. As long as the guns blazed away, the enemy would be hampered in their assault. Streams of rockets striking into fortified positions along the rows of large oak trees bordering the Mississippi River started late in the afternoon and continued until the last light disappeared beyond the horizon. Smoke from artillery still hung over the land miles from where they hit.

Gass, Ordway, and Pryor had been given command of a group of twenty men, while Bratton and Colter led another group of ten riflemen several yards to their rear. Pryor had walked tours through this plantation before, so Gass allowed him to navigate their push south. The light from the half moon was ideal for their purposes – not too bright to give away their positions but just enough to see where they were going. It was a tricky balance. If they engaged the British, the element of surprise would be essential.

By 9:30 Pryor stopped, holding up his hand as the tightly formed group came to a halt behind him. They could make out voices in front of them, speaking the King's English. The conversation was soft, as if coming across on the wisps of a light breeze, but as the men stood there listening, they could hear snippets of conversation. Men discussing cricket contests and one or two younger lads debating the aptitude of their pitching skills. It was casual and low-key, and Gass smiled. The element of surprise was still in their favor.

He waited for the prearranged signal, as the men silently took up positions beyond the trunks of large oaks, or behind bushes that pricked at them if they got too close. The air was cold and the sky partly cloudy. The visibility on the ground was near zero, forcing the men to rely on their hearing and smell to alert them to the enemy. Thirty-five men knelt waiting, holding in their hand their only real defense. Knives that would, in a few moments time, be used to slice and cut, maim and perhaps kill, were the weapons of choice for the evening. A few men slung rifles across their backs, but without decent visibility, they would not see any action tonight.

Across the fields an owl hooted, followed by another further away. Gass held his fingers to his lips and gave his own call to men further along the path. At his signal, twenty men rose with him, along with Pryor and Ordway, as they ran across the field hoping to catch the British patrol off guard. Distance was hard to accurately judge in the dark, and Gass was slightly off his estimate, but he had more experience in nighttime fighting than any man out here, and he knew they had to remain silent until the last possible moment.

The conversation of the men up ahead acted as a homing beacon to Patrick Gass and he smiled to himself. They made it easy for him and he was happy to take advantage of their mistake. He and his men were upon the red coats before they could stand up, knocking them down and taking their guns and weapons. He did not condone killing if he could avoid it, and instructed his men to take prisoners wherever possible. There was already too much loss of life in this damn war. But if they fought back…

A cry went up from his left as one British soldier came out of the woods ten feet away wielding a fixed bayonet on the end of his .75 caliber Brown Bess rifle, heading straight for Nathaniel Pryor. The captain held his position, twisting his body just in time to avoid being run through, as Ordway's knife flew out of his right hand in a single fluid motion. The weapon found purchase in the center of the soldier's chest and he stood for a moment transfixed, before falling backward.

Another British soldier two feet to the right, who had surrendered his rifle to one of men in Gass' unit, took advantage of the distraction and reached under his cloak, quickly bringing to bear a knife of his own. Gass caught the movement out of the corner of his eye and succeeded in tackling his own man to the ground just before the British soldier pounced. The coat of Englishman trailed behind him as he flew up to attack, but he tripped over the

American's body and hesitated for an instant, unsure of whom to go after. Another Tennessee rifleman in Gass' company, a young lad by the name of Saunders, took him down with a swing of his axe, blade flat. The man's arm cracked audibly and he cried out in pain, as the knife dropped from his fingers... but he would live.

Just as they were wrapping up this mess, Colter and Bratton led their ten men in a dead run past Gass, deeper into the British held plantation fields. They were silent as ghosts and carrying a deadly bite. Gass silently wished them luck.

There were five British men that were rounded up, not including the one that lay dead near the edge of the woods. Gass instructed five of the riflemen to watch over them, as he took the other seventeen men and headed off. They needed to cover as much ground as possible – with only a limited number of fighters at their disposal, General Coffee wanted them to make a big footprint on the British backside tonight.

The next English patrol they encountered was ready for them, the element of surprise gone by this time. Gass and Pryor did reconnaissance, trying to isolate them and come in where they were least expected. They almost succeeded...

Chapter 78

Within the hour, most of the Americans had retreated back to the territory of New Orleans but to their satisfaction, the British did not pursue them. It was left to the next day to find out how badly the Americans had hurt them. Patrick Gass was grateful that he had not lost any of his men that evening and only three had gotten hurt in the brutal fighting. Two had suffered stab wounds, and the third had been knocked unconscious by the wooden stock of a rifle. Gass was satisfied with knowing personally that one particular British soldier did not live long enough to finish off his attack on the young American lad.

General Jackson was soon back at his headquarters, piecing together the results of this nightly assault as more groups reported in. By morning's light, they had some solid numbers – only 24 men had been confirmed killed in the fighting, with a little more than 100 wounded. There were roughly 80 men that were missing, and some of these undoubtedly had been captured.

Gass and his men had brought back their five prisoners from their initial assault plus an additional seven. In all, 64 captured British soldiers were placed in the jails at the sheriff's office. Not exactly equipped to handle so many prisoners, Jackson had some of the younger lads released the next day and sent back to their units unarmed.

Even though the land assault had been completed, the *U.S. Carolina* took up her naval bombardment of the British troops across the Mississippi the next morning. It was Christmas Eve but the citizens of New Orleans, as well as the men defending her, thought little today of the holiday that night would bring. The threat of the thousands of British troops camped only a few miles away gave them a singular focus and a common bond between them.

Many of the citizens helped the Americans build their defenses that day, hoping they were not too late. Had the attack of the previous night bought them the time they needed? Scouts had been sent out to look for any sign of advancement but as of early afternoon, they had reported no sightings. The men began to relax a little. If any attack were to come, they reasoned, it would have already started before now. Unlike their American counterparts at times, the English relied on a disciplined and time-honored practice of warfare, for maximum strategic effectiveness. Their tactics often led others to view them as predictable but, with the largest army in the world, they obviously didn't see reason to change their ways.

"General, the forward defensive position is almost complete, thanks to the extra manpower the townspeople have provided," Major-General Jacques Villere said, as the top advisors sat around Jackson's long conference table on Christmas morning. His Louisiana militia had been tasked with leading the defense of the city, and the movement of their positions, from the northern swamp lands of Gentilly to the southern plains near the Mississippi, had taken a toll on his men.

"Thanks, Jacques," Jackson replied. "What do we have to fall back on?"

"We set up Line Jackson, the first of three defensive lines, right above an old unused canal that runs parallel to it. The line runs 1000 yards across, with the Mississippi River at one end and a large swamp at the other. This will force the Brits to come at us through this relatively narrow corridor, which will neutralize their great numbers.

"We have earthworks and fortified walls protecting eight gun batteries placed fairly evenly apart. The guns batteries are not fully established as of yet but they will be soon. We are working on establishing the other two lines behind the first. They will be Line Dupre, and behind that will be Line Montreuil. They will all have the same structure and size. With luck and God's grace, it will be enough to withstand whatever the Brits throw at us."

"Understood," Jackson said. "Thank you, Jacques. I also want to announce that, in light of the success of last night, I have decided to continue harassing the British outposts on a regular basis, in daylight and at dusk, to keep them off guard. I think we have seen what happens when we push the envelope against a predictable adversary. They are used to European ways of engagement, what they would call a more 'civilized' approach. When fighting the French, if both armies were nearby but idle at the time, they would stand down, safe in the knowledge that their outposts would remain unmolested. Not here! Our daily raids will keep them agitated, and indeed, might force them to make a mistake we can use to our advantage."

"Or it may force the Brits to deal with the problem we've created head-on and march on our positions sooner, when our defenses are not yet ready," said Colonel George Ross, commander of the 44th infantry division. "I recommend we let them be and solidify our defenses first. We don't want to make them any angrier than necessary."

"If we allow them to dictate the terms of the battle," Gass said jumping into the conversation, "we might as well hand over the keys to the city now. They have us outnumbered and outgunned on a field of battle, and we need to use whatever measures we have at our disposal to turn the advantage to our side. Skirmishes like General Jackson proposes will surely keep them off guard, will force them to question what assets and numbers we do have, and will not allow them to rest. No one wants a dog nipping at his heels all the time..."

"Until they get fed up with that dog and shoot 'em," Ross growled.

Chapter 79

The sun started to rise above the treetops Christmas morning in a slow arc, the chilly weather keeping everything in its tight and deadly grip. Major-General Edward Pakenham, commander of the British fleet, rode his white stallion along the foggy plains of the colonial Louisiana plantation known as Chalmette, observing his fine English soldiers sleeping in tents and huddled around fires to keep warm. His journey from the *R.M.S. Aleutia* that morning had been motivated more to uplift the men's morale than to address tactical situations. As he surveyed the current situation of his army, he grew increasingly disheartened by the progress they had made against a ragtag group of farmers and wilderness hicks.

As he made his way to the field officer's tent, cheers rang up sporadically from the bands of men as he passed. He was here and things would be alright. The message his presence suggested would offer them hope for a quick resolution to this conflict. It was the actions, or rather inactions, of his field commanders that he was most anxious to address.

"General Pakenham!" called a man who emerged from a large tent to their left. General Rudolph Gibbs came forward, pressing his thin hand over that of his commanding officer. Pakenham didn't respond immediately but slowly dismounted his steed, handing the reins to a youthful soldier standing at attention, his long red coat making a stark contrast to the film of white snow on the ground.

Without a word, the general entered the large tent, and was soon joined by five other field commanders, whom he had left in charge of cleaning up the little colonial port city. There were oil lanterns set on posts at intervals around the tent, and a makeshift table with maps that made up the bulk of the center.

There were only two chairs. Pakenham took one, and kicked the other into the far corner. No one else deserved to sit.

The room got quiet as the foul mood of the General permeated the atmosphere in an almost palpable fog. One of the men, a Colonel Rennie, tried to ease the tension by offering a "Merry Christmas" but it just produced a gruff dismissal from Pakenham.

"Gentlemen, I'd like to understand why I am sitting in a tent in the middle of a frozen tobacco field on Christmas Morning rather than in the Governor's mansion on Royal Ave in the heart of New Orleans? I thought my instructions were crystal clear. Am I to assume you are all deaf or are you incapable of following orders?"

General Gibbs cleared his throat nervously before stepping forward. "Sir, we made good progress until a few days ago. Admiral Cochrane's marines easily overran the five American gunboats protecting the entrance to Lake Borgne. We had plans to continue into Lake Pontchartrain and then down and enter New Orleans from the north. The idea was to push the Americans up against the Mississippi River and pin them while we fire from the northern ridge of the basin."

"And what happened?" Pakenham said, his voice dripping with acid.

"We captured a renegade American on Pea Island, where we established our initial garrison. His name is Frederick Bates and he claimed he was a former Lt Governor of the Louisiana Territories with knowledge of the American plans. He claims to be a British sympathizer, sir, and I felt it was advantageous to question him further."

"Was the information he revealed of use to you?"

"Quite frankly, yes, sir. He had information that the Americans had predicted our attack route and were building their defense at Gentilly. That in itself was not cause for any alarm – we expected something along those lines. But he gave us an alternative plan of attack, which frankly intrigued me. By marching across the marshy swamp directly west from Lake Borgne, we could attack New Orleans from the south – make our entrance with no resistance whatsoever."

"But that has not been the case, has it?"

Gibbs looked down for a moment, before lifting his head. "Well, not quite. The very afternoon of our arrival, their large gunship in the bay began an aerial assault on our forces that hit our positions hard. They have kept up the bombardment throughout yesterday and today. Frankly, without the big guns from our ships, we can't take it out. I've asked permission to get the guns moved up faster, but its slow progress transporting them through the swamplands."

"Why have you not sent your men directly north into the city? You wouldn't care as much about this little ship if you had control of the port. You have several thousand men here! Use them, for God's sake!"

"General, it was my position to do so, however, we came under a ferocious nighttime attack that gave us pause for concern. Their numbers were repelled but we lost 46 men, with another 160 wounded, and 64 reported captured. They attacked us along our northern outposts so they did not do much damage to our main body. But, without a clear picture of the enemy's positions, I took it upon myself to hold and wait for reinforcements that were due to join us in a matter of days."

"And now? General Keane arrived yesterday with his crack troops and still you wait. Am I to wonder if I chose the wrong man to lead the finest army in the world against a bunch of farmers? Tell me what I am missing, general."

"Well, the Americans…they've taken it upon themselves to change the rules of respectable warfare, sir. Unspoken rules, as it were, but still rules that govern a civilized conflict. Over the last four days, they have harassed our outposts, killed our men as they walk patrol, and given a general sense of chaos to the minds of our brave fighting men. The casualty estimates of these daring raids are not reassuring: about 50 brave men killed so far. They are not doing any real damage to the main body of our forces, as we see once again, but they will not allow anyone a decent rest and good night sleep. Our men have been complaining constantly that their behavior has been very… ungentlemanly."

Pakenham closed his eyes for a full ten seconds, as the men in the tent looked on. His body seemed so relaxed that Colonel Rennie wasn't sure if he had fallen asleep. He took a frightful step back when the general suddenly opened his eyes, and sprang to his feet. His eyes were lit like candelabras and there was a magical energy about him that defied reason. Where he showed anger and frustration just a moment ago, his mood had changed entirely.

"This is what we shall do, gentlemen. It is clear that our adversary is trying to play mind games with us, assaulting our outposts and harassing our men. We need to show them just who they are dealing with. We are the finest, most disciplined force in the entire world and our fleet of 18,000 men lay at their doorstep! We need to make these farmers tremble at the sight of us!"

"But what of the *U. S. Carolina* off our southern flank, sir?" General Gibbs asked. "We cannot move freely as long as she floats. She is taking advantage of the shallow marshlands and the islands around the bay to keep herself from our fleet."

"I will have cannons here within the next 48 hours and we will put her on the bottom of the ocean," Pakenham said. "Now I'd like to hear for myself just what information our Mr. Frederick Bates has to offer us. Please show him in and perhaps we can use his knowledge of the Americans to our advantage yet again."

Chapter 80

Two days after Christmas, General Jackson sat in his war room, finalizing the defenses of his remaining lines with two of his aides, Colonel Ross and Major-General Jacques Villere. The breastworks were almost complete and the British had shown no signs of advancements to this point. Jackson was almost ready to believe they would make it in time.

A knock at the door caused him to look up. His young aide, Lt. Higgins, came in slowly.

"Sorry to disturb you, sir, but I thought you should know. The British initiated a bombardment attack this morning against the *U. S. Carolina*. She responded in kind, but was hit with heated shot. She caught fire and sank in the bay an hour ago. All but five men were rescued, sir."

"I was led to believe the British did not possess their long range guns," Jackson said softly.

"They must have moved them into position last night, sir," Ross said. "The *Carolina* has protected our forces for days now. It was only a matter of time until the British would respond. Now that they have, is their next move far behind?"

"Colonel, the *Carolina* had long range guns on board – if we can salvage them from the wreck, we can put them to use on Line Jackson and let them feed on the Brits yet again. It would make the loss almost bearable. Please see to it."

"Aye, sir," he said as he quickly exited the room.

Jackson sat back, mulling over the maps on the table. *We know where you are. We're just about ready for you. Make your move.*

The next day, the British followed up their attack on the *Carolina* with a demonstration as impressive as anything witnessed by the men protecting

New Orleans. Tightly packed soldiers in long red coats, carrying .75 caliber Brown Bess rifles with extended bayonets, marched separately along both east and west sides of the battlefield heading north towards the recently finished Line Jackson barricades. The men defending the breastworks simply looked on in amazement, watching the spectacle unfold. Brilliant Congreve rockets lit the hazy sky, and thunderous booms from artillery cannons in the forward batteries gave the Americans lots to think about.

The thousands of red coated soldiers were startling to see up close and in daylight, the morning sun reflecting brilliant light off their muskets and bayonets. The men marched two abreast, in unrelenting formation.

At a signal from General Jackson, who stood at the center of his own defensive line, the Americans opened fire. Artillery shells shot away from the gun batteries, slamming into the sea of red coats as they advanced. Tennessee Riflemen took aim and delivered a withering display of hot lead of their own, bringing down dozens of the English troops. Still they advanced, unheeded.

In thirty minutes time, several columns of British soldiers had almost reached Line Jackson, despite the constant firepower from the Americans. However, it soon became evident to the British that they had a serious problem. The creative Americans had built their defensive line behind a canal that was filled with water several meters across. Without knowing how deep it really was, the red coats hesitated in the midst of a withering artillery assault. At a signal from a field commander, they took cover in various directions; some landing in the muddy water, while others took up positions around trees, bushes, or anything they could find.

Four men worked the small brass cannonade that made up the last gun battery on Line Jackson, almost a mile from the waters of the Mississippi. Swampy marshes to the east would make the going difficult for any British attempting to cut around their defenses and come up behind them, and a contingent of Colonel Henderson's Tennessee Riflemen were assigned to protect their flank.

The line of sight across the field was difficult at best as smoke from the rocket bombardment, cannon discharge, and small fires along the breastwork masked the movement of the British. 17 year old Titan McDaniel, from Nashville, grimaced as another shot from his brass dragon missed its mark again.

"Damn this carriage!" he cried out loud. The right wheel of the wooden gun support had been damaged ten minutes before by shrapnel from a closely aimed rocket, and the gun had been firing errant ever since. As much as he tried, he couldn't level the gun correctly, and he was frustrated every time shots from the English Brown Bessie's made him duck for cover.

He could barely see the double line of red coats through the smoke that lay like a haze across the battlefield, but noticed they were aiming to cross his path to the east. He lined up the cannonade once more as his battery teammate, a blond teen named Teddy, loaded the eight-inch muzzle with shot and black powder before dampening it down with the stout stick.

A newcomer to their ranks was tending to the wheel now, attempting to put a new wooden patch that might hold it for the duration. He was older than his teammates but Colonel Henderson was impressed with his marksmanship skills and resourcefulness and quickly put him to use. He wasn't military but so many civilians were assisting nowadays, that it was impossible to keep track anymore.

"Ready!" the man said loudly. Quickly, he backed away and stood beside Titan as he lit the fuse once more. The muzzle of the brass beast was aimed directly into the middle of the approaching line. A direct hit will cut their ranks in half and force them to scatter. Hopefully retreat. Titan crossed his fingers. He didn't notice the new cannon team member step away slowly and duck behind a large stone fence.

Titan watched the fuse go down, and knelt low behind the cannon to avoid a flash burn. He hoped this shot would be golden. He looked down, and absently looked at the right wheel the new man had worked on. His eyes grew wide as he saw a second smaller fuse next to…

The powerful explosion generated from the small vial of black powder disintegrated the right wheel a second before the cannonade discharged, the brass muzzle slamming hard into the solid stone base. The shock caused the hot metal and compact powder to detonate on the spot, and the cannon exploded in a piercing shriek of twisted metal and burning flesh. Five men, include young Titan McDaniel, died on the spot. The eyes of Joseph Richards blazed with delight.

The British saw the explosion and realized the misfiring battery was an opportunity they couldn't pass up. They took up a double-time march, passed the canal and the sporadic firing of the sharpshooters, until they cleared the breastworks and entered the marsh land. One hundred yards further along, the canal narrowed considerably. The men under General Gibbs' command made a clear jump over it without much difficulty. Quickly, they regrouped on the American side of the canal and proceeded with haste towards the rear of their enemy's fortifications.

Nathaniel Pryor had been working side by side with Colonel Henderson's regime of Tennessee riflemen, overseeing the execution of batteries seven and eight on the far end of Line Jackson, furthest from the river. When he heard the terrific explosion from battery eight, he ran over quickly to lend assistance. It did not take long to realize the deadly mishap had allowed a line of red coats to cross the canal further downstream. He sent a lieutenant to warn Henderson of the attack from their flank, and quickly organized his own group of riflemen to head them off.

Within minutes, Henderson rode up on his black mare beside the captain. His thin black mustache was set under a long nose and narrow brown eyes, and his hat was pulled low over his forehead. He wore a smart uniform of blue with the insignia of his Tennessee regime, and black gloves to ward off the chill in the air.

"Good work, Captain," Henderson said with earnest. "Now let's take it to them! I've gathered about 200 riflemen from my regime and I intend to sneak up behind the Brits and cut their line in half – with any luck they will never know what hit them! We'll need to drive them back and hard!"

Chapter 81

General Pakenham fumed as he saw his line of brave red coats return from their 'demonstration' battered and hurt, dirty and demoralized. This had not gone the way he had planned. He sent them back to their camps to the south as he met with his aides, just into the tree line that overlooked the defensive positions of the Americans.

"Are all units accounted for?" he asked.

"All except for General Gibbs' detachment," General Keane said.

"Without backup, they'll be cut down like pigeons," Pakenham said. "Send someone to notify them of the retreat at once. Send someone who is good at persuasion. I feel Gibbs may be out to prove himself to me at any costs. I admit, it's what I might have done in his shoes. Make it happen. I don't want to lose any more men."

"Of course, sir."

Within two minutes, a group of four junior officers headed out bravely across the battlefield to the last known positions taken by the missing general. Staying well back of the line and taking cover in the smoke, they navigated a safe passage before proceeding up the far side of the field near the last gun battery. The breastworks were silent for now, save for the moaning of the wounded. The massive guns that just minutes before had flung immense payloads of iron and lead into the ranks of human flesh stood silent, waiting, their sentries watching through the thick haze for any sign of attack.

Where were Colonel Rennie and General Gibbs? The four officers continued east, unseen and unmolested, until they saw the line of red coats off in the distance, the visibility somewhat clearer in that direction. Most were still on the south side of the canal, but there was a distinct body of men in long red jackets advancing westward along the far bank. The junior officers ran to a cluster of decorated men, finding the general in the midst of discussion with his advisors.

"General Gibbs!" one of them shouted. All heads turned to look upon the newcomers, who quickly stood up sharply. "Sir! General Pakenham has given us express orders to have your men stand down and retreat to base camp." He handed over a parchment upon which Pakenham had laid out his instructions to Gibbs, least the messenger not be believed.

"We're advancing well, found a hole in their defense!" Gibbs shouted angrily. "Why does he wish to stop us now?"

"General Pakenham cannot offer your men support in your assault and warns you that this advance today is a mere exercise, not an offensive attack. I have instructions to escort you and your men safely back."

Gibbs turned toward the northern bank, his eyes longing for a quick victory that seemed to elude him at every turn. He reluctantly ordered one of his men to inform Colonel Rennie to make a hasty retreat with his men. *Another day will come… and I'll be back to lay siege to your lines again.*

As Colonel Henderson and his American troops made their way east to intercept Rennie's detachment of red coats, Nathaniel Pryor kept pace with his commander on the back of a brown gelding. All the enlisted men walked carefully along the border of the swamp, sometimes finding themselves in mud and water up to their knees. His horse preferred the harder soil found along the tree line and Pryor couldn't blame him.

His men were a mixture of regular army and several volunteers from town. He was especially impressed with one, a newcomer who had given his name as Thatchiel Greenleaf. Dressed in a long black cloak, the man walked behind Colonel Henderson, his revolver out and ready for action. After the accident at the cannonade battery, he quickly stepped up to fill the ranks that Henderson was looking for. Pryor was pleased with his dedication and resourcefulness - a far cry from the average farm boy who appears on the scene, with little more than a pitchfork or short-handled hatchet.

Without warning two shots rang out, followed by three more. A young lieutenant fell to Pryor's right, clutching his chest. Pryor looked around quickly but was unable to find the source of the attack… until chaos erupted all around him.

British soldiers emerged from behind trees, taking aim and firing at Henderson's men, who scattered to avoid being hit. Pryor's horse was startled at the closeness of the firefight, rising in the air on his hind legs, almost throwing the captain into the swamp. He held on, trying to calm his mount down, while at the same time taking aim with his own Springfield musket. He fired once at a British soldier at point blank range who came alongside him attempting to take the reins of his horse. The shocked expression of the dead man's face stayed with the captain for a long time to come.

At the sound of the shot, Pryor's horse reared again, this time managing to loosen the grip of the rider and ditching him hard on the ground beside the body of the young British lad. Captain Pryor got up slowly, just in time to see the gelding disappear through the misty haze. He picked up his musket, quickly checked it for damage, and proceeded on foot towards the enemy's last known position, sloshing through water that swarmed around his shins.

Once he fell into an underwater trench that soaked him up to his waist in icy water. The mosquitoes were especially unbearable here, biting at any exposed flesh at every opportunity. He wanted to lash out at the large bugs but steeled himself to remain calm.

The firing seemed to have stopped and the men in the red jackets could be seen no more. Where had they gone? They had the advantage – why stop now? He continued to look around until he saw another body lying prone on the ground to his left, half submerged in the marshy water. He wore a blue uniform with the braided decorations of an officer. His hat lay floating in the water beside his head, caught on a few long reeds. His face was turned away from Pryor.

He slowly reached the dead man, grabbing him under the armpits and lifting him out of the water. His torso looked clean of bullet holes. Where was he hit? He gingerly turned him over onto his back, looking for any indication of injury to his person. There was a series of three red holes in his upper back, positioned in close proximity to each other, three rivulets of blood draining out of his body onto the soft clay soil beneath him. He had been shot at close range, judging by the display of the wounds. Pryor looked at the face and sighed deeply. He closed the eyes of Colonel Henderson before saying a prayer for him.

Chapter 82

January 1, 1816
New Orleans, Louisiana

T he piercing whistle of the Congreve rocket could be heard long before the explosion sent up a cloud of dirt and grass twenty yards from where Corporal Lance Steiner sat against a large rock cleaning his long barrel musket. Ducking his head down, he instinctively covered his ears from the shock of the powerful explosive. The boy raised his head tentatively and looked around before permitting himself a thin smile. He had survived... for the moment.

Joseph Richards looked over from his perch near battery two and tried to will the British to start the aerial bombardment in earnest. He was tired of the cat and mouse games the two sides had been playing for weeks, especially since the cowardly red coats had retreated despite the huge risks he had taken to help them advance three days ago. He took a long draft from his canteen and closed his eyes. It wouldn't be long now. Not even Pakenham would wait forever to clear the port city and advance up the Mississippi.

Another whistle shriek and...one...two...there it was! Richards tried to suppress a grin as he heard the satisfying explosion that struck at the nerve center of the infernal men in blue. Another followed soon after, and one more almost on top of it. He opened his eyes. The morning fog was beginning to lift, and with it the British were beginning to see the faces...and positions...of their foe. It won't be long now.

He heard voices to his left, and he dropped down off the high wall to the dirt walkway beneath. There must have been hundreds of men along the mile long perimeter that marked the first, and most formidable, of the American defenses. And yet he felt alone – without an equal. No one to challenge him as he walked among these backwoods lads whose only experience with war was hearing stories of their grandfathers, detailing their victory over the British in the Great Revolution. Oh, how he wished he had been born thirty years before! He has truly missed the most exciting time in history – even if the wrong side won.

Mercenary – that was the term they would have used for him back in the day. But he saw himself as more than that – he had more experience in war and battle than any man along this wall! But he was not just a gun for hire. He was a creative influence – an artist, if you will. Hiding behind disguises or manipulating others to do his terrible deeds had saved his bacon more times than he could count – and his presence now, walking freely among the enemy, was the most telling fact on his long life. Each time he struck – each time he got away. He had never seen the inside of a jail cell.

Well, almost never. He smiled at the thought of his youthful exuberance that had led to his first brush with the law. Poaching his neighbor's cattle when he was only a lad of twelve – now that he looked back on it, he marveled at his audacity. Mr. George Goodall – what a crotchety old bastard! - turned me in, tugging on my ear the entire two miles to the sheriff's office. When his father found out about his exploits, he was beside himself with anger.

Another rocket, this one closer to home. Men were scrambling now, running all over in a futile effort to escape from their path. Larger cannon fire began to accompany the smaller 32 pound Congreves, slamming into the breastworks and the waters of the canal in front of them. But as he looked around, he noticed something…strange. Not one American battery had fired back in response. He could see a man holding a lighted torch near the long 24 pounder near him but he simply looked to the east for the signal.

Richards followed his gaze and saw General Jackson on his horse riding between the batteries, holding his hand high in the air. He was dictating the rules they were to follow and his instructions were clear to the gunners at their stations. Wait…wait…just a little longer…

Now! His arm came down with a flourish and eight cannons roared as one, sending great tongues of fire across the frozen field into the fog, hoping their payload will strike at the heart of the enemy gun batteries. Immediately after firing, the gun crews got to work reloading and firing off more rounds.

Richards looked behind them and saw two ammunition wagons loaded with hundreds of pounds of explosives, gun powder, and metal shot. Several men were nearby unloading their deadly contents to a line of young soldiers standing ready to re-supply their gun batteries. He smiled to himself. A rocket exploded very close to his left, spraying him with dirt and small rocks. He covered his face from the assault and ran towards the rear. Another rocket hit again to his right as he zigzagged behind the lines.

He could see a small crowd from the town watching the action a short distance away, probably wondering what to make of all this excitement. With any luck, he thought, the British bombing would scare them off along with any soldier-wannabes that have swelled the ranks of the American defenses in recent weeks. This was a place for real soldiers, not farmers and simple townsfolk.

Despite the constant barrage of explosions going off in all directions from the aerial assault, he picked up a familiar voice from a group of men off to his left. He ducked his head down instinctively and turned his back to them, trying to hear what they were saying. It was that blasted Patrick Gass! He and his marshals had been the only ones to discover the truth about his boss' treachery and for that, Bates had marked them for assassination.

But to Richards' chagrin, these four men had repeatedly escaped from him, and the various methods he had employed. It was one of the reasons Mr. Bates had kept him behind enemy lines, as it were. Sabotage, assassination, and subterfuge had always been the hallmarks of his career as a soldier-for-hire. They were easy to accomplish when you had a reputable front – a position that would allow you free access to almost anywhere you needed to go in the colonies... or in the new territories around it. It was what he enjoyed the most out of life. It was an assignment that he would finish today.

"We need to take a 32 pounder from the *Carolina* and use it to shore up battery number 8, the last one down," Gass was saying to his audience.

"Commodore Patterson's men just got three of them up yesterday," someone replied back, "but they're still drying out from being submerged. They won't be ready for another day or two, I suspect."

"Ask General Jackson if we can put more men on preparing one of them now – we need it within an hour, not days! At this rate, the rockets will shell us all to death before the guns are ready."

"Fear not, Gass," another voice cut in. "The Brits are just trying to soften us up. The mortars and Congreve rockets look and sound impressive but Jackson wants us to hold fast..."

At that moment another explosion struck nearby, sending the group of men scurrying off to a safer distance. Richards remained where he was, deep in thought. He knew that ass Pryor was a friend of theirs, and it was all he could do to hold back his laughter as he shot Henderson right under his very nose. He was the perfect weapon! Richards prided himself in being the master of disguises, allowing him to strut around in plain view of the marshals without fear of capture. They had no idea who to look for! Joseph Richards was an enigma to them. Oh, the irony!

He looked around once more, and spotted Gass and the few captains with whom he was conversing standing to the rear of one of the large ammunition wagons that had just arrived on the scene a few minutes ago. It was still loaded and was relatively unattended. He reached into the inside pocket of his long black coat, and carefully pulled out a vial of black powder with a small fuse running from the corked top. He knew the value of such small incendiary devices – easily concealed, highly explosive, and best of all, they gave him time to clear the area before it went off. No one would know who did it – indeed, to the casual observer, it could easily be assumed that one of the Congreve rockets had finally found its mark.

The ammunition wagon was situated about thirty-five feet away, about twenty feet behind gun battery four, a medium size 24 pounder manned by a crew of four. Twenty or so men in blue were arranged around the large gun, firing their muskets at the unseen enemy. Acrid smoke from the incoming rockets and the resulting cannon fire of the Americans lay thick along Line Jackson and beyond, despite the bright light from the noonday sun.

He had found Gass – but he had no idea where the others in his unit were. No matter. Let's deal with them one at a time. Today, Mr. Gass was due a little payback. When he was no more than ten feet away, he pulled out the glass bottle carefully with his right hand, while his left hand revealed a wooden match and flint stick. Striking the match alongside the flint created the desired flame and he looked around carefully to make sure he was not observed. This part was tricky but he had performed this several times to date without injury to himself. He had long ago closed his mind off to the injuries he caused others. They were irrelevant. Only the target mattered.

He lit the wick protruding from the corked top which gave off a satisfying burn. He couldn't put it back in his pocket now – he had to walk the remaining ten feet to the wagon in full view of the men around it. He decided to walk as long as he could before making a quick dash before dropping it on top of the ammunition. Give his targets as little time to react as possible. The resulting explosion will take care of the rest.

Cradling the lit device in his left hand held down away from his body, he confidently approached the wagon, showing no fear, for in truth he felt nothing... nothing but a little anticipation, a small glowing of satisfaction.

Two feet from the wagon now and still the men were deep in discussions, not paying him any mind…

"Hey!" a shout coming from his left. "Get away from the wagon with that!"

Richards cursed under his breath and without looking at the caller, covered the remaining distance in two seconds, placing the glass bottle on top of one of the bigger wooden boxes that sat high in the wagon. The wick was already low, another few seconds…

Richards ran hard, up and away from the wagon, back towards town and away from the fighting. But immediately another shout came, followed by yet another. Things were not going quite as easily…

Chapter 83

The explosion seemed to rip away the very fabric of the air around them, sending fiery, hot shards of metal, wood, and black powder in all directions. Richards dove to the ground behind a rock that gave him but little protection. He dared a quick look behind him and smiled with satisfaction at the destruction he had left in his wake. Men were down all around, some trying to get up while others remained still. He looked for Gass but didn't find him immediately. Quickly, he got to his feet and brushed himself off.

The distance from his location to the scene of the carnage was perhaps sixty feet or so; between them laid the bodies of dozens of men. He wasn't sure if his ears were still ringing from the explosion he had set off, but it seemed to Richards the rocket bombardment had stopped altogether. No more high whistles or blind explosions from the Congreves. He looked around out towards the English line. Was that a faint cheer he heard above the deafening silence?

Many of the men before him were beginning to rise on unsteady feet, while several bloodied bodies remained lifeless. Others rushed by to help and soon men were running in different directions, helping the wounded or tending to the massive guns on the breastworks. He alone stood immobile against the chaos around him.

His focus returned. No one seemed to give him any heed, and he was used to it. His actions from mere moments ago were yet another anonymous nail in the coffin he was building. He walked slowly by the body of Patrick Gass, whose bloodied head was being held gently by another man, and it was all he could do to suppress a smile. There would be time for gloating later.

There was still much to be done. Amidst the chaos he created, the ultimate prize was within his reach.

A crowd of men surrounded the target who called out orders, and who galvanized men into action with his every word. The death of General Andrew Jackson at the height of the battle would spell doom for the rebels and put a swift end to the fighting. He would be a hero among the real loyalists of the Americas – ones who understood that bravery lay with the men in red and power was only granted to those who spoke the King's English. And the money Bates had tucked away for him all these years would buy him a lot of power.

He unholstered his pistol, walking calmly and swiftly towards the man barking orders. Three officers, a lieutenant and two captains by their uniforms, stood to Jackson's left, listening to his instructions. They paid no heed to the man in the long black coat who walked with an air of confidence. The battle was raging, men were dying, screams from the wounded filled their ears... Joseph Richards had lived his life cloaked in shadows. Now was the time to arise and take his place among the giants of his time....

The .45 caliber pistol was in his hand now, warm to the grip despite the chill in the air, and he brought it up in one smooth motion. *Bang, Bang, you're dead.* He was ten feet away now, nine feet, and he began measuring the distance in heartbeats. The power of the .45 would push the lead ball through the general's chest and out the other side before anyone would have time to blink. Five feet...four...

He heard a pistol shot go off to his right before he felt the sting of its bite deep in his left thigh. His knee buckled and he fell onto his back, his pistol flying out of his hand onto the ground beside him. Richards held his leg, cursing, his eyes closed off from the pain. Who had shot at him? How could...

"You picked a bad day to show up, James," a voice said coolly from above him. Richards tried to open his eyes, and the tears stung him. *James?* He hadn't heard that name in a while. When his vision cleared, he saw the familiar muzzle of another .45 caliber pistol aimed at him. The man holding it was John Colter, one of the marshals who had plagued him for months now. The trapper. Friend of Gass...doesn't he know he's too late to save the lout?

"You!" Richards sneered. "I should have killed you months ago!"

"You tried, remember?" Colter shot back. "Too bad for you, you're a poor excuse for a killer. Trying to take out General Jackson, and blame it on the British? I've got a problem with that. A big one." He pulled back the hammer of the large steel gray weapon in his palm and heard a satisfying click.

General Jackson stared at the two men who faced each other down less than ten feet from where he stood. All thoughts of the battle were momentarily lost, as he realized how closely he had faced death.

"Marshal Colter, is this the man responsible for killing Captain Lewis?"

"Yes sir, general, it seems we've finally met Joseph Richards. But that is just an alias, general, perhaps one of many. His real name is Captain James Neelly, and he is, or was, an Indian agent for the government stationed St. Louis. Now he is the right hand man, so to speak, of Frederick Bates, who is currently… but not for long, pray tell… at large. He accompanied Mr. Lewis along the Natchez Trace, then paid off the Cherokee for the hit, if the stories ring true."

"I've stayed up many an evening listening to tales of Captain Lewis' bravery and fortitude…under the most trying conditions. To allow the killer of such a man to breathe another day of life would be a mockery of all I hold dear." He snapped his fingers as the two captains ran to his side. "Gentlemen, assist this man to the stockade. We'll let the court system mete out its own justice."

Richards thought frantically, kicking out at Colter's legs while twisting his body away to the right, hoping to catch him off balance. The marshal saw the movement but was too late. His pistol spoke loudly, the bullet thudding harmlessly in the dirt, as his own body careened away from Richards.

The mercenary tried to hobble away on his good leg, until another British rocket exploded not far away to his left, causing him to hesitate for a fraction of a second. He fell onto his back, his right hand dug wildly for the gun in the dirt beside him, finding the stock, gripping the cold metal of the handle while bringing the business end up and out in one smooth motion…

The pistol fired like a thunderclap, a small red hole appearing between the eyes of his adversary, while the back of his head exploded like a watermelon on a hot summer day. The man fell back against the ground, the blood from his leg wound congealing in the dirt under him. Captain James Neelly, aka Joseph Richards, stared sightlessly skyward.

Colter came forward slowly, hesitant at first, but confident that there was no more threat from this godforsaken menace. He stood up straight, and looked at the general who gazed upon at the scene, his face grim and impassive.

"My apologizes, General, for the mess. I guess he didn't like prison food."

Chapter 84

Colter left the general to his aides as he turned around, surveying the scene. It was fortunate he has spotted the man in time – ever since Nathaniel had warned them of the man in the black cloak who had shot Colonel Henderson from behind – "able bodied, excellent with the side arm, and, I think experienced beyond his years in the art of warfare" – each of the marshals had been looking for him, waiting for him to make another move.

With Patrick helping the general with the men of the 44th infantry, filling in for the late colonel, and Ordway and Bratton stationed on post on either side of the great defensive line, it was up to Pryor and himself to look for one man among thousands milling along the middle breastwork fortifications. It was Colter who suggested he shadow the general in case an attempt was made to cut him down.

He breathed in deeply and closed his eyes. Just for a moment. He remembered now the explosion from the ammunition wagon that gave him concern for the general's immediate safety. Covering the general more closely at that moment allowed him to spot his quarry just in the nick of time. But what caused the explosion in the first place?

He looked over at the carnage, the blast zone about one hundred feet from the general's position, near gun battery four. Many of the men were getting up...a few were not. His eyes searched for his colleague, finally seeing someone kneeling beside the prostrate form of Patrick Gass, calling for help. *No, no, no...*

Putting the death of Richards out of his mind, he raced hard across the field to where his friend lay. Gass' head was covered in blood, lying in the hands of a young private, his own shell-shocked eyes belying the horrors he saw that terrible day. Colter took over for him, gently lifting his friend's head and cradled it in his own lap. The right side of Patrick's face looked particularly nasty. He must have taken a direct him from something in the wagon...he looked around, trying to decide what to do. He knelt down beside him, holding his head as best he could.

"Patrick, can you hear me? Patrick!"

He closed off all other sounds around him, wondering how he could staunch the flow of blood that continued to escape from this man from so many different holes. He pulled off his cotton shirt, tearing it in long strips, then tried his best to bandage the wounds of his friend. The head wound was the worst, and John wondered if he would survive. He looked once again at his chest – it rose up and down hesitantly, as if it wasn't sure if it would still function. How long could he survive?

Time seemed to stand still for John Colter, as the battle around him and the struggle for Patrick's life seemed inextricably joined together. The explosions of the furious aerial bombardment continued and Patrick's breathing grew shallow. The smoke and dust seemed to choke more life from the fragile grasp of the great Irishman, but he didn't let go completely. Somehow, he struggled to hold on to his presence in this world, as if telling God he had more work still to do.

"You're not ready, Patrick. You tell Him that! You hold on, you hear?"

The noise around the pair began to die down and Patrick's breathing seemed to improve along with it. Gass began choking violently and Colter turned him onto his side, seeing ribbons of bright red blood pour from his mouth, making small rivers in the dirt beside him. He was bleeding inside as well.

John Colter suddenly became aware of the silence that befell the air around him. Gone were the hideous shrieking whistles of the Congreve rockets, the loud explosions of the cannon balls as they slammed into rock abutments or packed earth, or the cries of the wounded both nearby and far away. A still wind had come in from the south, and the smoke that just an hour before lay impenetrable across the field now began to lift.

Colter looked up and saw an incredible sight. The British had vacated their gun positions along the far side of the plantation field, most of the cannons and support carriages lay broken or damaged. Bodies of the dead lay scattered in the field between the two armies, more red than blue he thought, but it scarcely mattered now. It appeared, at least for the moment, that the Americans had held off the mighty British for another day.

Suddenly there was movement from the man who lay on his side next to him. Patrick Gass fell over on his back, his one good eye looking up at the sky. John Colter gazed at him and smiled. Patrick squeezed his hand and blinked back.

Chapter 85

January 8, 1816
New Orleans, Louisiana

"What's the word on the 85th? I sent Thornton up the river hours ago! Has there been any news?" Major-General Edward Pakenham paced briskly back and forth outside his field command center, two hours before the first light of dawn would break over the horizon.

"Colonel Thorton and his 85th regiment were delayed, sir," General Gibbs declared. "The canal they attempted to dig, in order to advance their boats up the Mississippi, collapsed and they were forced to drag them over the mud instead. They did engage a company of Kentucky militia, and Admiral Cochrane gave them cover fire from his flotilla on the river, but they've not yet reached the point behind the American lines as we'd hoped. With daylight upon us, it might be worthwhile to consider withdrawal at this point."

"Damnation!" Pakenham shouted to all in earshot. "We can't withdraw – the Admiral already boasted he'd take his marines and wipe out the American defenses for me if I failed. I'll not give him the satisfaction! I hoped to set up a position behind their lines as well as in front, but we still sport a two to one advantage over them in numbers – not as much as I prefer in open combat, but I'll take it.

"We should continue our plan and advance General Keane's column up along the river's edge – initiate a decisive attack against a single point in their defenses in their first two gun batteries and overrun them. General Gibbs will take his 4th, 21st, and 44th infantry and come in behind General Keane, pushing their way through the weak American defenses. We'll keep Major-General Lambert's battalion in reserve. We must move now, while we still have the advantage of darkness and the fog to shield us. The closer we get to them before they see us, the closer we come to victory! Tell them to stand strong and proud!"

As Pakenham spoke, the captains who stood around him saw a degree of confidence return to their leader. He had been sullen and brusque with anyone within earshot, ever since the debacle of their rocket bombardment a week earlier. Today, as they went into battle, his military experience took over – he found ways to forge through setbacks and difficulties and get the job done. It was why his men respected him. Today, on the eve of battle, he was a changed man.

"Our attack will be a huge success and will deliver a key blow to this rebellious nation. Even as our two countries work out a treaty in Ghent, a victory this day would give us a huge advantage in negotiations. I also plan on taking the fleet up the Mississippi this week and seize as much land as we can hold, especially along the western shores. A renewed English presence will twist the knife in the wound we are inflicting today. I take full responsibility for the tactical delay, but it was necessary to get all available reinforcements on site and in position before we move on them. I only want to do this once."

He smiled as he looked upon the faces of his captains. "Our decisive attack will deliver the death knell to the enemy. As we did against the French, we will shove the frontal assault down their throats. They will be overwhelmed – they will break down and run for the hills! The men must remain strong and steadfast. The great British line of red will make them quiver in their boots. Thousands of English swarming their flimsy breastworks will send them running for cover... all the way back to Washington!"

A rousing cry from his captains gave him cause to smile. Only one man who stood along the side remained silent. Pakenham turned to address him directly.

"And you, Bates? I see you are not eager to come to our cause."

"On the contrary, general, I feel the British forces have an overwhelming advantage. I just fear a singular assault is not the best way to defeat the Americans. At least not here. We may have softened them with the aerial assault last week, but their guns and defenses remain strong. They have one advantage – they are fighting for their country, their homes, and their families. They will not run as easily as you think."

"And what do you propose?"

Bates smiled thinly. "As you know, I arrived here with a plan of my own. I have positioned a man behind their lines, intent on sabotage and… whenever possible, assassination. He will attempt to disrupt things as much as he can. I told him to blend in with them, pick a defensive position that would afford the British the greatest advantage, and then work his magic to give us the break we need at the right time. It almost worked during our demonstration, I believe. When Colonel Rennie was able to get around their defensive line through the swamp, I have to believe he was a key factor. The explosion of their gun battery at that precise moment was his signature. The fact that you ordered them to withdrawal was the only reason we are still standing here facing them yet again."

"So you propose that this man of yours can work his 'magic' one more time? Help give us the key advantage when we need it?"

"That's why I'm here, general. I know the Americans and I know how they think. Most of all, I came to you prepared and have done something none of you had even thought of all this time. I have played a mind game with the Americans for twenty years." He laughed. "If you want to beat the Americans, you need to think like them. I was born and raised here – much to my chagrin – but it has given me more money and perks than I could have gotten anywhere else. It will give you the keys to victory today."

"So you suggest we focus on the swamp area again?" General Gibbs spoke up. "You have played your mind games but we English play to win. We have tens of thousands of men ready to roll over the American defenses – we have no use of mind games. Put a gun in our hands and 10,000 men at my backs – we are unstoppable."

Pakenham put up his hand. "Gentlemen, the decision is mine. We will continue as planned and drive straight at their western end, towards the river. But, in deference to Mr. Bates' idea, perhaps we should send your detachment, Gibbs, to the swamp area and get around their defenses yet again. Give your man a chance to work his magic, so to speak. Create a two pronged attack. General Lambert will be held in reserve for either side. The timely death of General Jackson would make things much easier for us, if the fates align to grant us that request. Perhaps your man should be given a chance to do more damage."

Bates smiled. "Thank you sir. I think you'll find my man very capable of getting your forces through."

General Pakenham dismissed his captains, but called Bates to remain behind. Smiling, he pulled out two glasses from a trunk behind him and placed them on the table. He pulled a decanter of red wine off a makeshift shelf that was filled with books and map charts, and poured the expensive liquid into the glasses. Taking one for himself and handing the other to his guest, he said "I was saving this for after our victory today, but I'd like to take this time and give a toast to you. I was skeptical at first when you arrived, but your information has been invaluable to me, and your knowledge of these Americans, as well as the financial contributions you've provided, has been most eagerly received." He smiled coldly, his eyes unseen orbs that took in all light around them, revealing nothing. "Here is to victory."

"To victory," Bates replied. "To the British cause...and the pride of our homeland."

Pakenham put down his glass, and looked at Bates across the table. "When our forces have advanced to the American line and have taken it, you will ride with me as victors of a just cause. Your presence will let them know the depths of their defeat. Outnumbered, outsmarted, outmaneuvered...their defeat will be all encompassing. I am pleased to have you on our side."

Chapter 86

"General Jackson!" the voice of Captain McDermott filtered into his sleepy haze. Andrew Jackson sat up quickly on the sofa in his war room, the cobwebs of his fitful slumber already gone from his mind. He was all business.

"Yes, what is the matter, Captain?" he asked, getting up and pouring himself a drink of water from a decanter on the table.

"Sir, we have reports of British troop movement and feel you ought to attend to the situation. As you know, in the week since they withdrew from their aerial bombardment on our line, General Pakenham has brought ashore an additional 10,000 men. You've had us watching them for days now. Based on what our scouts can tell us, I believe this is the final assault – the one you've been anticipating."

Jackson looked hard at his aide-de-camp. "Philip, I appreciate your patience with me this week. If you're right and their primary attack is at hand, may God have mercy on us all."

The general arrived on the scene just before 8 o'clock that morning, but a thick fog still hung over the 1000 yards of plantation grounds that separated the armies of the British and American forces. Little could be seen, but the tension was high as word quickly spread among the gunners and riflemen in blue.

With Patrick Gass recovering from his serious wounds at the general's manor house, the remaining marshals had stayed in New Orleans until he could be moved. Jackson sent an aide to fetch them at once, requesting their presence and assistance if they saw fit to offer it.

The enemies they faced, and had vowed to bring down, were now joined together and had been for several weeks. The murderer Frederick Bates was still out there, protected by the English guns and thousands of soldiers that threatened the very country Jackson loved. Today's events would determine whether these Englishmen would crawl over the bodies of American blue or if the rivers would bleed the color of the English red coats. It was an opportunity Jackson knew the marshals would not pass up.

The American general surveyed the defensive line starting from the first gun battery on the road, about seventy feet from the Mississippi river. Its armament consisted of a six-inch howitzer, which fired high aerial shots into the back lines of the enemy, as well as two brass cannons that fired twelve pound balls. Ninety yards from battery one stood a cannon that fired twenty-four pound heavy shot from a short hill overlooking the field of battle. It was the highest elevation along the line. Manning it was a crew directly off the ill-fated *U.S. Carolina*, commanded by Lt. Norris.

Fifty yards further along, members of the French navy commanded gun battery three with two cannons firing twenty-four pound balls. Battery four had the largest cannon yet, a thirty-two pounder led by Lt. Crawley of the U.S. Navy, which was only twenty yards further east. Battery five, 190 yards away, had two small cannons firing six-pound shot.

Jackson walked past these placements and the hundreds of men that stood along the parapets, checking their muskets, talking to each other, or nervously looking out into the fog at the faceless enemy. When the time came for action, they would be ready...of that the general had no doubt. He patted some men on the shoulder and spoke words of encouragement.

The mighty forces of the English army would soon rise from the woods beyond the field and make their presence known. The British had moved in an additional 10,000 men? How would his meager forces stand up to such an assault? He only hoped he could gain a tactical advantage of some sort. He was heavily outmanned and outgunned – it would be up to sheer tenacity and God's will that would win out today.

When he got to gun battery six, he noticed the men were working on the brass twelve pounder. He inquired what the problem was.

"The powder got wet, sir," replied a young lad with black hair. "The powder is sticking when we pack it. I'm trying to dry out the barrel now – hope we won't be needing it too much today." He had the uniform of a French private, as did his three companions. Lt. Bertel was in charge here, Jackson remembered.

"Has your gun commander looked for an alternate powder cask? The battle will be upon us soon, I suspect, and I need all guns at the ready when the fog clears."

The lad assured the general that Lt. Bertel was working on getting it. A nervous smile crossed his face. "Ah, general?"

"Yes, private?"

"I just joined up, sir, only a few months ago. Haven't seen much action over in France before the Peninsular War ended. I've heard stories about the British army that...well, it's scary if it's true. I want to know...do we stand a chance in hell of holding them off? I know the Americans are good people – me and the boys are staying with one family in the village. But are they ready to fight to the death? Are they able to look the red coat in the eye and pull the trigger? Or are we fighting a losing cause?"

"Private, let me assure you that the Americans fighting alongside you today are among the bravest I have had the privilege to stand with. We will either win this battle today, or lay down our bodies for the good of our country. This is our home... there is no greater cause to fight for than to protect our property, our livelihood... our families. We stand strong with you."

Silently, Jackson continued down the line, stopping at battery seven, 190 yards east. It had two armaments, a long, brass eighteen pound cannon taken from the Spanish a decade earlier, and a smaller six pounder, both served by members of the U.S. artillery. Finally, sixty yards ahead was the last line of defense, the battery who suffered that fateful accident with the brass cannonade a few weeks earlier. Five people had died in the explosion that day. Four more had been badly injured and had been forced to take their leave of the battle. They had replaced the brass cannon with another six pounder, small but sturdy.

The batteries were in place – the men as ready as they could be. General Andrew Jackson looked out across the fog and saw that the sun had begun to slowly burn through the haze. He estimated the wait would be short indeed.

As he approached his command center located behind battery four, he was met by one of his captains, Marcus DelPaoli. He liked the man – strong and dependable. His artillery men looked up to him and they knew he had their backs in the thick of the fight. "Where do you want me to station the Kentuckians, general? The new crew under Thomas and Adair?"

"Hm, that lot," Jackson replied, his face barely able to conceal a smirk. "I wish they had half the firepower they should have brought with them! Can you imagine? We were expecting reinforcements of 2, 250 men – and only one man in five had a weapon of any sort!"

"Most of them needed clothes, as well, sir," DelPaoli said. "But you were able to bring the town together in a way I don't think anyone else could. You had the town purchase woolen blankets and all the ladies in New Orleans set about making clothes for them all. I've never seen the like!"

"Can't believe they arrived four days ago – seems a little longer to me. Has the last of them been properly outfitted?"

"Yes sir, I believe we've accounted for the vast majority of the men. Those with weapons, I suggest putting along the wall between batteries four and five, and between six and seven – those are the areas with the largest distance between guns. We'll need more snipers on the walls and they can fill in the gaps."

"As for the rest of the Kentucky men, you can position them on the rear lines, in case Line Jackson falls in vain. They'll have to use whatever muskets they might find or can pry off dead fingers."

"Yes sir, it will be done." Captain DelPaoli turned and bowed slightly before departing.

Jackson sighed. To have had the support of a properly outfitted unit to reinforce his own might have been the key ingredient to tip the scale in their favor. As it stands, it would be hit or miss. The odds were against them. Was fate as well?

Chapter 87

The first two conclave rockets shot high into the sky, bursting into a brilliant display that made the lifting fog almost shine red with color. Was it a signal? The fog was starting to lift slightly but not enough to see more than a few hundred yards at most. Andrew Jackson jumped on top of the nearest wall and called out as loud as he could. "Call to arms! All men prepare to fire! Hold on my command!"

All eyes were upon him as he stood his ground. It wouldn't be wise to waste ammunition firing blindly into the fog. Wait until they show themselves...have patience....

The long cannons can cover the distance of 1000 yards but are most effective inside of 500. Due to their higher trajectory, the howitzers have a shorter effective range. It would not do to fire them too early in the battle.

He looked at the men on the line. They were several men deep along the wall, each armed with a musket or a Springfield rifle. They would work as a four man team, the first man firing once and then dashing to the rear of the line to reload. The next man would take a shot and do the same. In this way, they could offer the enemy an almost continual assault of shot and ball, but their range also was limited to 400 feet.

Andrew Jackson was suddenly aware of the complete silence that surrounded him at that moment. It was with utmost clarity that he perceived the biting cold upon his exposed neck, yet he felt no discomfort. Adrenaline coursed through his body, bringing a warmth that often accompanied periods of action and excitement.

He heard the far off call of an owl, perched on a tree branch somewhere far to his flank. The acrid smell of gunpowder swirled across the defensive line as each gun battery prepared its mighty cannons. His eyes strained for any signs of the enemy. Patience was a virtue to those in command. He was calm...he was in control...he had vowed to win this day.

John Ordway stood along the wall near the sixth gun battery, studying the open field with a spyglass. Men were quietly standing by, ready and waiting for something – anything – to start. After the first rockets were seen fifteen minutes ago, the anticipation became almost palpable. Nerves were on edge...fingers sweaty on the stocks of their muskets...

"Red! I see red! Straightaway!" Ordway called out suddenly. "Estimate 600 yards, bearing left!" Others relayed the cry to the men all along the wall, and Captain Nathaniel Pryor, now a member of the 44th infantry manning gun battery six, ran up to report to General Jackson.

The commander stood up on top of the parapet, looking out across the field, his own spyglass held against his face. "I see them, captain. There appears to be a battalion heading for the swamps, another for the river. There might be more but I can't see them yet. Tell the men to continue to hold their rifle fire. We need to draw them in closer before we make our move."

On the wall, Ordway continued to look out with his spyglass, observing the approach of the British to the left. The fog was slowly lifting, revealing to all the defenders a long line of faint shadows approaching in an orderly pace.

"Four hundred yards away!" he cried.

Without warning the brass 12-pounder from battery six opened fire on the approaching column, sending grape-shot through the right side of the line. Several British soldiers fell but the line kept coming steadily. They were tightly packed alongside each other and were many rows deep. Their own muskets could be seen now, bayonets securely on the end for close range fighting. No rifle shots had yet been fired by either side. Don't waste the shot in haste – wait until they are a little closer...

John Ordway heard another cannon fire off to his left, closer to the swamp, and then one from the right, perhaps from battery two or one. He couldn't be sure. Gunners reloaded the cannon in battery six next to him and fired again. He looked out once again. This time there was no need of binoculars. The line of red coats was clearly visible in the lifting fog.

More and more cannons opened up on the approaching enemy, and several British soldiers dropped to the ground in the open field. Men in formation behind them quickly filled the gaps in the line with a calm and determined pace.

Soldiers in blue were pressed down against the stone wall, prepared to fire their muskets at the approaching English. But just as Ordway thought they were within musket range, a smoke thicker than the recent fog began drifting over from the leftmost batteries.

"Sir!" Ordway yelled. "The smoke from batteries Seven and Eight is blowing our way! It'll cause a problem for our riflemen to get a clear target!"

Captain Pryor relayed the issue to General Jackson, who immediately ordered cease fire from the left gun batteries. As the smoke began to clear from the field, the American commander surveyed the situation. The mile long stretch of flat, open prairie between the Mississippi River on the right to the swamp on the left contained three battalions of British soldiers, each behind the other, packed formations, several men deep.

One battalion was approximately two hundred yards to the left, trying to cross the terrain and hug the swamp. Another was forging its way towards the river on the right. Finally, he saw the third battalion, which was waiting behind in reserve, about a thousand yards distant, and more towards the river. The main open prairie between gun batteries four through six was relatively empty. The divisions of British soldiers in each battalion were organized in stiff columns four men deep, with 100 yards separating one group from one in front.

Jackson knew the British were smart enough to try and skirt around his breastworks rather than risk exposing themselves across open ground. Their attempt to advance under the cover of fog and darkness was a sound decision and the Brits captured more ground than he'd prefer to give them.

But the one tactical advantage Jackson had sought all morning had finally presented itself. Even the most formidable army in the world can not control nature as much as they would like to. The fog didn't quite last long enough for the British to completely cover the exposed ground. Many of their ranks were now left open to the close range of the American riflemen and artilleries.

General Andrew Jackson smiled grimly as he raised his left hand high then, with solemn determination, brought it down hard in the air. Captains relayed the 'Go' directive to the men on the wall, and those four-men teams began firing their lead shot at will.

The riflemen all along the fortified defenses sent volley after volley of round lead shot towards the advancing columns of redcoats, their numbers falling away under the withering assault. Those along the swamp tried to stay close to the trees, while their fife and drum corps started to play a formation step in a vain attempt to keep them in line. Within ten minutes, the first British division advancing along the swamp had completely collapsed, its members either dead, wounded, or scattered in all directions. The second division behind it moved up and immediately began to face the brunt of the American marksmanship.

Jackson barked orders to the captains along the defenses to keep the men in line, their four man teams coordinated and the bodies of their men covered from the return fire. He could see the level pitch of the battle field was making it impossible for the British caught in the open to find sufficient cover – only the trees by the swamp afforded any amount of protection.

Suddenly Jackson stopped, and looked carefully out towards the east. Batteries seven and eight were firing off explosives and lead balls, working in conjunction with the riflemen along the wall, but once the British hit the tree line of the marsh, the American artillery was proving to be less effective. The mighty cannons couldn't turn completely to face the trees because of the limited space in the breastworks, and the musket fire hit as many trees as they did bodies of British soldiers.

He called out to Captain Pryor who commanded the sixth gun battery near him. "Captain, I believe the enemy will try to push around the swamp and get behind the lines! Put someone in charge of Six, and take a company to head them off! Pour every ounce of lead into their positions and don't let them get around on us again!"

Chapter 88

P ryor saluted smartly, jumped on his horse which was tied up a short distance behind the line, and called to his lieutenants to gather men held in reserve. Within five minutes, he had a group of two hundred men at his disposal, and they set off at a run for gun battery eight. As he moved along he spotted William Bratton, who had taken charge of several rifle teams between six and seven, and told him to join them. He needed experience when he could find it.

When Pryor reached the end of the wall past battery eight, he saw several soldiers in red coats trying to advance through the marshy lands on the far side of the canal. He knew from experience that they would attempt to cross further down – and he vowed not one of them would.

He took half the men and marched them to the end of the swamp where the enemy had crossed two weeks back. When he passed the spot upon which Colonel Henderson had died, he bowed his head. *Your efforts were not in vain, colonel. We got your killer. And you have showed us the way to stop them today.*

About ten red coats appeared on the other side of the canal, which was at this point no larger than two feet across. But a single look at the one hundred muskets pointed in their direction was enough for all of them to put their hands up in surrender. Not a shot was fired. Pryor smiled in satisfaction. *This is just the beginning.*

William Bratton surveyed the scene before him standing behind the ramparts of gun battery eight. His long red hair swayed lazily in the wind, not the least bit contained by the beaver cap resting on his head. His face was haggard and his red whiskers hadn't been trimmed in several days. He wondered when this fighting was ever going to end. Would it be today? Next week? Next month? He was tired of the killing, on both sides. Too many lives lost.

He saw the several hundred bodies that lay on the ground in the field not more than 200 yards distant. Bratton thought of the reason he was here in the first place. To make sure the death of one man would not go unpunished. Who was to blame for the deaths of all these men here today?

A round slug struck the wall close to his face, and he winced as small stone slivers cut across his cheek. He touched his face and his fingers came away with traces of blood. Not too bad, he thought. He hefted his musket, hand crafted fifteen years ago in the back woods of Kentucky. It had dropped buffalo in their tracks, and caused bears to think twice before approaching... but in all that time, he could count the number of human lives his musket had claimed on one hand.

Even when he was in the midst of the Battle of the Thames, and saw Tecumseh fighting for his life and for his people, his thoughts had not gone to killing. He had fought several men that day and had killed a few. But taking someone's life was not something that he enjoyed or would do without a heavy conscience resting upon his soul.

He saw several men in the second division break almost immediately, scattering for the closest thing to protect them from the vicious onslaught of grape shot. Four of them ran straight towards the ramparts where he and his fellow men in blue were perched above, diving headfirst into the shallow waters of the canal right underneath the defender's position.

Bratton heard the four men in the water, just to the left and below the rampart he was behind, but was unwilling to expose himself long enough to get a visual. They were trapped, and he preferred they stay there. There were no commanders on horses that he could see – just the waves upon waves of men in red coats whose ranks were falling quickly asunder.

John Colter stood near gun battery two, calling to a four man team whose ranks had just been reduced by two, thanks to a well aimed British rocket. He pulled in reserves from those nearby, filling the spaces quickly and efficiently. He was not big on military discipline – John Colter would be the last man to tell you differently – but he understood the need to keep up the defenses, and he was as gruff and ornery with these lads as if he was back on the western trail of discovery.

To keep them on their toes, and thinking – that was his job today as much as wielding the big musket that he carried under his arm. His defenses would not allow a breach by the enemy. He would swear his life on it. It was a decision that was easy to make. The alternative was a swift death.

Suddenly, he saw amidst the sea of red trying mightily to withstand the hails of lead shot his men were delivering, several officers arriving on the scene of battle. They were easy to spot – riding horses, their uniforms stiffly pressed and their medals gleaming in the morning sun, they tried to rally their flagging men, spur them into an action that was both unwise and unhealthy.

Battery two was the highest point along the line of the American defenders, sitting on a short hill overlooking the flat fields beyond. Colter got up on a high stone ledge, and kneeling, took careful aim at the officer. The man was riding towards the Americans, his left arm lifting a sword high over his head. *I'm sure you look pretty impressive to the boys on the field. Let's see how good you look when I'm finished...*

He took aim for the center of the man's chest, no more than a hundred yards away now, and gently squeezed the trigger. The musket was filled with a round slug and the explosion of the powder sent it out across the field with a loud report. Colter waited a second to see if his aim was true. He saw the man continue as before, his left hand held high but then, without warning he leaned forward, toppling off his horse onto the packed earth. Three British soldiers near the fallen officer quickly grabbed him and tried to carry him back behind the line of fire. One of the rescuers was hit by shot and the group collapsed, before struggling to rise again. This time they made it back unmolested with their fallen officer.

As Colter reloaded his musket, he could see a curious thing. The men in red had stopped their advancement altogether, even though they were now within striking distance of the parapets. Several carried ladders, but these never made it against the walls, nor did any British soldiers gain ground beyond the last few yards. Those who were left had scattered, or been cut down. Colter jumped down from his perch and watched as the attackers retreated.

Chapter 89

"General Pakenham!" Captain Holester cried, running up to his commanding officer. "Colonel Rennie has been hit, leading the men against the first two batteries! The men have broken formation and many are retreating! The field is littered with our fallen brethren! What do you propose?"

"Have General Lambert's men shore up Keane's numbers. How does the battle go against the points east?"

"Many are trapped in the trees, and no one has been able to get around their defenses yet. They are cutting us down where we stand. Many have scattered or fallen in battle. We must retreat on all fronts, sir!"

"Never! I promised that I would deliver a victory this day and I shall do it, if it takes every man I have! We did it against the French – these Americans are no different! Keep the men moving forward. If Gibbs' detachment needs more men, send the 93rd Highlanders, as well as General Keane, over to help them. I'll also want Mullen's men from the 44th to assist as well. Remember this day, captain! It will be glorious!"

Pakenham ran to his horse, a prized white stallion he had brought with him on each of his overseas commands, and rode up to where several men stood together.

"Bates! Ride with me, now! You wanted me to take the eastern route – help me figure a way past their artillery and muskets. We'll go across with the 93rd and join General Gibbs and General Keane and make our breakthrough there!"

Frederick Bates looked hard at the man under whom he had pledged to serve and nodded his agreement. It was not in his nature to put himself in harm's way if it could be avoided – he had spent his life using others to perform the dirtiest of assignments that he required, but perhaps a victory here would secure him in good accord with his Majesty…

He took the reins of a black mare offered to him by a lieutenant and rode off towards the front behind his new commander. As they reached the southern edge of the battle, he saw hundreds of British soldiers nervously pacing and talking in whispered tones. These must be Lambert's men, he thought. They silently parted for the two riders, who rode through them and into the field of battle. To their left, men from the 93rd highlanders were already running over, their own muskets pointing cautiously towards the enemy a thousand yards to the north.

Major-General Edward Pakenham liked to lead by example and rode hard to the front of the line, his sword held out in front of him, calling out to the soldiers all around. Many were heartened by his presence and rallied around him, running hard on his heels, joining their own cries with his.

Frederick Bates rode thirty yards behind him, together with several British officers who did their best to encourage the men of the 93rd highlanders division. They were a tough lot, harking from the Scottish hills north of England, and went into the battle running hard and fast. There was no cover for them, and dozens were killed by artillery fire from the gun batteries three and four before they got too far. But they rallied on, heading northeast in a diagonal direction, getting closer to the defender's rifle fire with each step.

After several minutes, Bates was hard put to understand his commander's decision to forge this difficult route to the swamp. By the time they were within rifle fire from battery seven, now only 200 yards from the American wall, he could see hundreds of brave highlander soldiers lying on the ground behind him, stretching out across the field. Their coats of green and blue contrasted with the red worn by the British soldiers, but they all died the same way. Such a waste of fine men.

He spurred on his horse to overtake Pakenham, who had stopped briefly to rally what remained of the reinforcements he was supplying. Bates was a practical man and he did not mince words when he had the opportunity with his commander.

"General, I think this effort has been foolhardy at best!" he cried. "We've already lost two thirds of the men just getting here! We should take what we have and retreat now!"

"Withdrawal is not an option, Mr. Bates!" Pakenham declared vehemently. "I will not give anyone reason to doubt the resolve of the British army!"

"Then may I suggest an alternate approach? We storm the wall now – we'll never make the swamp at this rate! It's only a little over a hundred yards – I'm not one for a direct assault if we can get around them, but the swamp is still 300 yards away and we'll be in range of their artillery and rifles all the way!"

Pakenham looked at Bates, his eyes narrowing. "It was your idea to strike through the marshes and get around them. Don't back out on your ideas just because…"

The general felt the bite of the round lead ball hit his left arm seconds before the pain registered in his brain. He tried to move it, but it hung limply at his side, the forearm showing a red stain that grew quickly. Cursing loudly, Pakenham turned his horse around away from the direction of fire, but stopped short. His arm seemed to be on fire and he felt it difficult to concentrate through the pain. But he had been in difficult situations before…

The sudden bite of another slug into his right leg caught him off guard and the general fell from his horse in a heap. Seconds later the beautiful white stallion went down on its own, the victim of three shots to his chest and side. As the general witnessed the disaster unfold around him, he felt himself being helped up by a man behind him.

Frederick Bates stood by, handing the reins of his own mare to the general. "Only you can lead these men, general! I'll help you up. Give me your good leg. Once we're through with cleaning up this mess, we'll bandage you up in no time!"

The American turncoat helped his British commander into the saddle and guided his horse around, so he could face what remained of his men. Pakenham was losing blood and his face had turned pale. He was leaning heavily in the saddle but refused to give up command.

"Gentlemen! It's time to rally!" he tried to shout but his words became lost over the sound of the defender's attack. He turned to Bates, "Get General Keane to lead the men towards the swamp! We can't stand here any longer!"

"I'll do my best, sir," Bates said and he left the general and ran back towards where he saw Keane conversing with Captain Holester. Bates threw himself to the ground as he felt an explosion fall just yards away from them. General Keane barely flinched, riding high in the saddle of his horse. Bates got up and ran over. "General Keane," he announced. "Major-General Pakenham requests you take the rest of these men to aid General Gibbs. If my plan is to work, we need to get around their defensive line and quickly, before all is lost!"

General Keane was a short man, barely five foot and change, his hair already growing white despite being only thirty-five. He had fought Napoleon's army just a few months ago and was unperturbed by the turn of events here today.

"These are but farmers and country bumpkins – surely they can not hold up much longer!" He turned to the captain, telling him to gather the men for one last attempt to cross towards Gibb's position.

Keane looked out upon the remaining distance to the swamp and the limited protection the trees afforded him and his men. 300 yards at best, and the line would take them across the seventh and eighth gun batteries in the defensive line. He could already see Gibbs' men trying to overrun the last gun battery, but their men were falling under a furious response by the Americans.

Holding up his sword high over his head, General Keane called out to rally his troops and spurred his horse towards the marshes. Frederick Bates, having given up his own horse, ran behind him in company with several men from the Scottish hills. General Pakenham was making his progress as well, but it was slow and uneven. Bates ran to him when they were within seventy yards of the seventh gun battery. Pakenham seemed ready to collapse but he held a death grip on the reins of his horse. His face was a mask of concentration as he continued to bleed out.

Bates looked into the distance to see how Gibbs was progressing. In a few minutes time General Keane had come alongside the beleaguered commander. Seconds later Bates saw the body of the newly arrived general fall off his horse, taking a direct hit from an American musket. Bates closed his eyes. Things were getting worse and worse.

"Come general, we must retreat! This is madness to stay here! We have no defenses whatsoever – our men are falling all around us! General Keane has just been wounded, if not killed, and…"

Without warning, Major-General Edward Pakenham, commander of the British forces, was flung off his horse with great force, the body of the great black mare coming down on his legs as he lay there. Bates fell to the ground in surprise, gasping at the blood running in small rivers from both rider and mount. They had been hit by the same shot, having been positioned so close together.

Chapter 90

Bates looked up and saw the defenders along the American line no more than seventy feet away. He was a sitting duck, and he knew it. As others were lifting the general's inert form and attempting to retreat back towards relative safety, Bates looked around desperately. He stood up, and saw Captain Holester run towards the line just to the west of the seventh gun battery.

There were hundreds of Americans on the wall, taking turns shooting at the men in red, but there were at least a dozen or more of his countrymen holed up in the waters of the canal butting up against the wall. It was a place they could not get killed very easily – but that was a hollow victory.

Bates followed quickly on the heels of the captain, dodging bullets as fast as he could, and flung himself headfirst into the murky waters of the canal. He was surprised at how shallow the water really was. He was greeted with silent nods from a few soldiers in red coats. He noticed several of them had been hard at work using their bayonets to try and cut a hole through the earthworks in an attempt to get into the enemy lines. But they had not gotten far along in their attempt before giving up.

Frederick Bates sat up, and for the first time in what seemed forever, was able to look upon the field without fear of being cut in half by a well placed gunshot. He saw the great cannon of the seventh gun battery protruding out above his position and slightly to the east. He also turned in the other direction and saw General Gibbs shooting at someone along the wall. But riding his horse on to the battlefield allowed him to become an easy target and it was only a few moments later that Bates saw him fall, having taken several hits close together. Gibbs hit the ground hard and did not get up again. His horse ran off to the east, but it soon suffered a similar fate at the hands of these backwoods boys. *Damn them!*

The field was in total chaos, bodies in both red and green coats lying everywhere. Many were trying to move, but more of them were not. Frederick Bates realized to his chagrin that New Orleans was lost to the British. Their commanders had been killed, hundreds of men had been lost, and thousands most likely had been wounded. Perhaps more importantly, the resolve of the British army would not hold up for another round of fighting.

Suddenly, Captain Holester rose from his position, and called out to the Americans on the line. He had attached a white rag to the end of his rifle and was waving it in the air.

"Hold your fire! We surrender!"

"What are you doing, you fool!" Bates yelled. "Do you want us all to get killed?"

Holester looked down on the man sitting in the water. "I've just saved your life, Mr. Bates. That's what we British do at times of peril. We know when we've fought the good fight…and when we've lost."

"Hold fire!" someone yelled from above. Within a minute, all sounds of cannon and rifle fire had ceased on the line near the seventh gun battery. A few men leaned over the parapet and peered down at them. One of them, a large man with a shock of thick black hair, laughed heartily at the sight.

"Come on up, fellas! Get out of that water and get dry!"

Several offered hands to lift Holester up, followed by several of the British soldiers with him. As each was helped up, an American relieved them of their firearm. Bates came up last, ducking his head. He was a traitor and he wasn't sure how it would go over with the boys in blue.

A crowd of men stood around the captives, but none stepped forward. Captain Holester looked around but saw no high ranking officer in sight. "Is there no one who will accept my sword?"

Suddenly, a few men in blue parted and permitted William Bratton to walk slowly up to meet the British captain. "I am U.S. Marshal William Bratton. On behalf of the American government, I accept your surrender." He took the proffered sword and smiled.

Holester bowed deeply and Bratton was able to see for the first time all the men who had been captured by his company. His eyes widened in surprise at the sight of the man in the rear. He called out to him.

"You there, in back. Please come forward."

Bates stood his ground, but several pairs of arms grabbed him and thrust him toward the front. He held his head low and looked at the ground.

"Well, if it ain't the very man I've been hunting for all these months! Mr. Frederick Bates, former Lt. Governor of the Louisiana territory, traitor to an entire nation. You have been accused of stealing thousands of dollars from the American people of Louisiana...and for orchestrating the murder of Mr. Meriwether Lewis, your late governor and employer. Personal friend of mine and beloved by the nation. It will be a pleasure to take you into custody."

Bates looked up at the man before him, his eyes blazing with hatred. "I can't believe you're still alive, Bratton! I have a friend who will be sure to deliver a special parting treat from me..."

"You mean the late Joseph Richards? Or should I say James Neelly?"

Bates' eyes widened in surprise. "What...what do you mean late?"

"Oh, didn't anyone tell you? I'm really surprised – modern communication being what it is and all. We killed him a week ago, right after he bombed an ammunition wagon, and wounded a friend of mine. He told us to send you his regards right before Mr. Colter blew his head off."

Bates looked dumbstruck...but then an icy resolve grew in his face and he bent down, grabbing a small dagger hidden in his boot. Bringing it up with surprising quickness, he lunged at Bratton, trying to get inside his long arms and attack his vital organs. He managed to take a vicious stab just as the backwoodsman twisted away from him, the sharp blade making a long cut along the front of Bratton's soft, tanned shirt.

Bates wasn't going to let anyone get the better of him. He prepared for another swipe at the red haired giant before a loud shot rang out. Men looked about in confusion after hearing the sharp report of a pistol shot. Bratton looked at the face of his adversary which was twisted in rage and pain, before seeing a small, red, circular hole spread out on the chest of the traitor. Frederick Bates' fingers went numb and the dagger fell with a clatter on the stone beneath his feet. All strength had left him.

Falling to his knees, the traitor gingerly touched the red blood on his shirt, looking at his fingers in confusion and disbelief. *How can this be?* Bratton took his right boot and kicked the mortally wounded man on his back, where his eyes looked sightless upon the sun high above him.

In a moment, a man jumped down off the wall and stood next to the tall red haired giant. Bratton looked over to see John Ordway. "Good to see you, John. It's all over now."

"The battle is over. The search we thought would never end is finally over as well. Too bad Patrick missed out on all the fun today. We'll have to rub it in his face. He deserves it."

Bratton looked at his friend. "Was that your shot that brought him down? If so, I'd like to thank you."

"What are friends for? I heard you had yourselves a few bonafide prisoners down here so I came to take a look. Not as much action down my way. I did put a few holes in some general that was going too slow. Never do that on a battlefield – sure way to hell."

"Can you believe Bates came back? I mean, all he had to do was stay over on the other side and we couldn't touch him..."

"Maybe he got a little too big in the head...thought he could help win this war on his own. He was used to pulling strings from behind someone else... maybe this was his time to shine for his new country."

"Let's see how he shines from way down below."

Captain Holester stepped forward, his head bowed again. "I apologize for the actions of Mr. Bates. His misdeeds during a time of surrender go against all British principles. My sincere apologizes."

Bratton smiled. "No need, captain. Mr. Bates is now where he belongs. He had a very special man murdered in order to cover his own theft and criminal activities. He had compromised his conduct long before any of us knew him."

Ordway looked thoughtful. "Rest in peace, Mr. Lewis. Those who put an end to your life have been brought down now and...we will miss you," he said softly.

Epilogue

March 5, 1816
St. Louis, Missouri

"**H**ey little Lisette! Come see Uncle John!"

The three year old girl came running up to the front door, past the tall, black man holding it open, and threw herself into Colter's arms. He fell onto his back, laughing.

William Bratton carefully stepped over the pair, and looked around the hallway. It hadn't changed since their last visit to St. Louis, but...something was not quite the same. Perhaps it was he who had changed, he thought. They had fulfilled their mission, and lived through one of the fiercest battles of the war. He was glad to be back now among friends. Among family.

Governor William Clark emerged from the back room, a large smile on his face. He held out his hands and warmly shook them with his guests. When Colter finally managed to rise again, the last two men walked in.

John Ordway supported Patrick Gass, lightly holding him up by his left arm. His right arm used a cane to shuffle his feet slowly. There was a bandage over the right side of his head and his one good eye looked tired. But at the sight of Clark, he smiled broadly.

"Governor – it's good to see you again."

"Patrick, John. I couldn't be happier! Please let's sit and talk while York prepares dinner for us."

The five men walked into the drawing room, whose large glass windows let in a warm afternoon sun. The piano that Jean-Baptiste had played for them on their last visit sat off to one side. Ordway helped Patrick into a chair, while he sat nearby. Colter and Bratton took to the soft couch. Clark took a seat in a high-backed, red, velvet chair.

"Well, gentlemen, the stories from New Orleans that have trickled up this far north have made quite an impact. General Jackson is the hero of the nation now. I've even heard talk of higher aspiration for him if he wants it."

"The presidency?" Ordway asked. "If he can run the country the way he led the Americans in battle against such a large British force...he's got my vote!"

Clark smiled. "And you succeeded in tracking down Bates, and his man. That is quite the accomplishment unto itself."

"He actually made it behind British lines, Mr. Clark," Gass said slowly. "We had lost him..."

"Until he got too big for his britches and shows up again right under our very noses!" Ordway said laughing.

"And how are you feeling, Patrick? I know you took quite a beating down there."

"If you think this is bad, you should see the ammunition wagon," the Irishman said smiling. Then he took a more serious tone. "Actually it could have been a lot worse. I lived, and the only real, permanent injury is my right eye. But I do have another one so all is not lost. The rest of the cuts and bruises will heal – most have already."

"What about your head, though? You seem to have difficulty walking..."

Gass waved him off. "I think that's just temporary. I've seen men get hurt in battle...sometimes head injuries will heal themselves eventually. I've already improved a lot. The guys waited with me in New Orleans till I was well enough to travel. I just need more time to heal, I guess."

"Well you shall have all the time you need. I'd like you to stay on here at my house until you are recovered. After all, I feel responsible for you being there to start with."

"Thank you, sir. I think I may accept your offer on this occasion..."

"Good! It's settled then."

Bratton sat stiff on the couch, not quite used to such luxury. "Mr. Clark," he asked softly, "have you gotten any more information from Bates' servant while we were away? I'm terribly interested to know the extent of his...crimes. He attacked me again just before John killed him. He was a true menace but I think he harbored a great intelligence as well."

"William, you bring up a good point. Yes, I have made good use of my time while you were away, and uncovered some startling information. Some of it was gleaned from his manservant, and some of it from real detective work. I must say Mr. Bates, for all his faults, had quite a passionate place in his heart for his father's home country. He used it to fuel his crimes here – stealing from the people of the territory and funneling the money through Indian couriers – mainly the Sioux – that ended up in loyalist hands. He used Captain Neelly's contacts as an Indian agent to orchestrate his plans. From there it was sent to the British in Boston and some directly to his Majesty in England."

"But what sparked the idea to kill Mr. Lewis?"

"From what I could gather, when the federal government got wind of shortcomings from the governor's office, they started making inquiries. Bates held them off for a few years with falsified account books, and manipulating the fur company investments, but he had taken too much for it to escape totally. Naturally they started their inquiries with Mr. Lewis, and Bates decided then and there to use him as a scapegoat.

"He took advantage of Mr. Lewis' trustworthy nature, and used him to cover his tracks. When Mr. Lewis was sent to Washington to talk to the treasury department, Bates took it a step further and ordered his murder. It had to look like a robbery or an accident – anything that would keep his name out of it. Bates orchestrated this through Lewis' Indian agent, James Neelly, who paid off a few Cherokee who had a settlement near where Mr. Lewis would be staying. Once the formal inquiry was over and had died down, Neelly went to work for Bates on a more permanent basis, changing identities when it suited him – but he now worked for someone who appreciated the seedier sides to his resume."

Gass followed his lead. "But in order to make it work, Bates had to have inside help – someone from the government who could come down at a moment's notice and sweep everything under the rug. Suppress any evidence, pay off the Grinders..."

Clark nodded. "Yes, you're right. He had help from a few loyalists inside the army who came down from Fort Pickering and secreted away his belongings – including evidence that could have been used later. But they had to make an official report which made its way to the office of the president. Upon Jefferson's order, the diary of Mr. Lewis was sent to his office, where as you know, he keeps it in his library. Bates couldn't prevent that and keep his name out of the inquiry at the same time, so he let it go."

"Bates had everything he needed now – money, power, and a fall guy to take the rap for him," Colter said. "He just had one little problem. He never counted on you never giving up on Mr. Lewis."

"Thank you, John, but I can not take all the credit. You four were instrumental in getting under the problem, uncovering evidence he would kill to suppress. And he tried to, as you all know! But he couldn't shake you guys and in the end, he realized we were coming for him."

"So he ran," Bratton said. "I suppose to him, New Orleans represented the last place in the country he might feel safe. The British had retreated on all the other major fronts and the war was almost over. The treaty was being hammered out in France just as we were knocking on his door."

Clark continued, "To him, England was his real home – a place where he felt he belonged. He had given all he had to ensure England would remain in power and he saw it blowing up in his face…"

"But his own self importance became his undoing. He came back with the British officers into battle and we cut them down. He ended his life on his back, a prisoner of the American people. An ignoble end…surely someone upstairs had a good sense of humor." Ordway replied.

Clark stood up and walked into the kitchen parlor. In a minute, he returned with York, holding six glasses and two bottles of a red vintage wine. The governor proceeded to pour them each a glass and handed them out, including one to his servant who smiled broadly.

Governor William Clark held his glass up and smiled broadly. "Gentlemen, please allow me to give a toast. To Meriwether Lewis. Patriot. Countryman. Friend. You guided not just a group of men across the country, but an entire nation. The men who travel west owe you a debt of gratitude. You have shaped a new country, a better country, an indomitable country! We salute you, Meriwether Lewis! Your death is not the end, but simply the beginning…the country will never forget your contributions and we will not forget the friendships we have forged together. You are a great man and you deserve your peace. May God rest your soul."

Historical Appendix

<u>Meriwether Lewis:</u> Died on Oct 11, 1809, at the Grinder's Stand along the Natchez Trace. His death is shrouded in mystery, with many theories pointing to either suicide or murder.

<u>William Clark:</u> Clark served as governor of the Missouri Territory until 1820. Later, he was appointed Superintendent of Indian Affairs and lived the rest of his life in St. Louis. He died of natural causes on September 1 1838, at age 68.

<u>Patrick Gass:</u> With his own journals published in 1807, Gass was the first to coin the name "Corps of Discovery". The skilled carpenter served in the War of 1812 at the Battle of Lundy's Lane before loosing an eye at the Battle of New Orleans. The longest-living member of the Corps, he died April 2, 1870, at age 99 in Wellsburg, West Virginia.

<u>John Colter:</u> In 1806, Colter went back west with trappers Dixon and Hancock, before setting off on his own. He discovered the wonders of what later became the Yellowstone National Park, including Old Faithful and other geothermal spectacles, which he nicknamed 'Colter's Hell'. No one believed his tale until decades later. His escape from the Blackfoot in 1810 became legendary and he passed away from jaundice a few years later.

<u>William Bratton:</u> Served his country during the War of 1812 at the Battle of the Thames and witnessed the death of Tecumseh. He settled down to the life of a farmer, married in 1819 and fathered 10 children. He became the first

justice of the peace in Wayne Township, Indiana in 1824 and died November 11, 1841 in Waynetown, Indiana.

John Ordway: Ordway returned to New Hampshire, married, and later moved to Missouri to farm the 320 acres of land that he was awarded for his service in the Corps. Both he and his wife died in 1817 in Missouri.

Nathaniel Pryor: In 1807, he accompanied George Shannon to return Mandan Chief Big White to his home village. In 1811, he spied on Tecumseh and was captured, but escaped just before he was to be killed. After serving as a captain under General Jackson during the Battle of New Orleans, Pryor lived with the Osage Indian tribe, particularly the Clermont band in Oklahoma. He married a native Osage woman and had at least three children. He died June 10, 1831.

President Thomas Jefferson: Retired to his estate in Monticello, the former President died of natural causes on July 4, 1826. He was a firm believer that Lewis committed suicide.

Sacagawea: After returning to her Hidatsa village in 1806, she and her husband had another child, a girl named Lisette. Sacagawea died of an unknown sickness in 1812 at Fort Manuel in South Dakota. Clark adopted and cared for both of her children, Jean-Baptiste and Lisette, upon her death.

Touissant Charbonneau: The Canadian fur trapper moved his family to St. Louis in 1809 but returned in 1811 to take a position with the Missouri Fur Company, settling at a trading post at Fort Manuel in South Dakota. After the death of his wife, Sacagawea, Charbonneau used his services as an interpreter on several occasions for Clark. In 1839, at the age of 80, he was lost to the annals of history. His estate was settled in 1843 by his son, Jean-Baptiste.

Frederick Bates: Served as Lt. Governor of the Louisiana Territory under Lewis. Bates was an outspoken critic of his boss and his policies.

James Neelly: A government agent of Indian Affairs, Neelly accompanied Lewis along the Natchez Trace, staying behind to retrieve horses, and found Lewis at the Grinder's Stand. Priscella told her story of events to him. He fetched the authorities at Fort Pickering and wrote to both

Jefferson and Clark explaining Lewis' death. His name has come up during the initial inquiry as a possible suspect, but nothing was ever proven.

George Shannon: Shannon was appointed by Clark to return Mandan Chief Big White to his home village in 1807. While in North Dakota, his party was attacked by Arikara Indians and he was wounded in the leg, which he later lost due to infection. He finished his education, becoming a lawyer in 1818, and served three terms in the Kentucky House of Representatives from 1820-1823. He became a judge, presiding over a famous case of murder himself, where a popular governor's son stood accused. He eventually settled in St. Louis, Missouri with his family, before passing away August 30, 1836 in Palmyra, Missouri at the age of 49, while en route to try a new case.

George Drouillard: After the expedition's return, he worked as a bounty hunter and a trapper. In 1810, he returned to the Three Forks region for furs and was killed by the Blackfoot Indians. It is widely believed his death was retribution for the deadly encounter with Lewis' party in 1806.

Sgt. Charlie Floyd: He was the only member of the Corps to die during the expedition. At the time, the diagnosis was bilious colic but modern researchers speculate Floyd suffered from a burst appendix.

General Andrew Jackson: After enjoying immense national popularity after winning the Battle of New Orleans that effectively ended the War of 1812, Jackson was elected to the presidency and served from 1829 thru 1837. Upon retiring, Jackson, affectionately known as "Old Hickory" settled at his estate, the Hermitage, before passing away in June 1845.

General Edward Pakenham: Mortally wounded during the battle on Jan 8th, 1816, Pakenham was pulled behind the British lines by his aides, but died the next day. General Lambert assumed command of the British forces and withdrew from New Orleans shortly afterwards.

Jean-Baptiste "Pomp" Charbonneau: After finishing his education in St. Louis, Jean headed west. In 1823 at age 18, while living in a traders' village at the mouth of the Kansas River, he met Prince Paul Wilhelm of Wuertemberg, Germany, who was visiting the country. The prince took him under his patronage and they traveled through Europe together. Returning to America in 1829, he set aside his cultivated manners and turned to the mountains of the west, exploring, hunting, trapping, and serving as guide to those willing to pay for his services. In 1866, he left Auburn with two companions and headed toward new gold discoveries in Montana. En route, Jean-Baptiste, at the age of 61, died of pneumonia.